CHILD OF

HUMANITY

ISBN-10: 0-9979214-1-2

ISBN-13: 978-0-9979214-1-0

For my devoted parents, Andrea and Victor, who taught me what it is to love, sacrifice, live a life of compassion and empathy, and above all, to be and do good. I can only hope to become half the person you raised me to be.

For my little sister, Lauren, who has always been my inspiration. I was meant to be your role model, but over time, you became mine. Thank you for your lessons in embracing who you are and living life fearlessly.

Acknowledgments

Words cannot describe how grateful I am for:

Cindy Hochman of "100 Proof" Copyediting Services, who helped make this book flawless.

Drew 'Maijin' Lewis, graphic artist, designer, illustrator, and concept artist of "IMAIJIN" (www.maijintheartist.com), who did the gorgeous cover art. Thank you for turning my vision into reality.

My beta readers, Stephanie Jones, Lauren Steves, Danielle Ereddia, Amy Jurden, Brett Patterson, and Ben Maloney. You made this book what it is and gave me the courage to follow my dreams.

CHILD OF HUMANITY

Alyse N. Steves

PROLOGUE

When I was a child, my parents laid my siblings and me down to sleep and told us a story. Once upon a time, they told us, there was a beautiful city in a faraway land. It was made of precious metals and jewels, flowers, ribbons, lace, bows, and every other beautiful thing a wide-eyed and curious child could ever dream up. The people were happy. They had everything they could ever desire within the high walls of the city: food, toys, beautiful clothing, and handcrafted beauties—everything. Nobody wanted for anything. Nobody got sick. There was no strife. They danced and sang in the streets from dawn until dusk.

When little children got old enough, a stranger would tap them on the shoulder as they played and sang in the streets. He would smile and give them a treat, and then he would lead them away. They'd enter a palace, and he would take them down a beautiful hallway to a set of elaborate winding stairs. Together they would descend below the city. It would be dark below, and the child would be nervous as they walked down a narrow tunnel that grew gradually darker as they went. The stranger would lay a hand on the child's shoulder reassuringly and smile. They would come to a beautifully carved door, and the stranger would pull out an ornate key. The key would click in the lock, and the door would creak open just a bit. The child would be excited, wondering what marvels were hidden inside. He would stand on his tiptoes and peer inside, impatient and giddy.

The stranger would invite the child inside with a smile. The child would eagerly step within, and there he would see a figure in the center of the room, sickly and frail in the dark, its arms and legs bound to a chair, with coarse ropes chafing at its skin. It would be undothed, its bones sticking out beneath its skin, and its face haggard and dirty, streaked with tears. There would be no light to brighten the darkness and no windows for the nameless soul to see the joys that lay just outside. The room would smell of filth, and the very air would be saturated with pain.

The figure would cry out to the child, moaning and weeping unintelligibly, and then, just as the child would begin to feel truly frightened for the first time in his life, the stranger would take him by the hand and lead him back out. The stranger would give him another treat and a smile, and then he would leave him to play.

Most of the children chose to forget and went back to playing. They never saw the stranger or the figure again. Their lives went on blissfully. But every now and then, a child would not play. He would go home. He would pack a few things, hug his family, and go to the large, marvelous gates of the beautiful city. He would ask that they be opened for him.

And he would leave.

I didn't understand for many years.

CHAPTER 1

Through squinted eyes, I stared at the red fluorescence given off by the alarm clock. The light hurt in the darkness, but I didn't look away. As I lay there in the dark, numb and stiff from hours of sleeplessness, it seemed as if the red light seeping out of the electronic numbers, creeping across the face of the clock in a fuzzy red cloud, was almost unreal, like magic the way it transformed the dark. I stared at it until my eyes were dry and sore, and I was forced to blink. As the glow of the clock and the electronic numbers crept by, I felt small, insignificant, and empty.

It was 4:18 in the morning, and I hadn't slept all night.

It felt strangely cold. I almost always left the window open when I slept, and lately, a warm, humid breeze had crept in at night to lull me to sleep. Not tonight, though. I could feel the cold rain in the air, though it hadn't started yet. A chill crept up my spine, and I pulled the blankets closer. I heard the curtains whispering behind me. Most nights, the sound of the curtains rustling gently in the wind, the occasional voice echoing in the courtyard, the sound of crickets chirping and frogs singing in the bushes below the building, the rhythmic crash of waves from the ocean that lay not far from where I slept—all of those things usually helped ease me to sleep.

I didn't like to be alone. The noise carrying through the window usually comforted me, but not tonight. Tonight I felt isolated from the world, just the clock and me, staring at each other in the dark, cramped dorm room, waiting for the storm to begin.

I rolled over and stared at the ceiling—white, blank, and devoid of anything useful in my quest to quiet my mind and drift off to sleep. It wasn't long before I rolled back over to watch the red cloud creep off the clock, clutching my blankets in the hope that the softness and warmth would soothe my restlessness. The minutes dragged on, until finally I tossed the covers back with a defeated sigh and forced myself upright. The clock was still looking at me, so I shuffled my way into the hall and toward the bathroom, trying not to wake anyone.

I flipped the switch and the light blinded me as it reflected off the stark white bathroom tiles. I threw my hand up in a futile attempt to shield my eyes and wearily shuffled my way to the sink. Sighing, I looked in the mirror.

"Good morning, sunshine," I mumbled. The girl in the mirror simply stared back, her bright blue eyes bloodshot. The skin below her eyes was sagging, dragged down by the weight of the dark circles. Her red hair was sticking out at odd angles, and her freckles looked ghastly in the bathroom light, dark pinpoints on a sea of pale skin.

"You have no one to blame but yourself," I told her, before shoving a toothbrush in my mouth and groggily scrubbing. The pungent taste of cinnamon helped drive the fog from my head.

I threw my hair into a sloppy ponytail, pulled on my sneakers at the edge of the bathroom door where I had dumped them unceremoniously that evening, and quietly crept my way toward the front door, careful not to make any noise as I tiptoed past the two closed bedroom doors, the girls inside both sound asleep.

I heard, rather than saw, the third girl in the living room as I quietly crept around the corner. She was sitting on the floor, her back to me. I heard booming noises and other sound effects from the video game on the television. They masked the sound of me slipping out the door.

Two flights of stairs and a brisk walk across campus later, I had worn pavement under my feet and sea-grape trees lining either side of me, as my feet rhythmically carried me down the familiar jogging trail that connected Florida Eastern University to the coast. The cool morning air, heavy with moisture from the impending storm, filled my lungs. The crisp, clean smells of earth intermixed with salt had always been calming to me, as I hoped they would be now.

I always ran when I couldn't sleep. I liked to imagine that I was running away from all of my troubles, leaving them behind me for a place I knew they couldn't follow. I was running away to a place of peace and clarity, a place that I remembered from my childhood, when life was so very different.

My childhood felt like so long ago.

The pavement vanished beneath my feet as the jogging trail gave way to a beach of white sand, glowing softly in the moonlight. The crescent moon had fought its way out from behind the clouds and reflected off the waves in the dark water that lapped at the shore, leaving behind a hissing foam in their wake. The surface of the water was calm, and the waves that crashed to the shore were small, though I knew they wouldn't stay that way much longer with the storm approaching. I sat down in the sand and tucked my knees against my chest, thinking of home.

But today, the rhythmic roar of the waves, the salt in the air, and the nighttime wind teasing escaped strands of red hair didn't fill me with peace. The roar, though the waves that crashed weren't powerful at all, was deafening as I sat alone on the white beach with only the distant moon to keep me company, and the wind was becoming angry and violent, tossing hair, sand, and salty spray into my eyes.

When the moon surrendered to the clouds and the first few drops of rain kissed my face, I brushed the sand from my legs and surrendered as well.

I slipped back into the apartment in what felt like an eternity later, and was just as empty and numb as I had been staring at those glowing red numbers.

"You're soaking wet," Tori remarked, leaning against the kitchen counter with a cup of coffee in her hands. Because of the way the apartment-style dorm was laid out, she saw me before I saw her, making it too late for me to slip away to my room unnoticed before I even realized I was caught. I had no choice but to face her.

She was in her pajamas, her medium-length, black-dyed hair a mess. It was put up in a chaotic knot, in typical Tori fashion, adding to the aura of defiance that always seemed to radiate from the slender girl. Her eyes looked slightly bloodshot and glossy, and I knew she had been awake all night. It wasn't unusual for Tori, our resident night owl, to stay up into the wee hours of the morning playing video games. We had grown used to it, for the most part. I was guilty of the occasional attempt to coerce her into an early bedtime, though she hardly heard me when I did.

I managed to give her a weary nod. I made my way to the fridge, almost in a daze, but when I opened it, I found myself just staring at the contents, not really looking. The blast of cold hit my wet skin, and I felt the threat of uncontrollable shivering as a chill crept through my body and the hair on my arms stood on end.

"You're going to be sick," she said, giving me a disapproving look.

I just nodded again, the words not really registering.

"I made coffee," Tori said. She eyed me, sipping her beverage slowly.

"Thanks," I said weakly, though I knew I didn't want any. I shrugged off the cold as best I could.

"What's up? This is the third night in a row," Tori said, her voice equal parts demanding and concerned, maybe even a little on the irritated side. Tori was rough around the edges, but she meant well. Her concern was genuine, but that didn't mean she wouldn't try to forcibly extract an answer from me. As alone as I felt, Tori was not the person I needed to run into this morning. Warm and fuzzy was not her style, and I just wanted some peace, not an interrogation.

"Just can't sleep," I mumbled, trying to sound sincere. "I thought a run might make me tired."

"Bull," Tori mumbled into her coffee cup.

I sighed and grabbed a yogurt out of the fridge. I didn't want it, but "just tired" people still had an appetite. I dug around in the kitchen drawers for a spoon, only to find that there were none.

"It was your turn to do the dishes," Tori said, still watching me from behind her cup.

"Sorry," I sighed, as I went to dig one out of the dishwasher. I wiped it on a dishtowel before shoving a spoonful of strawberry yogurt in my mouth, and waited while Tori stared at me with her intense dark brown eyes. I felt the shivering start, but again I chose to ignore it.

She rolled her eyes and set down the cup of coffee, crossing her arms against her chest. "Look," she said. "Jillian and Marie may be willing to ignore your little mood and give you your space, but I'm not."

"I'm fine," I said, sighing. "It's the beginning of the semester. I'm just having a hard time adjusting to the new schedule. My classes are really hard."

She started to argue.

"I swear," I said.

I tried not to look guilty, but I couldn't help it, as my stomach clenched and my gaze dropped to the floor. I was anything but okay.

I set the yogurt down and crossed my arms. Tori eyed me. I was a terrible liar, and if it weren't for the shivering that could no longer be contained, she may have taken my closed-off stance as a sure sign that I was not telling the truth. Thankfully, the fact that I was freezing spared me any more grilling from her.

She sighed. "Fine," she said, tossing up her hands and rolling her eyes. "All this mothering and worrying about you has worn me out. It's out of my hands."

She gave me a grin. "I really don't know how you do it."

I couldn't help but smile. Tori was always getting on me about the way I "mothered" my roommates, as she put it. She was always complaining that I was too mature and never had any fun. When we first met, I irritated her, and it was her way of lashing out, but over time, it had become our little joke.

I felt as cold on the outside as I did on the inside, but I didn't move to do anything about it. The shock of it was oddly … poetic. It seemed unnatural to me that I might feel any other way considering the circumstances, so I just stood there and took it. Tori went back to sipping her coffee.

The silence was awkward. I stood there, trying to act normal, my eyes wandering around the kitchen in an attempt to avoid meeting Tori's gaze. I had never noticed how small our humble kitchen really was. Standing next to the refrigerator, with its low, consistent hum, the fluorescent kitchen lights purring their own low song in return, I felt claustrophobic. Whereas before I had felt alone, now everything was pressing in on me, staring at me with accusing eyes. I was dazed and far, far away from it all, and yet, at the same time, this feeling made my skin crawl in the most invasive way.

"All right, I can't fake it anymore. The coffee is terrible," Tori finally said, breaking the silence. At the sound of her voice, I snapped back to my senses. She dumped her cup down the drain. "You know, it took me a good five minutes to figure out which button made the stupid coffeemaker work. It took ten minutes before that to find the coffee in the cupboards. Don't even get me started on where the water goes. I can't handle this level of responsibility."

She threw her hands up in mock defeat.

I couldn't help it; I giggled, and for a split second I felt a gentle warmth in my chest.

"This place would fall apart without you, you know," Tori said, grinning. I knew she had said it to make me feel better, but her words had the opposite effect on me. Emotions hit me with full force, clawing at me from the inside and threatening to rip me apart. I couldn't breathe. I felt them wrapping around my throat and squeezing. I felt tears forming behind my eyes.

Marie's alarm went off and I knew everyone would be awake soon. I couldn't deal with them right now. I just wanted to curl up under the covers of my own bed and stay there, alone, and try to will some warmth back into myself.

I slowly put the spoon back in the dishwasher and tossed out the half-eaten yogurt, trying hard to make it look as if I weren't coming unglued.

"I need to get out of these clothes," I mumbled, and that's about as far as my resolve went. I tried to walk to my room calmly, but I was rushing for the comfort I hoped my blankets would provide.

"Hey, you!" Tori called behind me. I turned, trying not to look too desperate to get away. "You thought I forgot, didn't you?"

I smiled, but I felt my throat clench. I gritted my teeth. I decided I would go back to bed and stay there forever if I could. Forget the warmth; I just wanted to hide.

"Happy birthday!" Tori said, positively beaming—at least, it was beaming for Tori. Tori would always have that aura of cold reserve and strength—and perhaps bullheadedness—around her. I tried to give her a genuine smile through the clenched teeth, and mustered up enough strength to hug her. She didn't even complain about my wet clothes as she wrapped her arms around me in a genuine embrace.

With that little act I felt a pang go through my chest, as I realized how much she cared about me. I clenched my eyes shut and just prayed that I could get through it.

Once back in the confines of my room, I slammed both the door and the window shut, disregarding the wet carpet beneath the window; crawled in bed with my wet clothes still on; and stared at the red glow of the clock. I pulled the covers tightly around myself and listened to the rain beat against my window.

Neither peace nor sleep ever came, and an agonizing eternity later, I heard the door creak open. The bed sheets rustled as someone crawled beneath and found me wrapped up in my blanket cocoon. They were warm, and normally that warmth would be inviting, but I didn't move. I just clung to my blankets in the dark.

"Hey, Ally Cat," a voice whispered.

"Hey, Jilly Bean," I whispered back, trying not to sound as dreadful as I felt. There was a pause, punctuated by the distinct sound of the rain, which showed no sign of ending anytime soon. Beneath the sound of the rain hitting the window, I could hear both of us breathing. The warmth of her breath hit my face, and for the first time, I felt a little less numb.

"I heard this rumor," Jillian said, her voice trailing off.

"Yeah?"

"I heard that Tori made the coffee this morning."

"That's a pretty ugly one, isn't it?"

I heard, rather than saw, Jillian nodding.

"Marie was kind enough to drink it. You should have seen her face," Jillian said. There was a tone of genuine amusement in her voice.

I felt a grin tugging at the corner of my mouth. That was just like Marie.

"I didn't really feel like coffee this morning," I said.

"Hmm," Jillian said. "And then you missed all of your classes."

"I didn't really feel like classes," I whispered. I didn't feel like anything but lying in bed and waiting.

There was a long pause, both of us just lying there, breathing rhythmically in the dark. I closed my eyes, and I could remember the days long, long ago when I always fell asleep with someone by my side. I was never alone, but now, falling asleep each night isolated in a room with four walls and a door that locked …

Life was so different, so innocent, back then.

"What's going on, Ally?" Jillian said, snapping me back to reality. At the same time, I didn't want to lose this life, but I couldn't stop it. It was best in the long run.

"Just been tired. Really, really tired," I mumbled, feeling lost and detached. I was so tired of the waiting.

Jillian pulled the blankets down, exposing my head. The room was dark. No light came through the window, save for the lone floodlight outside. The streaks of water running down the windowpane glowed brightly as they reflected the stark light. The absence of sunlight was depressing, as if the day had died while I had hidden from it, but the fresh air filling my lungs after so long under the stuffy blankets made me feel more alert and alive than I had all day. It was an odd feeling.

Jillian was across from me, her gray eyes looking at me with confusion and concern, oblivious to the cause of my private torment. I didn't want to meet her gaze, so I focused on the glow of the dock behind her head.

After a few minutes, she spoke. "Did Eddie Johnson dip one of your pigtails in glue again?"

I couldn't help it; I laughed, and felt strangely better—maybe even a little happy. But, then, that was Jillian. Jillian could always make me feel better.

"*What*?"

"If he did, I'll go find another jungle gym to push him off of."

"Jillian, we were six—and you broke his wrist!" I said, and I was desperately trying not to smile.

"Little chump deserved it," Jillian muttered. "Mrs. Carmichael had to cut it out of your hair. You bawled."

"Because I was six!" I said. I threw my hands over my mouth in an attempt to quiet the giggles, but to no avail.

"Yeah, there you go, trying to be all polite. We both know it was funny."

I gasped and tossed a pillow at her head. "He was a six-year-old boy, and you broke his wrist!"

She tossed the pillow back at me. "He was seven, because he was held back! What are you going to do about it?"

Suddenly my miseries were forgotten, or at least temporarily set aside, while I pounced on her, fingers aiming for her ribs, which I happened to know were extremely ticklish.

"You want to start this, do you?" Jillian gasped, as she reached down for my equally ticklish feet. I squealed and kicked, but she was faster. "When you've lost, just remember that you started this!" she shouted between breaths, as she struggled to evade my flailing arms.

It didn't take me long to lose, two minutes, maybe, and only because she let it drag on that long.

"I'm stronger," Jillian said, grinning, as she pinned both of my arms above my head with one hand. I wiggled in a half-hearted attempt to escape, but not enough to encourage her to sit on me, which I knew she would not hesitate to do if it meant victory.

"Now tell me what's going on," she said, gently but firmly enough for me to know that she was done playing games.

"Nothing is going on," I said, trying to sound exasperated, as if the question were completely unfounded. "I've just been tired."

"Ally Cat, it's your birthday, and you've spent all day in your room," Jillian said, clearly not buying it.

"I know. It's just—I think I must be coming down with something."

It was a weak excuse, and we both knew it. I sighed. It was impossible to lie to her. It always had been.

Jillian sighed and settled down beside me. "You don't want to talk about it?"

"There's really nothing to talk about," I insisted.

She was quiet for a while, studying me with her gray eyes, but she finally propped herself up on her elbows, looking thoughtful.

"I think I know something that will make you feel better," she said. I raised an eyebrow at her.

"Stay right here," she said. She leapt from the bed, tossing yellow blankets in my face, and was out the door in a flash. She was back by the time I had managed to toss the blankets to the ground, entirely giving up on them and the shelter I was hoping they would provide.

She held a hand out toward me, looking meek. "I didn't wrap it," she said. "Sorry."

I propped myself up and opened my hand, curious. She dropped something in it; a piece of metal jewelry, from the feel of it.

I switched on the lamp on the nightstand to better examine my gift in the dim light. It was a necklace: a cute little pink half-heart with a tiny silver heart on one side, fake diamonds around the edge, and the letters "BE FRIE" in silver in the middle. A few of the fake gems were missing, but the chain was new.

"Is this—" I began, but she cut me off.

"The necklace I gave you when we were eight?" she finished. She sat down beside me, and I saw her pull out a necklace from beneath her shirt. It was the other half.

"I know it's a little childish, but … I found it when I was home over the summer. You know how my mom is always on my case about cleaning the junk in my closet. You wouldn't believe the crap I found in there."

"I've been holding on to it," she said quietly, taking in the expression on my face. "I thought you might want it back."

I just stared at it, speechless. There was a time when the necklaces had never come off either of us, but eventually they were outgrown and set aside. I thought they had been lost in time. A mixture of emotions churned in my chest, ranging from grief to nostalgia to insurmountable happiness. The gift was priceless.

"Thank you," I said, though the words alone couldn't convey how much the cheap, old necklace meant to me—nothing could.

"Now get up. We're going out," Jillian said firmly.

I started to say something, but she cut me off.

"You should know that Tori was hell-bent on dragging you out drinking, but I think Marie and I have convinced her to give up trying to corrupt you into a respectable member of society," she said, smirking. "We're going bowling. I know you'd rather be outside, but the weather says no, so suck it up. And try to keep the ball out of the gutter, okay?"

Again I tried to say something, but she stopped me.

"*No* is not an appropriate answer," she said.

"Marie made a cake," she added, giving me a stern look.

I sighed, staring at the half-heart necklace in my hand. I felt the inner war raging in my chest: part of me was in torment and just wanted to hide in the bed, but the other half was yearning for people, especially Jillian. At this point, I didn't know which would be easier for me to deal with, but I did know which one had the power to make me feel happy—for a little while, at least.

"Up," Jillian said, tossing a pillow at me.

"I'll be ready in a few minutes," I responded with a weak smile, though my heart wasn't entirely in it.

"I knew you'd see it my way," she said, smiling broadly.

"She's up!" Jillian shouted. I heard a "Hell yeah!" come from Tori in the living room.

Jillian made her way to the door, but she paused before she walked out. "Ally?"

20

"Yeah?" I said, still sitting on the bed, knees tucked against my chest.

"If there's something wrong, promise that you'll tell me? Don't shut me out."

The words cut like a knife.

"I promise," I said, but the truth was, she would never know. She nodded, smiling and trusting, and walked out the door.

I stood up but felt dizzy. I sat down and clutched at my head, feeling nauseated.

The familiar flash of light danced across my vision, the stars swirling in my field of view as I struggled to focus my eyes again. My ears popped, and I had to yawn to get the equilibrium back. The ringing, however, would only go away on its own. It was there and gone in a flash, but it was unmistakable.

I had forty-eight hours.

The necklace hadn't left my hand. I realized then that I had been clutching it since the moment Jillian had given it to me, so tightly that my knuckles were white. Hands trembling, I put it on. The warm metal pressed against my skin, and the effect was instantaneous. I felt tears behind my eyes as the rush of memories of a lifetime that was over engulfed me, but they didn't fall.

They never fell.

"Happy last birthday," I whispered to no one.

CHAPTER 2

Under the boom of thunder, I heard my bedroom door creak open, but I pretended not to hear it. I kept my eyes closed and breathing rhythmic, hoping that whoever it was would go away. I heard the sound of footsteps across carpet. They paused right at the edge of my bed, and I had to remind myself not to hold my breath or tense up, lest they realize I was awake.

"Rise and shine!" Jillian shouted, right in my ear. Still, I didn't move, hoping she would assume I was in a deep sleep and come back later—or not at all also worked. I didn't want to get up today. I knew that I had to, but I would put that moment off for as long as I could. Defeated and accepting of my fate, I had succumbed to hiding beneath my blankets once again, feeling worse today than I had during all of the previous days combined. All I had the strength to do was lay there and wait.

"Plan B," I heard Tori say. I had a feeling I wasn't going to like Plan B, especially if Tori had come up with it.

I felt the earthquake that was my roommates assaulting me—one with a pillow to the head, the other jumping on top of me, shaking me back and forth.

"Ally Cat, *get up!*" Jillian ordered, tickling my ribs. I pulled the blankets up over my head and rolled over. She responded by going for my feet.

"No," I moaned, pulling my feet away in the hope of escaping Jillian's fingers. "I'm sleeping."

"No, you're not. We've been standing outside your door. You've been tossing and turning for a while," Jillian said.

I groaned. "Then let me try to go back to sleep. *Please*. I'm tired."

"Don't care. It's noon, and we have breakfast. *Get up.*"

I lifted the blankets just enough to peek out. Tori was standing beside me, a pillow poised to strike again. Jillian was sitting on me. It was uncomfortable.

"You're both being immature," I said, from under the covers.

"Says the girl hiding under her blankets," Jillian replied.

"Ass out of bed," Tori said. "Marie just finished making the pancakes."

"Marie is in on this … this—" I whined pathetically. I groaned for emphasis. They were not going to get me out of bed, I decided stubbornly. I was exhausted and depressed, and I needed the day to go away. I had barely slept since I had received my notice, waiting for the moment to come.

Today was my last day. I knew that. But for some reason I thought I could make that reality disappear if I just hid under the blankets and ignored it. Life couldn't go on if I refused to participate in it, right?

When I was really young, I hated getting up for preschool. I just wanted to stay at home with my mom all day, doing whatever grownup things she did. When she'd come into my room in the morning, I'd be fast asleep, and nothing she could do would wake me. At least, that was the act I put on. At first it infuriated her, but eventually she learned how to play my game. She'd dress me, put my shoes on, and even brush my hair while I pretended to be asleep. She'd put me in the car, and I'd pretend to be asleep all the way to the classroom, sometimes even after she had dropped me off. The little-kid logic behind it was that the day couldn't start if I wasn't awake for it, so if I never woke up, I never had to leave my mom. If I got up, I was willingly going along with a reality I didn't want to accept, and I refused to be its accomplice.

I knew it was incredibly childish, but it was the only way I could have some control over the situation, and I was desperate to feel that my life wasn't slipping from my grasp.

"Interesting," Jillian said. "Marie sounded almost as whiny this morning."

Tori giggled maniacally.

I yanked the blankets off my head to give her a stern look. "What did you do to Marie?"

Tori laughed even harder. Jillian just raised her eyebrows and smirked, challenging me. I knew that look all too well. I had seen it for most of my life. Jillian had always been stronger and far braver than I would ever be. She had ambition and sought out challenges. She never let anything get in her way. I had always been the anchor she needed to keep her grounded, though she didn't always appreciate it.

"Did you blackmail Marie into cooking breakfast?" I asked her, eyes narrowing.

"No, she volunteered to do that herself. She seemed to be under the impression that we might poison you," Tori said sarcastically.

"*You* might poison her," Jillian corrected, shooting her a look.

"You two need to let that coffee thing go," Tori said irritably, rolling her eyes.

"Coffee grounds do not go *in* the pot," Jillian retorted.

"I really don't want to get up. I'm tired and I don't feel well," I said, as politely as I could, though I was not even remotely humored by my roommates' antics. Jillian and Tori always managed to bicker about everything or pick on each other. Normally, I would put myself in the middle of it and play the mediator, but today I couldn't bring myself to care.

I tried to pull the blankets back over my face, but Jillian snatched them away. "If you have any hope of finding your schoolbooks ever again, you'll come to breakfast."

"You didn't—"

"We didn't … what?" Tori said, grinning. "We didn't sneak into your room last night and make off with your book bag *and* all of your books? Why would we do a thing like that?"

I stared at them, mouth agape. "Marie will tell me where they are. She won't go along with this," I blurted in disbelief. Of all the things in the world, I didn't know why a few history books would get a reaction from me. I couldn't take them with me, any more than I could take anything else with me. But there was something about human history, interpreted and written down by humans over the ages, that I found precious and worthy of protection.

"No, I'm afraid she won't," Jillian said, looking mischievous.

"Because we have her books, too," Tori finished.

I groaned, covering my face with my hands. "Does your treachery know no bounds?"

"No, it doesn't," Tori said matter-of-factly. "Now get your depressed behind out of bed and come stuff your face with pancakes."

I stared at them, their faces hopeful and expectant. I had spent most of yesterday in bed, feigning aches and pains and other illness-related symptoms, then coming up with excuse after excuse when that failed to convince my roommates of anything. Jillian had come in multiple times to try to talk and force me out into the world. Marie brought me soup twice, and even Tori made her best attempt at getting me out of bed, in the form of inviting me to play video games with her. She even offered to let me have the good controller. They were trying so hard to help, despite the fact that they had absolutely no idea what was going on. They had no idea that, by the end of the day, I would have to give them up. It was just so much easier for me to withdraw in the end, rather than continue to immerse myself in their lives, only to be ripped away from them.

It was more than that, though. I was angry. I was hurt, and though I tried not to admit it, I felt betrayed. I wanted more time. I always wanted more time, but despite how much begging and pleading I did in the quiet confines of my blankets, whispering softly so that others wouldn't overhear, nothing ever changed. The deadline was set in stone, and it was just so unfair! This was the only protest I knew of, to lie under the blankets and refuse to participate. This was my only semblance of control. It was all I had! I knew it made no difference, but I did it anyway.

That's when it suddenly dawned on me that I was being incredibly selfish. My friends were ignorant in all of this, and my pain, as awful as it was, was temporary. The waiting was always the worst, but once it was over, I wouldn't hurt anymore. I just had to hold on until then. My role ended today, but they had to keep going, and I owed it to them to make the transition as painless as possible. I looked to Jillian, then to Tori. They had no idea, and I couldn't punish them. This wasn't their doing.

I didn't want my last day to be like this. This wasn't the me that everyone knew and loved. I wanted my friends' last memories of me to be good ones. Forget what I was feeling; they were the ones who mattered most. I took a deep breath and swallowed the pain.

For them.

"I think ..." I said, knocking Jillian aside and jumping out of bed, stealing Tori's skull pillow as I leapt past her. "You're both still immature."

All three of us came around the corner, giggling and shoving each other out of the way. Marie smiled when she saw us. She had tried to pull her wild brown curls back in place while she cooked, but more than a few had escaped. In typical Marie fashion, she attempted to tuck one behind her ear, which made her glasses slide down her nose. When she tried to fix her glasses, the unruly strand of hair broke free.

"I would just like to say that none of this was my idea," she announced, fiddling with the cross necklace around her neck. It was a subconscious habit she had when something was on her mind. If she got distracted enough, she'd put it in her teeth and play with it, which drove Tori nuts for some reason.

"Your involvement has been noted. Your innocence awaits further trial," I said, but I was smiling at the sweet girl with the unruly curls.

She smiled at me, still twirling the necklace in her fingertips.

"Thank you," I said, giving her a sincere hug. Her curls tickled my nose as I hugged her, but I was used to it by now.

We sat there eating chocolate chip pancakes and talking about classes and whatever else was relevant for what felt like the longest time. I didn't really keep track of where the conversation went. I just talked. A pancake war broke out when Jillian and Tori attempted to steal them off each other's plates.

"*No*," I scolded, as the first bit of pancake flew past my face, and Marie leapt out of the way, squeaking her own little protest, but there was no controlling Jillian and Tori when they got going—there was only minimizing the chaos.

I don't know how it happened, but Marie and I got caught in the mix, and the end result was all of us covered in pancakes, pieces of them strewn across the counter and floor.

"Jillian! Tori! Look at what you've done!" I squealed at the mess, but I was laughing so hard I could barely stay in my seat. When I saw the chocolate smear across Marie's cheek, I laughed even harder.

I got up and grabbed the paper towels from beneath the sink, tossing them in Tori's direction. She caught them and promptly tossed them back.

"Hey!" she said. "You're guilty, too!"

The war resumed, only this time, pancakes and an entire roll of paper towels ended up not only in the kitchen but also in the adjacent living room.

When the clock on the microwave started flashing, we almost didn't notice.

"Shit," I heard Tori say. "The damn microwave is on the fritz. Does everything around here have to break?"

I turned and watched as the time flashed repeatedly, followed by the chaos of digital numbers flashing across the screen in fragments, one after the other in a jumbled mess. Jillian hopped up and started pressing buttons, but it had no effect.

"Power surge?" she asked, giving us a confused look. Marie and Tori shrugged, while I sat there staring at the clock transfixed, waiting. A split second later, the clock flashed a string of eights and died completely.

"Great," Jillian said, throwing her hands up in exasperation. "I guess I'll call the maintenance guys tomorrow."

I stared down into my cup of orange juice, feeling claustrophobic. I would be strong for my friends, I told myself. No moping. The clock told me I had eight hours left. I would make the last eight hours of my life count.

"I feel like movies," I said, forcing myself to smile brightly.

"Really?" Jillian asked skeptically, eyeing me. I may have actually succeeded in convincing her that I was sick. "You want to watch movies?"

"Well," I said dejectedly. "It's not like we can go outside."

A flash of lightning lit up the sky. I briefly lamented that my last few hours would be spent away from the marvels of the outside world, but I pushed that disappointment aside. I had what I needed right beside me.

"I want movies and popcorn," I said, hopping up and making my way to the living room.

"Are you forgetting something?" Tori asked, picking a piece of limp pancake off the counter and staring at me, eyebrows raised.

"It can wait until later," I said, settling in on the couch.

They all stared at me.

"What?" I asked them.

"Who are you, and what have you done with my best friend?" Jillian said, her mouth wide open.

"First, *what*?" Tori said, still holding the tragic-looking pancake. "And in case you've forgotten, you hate movies. And TV shows. And video games. If it involves the TV, you don't like it."

"I do not *hate* the TV," I said, rolling my eyes. "I like some stuff."

"Documentaries are not TV," Tori remarked, a disgusted look crossing her face.

"Come on!" I whined, now determined to find a few decent movies just to prove them wrong.

I was genuinely surprised by what happened next.

Tori shrugged. "Why the hell not?" she said, hopping down from where she had been perched on the counter and tossing the pancake away. "But for each boring documentary you pick, you owe me at least one round as a video-game partner. You've been warned."

Jillian looked confused. I crossed my arms and gave her a mock glare.

"I've got the popcorn," she finally said, grinning.

It was nice. By the middle of the afternoon, we had made a sort of blanket cocoon, with the four of us wrapped up inside it. We watched a lot of movies, though none of us were paying that much attention to them. Mostly, we just talked. We painted each other's nails, something I hadn't done since I was a teenager. I chose a bright yellow, Jillian chose blue, and Marie chose pink. Tori refused at first, but when Jillian held up the black nail polish, Tori's eyes lit up, and she painted her nails purple and black. We probably consumed enough popcorn and cookie dough to meet our calorie requirements for the next week, but we didn't care. Marie was the one who suggested board games, and we spent the last few hours of our time laughing and shouting at each other. Most people could have come up with more exciting ways to spend their last day, but for me, it was the best last day I had ever had. Nothing could have made it better.

The sun had just gone down when the power cut off, leaving us in almost complete darkness.

"Damn it!" Tori spat, tossing her hands up. "*Every single time it rains!*"

I sighed. They always cut the power when it was time. The electricity got in the way of their instruments.

Despite being tangled up in three warm bodies, I suddenly felt frozen. My stomach started churning. I had been happy. I had almost forgotten. Now, all of the anguish I had pushed aside came flooding back.

"Hang on," I said, working hard to keep my voice steady and even. "I have a flashlight in my room."

I got up and walked away. Each step I took away from them felt like a distance of a thousand miles. My legs were wobbly, and I knew it wasn't because I had spent the past few hours sitting on them. I felt completely desolate.

Once in the confines of my room, I just stood there, waiting. I didn't have to wait long. There was a flash of light, kind of like a camera flash. I had almost mistaken it for another bolt of lightning, but out of the corner of my eye, I saw something floating in the air. I caught it with one hand, and that's when I noticed how cold and clammy my palms were.

I looked down. A single scrap of paper was in my hand. There was just one word written on it:

DRIVE

I sighed, shakily, almost choking from the tightness of my throat. I figured that would be it; after all, it was the easiest way to do these things. I grabbed the flashlight out of my closet and slipped the piece of paper into my pocket, wiping the sweat off my palms as I did so, and went back to the living room.

"I'm going to go ask the R.A. what's going on," I said, tossing the flashlight onto the blanket cocoon.

Tori flipped it on and pointed it at me. "It's fine," she said. "It'll be back on soon."

"I'll be gone for two minutes," I replied. I felt my heart breaking, but my face somehow managed not to betray any emotion.

The result of plenty of practice, I thought bitterly.

I forced a smile. "Cross my heart," I said, playfully crossing my heart for emphasis.

Was it really me standing there in the living room? I felt like I was standing in the background, just watching the scene unfold. I felt removed from everything.

"Fine," Jillian said. "But hurry back."

I looked into her gray eyes and smiled. This was my biggest betrayal ever. Of course it wasn't, but now was absolutely the wrong time to be remembering that. It was so hard, though, considering how this had gone before.

I shook my head. Why did I have to remember that *now*? I hadn't thought about it in years.

I turned and walked away, refusing to let myself think. I was on autopilot. My legs were heavy as lead, and I already felt the tears behind my eyes, though I knew they wouldn't fall. I vowed not to look back, but as I slipped through the door, I couldn't stop myself. I took one last look at Marie, with her legs tucked against her chest, Jillian beside her, and Tori sprawled across the couch. They were talking about something, smiling. When they all started laughing, I knew I couldn't linger any longer. I closed the door behind me.

And, with that, I removed them from my life forever.

How sad that I couldn't even shed tears for them.

I waited until I was at the end of the hall before I broke into a run. Two flights of stairs later and the rain hit me, pelting me with a cold, angry force. The wind howled sideways, lightning lighting up the black sky. I grabbed the scrap of paper out of my pocket, and dropped it as I raced across the parking lot, my footfalls splashing in ankle-deep puddles that soaked my shoes. No one would find the paper. Even if they did, they wouldn't know what it meant.

I flung my car door open and, once inside, finally noticed the heaving sobs.

"Calm down," I whispered to myself. "Just calm down. You've done all of this before, and it's better this time."

They would make the pain go away, if only I could find the strength to turn on the car. Unfortunately, I had never made a particularly strong person. I was sure I was going to be sick. My head was swimming, and I felt weak and shaky. It was hard to breathe between the sobs.

I waited a few minutes so that I could quiet myself. I turned on the car and put the heat on to lessen my shivering. Then, resigned to my fate, I turned on the radio and sat there, waiting. After a few seconds, I saw the repeating string of numbers across the radio: latitude and longitude coordinates of a place not far from campus. If I remembered correctly, the set of coordinates would lead me to a crossroad in the middle of nowhere, right beside the train tracks.

"Oh, not a train," I muttered. "*Please* don't be a train."

I didn't have enough nerves left to handle a train.

I put the car in reverse and gave one last fleeting look at the dorms. The buildings were still dark, making them almost completely invisible against the night sky, but the lights would be back on at any second. Not long after that, my roommates would realize I had been gone a while—purse, phone, and everything else left behind. I couldn't think about that, or I would never make it. I pushed the thought from my mind.

"Goodbye," I whispered, and I was gone.

The crossroad was only ten minutes away, and I was relieved when I made it over the train tracks without incident.

"*Thank you*," I whispered, letting out a sigh of relief. I should have known better. Drama at that level wasn't exactly our forte.

I stopped at the crossroad and glanced down at the radio, but it had shorted out.

"I guess I'm in the right place," I said to no one in particular. A flash of light caught my attention, and that is when I noticed the truck parked a few yards to my right, almost hidden by the wall of rain and the darkness. I flashed my lights in return.

I pulled the car into the intersection and unbuckled my seat belt. I saw the truck start up, then continue down the road at an ever-increasing speed. The driver's lights glared at me through the rain. I became all too aware of the hum of the car's engine and the squeak of the windshield wipers as they moved across the glass. Everything was moving in slow motion. A bolt of lightning tore through the night sky before me, and it seemed like forever before it kissed the ground.

My breath caught in my throat as I saw the lights outside the passenger's side window, and I clenched my eyes shut. I always wondered how I had the strength to do this over and over again.

As the truck hit me, I clutched at the half-heart necklace around my neck.

A white light blinded me. I found myself falling as the transport beam reassembled my body thousands of miles above where it had been sitting on the planet only moments before. A pair of strong arms grabbed me before I could hit the ground.

"Whoa!" a man said, his voice gruff. I looked up to see a plump man in a stained shirt and an old ball cap. I could smell the remnants of alcohol and cigarettes on his clothes. The smell of him made my weakened stomach churn.

I brushed a strand of red hair, which had been tossed wildly about after being disassembled and reassembled in an immeasurably short blink of time, behind my ear. A red blush, nearly rivaling the color of my hair, crept across my freckled face.

"You'd think I'd be used to that," I said, looking embarrassed. The transport beam always messed with our heads for reasons I didn't totally understand, and I always seemed especially susceptible.

"Happens to the best of us," he said, offering a hand for me to shake. "Jo'sha."

"Saira," I said, extending a shaky hand out to him.

"I'll be! Haven't I had the privilege of hitting you before?" Jo'sha exclaimed, beaming and grabbing my hand vigorously.

He smiled at me, but the only thing I could process was how wrong this all felt.

"You spooked my horse into throwing me once," I said, forcing a weak smile.

I had never been on a horse, though. At least, *this* me had never been on a horse. I had been a different girl, in a different time and place that seemed more like a dream than a memory. I hadn't thought about that life in a long time.

This part was always so confusing. How could I make sense of two realities when they were both, though completely opposite to each other, the picture of normalcy for me? Inside my head I felt the pull of opposing worlds, threatening to yank me apart.

I knew they needed to move me, and they needed to do it quickly. It was already becoming too much.

"That's right," he said, either oblivious to my inner torment or completely ignoring it. "I have to tell you, I don't think I could have done that. You sure put a lot of faith in these jokers."

Truthfully, I had been clutching my horse Sebastian's mane the entire time, begging him to be a good boy. He hadn't.

Papa always told me not to ride him near the river. I couldn't swim …

Jo'sha winked at me, but I felt far, far away.

I forced a laugh and a smile, trying to look professional—trying to look like I wasn't starting to unravel right there where I stood.

"Who have you been? That's a strong Southern accent," I said, doing my best to shake off the past and keep my composure.

"Yes, ma'am," Jo'sha said, laying it on thick. "I've had the privilege of being this unpleasant gentleman for the past six weeks. A real piece of work, this one. He likes his alcohol and hitting his poor wife more than I can handle. Definitely a hard act."

I cringed.

"He didn't make it," Jo'sha said, eyes straying toward the ground. I could see the guilt, but of course it wasn't his fault.

I sighed and closed my eyes. "And Allyson?" I asked, though I wasn't sure I wanted to know.

"Seems I remember something about a hard knock on the head, but I think she'll come out of it just fine."

I sighed in relief. "That's good to hear. She has a good life ahead of her. A lot of really wonderful people are in it."

This time, Jo'sha must have understood the look on my face, because he placed his hand on my shoulder and gave it a good squeeze.

I took a second to survey my surroundings but quickly realized it was nothing new. Same warm, white, padded room with no doors or windows visible, though I knew one would be sliding open at any second. The same itch, too. I rubbed my skin and felt the hair on the back of my neck stand on end as the nanotechnology crawled across me, sterilizing me of my earthly microbes. The ship, *Moga*, was home to thousands of different species, each with their own germs, but each species had had thousands upon thousands of years to adapt to each other. None of them had developed an immunity to the Earth's natural biomass yet, and though we had the ability to create vaccinations for everything, our bodies would hardly be able to handle it all at once. Besides, at this point, it was an unnecessary nuisance to try to protect ourselves against Earth germs. Still, a simple bacterium could potentially sicken us all; hence, the very itchy but convenient nanotechnology crawling all over my skin.

"Welcome back!" I heard a familiar voice call, though the language was decidedly not English. I spun around, and suddenly all of my heartache vanished.

In front of me stood one of the tallest creatures I had ever seen. His twelve-foot- tall body was easily twice my height, with arms and legs much longer than any human's. He was a deep royal-blue, with off-white patches and silver flecks of skin from the top of his head to the tips of his fingers and toes. His eyes were a golden yellow, and I could have sworn they were smiling at me.

Of course, Thellessians always looked happy. That was their nature.

"Dorain!" I shouted, my voice overcome with emotion. I ran to him, leaping into his arms. He scooped me up easily, and I planted a kiss on the top of his hairless head.

"How's my little sister?" he asked in Darcii, and I could see the flood of happiness sweeping through him. I hadn't realized until now how much I had missed him, and I felt like my heart would burst from pure elation.

"*Little* sister?" I asked him in our language, giving him a mock glare, although the smile that stretched across my face defeated the effect.

"Look at it from my perspective. You are quite little right now."

"And your accent sounds horrible in that body," he added.

I narrowed my eyes at him. "I'm half a minute older than you, and don't you forget it."

"But I am half an inch taller, *little* sister," he responded.

I touched my finger to my lips. For us, this was the equivalent of a human sticking out its tongue. Our tongues weren't long enough to leave our mouths like a human's was.

"That's my sister," he said, laughing. I planted kisses on each side of his face in human fashion and wrapped my arms around him tighter. I was acting completely childish, but I was just so happy!

"What are you doing here?" I asked, my face pressed against his neck, breathing in his familiar smell. My human nose couldn't place the unique odor, but part of me still recognized it as family. "Who authorized you for retrieval?"

"They thought it might be easier," Dorain said, delicately attempting to gauge my emotional status.

"After what happened last time," I added. Dorain watched me, his yellow eyes filled with concern.

"It wasn't like that," I said.

True as that might be, I wasn't okay, but I had my brother, and he made all the difference in a thousand universes.

I let him carry me through the ship, much like a human parent would carry a sleeping child. I rested my head on his shoulder and took a deep breath. He smelled like sunlight, I decided. I felt the rhythmic beating of his hearts in his chest. His skin felt like satin against my own. I briefly wondered if the hair on my arms tickled him. My mammalian body must have felt so strange to him. I giggled under my breath, wondering what must have been going through his head.

"I missed you," I whispered.

"I missed you more. How are you doing? Tell me the truth."

"It hurts," I said, my voice choking. I buried my face into his neck. If leaving my friends was the hardest part, this came in second. This was the part where someone would lead me away to have the pain washed away, but not just the pain. The first time, I had begged them not to do it. I wanted to beg my brother this time, but I didn't. I just gripped him tighter, closing my eyes and remembering the days when we used to chase each other in the never-ending sunlight, racing each other on glimmering beaches.

"Do you want to tell me about them?" Dorain asked softly.

"Please don't talk about it," I begged. "Right now I just want you to hold me. It doesn't hurt as much if you hold me."

For the moment, the joy of seeing my brother was washing away the pain of losing my loved ones on Earth. I wanted to ride the wave of happiness for as long as I could.

"Oh, my sister," he said. "You always get so attached."

I didn't say anything. I just let him carry me as we weaved through the maze that was *Moga*, listening to the sounds of thousands of alien voices in strange dialects, and the strange, unusual faces, yet all so comforting and familiar, passing us in the halls.

The medical room was just as I figured it would be. I think they brought me to the same one each time. It was white and sterile, much like the retrieval room. The only difference was the stainless disk in the center, and of course, the medical supplies that lined the walls. On the ceiling there was a strange apparatus of some kind. At the moment, it was the source of the bright light in the room, but I had always suspected that it somehow helped with the Transference.

My brother set me down on the table and I relaxed, laying out flat. The table looked cold, but it was actually quite warm. I sighed, taking in the scent of the sterile room. All medical rooms smelled the same, regardless of whether they were alien or human. It set me on edge. There were memories I associated with the smell, and the last thing I wanted was for them to surface now. I looked up at my brother and he saw the look in my eyes. He placed his hand on mine and squeezed. It helped. I felt my mind quiet down.

"Saira! If it isn't my favorite Doppelganger!" said a small, stout alien with two tiny, sparsely fingered arms. He was so short that he needed a hover chair to reach me. His beady eyes, each one positioned at the end of his hammerhead-like face, looked me over carefully. His skin was rough and an odd orange-brown color, but he looked warm and friendly.

"Ah, yes! Little Saira! I was wondering when I might have the pleasure of seeing you again," said the other, female, half of the conjoined twins.

I laughed. "Who are you two to call me *little*?"

"She always gets so offended," Dorain remarked.

He leaned against the table and said, with a wry smile, "I'd play nice with the two who are going to cut your head open."

I rolled my eyes at my brother, but I was smiling too. Any nervousness I'd had was gone. I trusted the beings in this room. I was excited to be home.

"Saira, you know the drill. The sooner we get these formalities out of the way, the sooner you get a growth spurt."

I nodded giddily.

"Name?"

"Allyson Owens," I said, without thinking.

There was a short pause before I realized what I'd said. Dorain stared at me. If he had eyebrows, they would have been raised. There was no mistaking his smirk, though, even if he didn't have true lips.

I saw one of the doctors turn his—or was that half a her?—torso to give the other one a look.

"Saira Ta'u," I said. "My name is Saira Ta'u. I'm a Peacemaker of the Doppelganger class. I was assigned to the Southern United States with the four hundred and eighteenth division. My identification number is nine-one-three-seven-nine."

"Very good, Saira," the left head, whom I now remembered was a female called Pask, said. The male half, Pashka, gently encouraged me to turn my head and look the other way. I felt a sting behind my ear, followed quickly by an icy numbness.

We ran through the other formalities: mission, species, home planet, family, education, years of service, etc. I had done it so many times that I sometimes answered the next question before Pask had a chance to ask it.

"Done," I heard Pashka say. I turned my head to look at the gleaming metallic chip he held between surgical tweezers.

I looked toward Dorain and noticed the slightly queasy look on his face. Well, it might have been queasy if he had a stomach.

"What?" I asked.

"You bleed red," he said, and shuddered. "It's just strange."

I laughed. "I would think that you of all beings would have seen enough of it."

"Not from you," he replied.

"I have bled red for twenty years. You get used to it."

"We're through here, Saira. It's time to prepare for the next part. Dorain, would you like to sit with your sister for a few minutes?" Pashka asked. Dorain nodded. Pask slipped a mask over my face and I heard the hiss of the sedative rushing out. It left a funny taste in my mouth, like the time I had put a quarter in my mouth as a three-year-old human. Mom had freaked out and pried my mouth open to get it out, terrified that I would swallow it. It had scared me badly.

The sudden memory depressed me, and I felt hysterical sobs rising in my throat. I clenched Dorain's hand tighter. He knelt down beside me, pressing his forehead against mine.

"When you wake up, you'll feel better," he said, giving me an encouraging smile.

"I know," I said. The mask distorted my voice. I closed my eyes and focused on my breathing. I only had minutes now and I would be okay. Everything would be back to normal, and another cycle of service would be behind me.

I kept telling myself that, but it was never that simple. I missed my mom. I missed my dad and sister. I missed Jillian, Marie, and Tori. I missed the Earth.

But I only had to be strong for a few more minutes. I could be strong for that long, couldn't I?

"She's nice," Dorain said.

"Who?" I asked, focusing on my brother. I tightened my grip on his hand. My wonderful brother … he had always been there for me.

"Allyson. I looked in on her a few times. I knew you would want to know. She'll be fine in a few months. The doctors did a number on her head. She won't have any memories."

"She's going back to some really special people. They'll take care of her."

"Did they give you this?" Dorain asked, pulling the half-heart out from under my shirt.

Hands shaking, I undid the clasp from my neck and held it out to my brother.

"Take it, please. Keep it safe for me," I said, my voice breaking, "It means a lot."

I started crying. The sound of my sobs was ugly and distorted behind the mask.

Dorain nodded.

"I don't know how you do it," he said, gently stroking my hair. I had told him a long time ago that it was a comfort to humans, as it was now. It was comforting enough that I succeeded in swallowing the sobs. "You always manage to be so strong, especially after—"

"Please don't talk about it. Not right now," I begged. I was starting to feel dazed, much to my relief.

He nodded and was quiet.

"I'm sleepy," I said, my voice barely a whisper.

"It's okay. I'll be here when you wake up."

"Tell me about her until I fall asleep. Please?"

"Sure," Dorain said, smiling. "She likes sports. She can play basketball really well. She plays soccer, too. She likes—"

But, by then, I was asleep. When I woke up, I would be someone else.

CHAPTER 3

From the moment I opened my eyes, I knew things hadn't gone as planned, though, strangely enough, it wasn't because of the narrowed field of vision from the too-close spacing of human eyes, the slight growling of a hungry stomach because the human body couldn't use the light in the room to photosynthesize energy—not even the strange, slow rhythm of the heart beating on the left side of the body, rather than the two I was used to fluttering in the center of my chest. No, what alerted me to the fact that I was still in the Ganger body was the flood of emotions I immediately felt. I still had them, and as beautiful as they were, they hurt. They hurt *so* much.

When the doctors performed a Transference, they put my mind back into my body, but not completely. I kept the memories of my human life, but I couldn't keep the emotions that were attached to them. I would still remember my family and friends, but all of the fond feelings I had for them should have been stripped away. It was the price Peacemakers were obligated to pay. If we lived each lifetime with the emotions associated with past families and friends, we wouldn't be able to perform our jobs. Some had tried, but the results were disastrous. None of us ever wanted to lose our emotions—even I had fought more than a few times—so the doctors made it easy for us and took them away as we slept.

Of course, that was only half of it. No one ever wanted to be awake for a Transference. Though I hadn't experienced it, I'd heard the rumors of those who had been awake for the Transference and had suffered anguish and near-madness.

Dorain's blue face swam into view. Behind him, I could see Pashka and Pask hovering, looking confused and more than a little concerned.

"What went wrong?" I asked. My voice sounded a million miles away.

"Nothing went wrong," Dorain said, stroking my hair.

"Your presence has been requested by the Elders," Pask explained.

"They asked that we not continue with the procedure," Pashka said.

"Was something wrong with the chip?" I asked. The thought made my head swim. If we had just lost twenty years' worth of information … If I had spent twenty years on Earth for nothing …

I loved my time on Earth. I cherished every minute of it, but it meant giving up a life here, not to mention the price that was paid at the end. Something had to come from that cost.

"We were not given that information. We were asked to wake you and get you to the Elders as soon as possible."

I nodded, though I didn't really understand. I was starting to feel a wave of nausea, though I figured it was just a side effect from the gas.

"The room is spinning," I slurred.

"I'll take you," Dorain said.

"The effects of the sleeping agent will dissipate shortly," Pashka added.

I nodded, and Dorain scooped me into his arms. My head spun. I had my wisdom teeth out when I was seventeen and had been put under anesthesia. This was even more disorienting than waking up from that. I wasn't sure how I was speaking, let alone comprehending anything that was spoken to me. During my first Transference, Pask and Pashka had tried to explain the process to me. They said that, when they put me to sleep, I was so far under that even my consciousness became unaware. It was the only way they could strip emotions from it without causing permanent damage. I didn't understand it, but whatever they did, it always worked.

Now I had to come out of that deep, soul-numbing sleep, and it was hard.

"Do you have any idea what's going on?" I asked Dorain, as he worked his way through the ship's maze. My Darcii was bad enough coming from human vocal cords, but with my barely coherent speech, it was taking my brother a moment to figure out what I was saying.

"No, but I was waiting outside when the messenger came. I saw another Ganger being led by. It looked like he had also just been woken up. Something is going on."

"I don't understand. If they have the chip, why do they need me? Now? As a Ganger? This has never happened before," I mumbled into Dorain's chest. Even in my dazed state, I felt panic rising. I tried to calm down, but I couldn't shake it off.

"I know," Dorain said, and that was all he could offer as an explanation.

My head was mostly clear by the time the large door appeared around a corner in the labyrinth that was *Moga*. From the outside, the only thing that would alert anyone to the significance of the room inside was the size of the entrance. Aside from that, it was as plain and white as any other door in the ship.

"I'll be close," Dorain said, as he gently set me on my feet. I was still unsteady, but at least I was capable of walking. I had seen Tori drunk on a few occasions. I wondered if this was how she felt.

I reprimanded myself. I shouldn't be focusing on Earth. I shoved the emotions away before they could overtake me—I knew I had to have a clear mind for what was coming. The anxiety building in my chest actually helped, pumping adrenaline through my body that drove all thoughts of my past to the farthest corners of my mind.

I approached the door but hesitated before placing my hand on the palm scanner. It wouldn't recognize Allyson Owens. I chewed on my bottom lip, but just before I could look to Dorain for help, the door slid open of its own accord.

Inside, there were several dozen Gangers already waiting, all looking as confused as I felt. Some seemed to be in worse shape than I. They must have been very deeply sedated when they got pulled back, perhaps even to the brink of a Transference. Somehow I knew this was my division, but I didn't recognize a single face. I had never met any of them as Gangers, and even if I had met them as their human Gangers once upon a time, we were never the same person twice. I looked for tell-tale mannerisms, but all I could see was a sea of human strangers.

I chose a spot between a blond male and a brunette female. We glanced at each other uneasily. We were all trying to figure out what we were doing here and who the people were beside us, but we were either too uneasy to speak or still too disoriented to make sense of our surroundings, so we just stood there, silent and uncomfortable.

People trickled in and found places to hover quietly. We were in a white room, just like any other room on *Moga*. This one, however, was not used to having occupants. There was nowhere to sit, so we all stood. While the room had looked massive on the outside, I felt claustrophobic. And it was incredibly dark—I couldn't even tell where the ceiling was. The white walls, though they had looked normal until closer inspection, were glossy and semi-reflective, almost like mirrors. There was a hum in the air, and the room had one of the strangest odors I had ever smelled: a combination of a hospital, hot rubber, and something else I couldn't place. I wasn't certain that I wanted to.

When the room erupted in color and noise, I jumped. We all did. We had been standing there silently for so long that there was more than enough time for the drugs to clear our systems. All around the room, images flashed across the walls. Thousands upon thousands of images, all of humans, dancing across my eyes so quickly I could barely make sense of one before another took its place. The chaotic movements gave me motion sickness. Some of the images I recognized as memories from Gangers, others were direct surveillance from *Moga*, and still others were TV shows, news, and movies from the planet Earth. They all went by in a blur, but I was certain that at least a few of the glimpses I caught were my memories.

Just once, I could have sworn that I saw Jillian's face. Maybe even Marie's and Tori's.

My throat tightened, but I closed my eyes and forced the emotions away.

"We have an unprecedented situation," said voices from above us, all speaking at once. The language was Common Tongue, the universal language used in the presence of multiple species.

I looked up, and what sat above me was startling. With the lights on, we could finally see them. Above us, seated at what I could only think of as a gigantic computer, with various wires and tubes protruding from it, was the Council of Elders, a group of dozens, each belonging to a species known for its phenomenal capacity for processing information, multitasking, critical thinking, and other intellectual processes on such an extraordinary scale that I would never, for as long as I lived, be capable of. They were not called the Elders because they were old, per se, though I knew some of the beings above me had lived long enough to remember the first generations of Peacemakers. The Elders represented the first species to make up the Higher Planets, a coalition of planets deemed advanced by galactic standards. The species above me were the first in everything: life, science, math, religion, medicine—everything. My own people hadn't even crawled out of the ocean before these beings had established order in the universe. I could not even begin to comprehend the knowledge and wisdom each species possessed. Not every being from these oldest species were Elders, but those that chose to serve as Peacemakers certainly were.

One of the Elders' duties as Peacemakers was to process the memory chips each of us carried in our heads for twenty years, along with knowledge taken from surveillance by our other technologies and what was available from humans themselves, namely, their media and literature. I had never seen the Elders before. No one had. They kept to themselves, tasked with the vitally important job of translating and interpreting everything there was to know about the human race. Not only that, but, given the Elders' knowledge and wisdom as a species and as individual beings, they alone were responsible for making every decision concerning Peacemaker activity on Earth. Almost every action I had ever taken as a Ganger had been ordered by these beings. The amount of foresight alone that these beings had …

Without them, the Peacemakers would not exist.

I realized, though, that such a job came with an enormous price. I looked from creature to creature and I felt my stomach twisting. They didn't move or blink. Their eyes looked dead, wandering around the room blankly and aimlessly. The wires and tubes that erupted from the gigantic computer fed directly into the heads and other body parts of each creature, twisting and snarling among them like a tentacled monster. The tubes and wires were permanent, I realized, when I saw the skin, or scales, that had grown around them. No wonder I had never seen an Elder. They never left this room.

The realization stole the air from my lungs.

For the first time in my life, I truly appreciated the purpose of the Peacemakers. For a creature to give up not only its life, but the quality of its life, for *this*, for a lesser species that didn't even know what we were doing, let alone that we existed …

My head was spinning from the magnitude of the thoughts rushing through me. The admiration, awe, and even horror that arose from what I was seeing threatened to overwhelm me. It would be a long time before I could fully digest what I was being allowed to see.

The images flashing on the walls were the material they were processing from us: twenty years of living with humans as humans. Whatever they had called us together for was so important that they hadn't even given themselves time to process all of our knowledge.

"We apologize for the abrupt termination of your Transferences, but we need you as you are," said the voices.

I had thought all of the Elders were speaking, but I realized that it was only one being, its voice projecting the thoughts of the collective. It was a species I had not encountered before, as were many of the beings I could see. This one was sightless, as far as I could tell. At least, it had no eyes that I could see.

The hair rose on the back of my neck. This day had already given me more information than I could possibly comprehend, and the Elders had just started speaking.

"We are disturbed by the developments of the human race. Despite our best efforts, they are not progressing as we had hoped. They are only decades away from being considered a Level Three planet. As we speak, their technologies are moving outward from their home planet. From there, it will not be long before their fate is out of our hands."

Peacemakers classified each planet based on levels, each level dictating our level of involvement. A Level Zero planet either did not have life or did not have life that was potentially intelligent; thus, our involvement was not necessary. A Level One planet was inhabited by beings that were considered intelligent, but they did not have technology. Level One planets tended to be monitored from afar, with very little involvement from Peacemakers. Level Two planets had beings that were intelligent and had developed knowledge in science, math, medicine, and other fields. Once a planet was considered a Level Two, the Peacemakers moved in, sending in Gangers and Impersonators to monitor and influence their development. It was a wide-ranging level, with more sub-classifications than I could remember. A planet could be considered a Level Two for millennia. A Level Three planet had the technology capable of reaching out to other planets with life, and once they did so, they were considered a Level Four planet. Once a planet reached

Level Four, the Peacemakers pulled out. Our work was done. There was nothing left for us to do but hope that we had helped raise an intelligent, benign race.

"Speak your opinion of this," the eyeless alien said in a hundred different voices. It wasn't forceful, just impersonal, as if a computer were speaking. But, then, after so many years confined to this room with wires embedded in them, maybe it *was* a machine that was speaking now.

We all shifted in place uncomfortably. Surely they could not be concerned about simple space technology …

A man spoke. "It's like you said. They are still decades away from having the technology to be considered a Level Three race. They remain oblivious to the existence of species outside their own planet. If your concern is that they are not equipped to handle the knowledge their technology brings them, destroying it is simple enough. They won't understand the reason for its failure."

"That order has been given and is being carried out. That is not our concern," the alien said. They were quiet, waiting, and we looked at each other with puzzled expressions.

"We don't understand," said another man, who stood only a few feet from me.

"The human race has technology beyond its ability. They should not be at the level of development that they are. Humans, despite their great knowledge, have yet to evolve beyond their primal instincts. They still cling to rudimentary origins. They follow the instinctual urge to produce offspring at unacceptable rates. Their planet is at capacity, yet their reproduction has increased. They are still given to consuming animal matter as a means of survival. The population of food animals has grown large enough to defeat its purpose. It is now destroying more than it sustains, while the ability to sustain the planet with plant foods has existed for decades. They have made great progress in science, yet they use this against each other. They use arbitrary borders, outdated beliefs—even morphological features are excuses for malevolence. The list of grievances committed by the human race is endless."

"None of these things are unique for a race in its childhood," said a woman. "These things are what the Peacemakers exist for."

"None of these things are cause for concern," a man echoed. "The humans are isolated, and we have the means to ensure that they remain so."

"We have watched them for many centuries now. The humans are a violent race," the Elders said.

We paused, unable to fathom what they were implying. There was a chill in the room; something was wrong here. I looked around. The others sensed it, too. I could see it in their eyes and in the way they shifted anxiously where they stood.

"Humans are not violent, merely young. They are a child throwing a temper tantrum, nothing more," said the woman beside me. I jumped slightly when she spoke. I remained silent, listening and waiting, as was my way. I was a curious creature, not a forward one.

"They are violent," the Elders repeated. I felt my heart begin to race. What was the purpose of this conversation? Why were we here? What use could the Elders possibly have for a group of Gangers, when they had access to *all* of the information, and the foresight to make all of the decisions?

"Human television, music, media—we have had access to it from its inception. It is disturbing. Humans are in love with violence. They use it as sport. Even their children's entertainment has become increasingly violent. They have become desensitized to the pain of others. They are apathetic. They view themselves only as individual beings. They do not care for the plight of others. They wage wars against themselves, slaughter each other for transparent reasons. They lust for the speed of bloodshed over the patience of diplomacy. They are violent," the Elders said.

I was scared now. No, I wasn't just scared, I was terrified. I felt as if the world were spinning out of control, and there was nothing for me to hold on to. I heard my human heart pounding in my ears. I was trying to control my facial expressions in the presence of such powerful creatures, but I could feel the blood draining from my face. I was sweating and shaking. My stomach was clenching forcefully, and I was afraid that I would be sick.

I tried to reassure myself. The Council of Elders was benevolent. Whatever they did, it was in the best interests of the lower beings. Their very existence was dedicated to them. The Elders were the most harmless body in the universe when it came to the humans.

I kept telling myself that, but something still felt wrong.

Very wrong.

"Humans have created music, art, dance, and theater. They write. Some of the images and stories they create are awe-inspiring," a woman said earnestly.

"The human race is digressing. It is falling apart," the Elders retorted.

There was silence. All around us, images flickered across the walls. There were distinct images of war, famine, genocide, TV shows, video games, mass shootings, terror, pain, hatred ... I couldn't help but wonder how many of them were from my own mind, and how many of those were feeding the Elders' words.

"All of your concerns can be handled. We have handled them before with other races. Animals, technology, populations—we have the ability to influence these matters as we see fit," someone said.

"No," said the Elders. "Humans are unlike other species we have encountered. They are too slow."

Again there was silence. The Gangers looked back and forth among one another. We didn't understand. Before us sat some of the most powerful and capable beings in the universe, and they were— what were they doing? These were not the words of advanced thinkers, I realized. These were not the thoughts of altruistic beings dedicated to raising lower beings. Their arguments were one-sided, as if they couldn't see the whole picture, but that wasn't true. They were being stubborn, blocking our arguments at every turn as if their minds had been made up, and no matter what we said, they would remain steadfast. Their words were arrogant and haughty.

This argument did not stem from them. The realization hit me with the force of Jo'sha's truck.

"What don't we know?" someone had the clarity to ask.

I was transfixed by the Elders. I realized that all of the Elders had adjusted their eyes to stare down at us, though their eyes were empty. They saw past us. All but the eyeless being were elsewhere, perhaps in our memories, but I couldn't help but think that their eyes were looking to us for the answers, as if we, not they, were expected to act.

"The Council of Traltix has convened," the Elders said.

"The Peacemakers are independent of their politics," said a male voice.

"Yes, and the Council of Traltix remains independent of us. There has been no change in this status," said the Elders.

The Council of Traltix was the government established to rule over the Higher Planets, each race electing delegates to represent their own planets. Each planet had a discrete government that acted for that planet alone, but even those governments answered to the Council of Traltix. The Council was a body of tens of thousands of members, each with the collective knowledge of their species. Their power was enormous, but they were as benign as the Council of Elders. If the Peacemakers were responsible for creating peace among the lesser planets, the Council was responsible for protecting it among the Higher Planets. This was how it had been for eons, each one working independently of the other, sharing information but never interfering.

"The Quintatinks declared war on the Sebicans. The Council of Traltix was quick to act, though not quick enough. Multiple worlds sent ships to intervene at the battle line. The battle that occurred was brief, but lives were lost. Peace has since been restored."

The words fell, and a deathly chill permeated the room. We stood there, frozen, each of us wondering if we had heard correctly. Where my heart had been racing before, it was completely silent now. I had stopped breathing. Everything was far away. I was afraid I might be passing out, the shock was so intense.

"War?"

I heard the word echo around the room, though I didn't think my mind could fully register it, I was so shaken. I managed to breathe again, but I felt like sobbing. Clearly, I wasn't the only one. I could hear Gangers around me begin to weep. It was a terrible sound in that eerie room, with the massive computer blinking and whirring and smelling of burning plastic and other unnatural things.

Earth had war. Actually, Earth had *wars*. Somewhere on the planet, at any given time, a war was raging. Some of them would last for decades. But off that planet ...

"It was the first war among the Higher Planets in over twenty-one thousand years," the Elders said.

"What was the cause?" someone whispered, nearly choking on the words.

"Fear," the Elders said. "Anger. Aggression. They give their reasons, but those are irrelevant."

That hardly helped. We all knew the primal causes for war. It was a cowardly strategy for creatures who were not advanced enough to understand true diplomacy and the sanctity of one another's lives. Still, the connection to Earth, and why we would be called to a meeting for such a thing, begged a more specific answer, I thought.

"What significance does this hold for Earth?" someone asked.

"The Council of Traltix has convened all of its members to the *Allisandre*. It is the largest Council meeting in history," the Elders said. They paused before they continued. "The Quintatinks were under Peacemaker guidance until ten thousand years ago."

"Are they holding us responsible?" someone asked.

"They cannot hold us responsible!" a different voice cried. "Once a species has passed Level Four, we cannot be held accountable for any relapse. The Quintatinks are responsible for their own fate, and the Council must hold them liable if a war could not be reconciled in time."

"Yes," said the Elders. "They do not hold us responsible for the act of war. They are, however, afraid. As the youngest species of the Higher Planets, they question our methods. They fear further relapses. They worry that our methods are not adept for species of ... a more aggressive nature."

"We have provided guidance for thousands of species. Retrogression does occur, but how many out of the thousands of centuries we have stood watch over budding worlds? Perfection is not our goal. In fact, it is unrealistic. Every species has its faults, but they learn to manage them."

"We share your view," the Elders said.

They shared our view, but it was clear that others did not.

"Then what significance does an act of war have for the planet Earth?" someone asked in a desperate voice. We were all distraught and very, *very* frightened. My stomach was twisting inside me and my legs were growing weak, and I was surprised that I did not pass out.

I had to be strong. I was a Peacemaker. I was a leader. I was trusted to watch over a people in their infancy. I called on my training to give me strength. Surely I had been through harder trials than this.

The human race was in no danger, I told myself. The human race wasn't even a threat. They were, without a doubt, a young, frustrating race, but certainly they did not deserve conviction. There was still time—and hope.

"Knowledge of Earth's development is not exclusive to the Peacemakers. Other worlds know what we know. They have seen many of the things that we have seen. Human technology is easy to access. They are not, however, capable of accessing all knowledge. They see only what the humans give them. This includes the Council of Traltix. They know that the humans have developed too slowly. They see the inborn tendency toward violence more clearly than any other human trait. As such, the Council of Traltix has requested that their race be reclassified."

"*As what?*" someone shouted abruptly.

"Between an animal and a sentient being. They would be their own class, and thus, no longer the concern of the Peacemakers."

"No!"

"That's ridiculous!"

"There is nothing wrong with the humans!"

"They're young!"

Suddenly, the room had erupted. At least, this was an eruption for a group of Gangers. Voices were raised. People exchanged words back and forth, their eyes frantic. Reclassifying humans did not take away their technology or their behaviors. If the Peacemakers were forced to abandon Earth, what did that mean for the humans?

What did that mean for *my* humans? What would happen to my family and friends if we left them to their own devices?

I was not doing a good job of being professional. My lips quivered. I was going to collapse into a heap soon, under the weight of this nightmare.

I was stunned, but somehow I managed to stand there. I looked up and nearly jumped. I only saw it out of the corner of my eye, but I could have sworn that the eyeless being was *staring at me*. I shrugged off the feeling. It didn't even have eyes to see me. Clearly, hysteria was setting in. I wanted to leave. I wanted to run.

But I was a Peacemaker, so I stood still. It took all of the strength I had.

"We told them as much," the Elders said.

"And what was their response?"

"The Council has asked if we would consider a Cleansing or Purge."

There was no shouting this time. It was as if all the air had been sucked out of the room. I felt the room swaying—this was the final straw for me.

In the history of the Peacemakers, there had only been two Cleansings. One Purge. After thousands upon thousands of years, and more planets than I could remember, the Peacemakers had only been pushed to desperation by three species. The humans were not like them, I told myself. It was too horrific to even consider.

"No," I said. My voice was driven by pure willpower. I didn't know what was propelling me, but I was still standing, and as long as I was, they would hear me on this.

I heard the word whispered throughout the room, the word passing through many lips. The answer was *no*.

"You think the human race is worthy of our efforts?" the Elders asked.

Not a single one of us showed signs of confliction. "Yes," we said, almost in unison.

The Elders were quiet. They stared down at us, and I realized that somewhere in the conversation they had all tuned in and were watching us with earnest interest. It was terribly eerie. Again I had the distinct feeling that this room full of Gangers was more vital than I could ever know. There was something about us that was unique—something the Elders knew was so powerful and necessary that they had felt the need to summon us, look upon us, and speak with us.

I looked around, but all I saw was a room full of pseudo-humans, alien on the inside, human to the eyes.

"Then we must ask more of you than ever before," the Elders said.

Chapter 4

I had been staring at the silver cylinder for who knows how long. I could see the panel just above my head, displaying strong, healthy vitals. I could not, however, look through the glass window high above my head. I could not see the blue face with her eyes closed, frozen in a complete stasis, almost as if she were sleeping. The only thing I could see coming out of the glass was a bright artificial light. In the dark, still hallway, it was comforting to know that I was sleeping in a bed of light, safe and warm. Of course, that was just my body.

I shivered and rubbed my hands up and down my arms, my teeth chattering slightly. The cold of the seemingly never-ending hall of cylinders penetrated straight through my skin to the bone. The silver pod would have to be heated, too. If I were my true self, I wouldn't survive an extended period of time exposed to this temperature. I could only regulate my body temperature for so long, after all.

"Back again?" Dorain asked. I should have been startled—I certainly hadn't heard him coming up behind me in the dark, his footfalls masked by the mechanical sounds made by the pods, but somehow I always knew when he was near.

"I have never been in here before," I said, my eyes still on the cylinder. "Five cycles and I never know where it is they put me. I always go to sleep and wake up in a medical unit."

"It's dark," Dorain said, sounding mildly anxious.

I nodded. "The dark doesn't bother me as much anymore. Earth gets dark a lot."

They didn't bother to keep this room well lit, since its main residents spent their twenty years here with their eyes closed. The whir of the life-support machines was deafening, but of course we didn't hear anything either. Occasionally, there was a light emitted from one of the pods, indicating that the being inside was photosynthetic. As a courtesy, there was a window for us to look out of when we first awoke. I liked it. It made me feel a bit less confined before the doctors got around to opening the pod. But here, in this dark, loud room, the sleeping faces that looked out from the pods made me feel as if I were standing in the middle of a morgue.

"I visit you sometimes," Dorain said.

"You do? Even in the dark?" I joked.

"I usually bring a light," he said, chuckling a little. "I hate the idea of you being down here alone all the time. I come down when I can. I sing and read to you."

My smile widened. "I have dreams of you singing to me. What do you sing?"

"Mostly songs the colony used to sing to us when we were kids."

"I like those."

Dorain laughed. "I know, my sister. That's why I sing them."

We were quiet for a while, staring at the silver pod with the light emanating from the top. It was surreal, knowing that I was sleeping within arm's reach. I was so close, and yet ... I was detached. A part of me didn't accept that the blue creature within was me. It was like looking at old photographs of my childhood self. I knew the child in the pictures was me, but I had grown into a new person, and the child in the pictures had been left behind so long ago that I didn't know her anymore.

I was that child just as much as I was the alien in the pod—I wasn't. The thought was slightly disturbing. I had never felt so disconnected from myself. Was this what happened when you kept your emotions for too long?

"What are you doing?" Dorain asked me, eyeing me curiously. I snapped out of my reverie, looking at him with a bewildered expression.

"What?"

"You're ... clicking your teeth and ... twitching," Dorain said, trying to find the words. "What kind of human trait is that?"

I laughed, genuinely amused. Human behavior was not my brother's forte as it was mine. I must have appeared, well, alien to him. Whereas I considered myself an anthropologist and a historian, Dorain had always been a scientist of a different sort. I understood languages and cultures, but Dorain's world was made up of numbers and facts. He could understand the computers and machinery on board *Moga* with the same ease that I spoke certain human languages and controlled five human fingers. The various tools of biology, chemistry, and physics were as captivating to him as the rhythm of a human heartbeat or the various expressions of a human face were to me. I guess that's why Dorain built the Gangers, but I was the one who walked in them. Twins we may have been, but my brother and I had always been such different creatures.

Even so, my brother was as comfortable with the red-headed human me as he would have been with his sisterly double. He never looked at me as if I was different. The bond between us had been fierce since birth, and my strange shell had done nothing to change that.

"I'm shivering! I'm cold!" I said, giggling. "Humans can't regulate their temperature, so they do this when they get cold."

Dorain's face grew thoughtful. He bent down and wrapped his arms around me, enveloping me in his warm embrace. I sighed in relief, feeling the heat radiate from his skin. His body temperature ran much hotter than any human's. I closed my eyes and rested my head against his chest, listening to his hearts beating.

I felt myself rising from the floor as Dorain picked me up and held me in his arms. I opened my eyes and turned my head, and when I saw her ...

I really don't know what I felt.

"There you are," Dorain said.

The sound of his hearts beating echoed in my ears. They reminded me of the hummingbirds on Earth; with their wings moving so fast, they appeared as a blur.

I looked at the blue face in the silver pod, eyes closed as if she were sleeping. The silver flecks on my skin reflected the bright light, while the white patches seemed to glow. I sighed, conflicted.

Actually seeing myself hadn't helped anything. Part of me yearned for her—for the familiarity and stability of the body I had walked in for so much of my existence, for the idea of me that I clung to as my true identity, but another part of me vehemently rejected the notion that the being in the pod was me at all. *I* was right there, after all, an outsider looking in. After two decades away, I had grown and left her behind, just as I had left my human-child self behind, and I found that I didn't know the shell anymore. I squirmed, uncomfortable in my brother's arms.

"What are you thinking?" Dorain asked.

I reached out to myself. I pressed my palm against the glass and held it there, praying for a connection, some familiar spark to remind me of my lost identity.

Nothing happened. I pulled my hand away. A single human handprint lingered on the glass, distorting her face, before slowly fading away.

"I've been thinking about home," I said.

"What about it?"

"Maybe it's time to go back," I said.

The Peacemakers was a volunteer organization. I had not been recruited; this was not a job. As a child, I learned about the younger planets in school. I read books about them and even got to see some of the images the Peacemakers collected. I loved them from the start. I knew from the first time I saw an image of a human that I would do anything to see one up close. I loved the Earth; so different from my home planet, which—although Maegora was breathtakingly beautiful in its own way—was almost all ocean, and what was land did not support much of anything outside of my own species. Earth was teeming with not only humans, but also plants and animals. They were everywhere! Birds, dogs, cats, snakes, trees, grass—Earth had everything, and I wanted to see it all!

As soon as I was old enough, I volunteered, but volunteering for the Peacemakers on my planet was like volunteering for the army on Earth. The Peacemakers did not just throw you in a Ganger and leave you to play make-believe. To be a Peacemaker, you had to give up your life while you served. That meant leaving your home, your family, and your friends. You could not start a family of your own, and that rule applied to my own self and my human Gangers that went down to Earth and lived there. Aside from your mission, you could hardly ever leave the ship. Even Dorain, who had never served as an Impersonator or a Ganger, wasn't given much of an opportunity to leave the ship, though he did so more than I. That was not the hardest part, though. My species had already been among the Higher Planets for longer than I could comprehend when I joined the Peacemakers. At the time, I did not understand the struggles younger planets endured. As much beauty as Earth had, it also had more ugliness than I knew existed in the universe. It was a terrible shock the first time I saw it. My family and friends worried for me. They thought the darkness might be too much. Some beings that entered the Peacemakers did not come out the same. It was a demanding life.

But I had loved the humans, and both the horrors and the beauty that I saw only proved to me how much they needed me and how much I was meant to walk among them. The harder I worked to get to them, the more I loved them. When I finally set foot on Earth, I knew I was where I belonged.

At least, I had belonged down there then. Now ...

I was getting close to the age when my own people began thinking about starting families. I hadn't seen mine in a very long time.

"You want to retire?" Dorain asked.

"I don't know," I said. "I don't know what I'm thinking, but what I feel ... Dorain, I miss having a family I can keep."

I turned my head and looked at Dorain, with his warm, golden eyes, my own eyes glistening. He nodded, understanding.

"I think of home all the time," he said. "But I know how you love the humans. Do you really think it's time to be done, Saira? I know you. You have all but given away your second heart to them. If you left, I think you would leave it with them."

I smiled at him. On my planet, it was said that we needed two hearts for all the love contained within us: one kept us alive, but we used the other heart for our love of others. If we had one heart like the humans, we would rather love than live.

"And what about you, Dorain?" I asked. "I'm sure Orna and Laina would not hesitate to take you into their home if you left."

"You are not the only one with curiosity and a sense of adventure, sister," Dorain said playfully. "And I happen to know that Solair is equally interested in you."

I rolled my eyes, blushing. "He is not!"

"I don't know," Dorain said playfully. "He asked about you quite a bit when I was home. I think he is quite taken by Saira, the girl who walks with humans."

I laughed. "Please tell me no one calls me that!"

Dorain grinned a lipless smirk. "It's quite popular among the younglings. They tell stories about you at bedtime."

"They do not!"

Dorain just smiled at me.

"I miss them," I said, resting my head against his neck. "I bet they are getting big."

"They are," he said. "Izra says she wants to be a Peacemaker, just like her big sister. She has the same curious spark as you, you know. She has the same hearts."

I looked back to the frozen girl in the silver tube and sighed. My littlest siblings were only a few decades old. Being a Peacemaker, I had missed so much of their lives.

"So, you would stay?" I almost whispered, staring at the girl in the pod.

We stood there in silence for a few minutes before Dorain spoke. "You know our work here is not done," he said.

"I know," I sighed, and I meant it. "I leave you alone for two decades, and look at what I come back to. Who said you could grow up and get so wise without me?"

"Don't worry, Saira. We are young yet. We have eons of life ahead of us, but for now we are needed here. In the grand scheme of things, it's such a short time to serve.

I leaned forward and, in the human manner, gave him a kiss on the cheek. "You sound like our parents. They told me the same thing."

"Tell me the truth," Dorain said. "How are you doing?"

"I've been better," I sighed.

I met his warm eyes and held them, my expression pained.

"I don't know if I can do this again," I said. "I said my goodbyes. I called Mom and Dad and my sister. I talked to her two boys, even her husband. My friends ... I'm happy with the way I left things. I made my peace."

"I could say something to try to make you feel better. Maybe something about them not really being your family? Maybe something about how I'm your brother and your family, but that isn't entirely true, is it? The little humans are also your family. You love them."

"I don't want to have to say goodbye again! Leaving them once was hard enough!" I said, in a trembling voice.

"Just remember that you're helping them. What you're doing is important for them."

"I don't even know what I'm doing!" I said. "What could the Elders possibly need *me* to go back for? I'm not an Impersonator!"

There were two classes of Peacemakers on Earth: one was a Doppelganger. Doppelgangers lived with humans for twenty years at a time as a human, all the while subtly influencing the humans around us and bearing witness to human history. Not only were we anthropologists, we were also actors and mentors. We replaced young children and were raised by human parents. Gangers were not the same as Impersonators. Impersonators were highly trained Peacemakers who were deployed when direct influence was needed and specific tasks had to be carried out. They were short-term, and they simply took the place of an adult human for a while. They got in, did their job, and left just as quickly. Though they were the minority, most of the influence on human history and behavior was the work of the Impersonators.

"I know," Dorain said, giving me a gentle squeeze. "I don't get it either, but the Elders wouldn't order it unless it was necessary. They see the big picture much clearer than we do."

"I'm afraid that I can't see the big picture at all. Not this time," I said. "What will this even do for the Council? *Why does it have to be me?*"

"Just remember that you are helping people you love."

"I hope so," I whispered.

Dorain eyed me, his expression sympathetic. "If you really can't bring yourself to go back—" he began.

"It isn't the going back," I said. "It's—"

"It's saying goodbye," Dorain finished. I nodded, feeling my heart sink in my chest.

Dorain held me tighter, and I took in the scent of him, letting his familiar smell serve as an anchor. I would focus on the *now*, I told myself. I would not think about what would eventually come until I absolutely had to.

"You're going to be okay," Dorain whispered. I didn't say anything back. I just let him hold me for a long time.

Finally, Dorain said, "Do you remember what you have to do?"

I shuddered. Though they had healed countless times and bore only the necessary marks, my arms still screamed in protest when I recalled some recent training-related events. I rubbed them and tried not to feel queasy.

"Yes," I whispered. "But Dorain ..."

I paused. Fear was coursing through my body. My heart began to race. I felt the blood draining from my face as I thought about the next phase of my job.

"Dorain," I choked. "I am *not* brave. I am not strong. Maybe I can't—maybe I really shouldn't—"

My brother took in the panicked look on my face and read the terror in my eyes. He spent a long time just looking at me. I was surprised when he smiled.

"Little sister," he said, and his voice was genuine. "I wish you could see yourself as I do."

I smiled back, though weakly. My throat tightening, I took his face in my hands and planted a kiss on his forehead.

"Are you ready?" he asked gently.

I took a deep breath and nodded. "As ready as I'll ever be."

"You know you have—"

"Less than a minute. I know."

"You are brave, Saira who walks with humans," Dorain said.

"I hope so."

I sighed heavily. "I just wish it didn't have to be today."

"You know we can't wait any longer. Allyson will wake up in a day or two. She needs to be back here."

"And I need to be back down there."

Dorain nodded.

"Okay," I said, taking a deep breath. "I guess that means it's time to go."

I took one last look at the metal cylinder as we left.

I stood in the white room, clad in the most unflattering hospital gown I had ever seen. In the bright light, several new scars, courtesy of Pask and Pashka's genius work, stood out on the right side of my body. There was a slight ache in my right arm where the fracture was, and the bulky white cast they had put on was itchy. I eyed it with awe, wondering how they had ever managed to reproduce the squiggles and drawings all over it. I saw my nephews' names scrawled across the cast, and if I hadn't known any better, I would have sworn they had done it themselves.

It was silly of me to think it, but I was grateful that none of the wounds Allyson Owens had sustained in the car accident were gruesome. Almost all of them could easily be hidden by clothing, though the pale, faint line down my neck would be too high up to hide with a shirt collar. I would just have to live with it.

It's not like I would have to for long.

My heart was racing in my chest. I felt exposed and vulnerable as I stood there in the center of the white room. I didn't want to be standing. I wanted to be in the fetal position on the floor, but that was hardly protocol.

"You look great," Dorain said, trying to distract me.

"You wouldn't know a good-looking human if it jumped up and bit you," I replied, my voice coming out as a squeak.

"Humans don't bite," he said incredulously. "And I know enough to know that *that* looks terrible," he added, nodding his head toward the blue hospital gown. I tried to manage a smile for him, but I failed. I just stared at him, my eyes wide with panic.

He bent down and wrapped his arms around me. "Best-looking human I've ever seen," he whispered in my ear.

I wanted to cling to him. I wanted to beg him not to let me go. I wanted to tell him that I had changed my mind and couldn't do it. I wanted to scream and cry and pitch a fit about how unfair all of this was, but I didn't. It took more courage than I thought possible, but, in the way of my own people, I placed both shaking hands on either side of his face and pressed my forehead against his.

"Go," I whispered. "I'm ready."

"I'll be waiting for you," Dorain said, as he slipped out of the room.

"I'm going to hold you to that," I said.

"Saira Ta'u," I heard a voice say from the speaker above me. "You have less than one minute. Good luck."

I took a deep breath.

"Do it," I said, and I was suddenly blinded by a flash of light.

My first thought was that the hospital bed was very uncomfortable. Then I shook the confusion from my head and scrambled to collect the needles and tubes around me, some of them still gleaming red. It should have been hard with the bulky cast in the way, but I had already learned how to maneuver with it. All around me, machines chirped their alarms, though I knew *Moga* was giving me a short window before the machines' signals could alert the hospital staff to anything going amiss. Until then, no one would notice anything. Weeks of training made it easy to identify what was what, but that didn't make shoving them into my body any easier. I gritted my teeth as tubes and needles slid under my skin, my heart pounding in my chest. I tried not to remember how painful my first attempts had been.

I only had a split second to ponder all this.

Then it was over. I had done it. I had actually done it! I quickly lay down and closed my eyes, forcing my heart and breathing to quiet. So the training had not been wasted. By the time my one-minute window was gone, I was lying in the hospital bed as if I had actually been there for weeks, all of the tubes and needles where they were supposed to be before the signals from *Moga*'s interference equipment had to shut down, lest my hospital devices fry like my apartment's microwave.

I couldn't celebrate, though. I couldn't think about it. That was just the first minute in a very complicated process. I had a mission to finish, and a determination I didn't realize I had was propelling me forward. I was back on Earth, and I heard my duty calling me. The sound of its call would never fail to excite me.

Voices carried down the hall.

"Is Aunt Ally Cat awake today, Mom?" asked a child.

"No, baby, but the doctors are hoping she'll wake up soon," I heard my sister, Meredith, say. I didn't realize how difficult it would be not to get choked up at the sound of her voice. As hard as it was to come back, I had missed my human family desperately. I was excited to see them again, but right now it was imperative that I contain my excitement. The machines' chirping changed their tune for a second, and I mentally had to scold myself for losing focus.

"What if the flowers die before she wakes up?" another child asked.

"Then we'll just have to go get more, won't we?"

I couldn't help it. I opened one eye long enough to glimpse the vase full of sunflowers beside me. I shouldn't have. Sunflowers were my favorite. It was becoming impossible to keep my composure. The machines chirped again, and again I had to force myself to calm down. An Impersonator would have done a much better job.

I heard the pitter-patter of children's feet on tile as Michael and Aidan ran into the room.

"Hi, Aunt Ally Cat," Michael, the oldest, said, as if he were completely at ease with the comatose aunt in the room. "I drew you another picture today. It's a race car!"

I heard the rustle of paper. I felt something light land on my stomach.

"That's very sweet of you, Michael. Let's put it on the table with the others," Meredith said. I felt her picking up the paper, and I knew this was my chance. I twitched my hand.

"Mom! Mommy! Did you see that?" little Aidan, who was only four years old, squealed.

"Boys, go get the nurse! Go!" Meredith shouted, her breathless voice a mixture of excitement and urgency.

I heard two sets of feet run out of the room.

"Ally! Oh, my god. Al, can you hear me?"

Slowly, just as I was coached, I opened my eyes. I hoped they were registering a stunned expression, rather than excitement and the intense urge to grab my sister in a bear hug. I saw her strawberry blonde hair glowing in the fluorescent hospital lights, inconveniently placed right where they would blind me upon opening my eyes, though I didn't care. Her light blue eyes, similar to my own deep blue ones, were brimming with tears. I felt the edge of my lip twitch. If I wasn't careful, I would smile.

I blinked. "Merry?"

"Oh, my god! Allyson!"

My sister threw herself on me, sobbing.

I wanted to cry too. I had missed her more than I had realized.

My sister and I had never been very close. Meredith was seven years older than me, and for much of our childhood, I had been an inconvenience for her. When she was a teenager, having to babysit me all the time, watch children's shows on TV because I was too young to watch the shows she watched, and include me when her friends came over "ruined her social life," as she liked to shout at our mother quite often. When I started high school, she had already gone away to college. When I started college, my sister was married and had already had Michael. Jillian had been more my sister than Meredith ever had. Still, I loved her dearly, and after she got married and had kids, we actually started growing closer.

"Where am I?" I asked uncertainly, looking around with a slightly shocked expression. At least I hoped it was. Part of me just wanted to burst into laughter. Yes, I was an actress of sorts, but pretending to be an average human toddler and integrating myself into a family was a bit different than this. Being a Ganger had only one real rule: don't give away being a Ganger. The rest was just being yourself, only, as a human. It became second nature after a while, and with the limitations of the human body on our own consciousness, we essentially were human. If thoughts, feelings, and behaviors were under chemical control, we could only be as alien as the human anatomy would let us, which wasn't much.

This just felt like lying.

"Ally, you're in the hospital. You've been here for a little while."

The boys came back in, a very excited-looking nurse trailing after them.

"Ms. Owens?" she asked apprehensively.

What was it that Jo'sha had said? They had "done a number" on Allyson's head? The nurse was expecting the worst. I guess she was going to be pleasantly surprised.

That was, until Allyson ended up back here. I tried not to think about that, but she would have to.

I looked down at the tubes and needles in my body, then glanced at the machines around me.

"I hate hospitals," I said matter-of-factly. At least that much was true. My fourth cycle as a human had ruined me for places with sick people.

I shouldn't have thought about that.

The hysteria started rising. The needles under my skin were burning like flaming daggers.

No! I had to beat back those memories —they were not welcome here or anywhere else!

My sister laughed, tears streaming down her face. The sound of her voice pulled me back.

"I know you do," she said, brushing her finger against the old, small scar on my cheek, just beside my nose.

"Do you remember the car accident?" my sister asked.

"Car accident? What are—"

I was interrupted by a six-year-old and a four-year-old tossing pictures into my lap by the handfuls.

"Aunt Ally," Michael said. "Aidan and me made you pictures every day so you would get better."

I looked down at the pictures and, I couldn't help it, I started to cry. Thankfully, everyone just assumed I was overcome by the shock of waking up in a hospital. In truth, I was so incredibly happy. I was back with my family. Aidan and Michael sat on my bed, chatting on and on about their favorite TV shows, the family dog, their soccer teams, this friend and that friend, and whatever else little boys talk about. They showed me the dozens of pictures they had drawn for me. Meredith said they each drew at least one a day. I told her I would scrapbook them all.

When my parents arrived thirty minutes later, tears streaming down their cheeks and the biggest smiles I had ever seen on their faces, I lost it again. My mom threw herself on me, sobbing. She stroked my hair and kissed me repeatedly, as I laughed and held on to her, telling myself that I would never let go. Even my dad shed a few tears. He kissed my forehead and squeezed my shoulder, and I gave him a bear hug in return.

As I cried, the tears never fell from my eyes. They never did, and no one ever noticed.

The next few hours were like that. We'd be talking, and suddenly one of us would break down. Then the rest of us would start crying too. When Marie, Tori, and Jillian came by the first time, the nurse almost made them leave, I cried so hard. They bombarded me with balloons, flowers, and chocolate. I thought they had bought out every balloon in town, but it turned out that the entire dorm building had chipped in. Jillian told me they'd had to take two cars to get those balloons there. They even had a card that everyone in the building had signed.

When I wasn't being smothered by people, the doctors came in and did tests; wheeled me into strange rooms with strange machines and did tests; and when they finished with those, they did more tests. To their amazement, there was no sign of the brain swelling or mild brain damage. I had made a full recovery. A miracle, they called it.

"When can I go home?" I asked, after two days in that uncomfortable hospital bed.

"It seems you've developed a fever, Ms. Owens. Your white blood cell count is also higher than it should be. We're going to keep an eye on you a bit longer, just as a precaution," was the nurse's reply

I nodded. That was to be expected; after all, I did have a virus injected into my blood. It wasn't a human virus, or I wouldn't have carried it willingly. I had had enough experience with human viruses, and I wasn't going near them again. This virus was meant for the Earth's livestock—specifically, cattle. I didn't like that either, but it could have been worse. Dorain told me about it before they injected it into me. Aside from a few aches and chills, it was harmless in human hosts, but it became pathogenic once it found its target host. By mechanisms I didn't fully understand, they had engineered it so that any cow infected would be incapable of significant weight gain. It seemed harmless enough, but, in truth, it would be terrible. Within fifteen years, farmers would have a crisis on their hands. Most of the world's cattle would be infected. There would be a shortage of meat. Humans would have two choices: devote more land and resources to meet the demand of meat or begin researching alternative food choices. I knew what would happen. Humans would push the Earth's capacity to hold all of their livestock, attempting to meet demand rather than change. They would destroy, pollute, and waste land until their entire system fell apart and they were finally forced to make changes to their way of life. It would be a hard lesson with a high price. I could only begin to imagine the effects, but it had to be done.

What I couldn't understand was how a livestock virus would mitigate the Council's uncertainties about the human race, but then, there were many things I didn't have the wisdom or the background to understand. My brother was right. I had to have faith in the Elders and trust that they knew far more than I did.

"And after that?" I asked the nurse hopefully.

"I see no reason why you would need to stay."

The fever broke a few hours later, and the next morning, I was released. Mom almost started crying again as I got into the passenger's seat of the car. "We're so thankful to have you back," she said through her tears.

Dad put his hand on my shoulder and gave it a squeeze. "Ready to go home, kid?"

"Yeah," I said. "Let's go home."

I was happy. I was beaming.
But I couldn't stay.

CHAPTER 5

"**M**om!" I called, trying to put on an earring and run down the stairs at the same time. Mom always joked that she should have named me Grace, a misnomer that I fully lived up to as I tripped coming off the last step, dropped the earring. The little diamond stud skittered across the floor in a vain attempt to get away.

"Mom! Have you seen the keys? I'm going to be late!" I called, as I scooped up the runaway earring and forced it into submission. The cast had just come off my right arm only two days before, and I found that I was having a difficult time making my right hand do what I wanted it to do.

At least, that was the excuse I gave myself. In reality, Mom was probably right; I was a klutz.

"Mom!" I shouted again, as I dug through the couch cushions and searched the living room. "I swear I just had them. I don't know where they could have—oh."

I rounded the corner and saw Mom and Dad sitting in the dining room, the keys on the table between them. It was actually a familiar scene. As a teenager, my sister had gotten into a lot of trouble: breaking curfew, talking back, getting unimpressive grades, etc. Unlike me, whom my parents often *wished* would get into trouble, Meredith was a typical teenager. My parents developed a routine. Whenever Meredith would get into trouble and lock herself in her room, refusing to acknowledge our parents, they would take her car keys, which Merry never did remember *not* to toss on the kitchen table, place them on the dining room table, and wait. It usually wasn't long before Meredith would have to face our parents to get her keys back. I hadn't had those experiences. I had to admit, it was incredibly clever of them. It was also rather annoying. I felt like I had been trapped in a corner.

No wonder my sister had been such an overly dramatic teenager.

I looked at them uncertainly. "Am I in trouble?"

"No," Dad said, "but we need you to sit down for a minute."

"*Dad*," I whined, knowing perfectly well what this was about; we had only had this conversation a thousand times. "We've been through this. I don't even remember the crash. I swear I don't have any sort of trauma for you to be concerned about. I'll be *fine*."

Sometimes it surprised me how much I really was their child, at least on some level. I was older than they were. I was older than their great-great-grandparents, actually—even their great-great-grandparents were infants compared to me. And yet, here I was, pouting and asking them for permission to take the car, just like any other young adult. Actually, I was always a bit sassy to them, similar to Meredith but much more subtle. It must have been genetic. I always suspected that the real Allyson was quite the spitfire. I always wondered whether Mom and Dad would have been able to handle Meredith and Allyson both.

The thought made me smile. Dad would have more gray hair.

I remembered that they'd have that fiery girl back soon, and my smile fell, pulling me back to reality. I wondered if they'd like her. Or would they miss the girl she used to be? Would they miss *me*?

I was conflicted. Part of me hoped they would miss me. Part of me wanted them to accept Allyson back unconditionally.

Dad scooted a chair out with his foot and nodded for me to sit. I sighed, but complied.

"You're sure you feel up to driving?" Mom asked.

"Mom, it's been a month. I'm going absolutely crazy by myself. Just because I had to sit out the entire semester doesn't mean I have to sit out my social life. I miss my friends."

"We know," she said, and she hesitated. I felt bad for them. They felt as if they had almost lost a daughter, and they feared losing her again. I may not have suffered any lasting effects from the car accident except a few ugly scars given to me by alien doctors and a healed fracture that ached slightly when it rained, but they were still reeling. I had to remember that they weren't in on the secret like I was.

"Mom," I said, taking her hand. "You can't protect me forever. The longer we put off letting me get back in a car, the harder it'll be for all of us. I don't want to spend the rest of my life being afraid of what *could* happen and missing out on my friends, on a life."

It always surprised me how genuine I came off. Of course, I *was* genuine. This *was* the real me. I just didn't tell them everything that was going through my head. That wasn't too different from the average human child, was it?

"We know—" Dad began, but Mom cut him off.

"It's just that it's *two and a half hours away*," she said. "Wouldn't you rather start with a short drive, maybe to the grocery store with me? Or we could go visit your sister again?"

I resisted the urge to sigh in exasperation. I had to remember that my family was not alien. They were not Peacemakers. Every member of my family was a human, and like every other human on the planet, they did not know who or what I was. They never would. When I was assigned to a mission as a Ganger, not only did the Peacemakers have to find a suitable human for me to take the place of, but they also had to screen the family that would raise me. I had replaced these people's child, and while a small child was, in some respects at least, easy enough for me to mimic, there were particular traits that my mother and father's true daughter had that I would never be able to copy. Yes, I had watched the child for a time and learned as much about her as I could before I replaced her, but there were things only her parents could know. When I took her place, they were faced with a stranger. They never knew it, but they sensed it. The hardest people in the world to bond with were always your human parents. On a deep, subconscious level, they knew from the start that the child in the crib was not their own, but their rational minds told them the opposite. They felt guilty for the thoughts they had, and I felt guilty because they were true.

It took the right kind of family to raise a Doppelganger. It took a family that was willing to work through anything, that was strong, and had an abundance of patience. Not everyone could handle having a Doppelganger introduced into their lives. It was determined that my surrogate family would love me, and over time, they did.

I adored my mom and dad. Mom loved to dress me in frilly dresses when I was a little girl. She would put my hair up in pigtails, and I would be the cutest thing anyone had ever seen. She made that part of my life last as long as she could. I think it broke her heart when I went from the little girl she could dress up in pigtails and dresses to the girl who threw on blue jeans, what she hoped was a cute shirt, and her hair in a ponytail as she ran out the door. I was never really one for style. The world was waiting for me out there, and my own race didn't wear clothing anyway. Clothes only blocked sunlight, and our planet was warm. Clothes were a concept that had never really caught on for me.

My mother was a stay-at-home mom for years. When she finally went back to work, I realized how much I missed her always being there. College was even worse. The first semester, I called her every day and came home every weekend to see her.

Dad didn't stay at home like Mom, but there was no denying that I was his little girl, even more than I was Mom's. We did everything together when I was a kid. It quickly became apparent that I did not have the competitive personality required for the world of team sports, but that never stopped the family backyard baseball games: Dad and I against Mom and Meredith. He took me to school in the mornings on his way to work. We had our favorite radio station that we listened to, and he would share his cinnamon breath mints with me. I thought they were candy. He would even walk me to the door, and on Fridays, he would surprise me by visiting me for lunch. Well, it was supposed to be a surprise, but every Friday I'd watch the door to see if he was standing there, waiting with whatever he had picked up.

I adored the parents who had given birth to the true Allyson but raised the Doppelganger. I always would. The humans had become my parents as much as the blue aliens that lived worlds away.

"Mom," I said firmly. "I'm going to go see my friends, and I'm going to be just fine."

"But you've been looking a bit pale lately, and you've got that cough. Maybe you ought to wait until you're feeling better," Mom said. She looked like she might cry. It broke my heart to see her worry over me so much.

"Mom, it's one weekend. I think I'll survive one little sleepover," I said. I gave her a reassuring smile.

I left out the part about how I was, in fact, dying; that is, the Ganger body was failing.

"All right," Dad said. "I'm sold." He tossed me the car keys.

I beamed at him as I caught the keys. Dad was so laid-back, even as far as letting his twenty-two-year-old baby get back behind the wheel of a car after an accident.

Mom opened her mouth to say something, but she hesitated when Dad gave her a look. She nodded. I knew it was hard for her. For her, I would always be that little girl with the cute dresses and pigtails.

"You'll call us as soon as you get there?" she asked.

"Mom, if it'll make you feel better, I'll talk to you the entire way there, so long as I can leave now. I'm *late*."

I stood up, but I was suddenly racked by a coughing fit. A side effect of having your lungs start to fail was my best guess. When it stopped, I wiped my hands on my jeans before Mom and Dad could see the speckles of blood. It didn't hurt, thank goodness, but I certainly didn't feel all that great. I had had slight asthma as a kid. Now my lungs and esophagus had that same raw, cold feeling as back then, only it didn't seem to be going away anytime soon.

I knew this was my last chance to see my friends. There was a reason Gangers only served for twenty years at a time. Any longer and the bodies began to fail. We could clone true human bodies that started as embryos and went through forty weeks of development. We could put Ganger minds in them once gestation was over. Those bodies didn't degrade over time, but it was too difficult for Gangers to live as infants. Starting off in a body with an underdeveloped brain had long-term side effects for the consciousness inside, let alone the frustration of having to teach a new, alien body how to function. Gangers started off as young as a year and a half, and even that was pushing things. The human bodies had to be cloned and grown as a being between the ages of eighteen months to three years, depending on the human model. No older, or replacing the child became almost impossible. Our technology was capable of making a brand new replica of a human toddler, but it was not perfect. Over time, the unnaturally produced body shut down. The life span for adults cloned for Impersonators was even shorter—a few months, at best. Dorain once tried to tell me why, but I hadn't understood. We had tried to fix the problem, but even with all of our technology and knowledge, we still hadn't found a way.

71

I was actually surprised by how quick the degradation process was. Luckily, Gangers didn't need more than a twenty-year time frame. It was more than enough time to serve out our missions.

I knew it was only a matter of time before I got my forty-eight-hour notice, and I wanted to see my friends. I knew I wouldn't be coming back again. I was amazed that I had been given this much time back on Earth as Allyson. I had thought I'd be on the planet for maybe a week, but it seemed to me that I was being given a maximal amount of time to spread my bovine virus.

I wasn't complaining. My friends and I had been talking and texting every day, and I knew I could live with leaving on those terms, but I still felt compelled to see them. They were the family I had created myself. When the other Allyson was sent back, she would come back to Meredith, Mom, and Dad—her family. She didn't have to re-create a relationship with my friends. Chances were that she wouldn't, and my friends would no longer be a part of Allyson Owens's family. This was my last chance to see my family complete. I had to see it whole one last time.

I smiled and twirled the keys on my finger, feigning perfect health before either of my parents could work up more concern.

"Thank you," I said, giving my dad a hug. I kissed Mom on the cheek and rushed for the door.

Something stopped me.

On the wall in the dining room was a family picture from years ago. I couldn't have been more than six or seven in it. In the picture, I was sitting in front of my dad, smiling radiantly. The photographer had somehow managed to coax a smile out of my brooding teenage sister, who was sitting in front of my mom. The photograph had always been one of my favorites. This was *my* family. This was *my* life. I felt a sense of longing as I looked into the eyes of each family member and the seven-year-old me, so happy to be a part of that family. I would always be so proud to have been a part of them.

Despite being late, I couldn't help myself. I turned and ran back to my parents, giving each of them a tight hug and a kiss.

"I'll be back Sunday night," I said to the bewildered pair. Then I left, the door clicking behind me.

I'll admit that I may have driven a bit too fast, but I still ended up very late to lunch. When I got to our favorite pizza place, Jillian,

Marie, and Tori had already ordered and were waiting impatiently with their food in front of them, untouched and cold. Jillian and Marie were having a conversation, and Tori was checking her phone, looking well beyond bored.

"I am so, so sorry," I said as I approached, but they didn't seem to care. They jumped up and nearly crushed me to death in a bear hug, even Tori. I held them tightly, breathing in the scent of each of them. I felt a weight I hadn't noticed before being lifted from my chest. I wanted to hold on to them forever, but of course, Tori broke away first, muttering something about making a scene, and even blushing a little.

"I got you macaroni and cheese, veggie pizza, and a strawberry shake. Enjoy," Jillian said. She had the half-heart necklace around her neck, and I was suddenly crushed when I remembered that Dorain still had mine, though I knew he was keeping it safe.

"Marry me, woman," I said, grinning. I sat down and grabbed the strawberry shake. One of the great things about being human was the food. I had no idea how much fun eating could be, being a photosynthetic being. I had never felt the urge. Earth had so many wonderful things, like cinnamon, strawberries, and chocolate. Fruit was amazing, and vegetables were also wonderful. The meat, however, I could do without. Not only did it disgust me, but I was morally opposed. My race was completely benign. The idea of eating an animal made my stomach turn. I had been a vegetarian all my life, much to my parents' surprise.

"Well, it's about damn time," Tori said, her mouth stuffed full of meat lover's pizza. "I've only been saying you two should be hitched for how long?"

"In that case," Jillian said, leaning back in her chair with a teasing look across her face, "you get to tell your mother. And where's my rock? I want a big one. They'll have to wheel it behind me in a wheelbarrow when I walk down the aisle."

"You want a diamond that fits in a wheelbarrow?" Marie asked, eyebrows raised.

"No," Jillian said. "I want a rock. Just get me a damn big rock."

We all laughed. I felt the warmth of it spread through my body.

"Speaking of wedding bells," Tori said, *almost* giggling. "*Marie met a boy!*" She all but blurted it out, her mouth still full of pizza.

"Tori!" Marie squealed, blushing.

"I just want to know when you're going to tell your dad," Tori said, with an undeniably mischievous tone in her voice.

"All I did was talk to him," Marie said quietly, her face bright red.

As strange as the pair were, Tori always seemed to take on a big sister role with Marie. It was touching.

We spent the next hour like that, talking about anything and everything that normal twenty-something-year-old girls talk about over too much pizza and shakes.

"You two should come stay with Jilly and me for a while over the break," I said. "Ever since we were kids, we've built gingerbread houses and decorated a tree at both of our houses. We leave cookies for Santa and carrots for the reindeer."

Tori tried to hide her amusement behind a look of repulsion. "Aren't you a bit old for that?"

"My little brother is eight," Jillian said. "He still loves that kind of stuff."

"Don't you use your brother as an excuse!" I said, shooting her a look. "Santa is real, and his reindeer love those carrots!"

Marie was giggling so much she was at risk of choking on her cookies-and-cream shake.

"You mean *you* love those carrots! You should have seen Tommy's face that year he came down and saw all the bite marks in them."

"I still had pieces of carrot in my teeth," I said, laughing. "I had to pick them out before he noticed!"

Marie had to put the shake down, she was laughing so hard. We all were. Even Tori was having a hard time feigning indifference; she too was laughing.

"You two are ridiculous," Tori said, as she rolled her eyes, though she was still chuckling as well.

"How close do you two live to each other?" Marie asked.

"We lived next door growing up," Jillian said. "After my folks divorced, my mom and I moved only a few miles away."

"Close enough for you to sneak—" I started to say.

But I started coughing. My coughing fits had only started a few days ago, and for the most part they were harmless, but annoying.

This one hurt. The cold ache was sharp now, stabbing in my chest. It was hard to breathe between coughs.

"You okay, Ally Cat?" Jillian asked, rising to her feet and putting a hand on my shoulder.

I nodded as I rose to my feet. I could taste the coppery blood in my mouth. I needed to step away before anyone saw.

"Here, drink this," Jillian said, thwarting my plans of escape as she grabbed my shoulder, spun me around, and forced a drink into my hand.

"You're kind of pale," Marie added. The look on their faces told me that I looked pretty bad.

"Sorry, guys," I coughed, trying to downplay the moment. "Swallowed the wrong way."

I took a sip of Jillian's soda in what I knew was a vain attempt to hide the cough, and I was relieved when it actually helped.

"There. Better," I said. I didn't show it, but inside I felt shaken. That one was bad. That one meant my time was growing ever shorter.

Tori rolled her eyes. "Way to go," she said drolly.

The flash of light came, only this time it made me very dizzy, and instead of ringing, my ears roared. I felt lightheaded. I would have to let the people upstairs know that the forty-eight-hour alert and a failing Ganger did *not* mix well. I braced myself on the table and couldn't help but groan.

"Ally?" Jillian said, alarmed. All three girls were on their feet. Lunch was turning into a disaster. I silently scolded myself for coming. I shouldn't have done this. I knew I would only get worse.

"I'm fine," I muttered. "Coughing fit gave me a headache."

I looked at Jillian, who was staring at me with genuine concern on her face.

"Seriously, all good," I said, forcing my voice to take on a normal cadence. In truth, it felt like someone was beating my head against concrete.

Jillian sat back down, looking relieved. I sighed. Perhaps I had managed to avert a crisis after all.

"Well, sit back down and—" she started to say.

There was a clattering sound behind us. I heard people gasping. Bodies rushed past me. Jillian was turning to identify the source of the sudden commotion, but I would never see what it was.

There was another flash of light. When I looked up, I was in a white room.

Alone.

"Jillian!" I shrieked, alarmed. No, I was more than alarmed. I felt terror rising in my throat. Blind confusion ransacked my brain. What had just happened? What was this?

I was going to be sick, I realized, as my knees gave way. While the particle beam that reduced my body to atoms and reassembled it in the retrieval room usually disoriented me, this was so much worse. I hit the ground hard, my head bouncing off the floor with a sickening thud. The effect it had on my already churning stomach was disastrous. I rolled over and heaved my lunch onto the floor. Then the coughing started again. Wet coughs racked my body. I couldn't breathe. I just lay there on the floor, gasping. The taste of blood was overwhelming. I was sure my lungs had finally had enough. They had failed. They had completely failed, and I was going to cough and choke to death on the floor right there.

Human suffering was a terrible thing to experience. I could still remember the first time I had felt pain, hunger, fear, and sickness. I had to be trained for years before I could fully handle suffering in a human form. The training had started slow. The first pain I had experienced was a gentle pinch—really no more than pressure on my skin. It had been strange, but it was not too bad. It had progressed from there—a gentle slap in various places, then harder. Some of the blows left light bruises, but they never went beyond that. Then I had to learn what sharp pains felt like. They started by poking me with blunt objects, but those objects quickly became sharper. At the end, they drew blood. They made me bite my own tongue. I intentionally stubbed my toes on things over and over again. I broke nails, jammed fingers, stepped on painful objects, fell down and hit my head, and scraped my knees. They gave me the stomach flu more than once, and I threw up for hours each time. I had suffered colds and headaches, toothaches, and gastrointestinal distress.

In the beginning, a stinging slap would leave me screaming until they pulled me out of my training Ganger. No one ever told me how different human pain felt compared to the way my own species processed pain; there was no comparison. Still, I never gave up, and one day, when they approached me with the needle that would pierce my skin, I whimpered and turned my head, and my eyes watered when it broke my skin, but I did not beg to go back to my body.

I had grown to accept that pain was part of being human, but that didn't make it any less awful. That didn't mean I was immune to suffering in a human body, and I was truly suffering right then.

That had to be why I was here. I had felt human death coming for me once before—real human death, not something that was ever practiced. This almost felt like it.

Almost.

The terror mounted as the memories flooded back. The white of the room looked like the white bed sheets. They were the last thing I saw before—

No! I clutched my head and groaned, digging my nails into my scalp. I told myself I wouldn't remember that.

I would never remember *that*!

The door slid open and two beings in blue-gray suits entered. They weren't Peacemakers. Peacemakers wore white, if they wore anything at all. The sight of them made me realize that something was terribly wrong. The creatures in gray did not belong here—not ever.

We were independent of them.

I told myself that it couldn't be.

This wasn't right! This entire situation wasn't right! I should have had forty-eight hours! And even if I was going to die right there on the planet, I shouldn't have been anywhere near people! They should have done something—anything but this! This was against protocol! What had Jillian, Marie, and Tori seen? What scenario had been set up that I could just be beamed out of a packed restaurant?

"Jillian ... Marie ..." I gasped between coughs.

It hurt too much to try to speak. Everything was going black. I had much bigger problems at that moment than worrying about my friends, but that didn't stop my mind from quietly racing as I continued to gasp on the floor.

"Help me," I managed to choke. *"Please."*

The strange beings came up on either side of me and took me by the arms, yanking me to my feet. The world spun as I was pulled upright, fading in and out. One of them placed a metal device under my neck. I only saw it out of the corner of my eye before I heard the hiss. I felt a sharp sting. The coughing stopped immediately. The nausea and lightheadedness disappeared. The throbbing from where my head had hit the ground, however, persisted.

"Saira Ta'u, you are under arrest for assisting in galactic crimes against the human species," one of the beings said.

What?

That was the only thought my disoriented mind could conjure. Had I heard them correctly?

I was so shocked I didn't even think to ask questions as they began dragging me forcefully out of the room. These beings weren't Peacemakers—that much I knew, but who I thought they were—

It couldn't be, and yet, I knew.

I looked at the sigil on their suits: a hollow moon with three stars inscribed in the middle, gleaming a metallic black in the light.

The sigil confirmed it. The beings represented the Council of Traltix.

I was in more trouble than I had previously thought. Failing lungs were bad, but this looked worse. The Council of Traltix had never boarded *Moga* for as long as I could remember. They had no authority here. And galactic crimes against the human race? Galactic crimes were considered among the worst crimes imaginable, and the human race was *fine*. Wasn't it? I had just been there, eating pizza! Nothing was wrong with the humans!

"Wait! Stop!" I shouted, dragging my feet, as my mental facilities began flooding back to me. "What's going on? I haven't done anything!"

They escorted me into a white room, almost identical to the retrieval room except it was darker and much smaller. I struggled, breaking free and whirling to face them. They moved to block the door.

"What's going on?" I shouted, shaken and desperate. They responded by slipping out the door.

"Wait!" I shouted, as the door slid closed. "At least tell me what I've done!"

But they were gone, and I was alone. I put my head in my hands and just stood there with my eyes clenched shut. My head was still throbbing and my chest ached. Mostly, though, I was exhausted, drained, and empty from the trauma. I leaned against the wall and slowly allowed myself to slide to the floor. I pulled my knees up to my chest and sat there, confused and more than slightly afraid.

It had all happened in an instant.

I wasn't sure what kind of room this was. *Moga* didn't have jail cells, but I got the impression that this one had been converted to serve as one. The thought sent a chill up my spine. Peacemakers weren't perfect creatures. Every now and then, one of them committed a crime, but no crime ever deserved containment. Whatever I had done, someone out there thought it warranted my being caged like an animal. The thought that that someone was the Council of Traltix—that they had boarded a Peacemaker ship to come after me—terrified me. *What had I done?* Why hadn't I seen any Peacemakers? Where were they?

The door slid open and a tall figure entered. My heart leapt in my throat when I saw him.

"Dorain!" I shouted, as my brother stepped into the room. I tried to stand, but the sudden movement made the room spin and my stomach protest. I was weak, and I realized that I had started trembling. Whatever the Traltix agents had given me, it had made me better, but it wasn't a cure. I decided that I would avoid moving as much as possible.

"Saira," Dorain said, relief flooding his voice. He knelt beside me and cupped my face in his hands, examining me with a look of deep concern. "What happened?"

"*Why are you asking me?*" I squeaked, my voice shrill. I felt hysteria rising. My heart was racing in my chest. I was shaking now, not trembling.

"It just happened," Dorain said. His behavior was something I had seen in both my own species and in humans. It was something one did when they were about to drop horrific news right on your unsuspecting head.

"What just happened, Dorain? What have I done? Why was I just plucked out of a restaurant with dozens of humans as witness? *What happened to protocol?*"

"It's the eastern half of North America, Saira," Dorain said gently. He was trying so hard not to make the news hurt. "Humans just started dying by the thousands. One minute, there was nothing wrong. The next, they just fell over. It's a virus, Saira."

"A virus?" I mumbled. Eastern half of North America? That was *my home*.

It only took a split second for it to register.

I felt hot and the room was spinning.

"Saira?" Dorain asked, distress written across his face.

"I'm going to be sick," I said, shoving him aside. I managed to crawl a few feet before I emptied my stomach yet again. It only made me feel worse.

I understood. It was a virus, like the one I carried back to Earth in my blood.

"No!" I said, still on my hands and knees. "We wouldn't! Why would we do that?"

"It wasn't us," Dorain said, and the tone of his voice was defensive and almost harsh. He had already spoken those words to others, though I didn't know which others. Had the Council questioned him? I knew he wanted to believe it wasn't us, but someone out there had to be saying otherwise, and just like me, he wouldn't accept that as truth.

"*Then why am I in here?*" I whimpered. I turned my head to my brother, looking for answers. His golden eyes just watched me. He looked haunted.

It hit me. Oh, I had realized that they were after me for the virus in my blood, but I hadn't thought ...

Slowly, I moved back to the wall. I pulled my knees to my chest and buried my face in them. I was quiet for a long time, my world crumbling around me.

"They don't think this was a Peacemaker decision. They think I did it," I finally said, meeting my brother's eyes. "They think I'm a traitor."

"No one knows anything. No one is accusing you of anything," Dorain said.

I knew he wasn't telling the truth. It was actually shocking. My brother had never once withheld the truth from me. It stung, even if I understood why.

He paused, and I saw him trying to choose the words he spoke next. "The Elders are under lockdown. No one can go in or out of their chamber. The Council of Traltix has taken control of *Moga*. We're to cooperate and obey until ... They've launched a full investigation. They're everywhere and in everything. We've been ordered to abandon our duties and stay out of their way."

"They can't do that! They don't have the right!" I said. The idea disturbed me more than the thought of the Council somehow thinking I could engineer a deadly virus and sneak it onto the planet. Galactic laws centuries old were disintegrating before us. "If this is our problem, *we* deal with it. We always have ..."

I didn't understand. How could a deadly virus make it to Earth? They had checked my blood right before I left. They had said I was okay. Was the machine wrong? Did they make a mistake building the virus and accidently engineer something deadly? Had there been a mix-up?

Even if any one of those things was true, that didn't explain why the Council was here. Was this the last straw? Some nerve I didn't know about that had been antagonized one too many times? The Council had already voiced concerns about humans, and now, the very species they wanted reclassified was at the center of a disaster. Did they think the humans' shaky status gave them the right to interfere?

"How could this have happened?" I asked.

Once again, I found myself thinking that it couldn't have been us. We couldn't make a mistake this grave, nor would someone intentionally do this. No Peacemaker was capable of this.

But then, I knew we were. Peacemakers had done whatever it took over the centuries to guide the human race. We had controlled natural disasters, genocides, wars, and diseases. We were singlehandedly responsible for the Black Death that had ravaged Europe. We were responsible for the influenza epidemic in the early 1900s.

I shuddered. I would not think of that. Not that one.

That didn't alter the truth, though. Peacemakers were more than capable of creating and deploying a virus that could cause astronomical destruction. We had already built them, perhaps even used them once, and kept them contained on this very ship. But if we ever chose to use something so destructive, there was always a plan of action. We always had backup plans and more than one fail-safe in case something went wrong. We would be able to stop this, perhaps in just a matter of days, and we would know how to repair the damage. This was terrible, but we would make it okay. If the Council of Traltix would only let us do our job, they would see that, and they would not have to get involved.

But they had interfered. They had stopped us from doing our job. They were coming after us. They were coming after *me*.

No, there was more to this virus, and the thought petrified me. If we couldn't control this, what would happen? What was the Council's plan?

"It just happened, Saira. No one has any idea what caused it."

"It wasn't us. At least, we wouldn't have—it wasn't *me*," I rambled. "The virus I carried—no one around me was sick! Not a single person!"

"They think it was engineered to incubate for an extended period of time. They think—they know it incubated for a month."

The words sank in. If there was anything left in my stomach, I would have vomited again. The room was going in and out again, and I thought I might pass out.

"Who is it targeting? Is it all of them?" I managed to sputter.

It was hitting where I lived. It was hitting where my family and friends lived. *If something happened to my family and friends …*

"No," Dorain said. "It's specifically targeting humans with severe illnesses. Anyone lacking an immune system can't fight it. Healthy humans are not affected so far."

"What—why would—"

That was oddly specific for an accidental virus, I thought, with a sinking feeling in the pit of my stomach.

"We don't know, Saira," Dorain said. He took my face in his hands. "Saira, do you know *anything*?"

I stared at him and felt a shock wave hit me. No, it was more than shock. I felt betrayed.

"Dorain," I whispered. "Do you think I did this?"

"No!" Dorain almost shouted. "No, Saira! This wasn't you! This is all just—I don't know. It's a mistake. It's a really terrible mistake."

"I'm so scared. My family …" I whispered.

"They'll be okay, Saira," he said, pulling me against him. I couldn't even register his warmth, I was so numb.

I broke then. I started sobbing.

"Shh," Dorain said. He stroked my hair. "They're bringing everyone back. There's going to be a trial. You'll be fine."

I felt relief sweep over me. Of course there would be a trial! Trials were fair and just. They saw truth as clear as day and revealed the darkest of lies as if they were shouted for all to hear. I hadn't done anything wrong. My innocence would shine out for all to see in minutes, and then I could help them fix this disaster. It was all going to be okay. I had that to reassure me, at least. The virus on Earth— what it had done was horrific but my family and friends would be okay, the Earth would heal, and the Peacemakers and the Council would go back to the way they were.

"What if it's natural?" I asked, trying to regain my composure. Everything would get better. Everything would be fixed. Maybe I had jumped to conclusions. Maybe no one was at fault here, and everyone was just scared and making rash accusations, when it was just one of Earth's natural tragedies. It had happened before.

Not every natural disaster on Earth was caused by the Peacemakers. If fact, most things that happened on Earth weren't. Our own actions stemmed from watching what happened on the planet. We merely mimicked the natural order of things.

I couldn't lose it now, I told myself. I would be needed. My human family would want me to be strong, and the Peacemakers would need me as soon as my innocence was proven. I had to be a Peacemaker. We would have to fix this.

But Dorain shook his head, and my heart fell. My heart ... singular.

"Dorain?" I asked, bewildered. "Why am I still a Ganger?"

If I was going to stand trial, I should have been in my own body, and to get back to my own body, I should be in a medical unit. Why had no one taken me to a medical unit yet?

The door slid open. More hollow moons and stars.

"Saira Ta'u," one of them said. "There is strong evidence suggesting your involvement in attempts to bring about the destruction of the human race. You will come with us without struggle."

"Are we going to a medical unit?" I asked. "Pask and Pashka—"

They approached me without saying a word.

"I'm not—I can't stay a human," I said, but as they approached me without speaking, I felt unease creeping down my throat.

"Please, I want to go back to my body!" I cried, as the two closed in on me.

Somehow I knew we weren't going to a medical unit.

"Dorain?" I pleaded, as they took me by the arms and dragged me ungraciously from the room. I didn't fight them. Innocent people didn't fight, and even if they didn't take me to see the kind doctors and their medical unit, they must have had their reasons. They served justice just the same as I did. They would want to see me treated fairly and proven innocent. Wouldn't they?

I really didn't know. I tried to tell myself that it would all be over soon, but I wasn't so sure.

"I'll be close," Dorain said.

He disappeared as the moons and stars took me away to a room filled with Gangers, all looking disconcerted and distraught, some of them openly weeping. It occurred to me that maybe no one blamed me specifically. They blamed my unit, but they were still looking for the true culprit. Right?

From there, they took us one by one into another room. Whoever went in didn't come back out. I tried to tell myself that this wasn't a bad sign; perhaps they were just exiting through another door. But as I stood there for hours in my human body in front of a room that clearly wasn't a medical unit, two Council agents gripping my arms on either side as my colleagues disappeared and didn't come back, I felt the hysteria rising. When the agents finally led me through the door, I had to resist the urge to fight against them, my heart lodged in my throat.

They led me to a table in the center of the room. At their request, I lay down.

"Why am I not in my body?" I whispered to one, but he didn't respond.

I felt vulnerable and exposed as they laid the metal band across my forehead and placed several square silver patches on my skin. I flinched slightly in discomfort as they embedded themselves into my skin, but the sensation soon passed.

"How does this work with humans?" I asked the other, but he was just as silent as his partner.

84

They both turned their heads to look at something on the other side of the room. They both gave a curt nod.

My trial had begun.

Higher Planets had evolved past the trial-by-jury method that the Earth predominantly used. With advanced technology at our disposal, we were able to transform the defendant into his own jury. The metal band on my head read my brainwaves, creating a perfect diagram on a computer that someone more educated than I would examine. Anyone could lie to another flawed being, but you could not trick something that did not have a brain. If anyone accused of a crime lied with the band on their head, it required certain sections of their brain. They would have to access areas of creativity and problem-solving. It would cause stress and a rush of adrenaline. All of these things and more would be read by the metal band on my head, and the sensors embedded into my skin would read the chemical signals in my blood, heart rate, breathing, muscle reactions—everything. Every action, feeling, or thought that I had painted a picture that someone could interpret. If someone was guilty, it was known in minutes, obviating the need for long trials and juries.

It was a flawless system.

It was also one that, to the best of my knowledge, had never before been used on a human.

"Saira Ta'u," I heard someone say. Out of the corner of my eye, I could see a row of individuals behind a dark panel of glass. The window was too dark for me to make out the features of those behind it.

The room, much like the room the Elders resided in, lit up. The screen directly in front of me showed brain activity and vital signs. They didn't make sense to me, but it was law that the accused be presented with the evidence that was either for or against them. Another screen lit up to my right. I turned to look, but I wished I hadn't.

The screen showed humans. They were dying. Thousands and thousands of images of people just falling over dead. They showed no signs of their impending demise, and then, they just fell over and didn't move. There was no way the death was natural.

I had to resist the urge to crawl off the table and hide. Looking at the images—they did something to me. I would never un-see them. They were branded into my mind forever.

"Saira Ta'u," the voice said again. "You have been accused of organizing the systematic genocide of members of the human race. Do you deny this?"

The people behind the glass were quick to get to the point. I, however, was deeply agitated. Things were not happening the way I had expected, but I decided I had to trust them. I didn't have all the information they had, and I had to accept that beings with more wisdom than me had decided that this was the right way to conduct my trial.

I took a deep breath and tried my best to block out the images all around me.

"Yes," I said firmly.

"We request that your blood be checked. Do you consent?"

I sighed in relief. I was so naïve! They thought the Ganger might be infected with the deadly virus! They needed to check and see if my Ganger was clean! I didn't know why they couldn't give me back my body and check the Ganger shell elsewhere, but I didn't need to know. Everything made sense now, and that clarity flooded me with reassurance.

"Yes," I said. One of the agents moved toward me, a strange metal device in its hand. I flinched as the needle pierced my skin, drawing blood. I held my breath, waiting as the machine analyzed it.

There was a series of rapid beeps. I didn't know what they meant.

"Positive," the agent said. His voice sounded like damnation.

"*Positive*?" I shouted, sitting up in a panic. The other agent moved to force me back down.

Hysteria consumed me. It was in my blood! It was in me! That deadly thing *was in me*! Throughout my peripheral vision, I saw the screen with the humans. They wouldn't stop dying.

"No, no, no, *no*!" I babbled insanely. "It's a cow virus! They checked it! They said—they said it—"

Someone had been wrong. Someone had made a mistake, and *I* had carried the evil to Earth myself.

What if I had helped someone do this to them? The thought came unbidden, but there it was. Up until that point, it had all felt like some tragic mistake, but now I knew it was *me*. All of my worst fears sprang to life right there. I lay there, hyperventilating, feeling like a cornered animal with a hunting rifle to its head. The agent wouldn't let me go. He had me pinned to the table.

I wondered when the bullet would come.

"Saira Ta'u, were you aware that you were harboring a deadly virus?"

"*No!*" I shrieked.

Something happened on the screen directly in front of me, but I couldn't read it.

"Did you go to the planet Earth carrying a deadly virus, with the intent to bring death to the human species?"

The voice was unmoved and unfeeling.

"*No!*"

Again, something happened on the screen. I looked toward the darkened glass, but I couldn't see through it. I turned to the agents that held me down, hoping I could read their faces, but they gave away nothing.

I wished my brother were with me.

"Were you in any way involved in the generation of this virus?"

"*No!*" I said, but it came out more like a sob. "I'm just a Ganger. I'm just—I don't know how to make a virus!"

"It's just a mistake," I wailed. "It has to be a mistake."

My skin was slick with sweat. I wanted to claw it off me. Evil was coursing beneath it …

There was a long pause. The screen in front of me displayed readings that I didn't understand. The agents wouldn't let me go. I wanted to plead with them to get off of me. I would be quiet. I could lay there *if they would just get off of me*. Their hands were holding me in my evil skin, and I'd never get out if they kept holding me in it! I felt the hysteria rising again. I knew it was making me crazy. I wasn't thinking rationally. I told myself to calm down. They would never let go of me if I couldn't calm down.

"Saira Ta'u, do you hate humans?"

The question caught me off-guard. Everything froze. I just lay there, blinking in confusion.

"What?" I whispered.

"In your years as a Peacemaker, you have been witness to unpleasant things. You have been forced to endure distressing events," they said. They didn't continue.

"Yes," I said. "But—"

"Do you hate humans? Do you hate the planet Earth for what you've seen and endured?"

"No!"

Again, everything was still, and the silence threatened to drive me insane.

"Do you think the Earth should be eliminated for the safety of our universe?"

"For our safety?" I erupted. "What could they possibly do to us?"

"Answer the question, Saira."

"No!" I shouted.

The screens blinked off. The white walls returned. I felt the metal plates release their grip, and one by one, the agents began removing them. I looked over toward the glass window, but still I could see nothing.

"Saira Ta'u," the voice said, and I knew the bullet was coming. "For your crimes against the human race, your status as a Peacemaker has been revoked. As punishment, all knowledge and memories of the human race shall be removed, and you will be transported to your native planet to receive further punishment, as deemed necessary by your own laws."

"No!" I shrieked. I hadn't lied! I hadn't done it! They couldn't judge me guilty!

I didn't even have time to wonder how it had happened before the agents yanked me up and pulled me off the table, dragging me toward a door at the farthest corner of the room. I resisted, fighting against them.

"Let me go!" I shrieked. They ignored me, pulling me closer to the door.

"I didn't do this!" I screamed. "You're wrong! This is wrong!"

I grabbed the doorframe, my fingernails digging hard into the metal.

Except *I* didn't have fingernails ...

It was the Ganger.

"Please," I cried. "Put me back in my body! Give me another trial! I'm in a human body! Our technology isn't meant to read humans!"

They ignored me. They weren't listening. As far as they were concerned, my judgment had been passed. Our technology was flawless, apparently even when faced with a human. They had given me my sentence, and that was the last they would have to see me.

My sentence …

As I was dragged out of the room, I started kicking and flailing violently. *They couldn't have my memories! They couldn't!*

Five generations of friends, families—they were going to take away my families!

"You read me wrong!" I screeched. "You read the human readings wrong!"

"No!" I shrieked, struggling to escape. I yanked and pulled at them, but their grips were strong. I had to get away from them, but I had no idea where to go. And then I screamed—a bloodcurdling scream that echoed down the halls.

"Saira!" I heard Dorain's voice call.

"Dorain! Dorain, help me! Please, Dorain, don't let them do this!"

I saw his face, desperate. His arms were reaching for me as they dragged me into a medical room. The door slid closed, separating me from my brother. The agents moved to lift me onto a table, but I broke free. I ran to the door, pounding on it with my fists.

"Dorain!" I screamed. *"Help me!"*

I wasn't Saira anymore. I was a wild animal, struggling to get away from its captors, clawing at the door.

An agent grabbed my midriff from behind, yanking me off my feet. The wind was knocked out of me as he threw me down onto the table. It hurt. Together, they held me down. Someone slid a mask over my face. The gas rushed out. I held my breath, but I couldn't hold it for long.

I gasped as the gas filled my lungs.

All the while, Dorain was banging on the door. "It's a Level Seventeen emergency! Do you understand me, Saira? Level Seventeen!"

I didn't. There was no such thing as a Level Seventeen emergency.

Pask and Pashka appeared, standing over me. They were saying something—shouting something at the moons and stars. The agents shouted back.

"Don't let them," I told the doctors, as my eyes rolled back in my head. This gas was stronger than what they usually used on me.

Humans were such fragile creatures. I couldn't fight the gas. I couldn't fight the creatures that held me down. The Ganger would lose this battle, and then there would be nothing to stop them from stripping my mind while I slept.

"Level Seventeen, Saira!" Dorain screamed from behind the door.

"It doesn't exist," I whispered. I tried to fight the gas. I wouldn't go to sleep, not willingly. I forced my eyes back open.

But I knew I couldn't win.

I wouldn't let them have my memories. I thought of everyone I had ever known: Mom, Dad, Meredith, Jillian, and every other family I had had during the four previous cycles. I reached out for a memory—any memory. I would cling to it so tightly, nothing would rip it from me. There was Dad, teaching me how to ride a bike. I had never ridden a bike before, not even in my previous lives. I was so excited, even when I fell off the first few times. Mom did my hair for my senior prom. She messed it up, and we had to go to the hair salon at the last minute. I thought of Jillian and I playing in the backyard as kids.

I remembered Jillian and I playing make-believe.

The memory came to me, and I understood:

"It's a Level Seventeen emergency, Ally Cat! Hurry!" Jillian yelled, shooting at the sky with her invisible gun.

"Don't shoot them, Jilly Bean! They could be friendly!"

"It's an alien invasion, Ally! Help me shoot them down! We have to save the Earth!"

"NO!" I screamed. "You leave them alone!"

I kicked and screamed. I thrashed, lashed out, and even tried to bite behind the terrible mask, but they held me down.

"I won't let you hurt them," I whispered, panting for air, my lungs smothered under the gas that was forcing me into unconsciousness.

But I had lost.

The last thing I heard as I fell unconscious was the screams of dozens of human voices carrying from countless medical units.

CHAPTER 6

Dorain navigated the maze of halls that made up *Moga*, his lengthy legs carrying him at a speed that, for most other beings, would be akin to running, though he carried himself in the languid manner of his people. Saira had once told him that he moved like an Earth creature called a sloth, and the only reason he got anywhere in a timely fashion was that the length of his limbs made up for the fact that he moved them so slowly. Dorain couldn't remember what a sloth was, but he found it amusing nonetheless. He would laugh, and Saira's face would light up. She told him he was much more graceful than a sloth, to which he just smiled. His sister was always telling him such sweet stories about Earth. He loved to hear the excited tone of her voice as she explained some Earth custom or what some strange alien beast looked and behaved like. She was typically sent to regions with similar heritages, but even so, time made each of her lifetimes drastically different. She always came back brimming with new stories, and it made his second heart glow with happiness to hear her speak so enthusiastically about her missions.

Dorain's face darkened. He had told his sister that he would stay close when the Council agents took her away, but after she disappeared behind the closed and sealed doors and had failed to reappear hours later, Dorain began to grow apprehensive at his continued separation from his sister. She had been so distressed when he last saw her. He only wanted to know that her discomfort was not continuing behind the doors. The idea of his gentle sister in lingering distress made his second heart ache with despondency. Other Gangers entered the room, but his sister never reappeared. No one had reappeared. He had approached the Council agents who stood watch at the doors, but none of the answers they gave him satisfied him as to where his sister, in her human shell, had been taken away to, or if she was well. And there was still no sign that Saira was going to reappear anytime soon.

He knew that the creatures meant her no harm. The Council of Traltix was just and amiable, the same as the Peacemakers. They did not mean to cause his sister such grief. A terrible thing had happened, and both sides were searching for answers. Dorain knew that it was a logical step to investigate his sister, and that in order to investigate her lack of a role in the devastation that was gripping the planet Earth, they had to cause her anxiety. Dorain knew this, but he didn't like it. He just wanted to know when his sister's sadness would end, and when he could have her back, to talk and sing to her and tell her that everything would be okay.

Dorain didn't remember when he began walking, but at one point he looked up and found that he was approaching the heart of the great ship. It was then that he realized where he was heading. The Council of Traltix was not the authority in this crisis. He knew this, yet they were taking a strange and unprecedented role in helping to solve the mystery of where the disaster on Earth had originated from. Still, they were not the masters of the ship, and Dorain had sought them out, if only to know that Saira was okay. He was being anxious, he told himself. The Elders had other matters on their hands to deal with, but there were many of them, and perhaps just one could spare a moment so that he could learn of his sister's fate. Perhaps he would be denied entrance to their chambers, as was understandable and their right, but they had always sounded like such sympathetic leaders, and surely they would understand a brother's concern for his sister. Perhaps he could also prove useful and help the situation in some way. Perhaps with his skills and knowledge, he could help design something to combat the wickedness that raged on the planet below.

Dorain swept past two beings in silver suits, metallic black moons and stars gleaming off their shoulders. He couldn't see their eyes behind their black reflective masks, and for some reason that only increased his discomfort, though he told himself that it shouldn't. Many species couldn't exist off their home worlds without carefully crafted survival suits, and it was no fault of their own if those suits obscured their features. Dorain himself often had difficulties aboard *Moga*, with its dim light and colder temperatures than he was accustomed to. If it weren't for the habitat of his sleeping chambers, he would find himself incredibly sick. Still, it seemed to him that there were far more Council agents aboard *Moga* than Peacemakers, and as time went on, the ratio was becoming more and more disproportionate. Those were not the first Council agents he had seen since he had entered the deeper portions of the ship, but had he seen other Peacemakers? He couldn't remember—he hadn't been actively looking, but he thought not. But why should he consider that unusual? The Council was helping investigate a disaster that had originated from this very ship. It made sense that they would investigate all Peacemakers.

Dorain thought then that maybe it was unwise to be wandering the ship—perhaps he was impeding the investigation, but no one had said anything yet, and he only wished to ask a very simple question. Certainly he wouldn't inconvenience anyone too much, would he?

Still, he couldn't shake the unease that lurked in the back of his mind. He kept his head down as he passed the two Council agents, and though he couldn't see the eyes behind the black masks, he felt them watching him as he rounded the corner and quietly slipped away. Somehow he knew they hadn't taken their eyes off him until he had disappeared out of sight.

Dorain saw the great white doors appear before him. He had always wondered why the Elders' chamber had doors so vast, but that wasn't his concern just then, so he let his curiosity pass. The doors stood open, a sight he was unaccustomed to seeing. In fact, the only time he had ever seen the doors open was when Saira had passed through them all those weeks ago.

Several Council agents swarmed around them, entering and leaving with rushed purpose. He hesitated then, watching as the foreign agents intruded upon the one area of the ship that had always been closed to him—to everyone. Well, it had never been closed, per se, but he had certainly never felt as if he were invited to enter the chambers. It was a place everyone respectfully left alone. The chamber of the Elders remained as mysterious to him as the farthest corners of the stars, and it occurred to him then that maybe there was a reason for that. He had never had cause to beg an audience with the Elders, with orders and information freely communicated among the Peacemakers. It seemed to him that everyone knew their purpose on the ship. Dorain himself awoke each morning to find that he, through one of the ship's great computers or someone higher than him, knew his day's work. He never questioned how they always knew what to do. It was known that the Elders were wise, and swift to make decisions. It was known that they made every decision on the ship, but Dorain had never asked how or to whom they communicated their orders.

Perhaps, he thought, they did not want to communicate directly with anyone. Perhaps they purposely kept their chambers sealed.

Dorain hesitated. He feared that it was not his place to entreat the Elders, nor would they want him in their presence, but he took a dubious step forward anyway. They were kindly beings, and his question was so innocuous, after all.

He would never make it to their chambers, though. Someone grabbed him from behind.

Two strong arms gripped him by the waist and pulled him back behind the corner. They may have reached for his mouth to silence his cry of shock had he made one, but it was not his species' way to cry out in fear, and he was too tall for his assailant anyway. Most beings evolved alongside some sort of hostile pressure that caused an innate fight-or-flight response. Most beings would have cried out, perhaps as a natural cry that would call others of the same species to come help. Dorain's ancestors had never been subjected to such things, so instead, his knees reflexively went out from under him, and he ended up sitting against the wall, his eyes staring up at the Council agent hovering over him.

The masked agent didn't hesitate to cover his mouth then, but still, Dorain sat there, stiff and quiet.

"One more step toward those doors and you can consider yourself a marked man," the agent said, his voice just loud enough for Dorain to make out the words.

Dorain didn't struggle. He sat there, golden eyes wide, and stared into the mask. He hadn't done anything, so why would the masked man hurt him? He calmly waited for him to release him and explain himself, as he assumed he would.

"Did they see you?"

Dorain eyed the masked figure. He couldn't be certain, but could he be the same Council agent he had just passed in the hall? Had he followed him all the way to the Elders' chambers? Why? And why would he care if the other Council agents had seen him?

"Did they see you?" the agent asked, this time with a hint of frustration under his breath.

Dorain saw no harm in answering him, so he shook his head. He was certain that the agents outside the door were too busy to have noticed him.

The Council agent sighed and dropped his hand.

"I would like to know where my sister is," Dorain said, the moment the hand was dropped from his mouth.

"Not there," the agent replied, almost briskly. "And don't speak so loudly."

"I would like to ask if—"

"They can't save Saira," the masked man said abruptly.

Dorain's eyes widened in sudden alarm. There was something about the man's voice ... and "save?" The word had not been lost on him. He did not say "help." No, this man was suggesting that his sister was in more peril than he thought.

Something else registered: the agent knew his sister's name. This was someone who knew them ... but how?

Dorain racked his brain, trying to pinpoint the being's accent. Relminish? Nanushk? Avinox? Ilkshin? It could have been any one of them, but the real question was how the Council agent knew of his sister and recognized that they were related. He had certainly never met a Council agent before.

The Council agent slowly peered around the corner, and what he saw must not have pleased him because he let loose a curse under his breath.

Only, he didn't speak Common Tongue. Though Dorain was not particularly fluent in it, he could recognize the human language English when it was spoken. This time he eyed the Council agent much closer, but now he was certain that this was not a Council agent. Council agents did not reflexively speak human languages. Only recently returned Impersonators and Gangers were known to accidentally slip into human tongues, and the accent ... Dorain was sure he had heard that particular dialect recently.

"Jo'sha?" Dorain asked, remembering the Impersonator who had stood beside his sister as she returned from her last mission. He hadn't spoken with the man directly, but he had heard him speak to his sister, and that accent was unmistakable.

The Council agent flinched noticeably, realizing that he had let his guard down.

"I wouldn't call me that around others," Jo'sha replied, leaning his head back to check down the hall for listening ears, and turning his head sharply in either direction. The visor of his mask was too narrow and thin for him to see out of properly, Dorain realized. He was wearing a suit designed for another species.

"What are you doing in that?" Dorain asked, cocking his head to one side curiously. Jo'sha was an Impersonator, but never before had Dorain seen an Impersonator imitate anything other than a lesser species.

"Keeping you out of the Council's hands," Jo'sha replied.

"I don't understand," Dorain replied, waiting patiently for a proper explanation.

Jo'sha didn't respond. Something caught his attention, and though Dorain couldn't hear anything, it appeared that Jo'sha had.

Dorain saw that the visor was pointing down in his direction, watching him. His body tensed slightly, but whatever it was that Jo'sha heard that had unnerved him, the moment passed, and a sense of urgency replaced it.

"Get up," Jo'sha said. "We need to move away from here."

Dorain started to ask another question, but Jo'sha was moving by then. He took Dorain by the wrist and pulled him up, leading him down the hall at a brisk pace. Dorain followed obligingly. Despite the hurried gait of the smaller man, Dorain tried not to outpace him.

"My sister has not returned," Dorain said, as he followed the Impersonator. "I'm growing worried."

"She isn't going to," was Jo'sha's reply.

Dorain stopped abruptly, startled. Jo'sha had expected it, though, and he gripped the large alien's wrist without breaking stride and pulled, urging him forward.

"You must follow me," Jo'sha said. "We must not linger here."

"My sister—"

"If you want to help your sister, you must follow me. *Quickly*."

Dorain didn't hesitate then. He nearly pressed against Jo'sha as he led him through the maze. On and on they went, farther and farther into the ship, descending into the lowest levels. Dorain thought they might never stop walking.

Everything was still now. It was the quietest Dorain had ever seen the great ship, which normally housed well over ten thousand

Peacemakers, give or take a few hundred, depending on incoming and outgoing missions. The ship was always bustling and lively. Monitoring an entire planet required that everyone on the ship be constantly moving and completing some vital task or another, but at that moment, he saw no Peacemakers. There were no Council agents either. If anyone was around, Jo'sha actively avoided any of the more trafficked routes, a curiosity Dorain picked up on quickly, though he had no more explanation for it than he did for why Jo'sha was in a Council suit made for another species.

When Jo'sha pulled him into a room at the end of a tight corridor and closed the door behind them, Dorain felt increasingly uneasy by the lack of life, and the room they entered did not calm his agitation. It comprised one of the oldest parts of the ship, Dorain surmised, and perhaps it had once been some sort of transport or control room. The old machinery and wiring looked like it could have come from technology centuries out of date, and as far as Dorain could tell, the room had been abandoned and lost to time. The lighting barely worked, and even then, it cast grotesque, twisting shadows just as often as it illuminated some small patch of the room. The airflow in the room was strange, too. Dorain shuddered as air currents whipped past his feet and out the door, a moaning whistle announcing the defect in the doorframe that allowed the frigid air to escape.

Dorain did not like the room. He cringed lower to the ground, the dark corners and cold setting him on edge.

And yet, despite his growing anxiety, Dorain could not help but notice the oddities of the various old computer screens, processors, motherboards, blinking lights and circuits, wires, and partially dissected panels. The snarled mess had all been retrofitted together and shoved into a dismantled portion of the ship's wall, with its various tubes and other innards that were deemed unnecessary chaotically exploding outward. Through the disorder, Dorain couldn't make out what the device was supposed to be, or its purpose.

"What is this?" he asked.

"Treason," Jo'sha replied calmly.

Dorain's eyes grew wide. It didn't make sense to him, but it was a word that immediately sent a thrill of terror down to his core. Jo'sha was good, he knew. He trusted him, but with one word, he realized he didn't want to know what was happening. Whatever it was, Jo'sha wasn't really doing anything wrong and had everyone's best interests in mind—this he knew, but Dorain didn't understand why he would say that, and he decided that he would not play a part in it. He backed away slowly, sliding closer to the door, his heart rates quickening.

He would leave, and he would find Saira, and everything would be okay soon, he told himself.

"Of course, this isn't the only one," Jo'sha continued as he watched Dorain back away, making no move to go after him. When Dorain turned to leave, he saw why.

The other Council agent was standing behind him, blocking the door. The air danced between the both of them, cool yet wild, like a storm.

"They may be enough ..." Jo'sha began, but he stopped and shook his head, sighing.

Dorain turned to look at him, his knees shaking, threatening to go out from under him. He didn't understand. Hadn't Jo'sha said he would help Saira? Dorain didn't see how the room with the strange devices would help her. He didn't understand why Jo'sha was in disguise. He didn't understand why the halls had gone empty or why they were moving about and speaking in secret, but Dorain did know that this was not his place, and he wanted to leave and find his sister.

"Whatever this is," Dorain said, "I just want my sister to be safe. I only came here for my sister—nothing else."

"Then there is something you need to see," Jo'sha said. He walked to the nearest disheveled piece of equipment and pressed a button. All around him, Dorain watched as screens flickered and whirred to life, groaning as they displayed their grainy images.

Dorain stepped forward to get a better look.

He promptly recoiled and dropped to his knees, gasping, as he watched the Ganger being held down on the medical room table, the mask forcefully held over his face as he screamed and clawed at the Council agents who entrapped him. The doctor was in the corner, shrieking, as he attempted to push past the agent who had him pressed up against the wall. The Ganger's eyes rolled back in his head and his body stilled as the gas overwhelmed his lungs. The Council agents reached up and pulled down the strange apparatus hanging from the ceiling and pressed it against the Ganger's temple. Its metal arms clamped down on his head, and where the light had once been, a long, slender needle appeared.

Dorain was aghast as he watched the needle pierce through the Ganger's skull. The human shell gave a shudder.

"He wasn't fully unconscious," Dorain whispered. "He wasn't—*Saira*."

Dorain moved from screen to screen, taking in each Ganger held against the medical tables. Others were on tables of other sorts, metal bands pressed against their foreheads. Still others were standing outside great doors, held on either side by Council agents.

"Which one is my sister?" Dorain cried, his voice almost rising to a shout. "They can't—they wouldn't do this to h—"

Jo'sha pointed to a screen, and Dorain gasped as he watched the red-headed girl being led into the interrogation room, her eyes wide with fright. They turned toward the screen, and for a brief moment Dorain could have sworn that she saw him. He had left her, and now she was begging him with her eyes to help her.

"What are they going to do to her?" Dorain whispered.

"The same thing they have done to each and every one of the others," Jo'sha replied, his voice cold.

Dorain turned to look at him, his eyes haunted. "All of them? *Why?*"

Jo'sha was still, watching him. Dorain tried to discern what Jo'sha was thinking, but the man behind the black mask was a veteran Impersonator, and he only let you know what he was thinking or doing when he wanted you to know.

"I can tell you, but are you sure you want to know?" he finally said.

Dorain watched him. He looked around the cold, shadowy room. He didn't want any part of whatever this was—that he knew. The room should not exist, Jo'sha should not be hidden, secrets should not be kept, and he knew that he would not be a part of the world that was slipping into this evil. He shook his head. If he knew, he could never not know, and he had no intention of fueling whatever was happening. He had sworn to protect peace and a way of life, and he would continue to do it the right way.

"I just want to help Saira," Dorain said. "Tell me how to help her."

"Treason," Jo'sha replied.

Dorain shook his head. "No," he said. "I won't do it. I'm a Peacemaker. I live by our way."

"Having a way does not stop the world from being what it is," Jo'sha said.

Dorain watched him, speechless. He didn't understand.

"Tell me," he continued. "What would you do if I told you that we have changed the rules? What would you do if I told you they are no longer who you think they are?" he said, pointing at a screen with another screaming Ganger.

"What are you saying?" Dorain asked. He turned his head before the Ganger could give his death shudder as his consciousness escaped from his human shell to return to its true form.

At least he hoped that was what was happening.

"Why are you showing me this? Why are you doing this?" he asked when Jo'sha didn't respond.

"In five minutes, this place is going to erupt in chaos. Where do you want to be?"

"What are you—?"

But Jo'sha straightened and met Dorain's eyes behind the mask. Something had changed, though Dorain wasn't sure what. The man in the suit had a sense of urgency and secrecy to him before, but now Dorain felt a wall come down. The man was rigid and as cold as ice.

Again, Dorain had the sneaking suspicion that Jo'sha could hear something that he could not.

"You have five minutes to get to your sister, Dorain Ta'u," Jo'sha said.

He flicked off the computer screens. Then he leaned over and picked up the stun gun that Dorain hadn't seen leaning up against the wall. He backed away, his eyes wide.

He didn't want to see this. He didn't want to know. It wasn't happening, he told himself. It couldn't happen. They had a way, and they all lived by it.

"When you get to her, tell her it's a Level Seventeen emergency," he added, not looking at Dorain.

"We don't have—"

"No, we don't, but I highly suggest that you tell her anyway."

Dorain heard the stun gun charging.

"Your sister is far away, Dorain. I suggest you run."

He didn't even realize that he had started running, but he burst past the Council agent behind him, and his long legs carried him through the ship at blinding speed. He didn't know what he would do, but Saira needed him, so he ran.

He never got a chance to help her, though. He was too late before he even started running.

Her desperate pleas led him to her. There was his sister, tiny, human, and fragile, being carried down the hall by two Council agents in suits. She fought against them, screaming and crying, but the suits showed no remorse as they carried her away.

"*No!*" he heard his sister cry. The sound of her terror nearly ripped his second heart from his chest.

"*Saira!*" Dorain called out to her.

She saw him. Their eyes met.

"Dorain! Dorain, help me! Please, Dorain, don't let them do this!"

She continued to wail as they dragged her away. He had never heard such sounds from her before.

Dorain's feet were carrying him forward, but the agents were surprisingly faster. Before he knew what had happened, she was gone. The door to the medical unit snapped closed, separating him from his sister.

"Dorain!" he heard her scream from within. "*Help me!*"

He stood there, panic rising in his throat. What could he do?

"Saira?" he whispered, frozen at the door.

She continued screaming.

"*Saira!*" he cried, his hearts racing. Still, the screaming continued. On and on it went, a desperate, mournful sound.

A memory flashed before Dorain's eyes: a male Ganger with a needle punching through his skull.

The sound of a fist slamming into the door jarred him back to reality. He looked up, and the Umber held his eyes. The giant creature grunted at him, black, beady eyes peering at him from beneath a heavy brow of callused gray skin, so tough and coarse that it looked like it could have been stone.

All around him, beings were streaming down the halls, running and shouting as thuds and ringing echoed through the halls. He looked left and right, and saw the Peacemakers—they wore the suits of the Council, but he knew who they really were now—beating on and prying open the medical chamber doors.

He looked back up, and the Umber held his gaze, waiting for him to make his decision.

"Do it," Dorain whispered. "Save her."

And he hoped he'd be forgiven for the choice he made.

The Umber's fists connected with the metal with a deafening thud. Then he raised it and struck again, over and over.

The lights cut out, plunging the hall into darkness. The only thing Dorain could hear was the ear-splitting clang of doors being broken down, and above it all there were the wails of so very many voices in pain. One in particular stood out among them all.

Dorain stepped closer to the door. He heard Jo'sha's words reverberating in his head.

"It's a Level Seventeen emergency! Do you understand me, Saira? Level Seventeen!"

The Umber slammed another fist into the door. The metal was caving, but it was giving far less than the Umber's bloody fists, which dripped fat black drops onto the ground more and more as the metal bit into his skin with each additional punch. Dorain knew the door would hold longer than the Umber and yet he didn't stop throwing punches. The black eyes showed no hint of pain, only determination.

The siren came on then, an ear-shattering shriek combined with flashing lights. Each pulse of the white light showed the movements of those around him, and he watched as the figures twisted and contorted in a grotesque dance. He watched in a daze as they rushed by, limp bodies cradled in their arms. The sirens muddled the sounds of their voices as they called back and forth to one another, and yet they weren't loud enough for Dorain to miss what he wasn't hearing.

The screaming had stopped.

"Level Seventeen, Saira!" Dorain cried, but he knew by then it was futile. He could hear nothing from behind the doors.

"*Saira!*" Dorain screamed. The Umber beat against the doors over and over and over again, but nothing happened.

"It's not working," Dorain whispered, but if the Umber heard him, he said nothing; he just kept beating against the door.

"Saira," Dorain whimpered, as he slid to his knees in the middle of the hall.

He heard nothing.

They had failed.

Someone leapt out of the darkness and grabbed the Umber's wrist, pulling him back. Dorain caught sight of the Council suit out of the corner of his eye, and then he heard the shrieking whistle as the lights suddenly flashed on, growing brighter and brighter until Dorain was blinded. Everything went dark again as the popping sounds signaled the end to the lights, and he heard the metal clanging as the surge in electricity short-circuited the internal locks of the medical room doors. When the sparks stopped leaping out from the doorframe, Dorain knew it was safe.

And then ... he heard the screaming again. It came from inside the medical room his sister had been dragged into, but this time, not one of the voices was his sister's. Then he heard the sickening thuds.

There was silence.

Dorain leapt to his feet.

"Saira!" he cried, as the Umber forced his thick, bloody fingers between the door and the wall and heaved it open, using all of his great strength. When it was wide enough, Dorain slipped through, and the Umber released the door, gasping from his great exertion.

Dorain slid to a halt when the gas hit his lungs.

He could hear it now that he was in the room, hissing out of the cracked tube and flooding the chamber. His lungs already felt raw and irritated. He coughed, trying to force the poison from his lungs, but he could feel more of it crawling its way down his throat, threatening to smother him.

The two Council agents were on the floor, the masks of their helmets cracked, allowing the gas to pass unrestricted through their protective gear and snake its way down into their lungs. They were already still, though Dorain couldn't be certain that it was a result of the sedative.

He saw the red-headed girl on the table. The mask had been displaced from her face and was hanging off her cheek, but even so, she was still. The gas had done its job.

"Saira!" Dorain gasped, rushing forward. The gas grew denser as he moved inward, but he didn't hesitate, even when he felt his head begin to spin.

"Wake up," Dorain said, giving her a gentle nudge. "Saira, *please*, you must wake up!"

"She needs—" a voice whispered from the other side of the table, but it gasped and choked, gurgling as it tried to force out the words.

Dorain saw them then, the two doctors, lying on the floor. One head was still, its eyes frozen open, but the other was still twitching, its limbs flinching uncontrollably. Clenched in her hand was a set of large metal forceps.

They were perfect for shattering the protective masks of the Council agents' suits.

"Pask!" Dorain cried, rushing to her side.

"Toxic," she managed to choke, before her eyes rolled back in her head and the foam erupted from her mouth.

Dorain didn't hesitate. He grabbed the doctors by the arms and heaved them up over his shoulder. With his free arm, he did the same with his prone sister. After he dropped them outside the door, he went back for the Council agents.

When he stepped outside the door again, his head was reeling. He collapsed to his knees, wheezing.

"Help!" he shouted, though it came out in a whisper. He saw the Umber down the hall, standing under one of the few lights that had not blown out, watching him with black eyes. All around him, the siren and flashing lights continued.

"Help me!" Dorain called, as he knelt among the four face-down bodies. The gas was escaping out the door, growing denser in the hall. He watched as the Umber groaned and retreated farther down the hall, clutching his bloody fists to his chest. Dorain saw the black blood giving off steam, and he understood. Each species aboard the ship was different biologically. Some were more different than others. While the gas was a sedative to humans, to other species, such as the Umber and Pask and Pashka, it was poisonous. The Umber would be of no help so long as the gas was there to burn him.

Dorain nodded and heaved himself to his feet. He braced himself against the wall and bent over. He threw his sister over his shoulder. The doctors went into the crook of his arm, and with what strength he had left, he dragged the two Council agents down the hall by their silver suits.

He collapsed at the Umber's feet, panting.

"The doctors," he gasped. They both stared at him with eyes wide open, their mouths dripping frothy saliva, but he told himself that they were not dead. That would not be the justice they deserved for what they had done for his sister, even if he did not agree with their methods. And the Council agents ... behind the masks, he could not tell if they were still alive.

The Umber did not hesitate, though. He reached down and gently tucked the doctors under one arm. He hoisted each Council agent under the other, letting them dangle limply in his grasp. He eyed the red-headed human who lay prostrate on the ground, her blue eyes closed, her hair splayed around her like a halo. Dorain thought she almost looked like she was sleeping, she looked so peaceful.

"I've got *her*," Dorain gasped. "Save *them*."

He was not likely to give his sister away so soon.

The Umber nodded and turned, lumbering away with the doctors and the Council agents in hand.

Dorain forced himself to his feet once more. The gas was leaving his lungs and he felt stronger, but not much. He bent over and carefully pulled his sister into his arms. Her eyes were closed and her face was still, but her chest was moving up and down, and Dorain knew that meant that she was still breathing. So long as she was breathing, he knew she would be okay.

"Saira, wake up," he begged, but if she heard him, she gave no sign. He gently pressed his hand against her cheek, but she didn't move. The flashing lights illuminated her, going back and forth between lighting up her face in a ghostly fashion, so white that she looked dead, to casting her face in dark shadows. Dorain did not like either look on her. He only wanted her to wake up, but he didn't know how to wake a human up. They had always injected the Gangers with something after someone's consciousness had been transferred to them. Would that work?

No, he realized. His sister needed to wake up, but not in the human body. He knew she would never be safe in it, so he pulled her closer to his chest, and he ran.

106

But when he entered the long, dark, narrow hall, what he saw nearly brought him to his knees. Where dozens upon dozens of life-supporting metal cylinders had once stood, wires and tubes dangled from raw wounds in the walls where the pods had once been connected. The hall was devoid of anything. The cylinders had been ripped from them.

His sister's true body was gone.

He looked down at the unconscious Saira and once again felt panic. He had to get her out of the human Ganger! In the smaller, weaker form, she was defenseless, but if he could just get her body back, she would stand a chance against the Council agents who had tried to hurt her. A human body was easy to manipulate, but not a Thellessian's. If he could just get her back in her body, she might get through this without harm, *but where had it gone?* What were they doing with it?

Dorain knew he didn't have the time to look for it. The wailing siren and flashing lights blared urgently at him, and though he did not know exactly what the warning meant, he turned and ran, heading to the one final place that held hope for him and his sister.

The lab was cast in shadows when he entered, but unlike most of the other parts of the ship, it had a backup generator, as the contents of the room were far too precious to lose to a power outage. Should the power ever be completely lost, months, perhaps even years, of work and research would be lost forever, and the Peacemakers as they were would come to a screeching halt—at least for a time. As it was, he heard the powerful generators roaring, pushed into overload to protect the contents of the room.

The priceless contents, however, did not include the main lights. Even the wailing siren, with its flashes of blinding light, was absent. It seemed to Dorain that the lab was even darker than Jo'sha's secret room, and his eyes, accustomed to a world of constant light, were useless. Nearly blind, he shuffled into the lab, almost bumping into the edge of a small pool. He looked down, and he could make out the body that lurked beneath the surface of the liquid. It was small—only a child—and just halfway to completion. He could tell that the bones were fully formed and solid, but the nervous and vascular systems were new, just beginning to infiltrate the budding organs in the body's gaping holes, which were held open by organic, degradable mesh networks. The skin, which was always the last to begin forming, was a transparent sheet—thinner than paper and so delicate that even a gentle bump could rupture it. The new eyes, just black pinpoints until they developed further, stared up at him. Dorain was grateful that he had seen the growth pool in time. It was hard to repair a body so underdeveloped. Had he damaged it, they would probably have to abandon it.

He avoided looking at the adjoining pool, the one with the empty adult vessel that was being enzymatically digested down to its most basic components. Dorain knew that the liquefaction of that body meant that they could simply reuse the nucleic acids, lipids, and amino acids for the new one, rather than going through the time-consuming process of synthesizing their own, but that didn't mean that he liked it. The sight was grisly, but it was the smell that he couldn't tolerate, so he made it a point to stay far away.

He looked up and saw the large glass cylinders that lined the walls. Each one was occupied by a tiny form—fully formed human bodies, each ready to be decanted and fully capable of accepting a consciousness. Dorain glanced down at Saira. Could he move her to one of those? Would she be safer in a different form?

He knew better, though. A smaller body would be easier to move and hide, but a child's body would be far more vulnerable than the young adult he held in his arms. No, he knew what he had come for.

The Transference ampules full of aether were stored at the farthest corner of the lab. Tiny glass vials filled with a viscous, shimmering, white-silver liquid, they had always mesmerized Dorain. Despite his depth of knowledge of biology, chemistry, physics, and a wide range of technologies, he still could not understand how they could hold an entire being's consciousness. Of course, that wasn't all they did. Each medical unit carried one ampule per Ganger they transferred, for more than one reason. Sometimes Transferences went awry, and in that case, ampules could safely store a Ganger or Impersonator's mind until they could be put back into their body. If a Transference did go as planned, they stored the indestructible emotions that the Gangers and Impersonators were not permitted to keep. The used ones carrying emotions were stored far away, in another part of the ship. Dorain had only laid eyes on them once.

Dorain did not seek to move emotions, though. Carefully, with his sister tucked into the crook of one arm, he took an ampule, watching with fascination as the silver-white liquid churned of its own accord, swirling around as if moved by an unseen current. With his prize in hand, he moved to the metal table that was concealed in the shadows. It was the only one the room contained, and it was meant to be used only in dire emergencies.

Dorain considered this situation to be an emergency.

Carefully, he set his sister down on the table, though he didn't position her right away. He looked at the panel at the top of the table. It was old, and Dorain did not quite recognize the purpose of each knob and button. He stepped forward, and it was then that he saw the thin, unassuming hole in the headrest. The sight of it unnerved him.

He recognized the power button easily enough, and when he pressed it, the panel whirred to life, blinking lights in various places. The largest switch, however, he did not understand the purpose of, so he threw it. When the long, slender needle leapt out of the headrest, he leapt back, and his legs nearly went out from under him. He regained his composure and carefully selected another switch. He watched as the translucent microfibers slid out of the needle, catching what little light there was and reflecting it, glowing eerily. Dorain pulled both switches back in order, and with frightened golden eyes, he watched the needle retreat back into its home.

He pulled his sister up, positioning the back of her head above the needle's resting place.

"Saira," he whispered. She didn't move.

He hesitated, watching the human face. How unconscious was she? If he flipped those switches, would she too give that horrible death shudder? Could he do this without harming her? Did he even have the skills to do this? He knew he had the scientific background and understood the theory, but theory and practice were hardly the same.

He didn't see what choice he had, so he stepped up to the control panel and placed the ampule in its proper slot at the head of the table. It clicked into place, and he watched the silver liquid drain out. He hoped it was supposed to do that. He placed his hand on the first switch.

"I wouldn't do that," came Jo'sha's voice, as a gloved hand closed around his own. Dorain, in his shock, almost collapsed to his knees.

"How did you—?" Dorain began to ask, but he knew it didn't matter.

"Help me," he insisted instead.

Jo'sha shook his concealed head. "You know she isn't fully sedated. She's going to suffer."

"Then what should I do?" Dorain asked. "If I leave her like this—"

"The only fighting chance she has is like this," Jo'sha said.

Dorain stared at him, his golden eyes pleading. "How? If I leave her like this, they will take her from me and hurt her."

"Not if we send her somewhere they can't find her," Jo'sha replied.

"How—?" Dorain began to ask, but that was when the floor beneath him began to rumble and shudder violently. He and Jo'sha both braced themselves against the table as the floor continued to rock and buck. Dorain thought it would never end, and when it finally did, everything seemed eerily still.

"What was that?" Dorain whispered.

Dorain had felt *Moga* lurch when the Council ship *Ezzeniel* had docked next to them. The ship had given a shudder. There had been some groaning and rumbling. This was not like that. Whatever had just happened, it was not another ship docking.

"Our primary plan has failed," Jo'sha replied. "They captured too many of us. They've taken back parts of the ship that we did not want them to have. We have no choice but to implement our next plan."

"Who? What plan?"

Jo'sha looked down at his sister. Dorain understood.

"You mean to send her down to the planet."

"I do."

"You can't!" Dorain said. "The planet has fallen into crisis, and her Ganger is too old! She's too weak! She can't survive down there!"

"Not for an extended period of time, no, but for a period of a few days, she will endure."

"You cannot send her to the planet," Dorain said. "She will come to harm."

"And you think she will be safe in a glass vial?" Jo'sha asked, his voice taking on a harsh tone. "You would trust her life to a thin wall of glass while the world she loves turns to ruins below? And, tell me, when they come for you, her *twin* brother, the person she is closest to in this world, to search for her, will you fight them? Or will they take her from you, conveniently packed in that fragile prison, to do whatever they like to her captive mind? You put her in that ampule and she is as good as lost. Which fate is truly worse?"

He was right, Dorain realized. Hysteria had clouded his judgment. If he put Saira in that vial, he could not protect her any more than he could protect the Ganger.

"Then help me hide her, but do not ask me to send her down to that planet alone."

"So you would trap her up here and let the planet go to ruins. How? Hide her in a stasis chamber? Make her sleep while the species she loves dies out? What do you think she will say when she awakens? How do you think she will feel?"

"She'll be safe ..." Dorain said weakly.

"She's a Peacemaker—a Doppelganger. She has devoted her life to protecting the people of the planet Earth. What do you think she would want *now*? The planet she loves is falling apart. The people she loves are in danger. Do you think your sister would be full of fear like you are? Do you think she would be so selfish?"

"What do you think she can do?" Dorain asked, watching Jo'sha's face in earnest. "What do you want of her? You must know that there is nothing she can possibly do to ameliorate the situation."

It occurred to him then that he could see his face—he had unmasked it, but he was thinking too quickly to linger on the curiosity.

Dorain watched as Jo'sha pursed his lips. It was a strangely human thing to do, and the expression looked out of place on his face. The flash in his eyes, though ... Dorain could recognize that. It was there and gone in an instant—gone before Dorain could make sense of it—but he saw the slip of a thought pass through Jo'sha's mind. It was one that he seemed quick to hide.

"Your sister loves people on that planet. The situation is lost, but let her go to them. Let her do something for them."

Dorain looked at his sister. Jo'sha was right. He *was* being selfish. What he was doing—he wasn't doing it for her, he was doing it for himself. He was so afraid of losing Saira, of watching her suffer, that he was making all the wrong choices.

But there was something else. Dorain had not forgotten the look that had passed across Jo'sha's face.

"You came for her," Dorain said. "Of all the Gangers to rescue, you came looking specifically for her. Why?"

Jo'sha hesitated for a moment, then quietly slipped his hand into a pocket. When it emerged, there was a small, pink half of a heart dangling by a silver chain in his grasp.

"How did you get that?" Dorain asked, immediately recognizing the necklace.

"Do you think she won't protect them," Jo'sha asked, "no matter the cost?"

Dorain watched him carefully now. "Why are they so important to you?"

"They're all we have left."

Dorain watched him, analyzing his face. It was a simple statement, and Dorain understood it clearly enough. The humans with whom his sister and others like her had lived with for so long— they were the only things left of the world they all had once known. They were the only things left to fight for and protect.

And, yet, the way Jo'sha said it made Dorain think that there was something more to his words.

"What is this plan of yours?" Dorain asked, watching his unconscious sister.

It was time that he accepted that nothing about this situation fit into his perception of the world, so he asked. He felt his ideals and beliefs drifting away.

"Do you truly want to know?" Jo'sha asked. It was the same thing he had asked in that dark, secret room, right before the calamity had begun. Dorain looked down. Jo'sha had the same stun gun in his grasp.

"It isn't meant for you," he said, but that didn't comfort Dorain at all. A Peacemaker Impersonator, hidden in a Council agent's suit, stood before him with a weapon, and Dorain knew there was something wrong.

112

At the last minute, he reached out and took back his ideals. He felt the walls of protection go up in his mind.

Some things were worth protecting, whatever the cost.

"No," Dorain said. "I only want to know that Saira will be safe."

"On my life," Jo'sha said. "All I want is to protect her—to protect all of them until this is over. They have done nothing to deserve this fate."

"Then send her to the planet," Dorain said.

Jo'sha moved with incredible speed then. Before Dorain knew what was happening, the masked man jabbed a needle into his sister's neck. It clicked and hissed, injecting something into her veins. There was another needle in his hand.

"We only have minutes until she wakes up, but I fear we have less time than that to get her out of here. *Move*," he said.

Dorain scooped his sister into his arms, and when Jo'sha ran, he did not hesitate to follow.

The wailing siren and flashing lights met them in the hall, signifying to Dorain that the world was still off-kilter. But Dorain ran, and when Jo'sha slipped into the transport room, he was right behind him.

His sister stirred in his arms, groaning.

"Saira?" he asked, but her eyes remained closed and there was no response.

"Get her into the room," Jo'sha commanded.

"Where are you sending her?" Dorain asked.

"If I recalibrate the machine to send her somewhere specific, it will take too long. They'll know we're in here and pull what little power is left. We can maintain control of the transport rooms, but only if we are quick."

"So what are you going to do?"

"One-way genetic signature," Jo'sha said. "She'll be gone before they know what's happened, and we'll be gone before they can send someone after us."

"One-way?" Dorain asked. "But that means—"

"It won't be a problem."

Dorain turned to stare at the suited man. "What happened to the girl?"

Jo'sha didn't acknowledge the question. Instead, he thrust a fist at Dorain. "Make sure she has these."

Dorain opened his palm, and Jo'sha pressed two objects into his hand: the necklace and a scrap of paper.

"And use this," he added, handing him the needle he had been clinging to.

"What is this for?"

"If she can get to those coordinates, her safety is guaranteed. I only wish I could send her directly there, but she has a better chance if she runs."

"How? How will she be safe there?"

In his arms, Saira groaned. Her eyes fluttered momentarily before closing again.

"She's waking up. What do I tell her?"

"I don't know, but whatever you say, you have fifteen seconds to say it, and it had best convince her to run for her life."

"What—?"

"I need your sister in that chamber, Dorain Ta'u. We are out of time."

Dorain looked at him, his eyes conflicted.

"Go!" the man said sternly. Dorain turned and rushed through the door, setting his sister down inside the room. Her eyes were opening again.

What should he tell her?

He glanced down at the necklace in his hand, and suddenly he knew. He knew what would make his sister run—what would make her protect herself, even if she didn't know that that was what she was doing. He knew what his sister would want if she had all the facts—what she would value most, even more than she valued her own well-being. He didn't have time to tell her everything. She wouldn't get the chance to make the decision herself, but then, it was Saira, and it was all Saira ever wanted.

So he said the words.

And then, it was over. He was standing on the other side of the wall, his sister gone in a flash of light.

He just stood there, not believing what he had just done.

"We have to go," Jo'sha said behind him, but Dorain didn't move.

"Dorain, run!" he shouted at him. "They're going to come for us!"

"No," Dorain said, still staring at the spot where his helpless sister had sat. He could only hope that he made the right choice.

Suddenly, something told him that he hadn't.

Then, Jo'sha was in his face. "Run, Thellessian, or they will take you and throw you in a dark cell!"

"I know," Dorain said.

He turned to look at the other Peacemaker. "You promised that she will not come to harm. I will hold you to your word."

The suited man stood there, rigid.

"What are you doing?" he asked.

"I have committed my sins to save my sister," he replied, "but no more. I will not follow you. Whatever you are doing, I will have no further part in it. I've tarnished myself enough, and it stops here."

"You do not know what you are doing," said the Impersonator.

"You are mistaken," Dorain said. "I am saving my way of life. I'm saving myself."

"You will suffer."

"It is not the type of suffering I fear," was his reply.

"It is true that I do not know true suffering. I recognize that I am naïve and childlike," he continued. "And there is nothing wrong with that. Is that not what we work for every day? For a time when all species and planets know true peace? When they don't know animosity? Let me remain as I am. Let me shelter myself from the wickedness that's out there. Let there be one being that does not know what hatred or anger is, so that whenever all of this ends— whatever this is—one creature will know what it is like to never know a world that is unsullied. Let there be one creature who will remember and keep working toward that future."

They heard the banging on the door then. Whoever was outside the door—be it the Council, the Peacemakers, or someone else—they had found them, and they were coming to take them away. Dorain turned to face the door, waiting for whatever was going to happen.

"I do not believe in this," Dorain said. "I do not understand it, and I do not agree with the path you have chosen, so I take no responsibility, but I beg of you, for whatever reason you came for my sister, don't make her a part of this. Just keep her safe."

Dorain fell to the ground. He never felt the burst of energy that came from behind.

Jo'sha walked up to his prone form, stun gun in hand.

"You speak the truth," Jo'sha said, sighing. "But I fear you are also misguided."

He knelt down and pulled out a pair of handcuffs.

"I apologize for lying about the gun," he said to the unconscious form as he clamped the cuffs around Dorain's wrists. "And for lying about everything else."

"You should know that I have never wished your sister harm," he added. "And I deeply regret her sacrifice."

CHAPTER 7

"**S**aira, wake up!" someone shouted. They were shaking me urgently. As awareness came flooding back, I realized I was sitting on a floor somewhere, slumped against a wall. My neck and back were stiff. I tried to open my eyes, but they felt so heavy. I tried to speak, but my mouth was dry. Just swallowing was a chore.

Whoever they were, I felt them slip their hand under my chin. I felt cold metal against my neck, followed by the biting kiss of a needle puncturing my skin. It burned. The sensation helped rouse me from my stupor, but just barely.

I became aware of the blare of an alarm, shrill and pulsating in the background. Behind closed eyelids, I could sense the pulses of light from a siren. It made my head hurt. I groaned, but the sound was a million miles away.

"Saira, open your eyes!"

Every instinct I had was telling me to just close my eyes and go back to sleep, that I didn't want to see what was waiting for me, but I did. The pulsating bright light in the background burned my eyes. Someone was crouched before me. They were still too tall for me to see their face, but the blue, white, and gray-speckled skin instantly gave away my brother.

Where was I? The last thing I remembered was the medical unit and the sounds of Dorain screaming behind the door. How had he gotten in? Where were we? All I could see were white walls, a white floor, and the steady strobe of the much-too-bright alarm.

"Saira, look at me."

I tried, but even crouching down, he was too tall. The effort to lift my head was too much, and I could only meet his eyes for a second. Still, it was enough. I had never before seen that look on his face. Again I tried to speak—tried to figure out what was happening, but my mouth wouldn't move. I managed a feeble squeak.

There was a noise outside the room, barely discernible under the blare of the siren. Someone was banging on the wall, but it wasn't the sound of someone breaking in. It was the sound of urgency, but I couldn't understand why. Dorain looked back, anxious. He slid something into my jeans pocket.

"Save them, Saira. Do you understand me? Save them!"

He jumped to his feet and ran to the wall. A door slid open for him. He gave me a fleeting look and lingered at the doorway.

At the last second, I found my voice.

"Dorain!" I cried, reaching for him. The gravity of what was happening suddenly dawned on me.

But he was gone. There was a flash of light.

My head spun. Nausea gripped at my stomach, and I thought for sure I would be sick. Again. I was going to be sick again. And—I had gone blind. The Ganger body had taken all it could take.

It hit me: Ganger body. Realization flooded my previously muddled mind as the shock of every fiber of my being protesting the effects of the transport beam forced me into an abrupt clarity. I was still a Ganger, with—as far as I could tell—all of my memories intact. I should have been in my own body, devoid of any knowledge of Earth, but I couldn't deny that, although I couldn't see them, I could count five fingers on each hand, not three. I counted multiple times to be sure it wasn't just confusion from my spinning head, but I was definitely fully alert now.

I became aware of how awful my body felt. I could feel all of my systems failing. I felt weak, and things hurt: joints, bones, organs— pretty much everything. It was just a dull ache for now, but I knew it would worsen before the end, and what an end it would be …

For whatever reason my brother had sent me back to Earth in a Ganger body, his efforts would prove useless. This body would fail soon. Once it did, my consciousness would be ejected, and I'd just end up back in myself, probably insane. I had heard that the Transference, when done properly, was a madness-inducing process to be awake for. If not done properly, you would be fortunate if parts of you even made it back.

I started to panic. I was emotionally and physically exhausted. What had happened? How did I get out of the medical unit? Why was I in a dying Ganger? Who was I supposed to save, and from what? Why? *And where was I?*

I was lying on my stomach—I knew that much. It was so cold; I was shivering uncontrollably. The ground was soft and lumpy beneath me, but whatever it was, it wasn't dirt. It felt more like wadded-up bed sheets. I tried to feel around, and I realized that there were walls and a ceiling not far from me, unyielding and like ice against my skin. I was in a box, and based on the stale air, it was a very tightly sealed box. *Why was I in a box?*

I didn't want to be here. I wanted to be anywhere else. I wanted my brother.

I forced myself to swallow the building hysteria; it wouldn't help me here. I continued to feel around, fingers tracing the outline of the fabric beneath me, until I touched something beneath the sheet that stopped my heart in my chest.

I felt a face: a very cold, still face. The realization hit me. I felt it seize in my chest, threatening to choke me to death with its weight. When a Ganger got sent to Earth or pulled back to *Moga*, there was usually an exchange with a human of identical genetic makeup. I had been sent to Earth following the genetic signature of Allyson Owens, but the human hadn't been pulled back. I was lying on Allyson Owens. The real one.

She was dead.

Terror gripped me. This was worse than the ship. This was monstrous. This was soulless. I screamed, the sound primal and uncontrollable. I didn't think I'd ever be able to stop, but the hyperventilating left me breathless. I pounded on the walls until I was sure my knuckles were bloody. I did everything I could to get away. I would rip that cold box filled with death, grief, and betrayal apart if I had to!

She was dead! She was supposed to live! She was supposed to be okay!

The door opened, and someone yanked us out of the tiny refrigerated box. I instinctively rolled and landed on the floor of the morgue with a thud, the wind knocked out of me. I crawled a few feet before I collapsed in a fit of sobs. As I lay there, trying to make the room stop spinning, I became aware of someone else screaming. A young man—an intern, maybe—tried to run, but I had the sense to grab his ankle. He collapsed in a heap.

"Wait!" I cried.

119

The young man stared at me, too petrified to move. His hair had receded years earlier, making him look older. He stared at me, too stunned to pry his ankle from my shaky grasp. The fear made him look even older.

He looked at me, then at Allyson, then back to me. "You—dead—two—"

He stared at me in confusion, and from the pale gray color of his face, I could tell he was about to faint.

"Hey!" I said, scrambling to my hands and knees. "I'm sorry. I'm sorry! Stay with me!"

He just watched me, dazed.

"I'm sorry. I'm so, *so* sorry," I repeated, crawling to his side.

He continued to gape, eyes wide and pupils dilated, on the verge of passing out. I touched his cheek. He recoiled, though I don't think he actually processed the touch.

"Dead," he mumbled.

"Yeah," I said. "She is."

I looked back at the dead girl. I had pulled the sheet off her when I took my tumble to the ground. There she was, red hair gleaming in the light, one gray hand hanging out to the side. It was more than I could bear. I squeezed my eyes closed and took a deep breath, trying to regain my composure.

I'm not sure where the strength came from; it certainly didn't come from me. I remembered by brother's face. He had gotten me here. My brother had been brave. The thought of what he had done for me renewed my strength. He had sent me here for a reason. I had to figure out that reason. I could be strong for him.

"I'm sorry I frightened you," I told the man. "Can you tell me how long she's been in there?"

He seemed to snap out of it a little bit. "What?"

"How long has she been here? Where is her family? Where are her friends? There were people with her when she died. Where can I find them?"

"Six ... um ... six hours," he said. He still looked frightened, but I could tell he was trying to pull himself together. "How—?"

"I don't know," I said, cutting him off. "I don't have any answers for you, and I'm sorry. I don't even know what I'm doing myself, but I *need* to know if her family is here."

120

Save them! The words echoed in my head. Save *who*? I didn't know, but a few faces immediately came to mind. I knew I had to find my family.

"Uh … no. No. We tried to call, but the phones went down right after we brought them in."

I hesitated, not missing his choice of words.

"Them?" I asked.

Slowly, I looked up. Allyson wasn't the only one in the morgue. A white sheet dangled off a metal table inches from my head. They were everywhere, filling and lining the small, cold room.

My breath caught in my throat. I felt the tears that would not fall welling in my eyes. All I could do was stare at the still, empty destruction. How could devastation be so quiet? And yet, it roared in my ears, accusing me.

It was my fault. I felt my heart beating in my chest, pushing contaminated blood through my veins. I saw the bodies lying all around me, and I knew I was the one who had killed them. Them and Allyson. I put my hand over my mouth, stifling the sobs.

I wanted to beg them for forgiveness. I didn't mean to; they had to know that I didn't mean to!

"They all came in at once," the man said, but I barely heard him.

I forced myself to look down at him, to focus on his face. He had brown eyes. I had to focus on his brown eyes.

I knew I would never forgive myself. I would never forget what I saw in that room, but it was over. I had already done it, and it could never be changed. There were still events to be changed, though. There were still lives I could spare. Isn't that why my brother sent me back?

"The phones?" I nearly whispered, but I didn't know who I was afraid of disturbing. The other people in the room couldn't hear me.

"Everything is down: phones, radio, television."

Save them, Saira! My brother's voice was ringing in my head. The hair on the back of my neck was standing on end.

"It's been six hours and her family hasn't shown up?"

"There's been no way to let them know," he said.

"I need you to listen to me," I said, staring him in the eye. "Get out of here. Take whoever you can and get out of town. Go to the country. Do you understand?"

121

"What? *Why?*"

"Go now," I said. I stood up and made my way toward the door. I knew I didn't have much time.

I forced myself not to look at the white sheets beside me.

"W-wait!" the guy called after me. "Your friends—her friends—they're here. They're in the waiting room. They wouldn't leave."

"*Thank you,*" I said, my voice breaking with relief. I took one look over my shoulder—I couldn't stop that. The red-headed girl on the table looked peaceful, as if she were sleeping. My throat tightened. Every bone in my body ached to tell that girl that I was sorry. I wanted to beg her forgiveness, tell her it wasn't my fault. I didn't know.

But I couldn't. She was dead, and it was my fault. I knew it was.

For a brief moment my head swam, and the girl on the table transformed. She became tiny and frail, her body racked by disease. I had wanted to apologize to her, too.

No! I wouldn't think about it! I wouldn't! I forced the memories back into oblivion.

I clenched my eyes shut and steadied myself. It was time to be brave. My brother was counting on me to be brave. I would do it for him.

It was time to be a Peacemaker. It was time to find my family.

I ran. I didn't look back.

I found them in the waiting room, right where the young man had said they would be. Marie was curled up in an uncomfortable-looking chair, fast asleep. Tori sat beside her. She had a cup of coffee in her hand that looked like it hadn't been touched in hours. Black streaks ran down her face where tears had made her thick black eyeliner run, though it looked as if she had run out of tears a long time ago. She stared at the wall ahead of her, unblinking.

I saw Jillian sitting across from them, her head in her hands, still weeping but trying to hide her tears behind her hands. She had always been reticent about showing her emotions.

"Jillian!" I screamed at the sight of her, loud enough that everyone around me turned to glare. We were in a hospital waiting room. It was so quiet, my voice seemed to pierce the air.

Tori jumped to her feet, startled beyond comprehension, eyes wild, trying to make sense of a dead girl's voice. The cup overturned and the coffee went everywhere. Marie startled awake. She looked around, confused. When she saw me, she started flailing in an attempt to get upright, making sounds of frightened desperation. All of the color drained from her face.

Jillian's head shot up, the look on her face one of hopeful disbelief. She looked toward me and our eyes met. Relief flooded her face, and then, she was running toward me. She grabbed me in the tightest hug I had ever felt.

"Oh, my god, Ally!" she sobbed.

Despite the urgency of my mission, I couldn't help it. I wrapped my arms around her and buried my face in her hair, remembering her human smell. She always smelled like spices. She was here. She was okay. They were all okay.

Marie and Tori appeared by her side, but they were too stunned to speak. They just stared at me.

Save them ...

Then I noticed the other people eyeing our emotional reunion, some trying their best to ignore us, others irritated or curious. What could I do? How could I save them all? I looked back at the faces of my friends.

I knew there was no time. The man had told me it had been six hours. Something told me that my window was about to close and that, once it did, it was over. I took one last look at the people in the room and prayed that I would not live to regret my actions, but I couldn't. I couldn't save them all.

I grabbed Jillian by the shoulders and forced her to look me in the eye. "We have to go. I need your keys."

"What?" Tori blurted out.

Jillian did as she was told. Confused and clearly shaken, she pulled the keys out of her pocket and handed them to me.

Save them ...

I would. Someone had already deemed my life over. Who, and for what reason, I didn't know, but my brother had given me this chance. I would save them from whatever was coming if it was the last thing I ever did.

"Go," I said, and then I was running for the parking lot. To my relief, I heard three pairs of running feet trailing me.

I left everyone else behind.

The car was right out front. I threw the door open and started the car. I was backing out before Marie had the back door closed.

"What the *hell*!" Tori shrieked as I exited the parking lot, a car throwing on its brakes and laying on its horn as I cut it off. "You're freaking dead!"

Tori had never been able to keep quiet long, grief-stricken or not. I ran a red light out of the parking lot—with yet another car squealing to a halt and honking its displeasure— and made my way toward the highway heading north, out of the city.

I ignored her. "Do any of you have cell phone service? Can you call your families?"

"They're down. They went down right after you—we called 911, and they went down maybe a minute later," Jillian said. She was staring at me, turning the same shade of gray as the poor guy in the morgue.

"I need you all to try." I put a hand on Jilly's shoulder. She jumped. "I need you to stay with me, okay?"

"You died," she whispered. "I turned around, and when I looked back, you were on the ground, too. What happened, Ally?"

"I'm right here," I said. "I'm right here, and I'm not going anywhere."

At least I hoped not. The truth was, I was expecting a flash of light and a swarm of uniforms from the Council of Traltix to rip me away at any moment, but I also trusted my brother. If he could somehow break me out of a medical unit and get me on the planet, he could keep me here, and I had to trust that I would be here long enough to do whatever I needed to do.

"Where are we going?" Marie squeaked from the back seat.

"Home," I said. "We're going to go get my family. Jillian's too. I need you to call yours. Call whoever you can."

I knew they wouldn't be able to, that Earth technology was dead, but doing nothing wasn't an option. Marie and Tori had families, too. Tori's might not have been the most exemplary people on the planet, but they were hers. They both lived out of the state. We'd never be able to get to them, but maybe …

There was no maybe. I knew the ending to this story, just as I knew the end for the people in the hospital, but we would try, for the sake of Tori and Marie.

I turned on the radio. There was nothing but static.

"The radios are down, too," Tori said. "Can you turn that damn thing off? It's irritating as hell."

"Sorry," I said. "I need it."

For what, I didn't know, but Earth technology was simplistic, and it was easily manipulated. We had been using it for decades to secretly communicate with Gangers and Impersonators, so why not now? Maybe my brother could send me a message. Maybe he could tell me what was going on.

"*You need it?*" Tori shouted. "What the hell is going on? I'm sorry, but have you *not* been dead for the past six hours?"

"You just fell over," Marie whimpered. "People just started falling down."

The morgue, together with their words, led me to the conclusion that it was the virus taking effect in the restaurant that provided the distraction the Council needed to beam me back to *Moga* unnoticed.

"No," I said firmly. "I'm okay. I'm fine."

There were two sets of eyes staring at me from the back seat. Jillian was also staring at me, chewing her nails as she always did when she was really anxious.

"I promise you that I'm fine," I said. "Everything is okay."

What was I saying? I knew that it wasn't. They had just watched who knew how many people fall over dead in a restaurant!

Adrenaline had taken away the pain and weakness I had been feeling, but glancing in the rearview mirror, I knew I wasn't okay. I was pale, my lips slightly blue. Beneath my eyes there were dark circles and a tint of yellow, which was more than worrisome. I looked sick. I was sick, but I couldn't tell them that. They couldn't know anything, though this would be easier said than done.

"Where the *hell* are you taking us?" Tori shouted.

"Please stop screaming," Marie begged, her voice breaking.

"Out of the city," I repeated. "We're going home."

"What the hell for? What's going on?" Tori fumed. "Is this an outbreak?"

"I'm not sure," I said. "I just—something happened at the hospital."

I reminded myself that I couldn't tell them anything, but I sure hadn't been doing the best job of keeping things from them so far. I had been trained for decades on how to properly infiltrate human society, but there was no training available for this situation, and my species was terrible at lying.

"Liar," Tori snapped, proving what I already knew. I cringed inwardly. This was not going to go well.

"Tori!" Jillian shouted. "Would you calm down and shut up!"

"I'm sorry, but, one minute she's dead, and the next minute she's alive and rushing us out of the city like a lunatic. I just want to know where I'm being kidnapped to and if *I'm* about to drop dead as well!"

"Just stop yelling!" Jillian snapped, turning around in her seat to glare daggers at Tori. "We've all had more than we can handle today, and you're not helping, so could you just *shut the hell up* until life starts making sense again?"

Jillian collapsed back into her seat and covered her face with her hands. This was out of character for her, as she had never been one to show vulnerability. I could hear sniffles behind her hands as she tried not to have a breakdown in the front seat. It broke my heart to see her in such a state. I wanted to put my hand on her and tell her that it would be okay, but I knew I couldn't lie to her like that, so I kept both hands on the wheel and looked straight ahead at the highway, willing myself to stay strong and resolute.

"No one is sick," I tried to say as reassuringly as possible. "It was an isolated incident, okay?"

"That's not what we heard at the hospital," Tori snapped.

"I promise you, you are *not* sick," I said more forcefully.

"Can we just stop for a minute?" Marie begged. "I think we need to go back to the hospital. You look really bad, and—"

"I'm sorry, Marie. We can't stop. We don't have a lot of time."

"*We don't have a lot of time*? Who the hell are you? What is going on? *You know something!*" Tori ranted.

"Ally, Marie's right. I think we need to go back to the hospital. I think you've had a rough day, and you're sick and confused, and you're worrying me. You don't look good. Let's go back. We'll call your parents once the phones come back up," Jillian said, trying to stay calm.

"Ally, *please!*" Marie pleaded, and she started crying. "You have to go back to the hospital."

"Stop crying, you wuss!" Tori shouted at her.

"*Tori*" I roared, my tone commanding. Everyone was instantly quiet. I never raised my voice—my species didn't have the ability to raise our voices in anger. For me, it was an unnatural response, and even I was startled.

"I'm not sick. *No one* is sick or dying," I said as calmly as I could, but the rush of adrenaline made it difficult. "I'm sorry you're frightened, but you have to trust me. Please get on your cell phones and try to call your families."

"Why?" Tori demanded. "You know what's going on."

"I don't know anything," I said matter-of-factly.

The radio static stopped and, in its place, a long, shrill tone.

"Oh, god!" Tori shouted. "That's worse! Turn the damn thing off!"

I turned it up and slammed my foot onto the gas pedal. I could hear my heart beating in my ears, adrenaline surging through my veins even stronger. I clutched at the steering wheel, clenching my teeth. I was right. I had an angel on *Moga*, and they were giving me the red alert. We were all in very real, imminent danger, and I prayed that I was going in the right direction. I prayed that I had enough time. Drivers lay on their horns as I weaved dangerously in and out of traffic. I prayed I wouldn't kill us then and there. I prayed a lot of things.

"Ally, what does that mean?" Jillian asked, with a pleading look aimed at *me*.

"Call your families," I said.

"What the f—" Tori started.

"Call. Your. Families. NOW," I said between clenched teeth.

There was silence for a few minutes, followed by Tori smashing her phone into the floor of the car. "The phones have the same damned noise!"

"Would you calm down?" Jillian hissed.

"I'm sorry. I'm being kidnapped by my undead roommate, who just happens to be driving well over one hundred miles an hour, in case you hadn't noticed! Oh, and the world has gone to shit. You're right, I should calm down. I'm sorry for my selfish behavior."

She threw herself against the back seat and crossed her arms.

"I'm not undead," I muttered.

"Could've fooled me!" Tori snapped. "You certainly look it."

127

"I'm fine," I said. Tori scoffed.

"Tori, stop being an asshole," Jillian said, rubbing her temples.

"Can we all just stop cursing at each other?" Marie squealed. "And could you please slow down?"

I glanced at her through the rearview mirror. "Watch for cops."

"That's a *no*," Tori muttered petulantly.

Everyone was quiet after that, as their animosity gave way to exhaustion. I wasn't the only one who had had a day that would put any nightmare to shame. Today their world changed forever, and I feared that they had yet to figure out just how much. That wasn't to say they were calm, but at least the yelling stopped.

Marie curled up in the back and stared out the window, and every once in a while I heard her sniffle. Tori crossed her arms and glared at the back of my seat. I felt it more than I saw it. Her silence was just as loud as the shouting. Jillian scanned the channels for a while, but she finally gave up and just sat there, eyes closed as she tried to block out the world for a while. Actually, she was probably trying to block out my wild driving strategy. I had yet to stop weaving in and out of traffic at a ridiculous speed, and each time the car jerked or I was forced to throw on the brakes to keep from rear-ending someone, she clenched her fists. Marie and Tori didn't like it any better. Marie let out the occasional squeak, and I heard a colorful assortment of profanities muttered under Tori's breath when she wasn't being deathly silent. More like *deadly*. I was fairly certain she was waiting to explode on someone, but I did my best to ignore that thought.

"What are we going to do when we get home?" Jillian asked, her eyes still closed. I could tell from her voice that she was putting considerable effort into keeping it together.

"We're going to get our families and find someplace safe."

"From what?" she asked.

"I don't know."

"Then what are we doing?" she said, her eyes still closed.

She knew she wouldn't get anything from me. She knew I was lying, or at the very least, not giving them the whole story. Of course she did. She was my best friend since childhood, and it was absolutely killing me to do this, but they could know nothing, or they would be at risk.

"Why don't you get some rest? You must be exhausted."

"Ally," she sighed. Her voice was strained. "I'm trying really hard to trust you over here, but you aren't giving me anything to work with. Please talk to me before I decide you're a crazy person."

I felt my heart breaking. I felt eighteen years of trust slipping away.

"She *is* a crazy person," Tori hissed.

"I'm telling you that I don't know what's going on," I said, my voice resolved. Honestly, I could only guess at what was going on, and even then, I hoped I was wrong.

"Ally, I watched you and quite a few other people die today. I watched my *best friend* fall over dead."

"I've had an interesting day, too," I muttered. I could think of far better ways to describe the hell I had endured that day, but I decided to stick with that.

"You are Ally, right?" Jillian asked. I felt my heart stop.

"*What?*" I asked. But her question was not that far-fetched. The cold corpse that was the real Allyson Owens flashed in front of my eyes, one icy hand hanging to the side. I knew this would haunt my nightmares forever, and I knew that the same dead girl would haunt my three best friends as well.

Jillian was staring at me now, tears in her eyes. I saw the trust shattering like glass. I couldn't keep eye contact; it hurt too much.

"Jilly, of course it's me," I said, and I didn't try to hide the wounded tone in my voice. "Who else would I be?"

"Then why won't you tell me what's going on? You know *something*. What? You took a nap in the morgue for a little while and woke up knowing that we were in some kind of mortal danger? Or did you know beforehand, and the whole dying thing was just for shits and giggles?"

She broke down at the end, sobs racking her body. I wasn't expecting that. For the eighteen years that I had known her, I had only seen Jilly cry a few times. I wanted to pull over and stop, but I knew I couldn't. I knew we had to keep going, so I took a deep, shuddering breath and gripped the wheel tighter.

It was torture.

"Well, great," Tori muttered. "The annoying jingle from hell stops, and now we get to listen to more sobbing ..."

"What?" I said.

"Do you not hear her crying? Jesus!" Tori shouted.

By then, I had noticed it. The radio was silent.

We were about to pass a rest stop. I jerked the car into an almost ninety-degree turn, causing the driver behind me to lay on his horn as he went by. I ignored it and slammed on the brakes, stopping the car at a horizontal angle that took up three parking spaces. I could smell the burning rubber.

"*Are you trying to kill us?*" Tori shrieked. "I'm out! I'm getting out! I'm done with this shit!"

She unbuckled her seat belt, but by now I had already leapt out of the car. People were staring. I noticed one person pull out a cell phone, only to realize that they had no service, then shake their head with a disapproving scowl. I'm sure I looked insane as I wandered into the middle of the parking lot, staring above the trees, my friends leaping out of the car to shout at me, asking what on earth I was doing. I ignored them all. It didn't matter. I looked up at the sky. The sun had started going down and it was getting hard to see. I nearly tripped over the curb as I found the sidewalk and stumbled into a picnic area, never taking my eyes off the sky.

"Please, please, please," I whispered, but there it was, way off in the distance: the clouds formed a perfect circle, slowly churning in the atmosphere.

"*No,*" I said. My heart stopped. Everything stopped ...

You couldn't see the pulse, but we all felt it. It shook the ground with the force of an earthquake, but it was there and gone in an instant. Just one quick pulse in the ground, its aftershock trailing behind and almost as intense, but the world as we knew it was over.

I just stood there. I couldn't move. I couldn't breathe. I couldn't think. I couldn't comprehend anything. It had all stopped making sense.

"What was that?" Jillian asked warily, sidling up beside me. She was looking to me for an answer, but the only one I could give her was the one I was so desperately trying to deny.

"Close your eyes, Jillian," I said numbly, my eyes transfixed on the sky.

It wasn't over yet.

"You don't want to see this," I whispered, yet I myself didn't blink. I couldn't stop watching the clouds.

She looked at me, her face a mixture of confusion and terror. I wanted so badly to save her from what was coming.

"Close your eyes! Look away!" I shrieked at her.

The blinding light fell from the sky. It was miles and miles away, but it still burned my eyes, like looking into the sun. I was forced to shield my face.

It was over in less than a minute. Then, there was nothing.

It took me a few seconds to recognize the sound of my own heaving sobs.

"Ally, what was that?" Jillian asked me, genuinely terrified. I turned and walked away, shaking my head. She clutched at my hand, but I pulled away. I couldn't face her. I didn't want to deal with this. I stumbled around in a daze, until I sank to the ground, my knees too weak to support me. All I could do was sit there in disbelief in the middle of a mulch pile.

Sobbing. Wondering why.

Everything was chaos. People were screaming. They were running. There was no point now, though. There was nowhere they could run.

"Ally!" Jillian wailed, dropping to the ground beside me. "Please!"

I couldn't stop crying. I couldn't speak. I couldn't bring myself to tell them that it was a Cleansing.

CHAPTER 8

I stared into the distance, where millions of people used to live in a busy, lively city.

Not anymore. In less than five minutes, more than half of the world's population of humans was gone. Anyone living in a large city, on a military base, or at a nation's capital—they were gone. All over the world, cities had been emptied of their people. Not even their remains would inhabit it.

"*What was that*?" Tori screamed. I could hear Marie crying. People were screaming and crying everywhere.

I clamped my hands over my ears, digging my fingernails into my scalp so hard I was certain they would come back bloody. I couldn't listen to it. I couldn't see it anymore. I clenched my eyes shut. So much crying. So much grief, and it had just started. This horrible nightmare had just started for us. I couldn't fathom it. *I wouldn't.* I just wanted to go home and be safe. I didn't want this to be real. I couldn't handle this. I just couldn't.

Faces flashed before my eyes: Mom, Dad, Meredith, Aidan, Michael …

They were gone forever. I would never see them again.

I never really thought it would happen. I thought that I could get to them. I really thought I could save them.

I had failed them. The reality settled in my chest, cold and rigid. It was getting hard to breathe. The grief would surely suffocate me. I had never felt pain like this before.

Oh, but I had, I realized, and suddenly it was all driving me very mad.

"Tori, for the last time, *shut up and calm down*!" I heard Jillian hiss beside me. Everything was muffled behind my hands, but I could still make out guttural, angry sounds coming from behind me. "Take Marie over there and just *chill out*."

Jillian's voice was on edge. Her voice was desperate. Of course it was.

I could hear the sounds of squealing car tires. People were fleeing, getting back on the highway. I wondered where they would go now. They probably didn't know themselves. They were just running.

I wanted to run too, but I had no idea where to. No place was untouched. I gripped my head tighter, desperately trying to block everything out. I would crush the very thoughts from my head. I would squeeze away the memories of what I had just seen and the demons that were creeping up from the depths of my own personal hell. But no matter how hard I squeezed, I could still hear the chaos. I couldn't even feel the pain.

"Allyson!" Jillian shouted. She grabbed one of my wrists and ripped it away. "*Stop it*! You're hurting yourself!"

She startled me. I found myself staring into her gray eyes, which were dilated with fear. She was trying to keep her face still and calm, but her eyes betrayed her. She was terrified. I could feel her hand around my wrist, shaking.

Numb, I looked down. My nails were stained red. It wasn't bad, but the sight of it made my breath catch in my throat. I was choking, and then I was hyperventilating. I rose to my feet. The world was spinning. The world was madness.

My hands were red in this. The blood was on my fingertips. I could have stopped this. I didn't know how, but I could have! I was right there, on the very ship that did this! I should have said something! I should have fought harder!

I don't know how long I had been screaming when the sound finally registered in my reeling mind.

"*Why?*" I shrieked at the sky, over and over again. I couldn't stop myself. I just stood there, screaming.

"Allyson! STOP IT!" Jillian yelled in my face. She had me by both shoulders, forcing me to hold her gaze.

"You stop this," she whispered, never looking away. "Please stop this."

By some miracle, I did. I was quiet. She let me collapse against her, and I buried my face into her neck, clinging to her for dear life. She was the only thing that made sense anymore. She was all I had left. It was just her, Marie, and Tori now.

"Something awful just happened," Jillian whispered.

I would have to tell her, I realized. She didn't understand the full gravity of the situation, and I was going to have to be the one she heard it from. My stomach turned into a hard knot at the thought of it. I was going to have to shatter her entire world, just as mine had been. I would have to do the same thing to Marie and Tori, too.

"It's too much," I whispered into Jillian's neck. "I ca—I *can't*.

"You're okay," Jillian whispered.

"No, Jilly. We're *not*," I choked. My voice was raspy from all the screaming.

"We're all still here, Ally," Jillian said. "We're right here."

I could hear her heart racing in her chest. She was so scared. I could hear Marie weeping behind me. The sound of it drew me away from the comfort of Jillian's arms. I turned to see the two girls by the car, Marie leaning against the back of it, her face hidden behind her hands. Tori had her back to us, sitting in the shadow of the car with her head leaning against the passenger's door. They looked so little. It occurred to me how easily broken they could be.

I had lost my parents. I had lost my sister and her family. I had lost everyone I had ever known. The only people left whom I loved were right here, but they could be ripped away from me, too. It would be too easy, I realized. They were helpless and fragile.

All they had was me.

I looked at Marie and Tori, then to Jillian. I met her frightened gaze. I was the only thing between them and death, wasn't I?

"I have to protect you now," I whispered. I had just become fully responsible for three human lives. I let the weight of it settle on me, and much to my own surprise, I felt raw determination.

I would not let them die. Whoever had done this would rip me from this body and steal my mind before they took my friends' lives away.

"Okay," Jillian said. "Then let's go home. Let's go home and get our families, and we'll go from there, okay?"

I took a deep breath. I would be strong now, I told myself. No more crying. I pushed the grief away and focused on what I had to do. I met Jillian's eyes.

"It wasn't just that city, Jillian," I said as gently as I could.

"What?" she asked. I saw the understanding flash across her eyes, but I also saw the denial. She withdrew back a step, her fists clenched. I saw the fight in her eyes—how she refused to believe the conclusion her mind had instantly jumped to.

"Home is gone, Jillian. Everything is gone," I said. I saw her shatter.

"My mom …" Jillian began. "My little brother—Ally, he's only eight years old." The look on her face—I had to look away. I couldn't bear to see this. I couldn't watch as my best friend's entire world was ripped away from her.

"My mom. My dad. My sister. My nephews," I said. In one day, I had had my entire life ripped away from me over and over and *over* again. I wished then that my Ganger body *would* fail. I wanted to be as dead as Allyson Owens in that morgue, my mind sent back to my body on *Moga*, where the Council of Traltix would make me pay for imaginary crimes and take all of this pain away from me. I didn't want to be the heroine my brother had asked me to be. I couldn't be a heroine. My race didn't know how to fight to live—we couldn't, even if we wanted to. We just weren't made that way. I *could not* do this.

I clenched my fists. No, I wouldn't think that. I was here and I had made my choice. I knew I couldn't be strong for myself, but I would keep going for them. I had kept us alive so far. I could keep doing it somehow.

"We have to go," Jillian said, trying to push past me in her panic. "We need to find them!"

I heard the hysteria rising in her voice. I grabbed her as she tried to push past and pulled her to my chest. "The whole city is gone, Jilly. Everyone is gone."

I closed my eyes, willing myself not to cry. Our families lived in Jacksonville. It was the largest city in Florida. There was no chance that it had been spared.

"You don't know that!" Jillian exclaimed. She tried to push against me, but her heart wasn't in it. When I didn't let go, she fell against me. I felt the life draining out of her as the despair set in.

Behind my closed eyes, I saw it almost as if I were standing in the streets, looking at everything we had ever known laid to waste. Jacksonville was nothing more than a burn mark on the planet. In the streets, empty cars would clog the arteries of the city. Perhaps a few would have their doors thrown open from when people got out to watch the clouds churning in a near-perfect circle just before the pulse tore through and hit the ground with a force unknown to this world. The rest of the cars would have come to a rest on the roads, their windshields smashed from the impact of the blast, glass scattered across the ground. Homes and businesses would have had their windows blown out as well; perhaps a few had even collapsed as the pulse cannon hit the ground with the force of an earthquake. There would be no people. There would be no animals. Even the plant life was gone. Grass, trees, and flowers – everything living in the city had been erased in a flash of light. There would be only burn marks and ash.

"There is nothing there, Jillian," I whispered. "We can't go back there. Our families aren't there."

"You don't know that!" Jillian nearly shouted in my ear. "We have to go! We have to look for them! We can't just leave them behind!"

I couldn't answer. I was choking on grief. I wanted nothing more than to hold on to the hope that I was wrong. I wanted so badly to race back home to find my family spared and to save them, too, but I also knew what was waiting for us if we did. Could I really step through the front door of my family's home, only to see it destroyed and my parents erased from this world? Could I bear to go to my sister's house and see my nephews' rooms as still and empty as a tomb?

Could I bear not to? Would I forever hate myself if I abandoned them to an uncertain fate?

"Ally, *why*? Why would someone do this?" Jillian asked.

"I don't know," I said. At least that part was the truth. I could think of no explanation for this.

She couldn't handle it. She forced her way out of my arms and rushed away, where she could process her emotions without an audience. I didn't follow. There was nothing more I could say. The only thing I could do was give her time to grieve. That was her way.

I became aware of something in my pocket. The weight was subtle but noticeable. That was when I remembered that Dorain had slipped something in it right before I was sent back to Earth. I reached in and pulled out a scrap of paper and the half-heart necklace. Written on the paper were two lines of numbers: latitude and longitude. It was a national park in Tennessee, if I remembered correctly. Decades of watching this small blue planet from *Moga* gave me a wealth of knowledge about its surface. No, I remembered, the coordinates were a system of caverns.

We were in Florida, two states away. It would take forever to get there!

"What am I supposed to do, Dorain?" I whispered. The caverns were so far away, and I didn't even know if I had the time. I didn't even know what was waiting for me there.

The half-heart necklace was warm in the palm of my hand. It was such a simple little thing: fake diamonds on a gaudy hot-pink background, BE FRIE written in silver letters. How could such a little thing mean so much? I looked toward Jillian. It was dark now, and in the light of the moon, as she leaned against a picnic table with her head hung in despair and her dark brown hair covering her face, I saw the chain around her neck glint. My eyes went from her to Marie and Tori a few yards away.

I slipped the necklace on. It was true that my race was not brave. We were not warriors or fighters, but we could love, and I loved my friends.

I stood up and brushed the dirt off my pants. I clutched my half-heart in my hand. We were going to Tennessee.

I became aware of Marie and Tori arguing.

"I don't see anything," Tori muttered.

"I'm telling you, I see something. Look over there," Marie argued back.

"You're practically blind, Four Eyes. You can't see that far in the dark."

My blood ran cold. In my grief, I had forgotten something so terribly important.

"Where, Marie? What do you see?"

"Over there, where the light was," Marie said. "There's something in the clouds."

I didn't need to look. I knew what they were. "Get in the car! Now!"

I was an irresponsible fool. I never should have stopped. I had forgotten about the second phase. Half of the humans on the planet were gone, but this was a Cleansing, and so many more were left to be eliminated.

They didn't use a pulse cannon for that.

137

"*Again?* Are you out of you mind?" Tori snapped.

"Get in the car, Tori," Jillian said as she marched past me. Her red-rimmed eyes briefly met mine as she rushed past. There was something hidden behind them, but I didn't catch it before she slid into the passenger's seat. I was too busy staring down the petulant human before me.

Tori glared at me, eyes burning, and for a minute I thought she would resist me.

"Screw it," she spat. She flung the back door open and crawled inside, Marie quietly following after her. It was Tori who made sure to slam the door closed, though. I practically threw myself into the driver's seat.

"What is it?" Marie asked as I hit the gas.

As I pulled onto the highway, I couldn't help but notice the lack of cars coming from the south.

Marie braced herself in the back seat, clearly uncomfortable, but she decided against commenting on my reckless driving. They understood that we were running, even if they didn't know what from or why. I hoped they would never have to find out.

They couldn't, actually. They couldn't know anything, I remembered. Humans who knew too much were a risk to our entire operation. Humans knowing about Peacemakers—about alien life in general—would destroy any progress their race had made. Such humans were considered dangerous. They were dealt with swiftly, either by having their short-term memories altered, or, if that didn't work, an accident could take away a larger span of knowledge.

The thought made the hair on the back of my neck stand on end.

"I just don't think we should stay here," I said hastily. "I don't want whatever that was coming for us."

I was a terrible liar.

Tori opened her mouth, poised to strike, but Marie gave her a look. Much to my surprise, Tori was quiet. Marie was a gentle creature, and Tori had always had a soft spot for the girl, even if she pretended that Marie's pious mannerisms drove her up the wall. The two couldn't have been more different, yet Tori watched over her like a big sister. The look in Marie's eyes told us all that she had had enough, and it left Tori silent in the back seat.

For the moment, at least.

"When will we get to your house?" Marie asked, innocently enough. I noticed something in her voice, though. I glanced in the rearview mirror to see her watching me, her cross necklace clutched in one hand. The look in her eyes told me that the question I heard was not the one she was truly asking. I couldn't see what she really wanted to know, though. Whatever it was, it was hidden behind square-framed glasses that slid down her nose.

"We aren't going home," I whispered. My guilt made me choke on the words. I could never forgive myself for abandoning my family, I knew that, but I couldn't sacrifice my friends to ease my conscience. "There's a system of caverns in Tennessee. We're going there."

"*We're doing what?*" Tori exploded. "Have you completely lost it? *Caverns?* In freaking *Tennessee?*"

That didn't take long. This was already turning out to be a long, terrible car ride. Tori was in a raging fit, Jillian had gone catatonic in the passenger's seat, and Marie—well, Marie just had this look, and she kept watching me, twirling her necklace. I didn't know what to think about her.

"Just tell me if you see anything," I mumbled.

"Like what?" she snapped.

"Tori, please—" Marie began.

"I'M NOT SHUTTING UP!" Tori bellowed. "I'm scared to death! I've watched people die today. I've been essentially kidnapped. The world has gone to hell, and Sleeper Cell up there won't tell us anything! I just want to know what the hell is going on!"

Jillian sighed in the passenger's seat and looked at me, exasperated. "What could it hurt to tell us what you're looking for?"

She said that, but what I really heard was "say something to make her calm down so I can have a moment's quiet, because I'm at risk for losing it, too." She looked like she was holding it together, but in truth she had just swallowed everything, and she was dying on the inside. She was barely holding it together, and she knew it. We both knew it.

I glanced back in the mirror. Marie was watching me with that look of hers. Tori was bright red. I hadn't even told them the worst of it yet, and already everything was turning into madness.

I was quiet. If I told them too much, I could make them a target.

I saw Marie's face in the rearview mirror, and this time I looked hard at her. She was pale and her eyes had a glazed-over look to them, but I could tell she was trying to be brave. Marie, who was so sweet and shy and naïve, was being so strong. She didn't deserve to be so terrified. And as horribly as Tori was behaving, I knew she was just scared. And Jillian … I looked into her eyes. There was that look again. It was the same one I had seen as she was getting into the car. She was withdrawing from us—from me. Something deep inside her had snapped.

She didn't trust me. The realization dawned on me, cold and shocking. The look in her eyes—it wasn't the same look of warmth and familiarity that she normally gave me. It was as if she didn't recognize me. She may not even have realized it yet, but she had begun to view me as a stranger. Something I had done had triggered some sort of suspicion in her. I looked back at Marie. Was that the same look she had been giving me? Certainly I had never seen Marie look at me that way. They were all seeing me differently.

I was losing them. And how could I blame them? Would I have viewed myself the same way if I had suddenly popped out of a morgue, hijacked a car, and fled a city just in time for the equivalent of a nuclear bomb to be dropped on it? I realized how ludicrous all of this was to them. They were frightened and confused, and I had yet to help them deal with any of it.

"If you see a weird sort of silver machine, yell, even if you're not sure," I said. That wasn't dangerous to tell them, I decided. Earth had plenty of silver machines.

"A silver machine?" Marie said.

"They're about the size of a microwave and *very fast*."

"We're looking for evil microwaves?" Tori asked, incredulous.

"In a nutshell," I muttered. None of that was odd, right? It was still human enough.

"That came out of the sky," Marie said. It wasn't a question. I realized that perhaps I was wrong.

The curly-haired girl saw more than I gave her credit for.

"Yes," I said. There was no denying that one, but humans had control of the skies, too. The conversation was still safe, wasn't it?

"That light came out of the sky, too," Marie said. "From really high up. Wherever it came from, it was way above the clouds. I saw it rip right through them."

Marie was in the back of the car, still twirling that necklace. No, nothing was getting past her. That last part was not safe at all.

"Marie, it's really important that we watch out the windows," I said. The conversation needed to end. I needed more time to think about how I was going to do this.

Much to my relief, Marie complied. Slowly, she sat back and curled against the window, staring outside. Still, the way she chewed on her cross necklace didn't slip past me.

"You know what it was, though, don't you?" Tori asked.

I chewed my lips. I hadn't thought about this part at all. They were still in shock and not really thinking, but when things calmed down, my cryptic rambling wasn't going to cut it. I was being cornered, and it was more than obvious by now that I knew things. The problem was that I couldn't tell them what I knew. I had to make something up, and sooner would be better than later.

"Was it a bomb?" Tori asked.

Jillian was looking at me. It was the look of someone burdened. I had already told her the worst of it, but the two girls behind me didn't know. I gave her a look back, begging. Not now. I just couldn't tell them now.

This was going terribly. What I wouldn't have given to have had just a few minutes to come up with something coherent!

"Yeah," I said, and that was all I could think of.

"Where'd it come from?" Tori said, grilling me.

I just shook my head and ran my hand through my hair. I took a deep breath. I felt trapped. I didn't know what to say.

"I don't know," I said.

"Yes, you do," Tori snapped. "Don't lie to us!"

I felt my pulse throbbing in my neck, a pressure in my head.

"Tori—" I began, but I never got to finish.

"Tori, just shut up," Jillian said, and her voice was as cold as ice. "Just *shut up*. Just—just—"

Her voice was breaking. She squeezed her eyes shut and clenched her fists, fighting for control.

"Maybe we all just need a minute to be quiet," Marie whispered.

"I think that's a great idea," I said with a tired sigh.

There was a steely silence, but, slowly, Tori sat back. Tori was not heartless. She could be rude and incredibly selfish at times, but she was not heartless. She gave in for them, and I sat there, counting my blessings. They would need answers, but I didn't have to give them now. I knew the downside to the silence, though. The longer I went without talking circles at them, the more time they had to think and come up with more questions. I would have to come up with lies for now *and* later, and I didn't think I could do it. I wouldn't be able to stay ahead of all three of them.

We were all deathly quiet after that, the fight gone from us. Tori sat in the back seat with her arms crossed, glaring out of the window. Marie and Jillian also watched out the window, but after a while I noticed Jillian's head begin to droop. She finally fell asleep against the window.

I chose to stay on the back roads. Even under normal circumstances there would be fewer cars and people to run into. Now we passed almost no one, and I was grateful. Fewer people meant less danger. There weren't many other cars traveling country roads in the middle of the night, regardless of whether or not they realized yet that the world had ended. Way out here, people might not have even realized it. We were hours away from the closest big city. No one would have seen the light in the sky, piercing through the clouds to erase the death caused by the pulse cannon. They probably felt the pulse, but they certainly weren't going to attribute a brief shaking of the ground with an alien attack. They had probably already forgotten about it. The radios and television sets would still be useless. I wondered how long it would take before people would figure out how to make them operational again, but then, maybe it was for the best that they stay dead. Once, human entertainment had been fascinating to me, but not anymore. Maybe I would never have to see their chainsaw massacres and murders ever again.

I shook my head. Those were not the kinds of thoughts I should be having. There was no bright side to this. As childish as the human species was, and as much as some of their habits disturbed me, this was wrong. Anyone who saw this would know this was just wrong. So why was it happening?

For the first time I found myself wondering what had gone wrong. Hadn't the Elders said no? Hadn't they asked our advice, taken our words to heart? They sent us back here to help the humans, not kill them. What had happened during my short time on Earth that would force them to do this?

Unless it wasn't the Council of Elders.

I felt my blood run cold. This couldn't be the doing of Peacemakers. But if it wasn't us, who was it? Who had the technology and knew the protocols for an organized Cleansing? Who would want to harm the humans?

"Ally?" Marie said from the back seat. Her tiny voice snapped me out of my stupor.

"Do you see something?" I asked, glancing in all the mirrors. The roads looked vacant.

"The gas light has been on for a while," she said.

She was right. The bright orange light was glaring at me, telling me that we had to stop. For the past few hours, every lonely car that had passed us made my heart stop. My sole focus had been getting farther and farther away from people, pushing the car closer to where my brother told me we would be safe, and now a little light in the corner of my dashboard was telling me that I had to seek out people and *stop*. The idea made my stomach churn, but one way or another, I knew this car was stopping, preferably not broken down on the side of the highway.

I pulled in at a little gas station in the middle of nowhere. There were four gas pumps, one of them already occupied. I chose the pump farthest from the old red pickup truck and shut the car off. I looked at the little store, a brick box with the windows covered with faded advertisements for various foods, drinks, and cigarettes, and signs advertising the lunch and breakfast specials. I chewed on my lip as I glanced back at the humans in the back seat. Lunch was a while ago, and I didn't plan on stopping again unless I had to.

"I need you two to do me a favor," I whispered, trying not to wake Jillian. "I want you to go get food, drinks—anything you think we might need."

Tori had gotten out of the car before I even finished speaking, slamming the car door. I winced.

Marie glanced through the rear window as the dark-haired girl stormed toward the building. She looked back at me, looking helpless.

"What do we say to the people in there? They can't possibly know ..."

I watched as Tori entered the building. I really didn't like letting her get so far away from me. I shifted uncomfortably in my seat, feeling the anxiety rise as she disappeared. Anything could happen to her now. I hated this stopping thing more and more as the milliseconds passed. Every fiber of my being wanted to run in there after her and drag her back to the car.

Marie must have understood the look on my face.

"I'll figure it out," she said, as she opened the car door. "We'll be fast. I promise."

I grabbed her wrist before she could get out.

"Thank you," I whispered.

She gave me a weak smile. "We'll be right back."

I watched her disappear into the building, too. My stomach turned to knots.

"They're fine," I muttered under my breath, but I couldn't shake the feeling that letting them out of my sight had been a bad idea.

The moment I stood up outside, my head started spinning. I leaned against the side of the car and felt my stomach rebel, trying to force its contents up. My stomach was empty, though, and the end result was a set of dry heaves that left my abdomen sore and my eyes watering. I leaned against the side of the car, gasping, and I was relieved to see Jillian still asleep in the car.

That was my friendly reminder that I was still a dead girl, I surmised. I would have to be more careful. My body was failing; it couldn't handle all the stress I was experiencing. Message noted.

The entire time the gas was pumping, I leaned against the car wearily, watching the building, waiting for Marie and Tori to come back out. Overhead, a light flickered on and off, threatening to burn out. An odd assortment of insects buzzed around it, mesmerized by the light.

Something caught my eye in the dark, a quick flash when the light blinked. It was there and gone in an instant, and when I turned my head to look, I saw nothing. It was probably a raccoon or some other creature of the night, I told myself. Still, I couldn't stop the hair from rising on the back of my neck. The girls weren't back yet. The gas nozzle clicked, and I hurriedly replaced it at the pump, slamming the gas tank closed.

"What are you doing?" Jillian said groggily. I jumped. I hadn't even heard the car door open. She had cracked it just enough to poke her head out and was blinking her eyes, dazed by the flickering light overhead.

"Go back to sleep," I said. "I'm just going to get Tori and Marie."

She nodded wearily and closed the door. Leaning back in her seat, she closed her eyes, spent.

I made my way to the small brick building. A bell jingled as I pushed the door open. There was a man at the counter to my right, and Tori and Marie were in the aisles, weaving between bags of potato chips and candy bars. Half of the store looked like a typical gas station and the other half had been converted into a makeshift restaurant, a small kitchen at the back and various tables—the chairs put up for the night—scattered around the floor. In the corner, mounted to the wall, was a television, but it had been muted, and all it showed was snowy static.

"Sorry," a boy who looked to be in his late teens said to a bearded man at the register. "It's temperamental sometimes."

The man grunted, clearly growing impatient.

"Tori! Marie!" I called.

"Yeah, yeah, yeah," Tori muttered. "We're done."

"You ladies find everything you need?" the boy asked. Out of the corner of my eye, I saw him give me a look. He glanced warily at Tori, who just looked petulant. She shrugged, and wandered to the magazines by the front door, flipping through them irritably.

"Sorry about the phone," the boy said. "Everything's kind of a mess today."

Phone? I glanced at Marie. She lowered her eyes and dug through her purse, clearly avoiding looking at me. Tori kept her back to me, flipping furiously.

"It's okay," Marie said, as she dug out her credit card. "It seems to be kind of a problem today."

"It's the weirdest thing," the boy said, as he took the card and swiped it.

Marie looked at me, the expression on her face helpless. I didn't know what to say either. Should I warn him? Should I tell him what had happened? Or should I leave him to let fate sort things out? He was all alone.

Could I take him with me? We had the room.

"Sorry," he muttered. "This thing is kind of finicky. You don't have cash, do you?"

I looked at the boy. He had blue eyes and shaggy blond hair that came down to his shoulders. He was trying his best to grow a mustache, but he had only managed a few long, wispy hairs. Still, by the way he brushed them as he fought with the erratic piece of technology, I could tell he was quite proud of them.

I looked at Marie and Tori, then back to the boy. He had no idea anything was wrong. No one around here did. These people were still alive. Should I do something? Could I? Was I going about this the wrong way, racing two states over with just my three humans? Should I be knocking on doors, leaving notes in every window, warning people that the world was ending and death was coming for them? This boy–Chad, based on the name tag—had a family. They were probably still alive in their home, waiting for him to get off work.

I couldn't possibly save them all, I knew that, but I could send this boy home to be with his family. It was all I had the power to do.

I moved toward him, but I never got the chance to say anything.

Tori dropped a magazine at the front door. She stood there, staring out into the parking lot. "Do your evil microwaves have wings?" she asked.

I felt the pulse. It came from the parking lot. I felt the world collapse around me with it. We weren't fast enough. They were here.

"Tori!" I screamed. "Get away from the door!"

She didn't hesitate. She dove away, scrambling on her hands and knees to where we had crouched at the base of the counter.

"It's silver," she panted. "It has wings. It's some kind of machine."

"I know," I said, pulling her behind me, as far from the fragile glass door as I could.

Then it dawned on me. *It was in the parking lot.*

"Jillian!" I screamed. I scrambled to the front door on my hands and knees. I saw the car at the pump. The passenger door was open. She wasn't there.

Blind panic consumed me. I leapt to my feet, and without thinking, pushed the door open. I felt hands grip my shoulders before I could run out. Tori pulled me back behind the counter.

"Are you insane?" she hissed.

"Let me go!" I screamed. "Jillian's out there!"

"Shut up! It'll hear you!" Tori hissed.

"It already knows we're here!" I snapped. I knew the sounds of the four human hearts—no, five—there were still five, and one of them had to be Jillian's!—beating couldn't be ignored. It wouldn't take long for it to find us. I had to hurry. I had to get Jillian. I had to get us away.

The boy, Chad, leapt out from behind the counter and locked the door.

"What are you doing?" I screamed. "Jillian is out there!"

"What the *hell* is going on?" the boy asked, his eyes wide.

But I wasn't listening. "Let me go!" I snapped at Tori. I struggled against her, but I wasn't a very strong human. Tori was. She grabbed hold of my wrists and pulled me against her chest, trapping me.

Marie crawled to the front door. "I don't see anything," she whispered. "I think it left."

"Marie, get away from the door!" I shrieked. "Tori, *let me go*!"

"We should run," the boy whispered.

"Are you listening to me?" I screamed, fighting against Tori's clutches. "I have to get Jillian!"

"Shut *up*!" Tori snapped. "We're going to go get her, but we have to see what that thing is doing!"

Someone dropped down beside us, panting. "Jillian is fine. Shut up," Jillian muttered.

Tori released me with a sigh of relief, and I sprang forward. I threw my arms around Jillian, sobbing, "Where were you?"

"I saw it. It was on the other side of the parking lot. I ran. The man—he just fell over. He didn't even see it. Back door," Jillian gasped. "I came in through the back door, through the kitchen. I don't think it saw me."

147

It saw her. It still saw her. It saw all of us. We had to get away. One little building wouldn't stop it. I had to regain my composure. Jillian was safe. Marie and Tori were safe. The boy, Chad—I had to keep him safe, too.

"Is anyone else here," I asked him.

"V-Vince is out back," he stammered.

"There wasn't anyone out there," Jillian said.

"He just stepped outside," Chad said. "He said he'd be right back. I—I have to go get him."

I grabbed him as he stood to run. "He isn't out back," I said, pulling him down. It was just my roommates and the boy then. The car wasn't far. All of us could make it. But what then? A car couldn't outrun a Cleansing bot.

"*Ally*," Jillian said, her face pale.

I saw it.

It was at the door, its silver surface reflecting the lights of the gas station, hovering silently about five feet off the ground. It was a beautiful piece of technology: winged, sleek, and seamless, but as I stared down the barrel of death, all I felt was terror.

Chad leapt to his feet and ran, heading to the back of the store.

"No!" I shouted, leaping to my feet. But what could we do? It was at the door. It was within reach. There was no time to think; we had to move.

"Run!" I shouted. "Run for the car! Stay away from it!"

We ran, heading out through the kitchen. We burst through the back door, out into the open. I felt the night air hit me, filling my lungs, pushing me forward. I felt my heart pounding in my ears. We rounded the corner of the building. It wasn't there. I slid to a halt, scanning the parking lot. Where was it?

Cleansing bots never just left.

"Allyson!" Tori shouted from near the car. I counted three girls. Where was the boy?

I heard screaming. Chad ran around the other side of the building. The bot was behind him. He never had a chance. He fell. We felt the pulse in the ground only a split second later, its aftershock following. The pulse came after the bot fired. If you felt it, it meant you were still alive.

We were already dead, though. We would never get in the car in time, let alone leave the parking lot.

Everything was moving in slow motion. The bot turned and faced us, and my friends' faces froze in terror as they realized the gravity of the situation.

There was a rock at my feet. It wasn't very big, but it would be enough. There was a human heart beating in my chest. That would definitely be enough.

"Get in the—"

Again, there was screaming. My blood turned to ice as the sound permeated my mind. It was a sound I never wanted to hear, the sound of my friends afraid for their lives. The world was moving again, but it was too quick. The bot was coming directly at us.

"Tori!" I heard Marie scream.

I turned to see the girl darting across the parking lot, away from the bot. Still, it was coming at us. It would go where the highest human density was, and at that moment, it was focusing on three humans, ignoring the one. Not for long, though. Once it was done with us, it would go for her. On foot, no one stood a chance.

Jillian's eyes met mine for a split second. I saw the look in them.

"No!" I shouted, but I was too late.

"Tori!" Jillian shouted, and she was running too, in the opposite direction of the car, my only hope of getting them away alive. They were running the wrong way.

"Jillian, no! Tori!" I shrieked, but they were gone, disappearing into the dark trees surrounding the gas station.

"Allyson!" Marie cried, as the bot raced toward us. The rock was still at my feet.

"Marie. Run!" I shouted, and I scooped up the rock and chucked it at the bot. It was the only thing in my arsenal. The rock would have hit had the bot not been protected by a translucent force field, a soft, fluid gray against the dark background of the night. Still, the effect was as expected. The bot focused on me, the aggressor, all other human targets forgotten until the hostile being had been removed. It was a special program, ensuring that the overly aggressive members of the species, those who fought instead of ran, those who were a threat to rebuilding a peaceful species once the Cleansing was completed, were removed.

149

It bought my friends a few minutes, but as for me, I was a dead girl. I ran but in the opposite direction of my friends, drawing it away. At least I thought I was.

"Hey!" I heard Marie's mousy cry, followed by the clatter of stones on pavement, one after the other. My heart caught in my throat as the bot turned away from me to face her.

"No!" I screamed, but the more aggressive target had been marked. It went for her.

Marie ran, the bot pursuing her. She would never be able to outrun it. And, unlike me, when it killed her she didn't get to wake up in another body on a ship thousands of miles away from here.

I ran, but they disappeared behind the corner of the convenience store, and by the time I got there, they were lost in the trees, the darkness swallowing them whole. I heard the rustle of leaves, and I dove into the trees, running blindly for the sound.

"Marie!" I shrieked.

"Ally! Help!" I heard her voice cry out in the distance.

It was impossible to run in the woods. It was dark, and the ground was uneven, the rocks, vines, and fallen branches threatening to pull me down at any moment, and I was suddenly very weak. Breathing was incredibly painful, and I found it hard to keep my balance. An overwhelming sense of vertigo consumed me, and I had to grab at trees and limbs in an attempt to stay upright as I ran. I could hear my heart beating in my ears. I couldn't keep this up, but I had to. I had to get to Marie. I had to find Tori and Jillian. What if the bot found them first, lost and helpless in these dark trees?

I saw her. She was only a few yards away, the bot right behind her, but she was small and quick, and the bot was having trouble maneuvering between the trees. Bots were fast, but they weren't agile. They didn't need to be; they were designed to seek out regions of high population density, and that tended to exclude dense woods.

They also had very localized short-range pulses, I realized. They may have been accurate at picking up human vital signs, but unless their target was right in front of them, their aim was terrible. It couldn't lock onto her. So long as she stayed in the trees, so long as she kept running, she would live, but she could only run for so long. Once she succumbed to fatigue, the bot would catch up to her.

"Marie! Here!" I called to her. Without hesitation, she ran for me. There was a large branch at my feet. I grabbed it, and with a deep breath, I ran for the bot. Marie ran past, and I swung. The branch shattered upon impact with the shield, sending wood debris flying. The impact was jarring, and I stumbled, falling to the ground.

"Ally!" Marie shouted, as the bot turned toward me. I was done, I realized.

"Run, Marie!" I shouted, but she just stood there, her eyes locked with mine, petrified as the bot drew closer.

"Hey, asshole!" Jillian shouted, nailing the bot with a large rock. From behind me, another rock flew past.

There was a gun blast. The sound of it was loud and sharp, like a crack of lightning between the trees. The bot's shield went up, followed by the sound of a bullet striking a nearby tree.

I panicked. Guns were bad. Guns were very, *very* bad. *Who in their right mind had a gun?*

There was another shot. Another bullet ricocheted into the trees. A man stood not far from us, a shotgun in his hands.

"Get up," Jillian said, yanking me to my feet from behind. "Run."

We ran. I put myself behind them, between them and the bot, as best I could. Jillian had me by the wrist, pulling me forward as much as she could, but I was weak and slow. Tori and Marie took the lead. There was another gun blast. I wanted to scream at the unknown man, tell him to drop the gun, to run for his life, but I couldn't see where he was. He wasn't running with us. The bot would kill him. A gun would do nothing but make the bot single him out.

There was a pulse. There were no more gun blasts.

I had to think. I had to come up with a way to make it turn away from the humans. Bots were extremely sensitive devices. I knew from past Cleansings that they were sensitive to their target's vital signs: temperature, heartbeat—even brainwaves. A bot could detect a human from a quarter of a mile away. I had to mask their vital signs, but I didn't know how.

Too late. We were back at the store.

The car! We had to get to the car!

But we couldn't; the bot was right behind us.

"Get inside!" I shouted. We ran into the store through the back. I dead-bolted the lock. It wouldn't do anything but slow it down, though. The bot had locked onto an area of human density. It would break through the door to thin it out. I briefly wondered if it would leave one of us alive or just kill us all.

"Where's Vince?" Tori asked, gasping.

"Where do you think Vince is?" I snapped, tasting blood in my mouth.

"Don't yell at me!" Tori shouted. "You just brought us right back to where we started!"

"Stop shouting!" Marie whimpered. "It'll hear us!"

"Doesn't matter," I said, doubled over, trying to catch my breath. "We have to mask our vital signs. It's following our vital signs."

"How?" Jillian asked. She was staring at me, her eyes pleading, begging me to have the answer.

"I don't know," I sobbed.

There was a thud. The sound of the impact was jarring. We leapt back, startled, backing away. The bot was at the door. I could see it through the vertical slit of glass that was the window. It was going to break the door down. We were cornered. They were going to die if I didn't do something. But what could I do? What could shield three humans from a bot? What could block its sensors? Despair gripped me. I met my friends' eyes. I had failed.

No, I realized. I couldn't block their vital signs. That was impossible, but I had the power to give it something else. The bots weren't fully automated. Somewhere, thousands of miles away, there was someone monitoring the status of each bot on the planet. What would happen when one of them sent back information that they simply couldn't ignore?

"Tori," I said. She looked at me, tears in her eyes. "I need you to take the car and go. Drive as fast as you can. Get to Tennessee."

"What—no—"

I grabbed her by the shoulders and held her gaze.

"*You make them both leave*," I told her. I let her go. I turned. There was the bot, right in front of me. I took one step toward it.

"Allyson!" Jillian shouted, grabbing my wrist. I met her eyes.

152

"I'm so sorry," I told her, and there were so many things I was apologizing for. I averted my gaze. I couldn't see the look in her eyes. I pried my wrist from her grasp, my heart broken.

I walked toward the door. "Stop!" I shouted; only, I wasn't speaking English.

I couldn't tell if it had focused on me or not. It was unreadable. I took another step forward, then another. I was at the door. I unlocked the deadbolt.

I wasn't dead yet, so something was happening.

"My name is Saira Ta'u. I am wanted for galactic crimes against the human race," I said in Darci.

Still alive.

I took a deep breath and prayed that I was doing the right thing. It was all I could do.

"Come and get me," I whispered. I burst out the door and ran past it. It pursued without hesitation.

My friends were screaming my name, but I didn't look back. I ran into the dark.

CHAPTER 9

Before the universe stopped making sense, I loved to run. Running helped me clear my head. Running made me feel as if I could leave my troubles far behind me, at least for a little while.

Well, now my problems were chasing me, and they were fast.

This was a ridiculous plan. The searing pain in my lungs reminded me just how inept I was in carrying out this futile idea. It wasn't even a plan—I hadn't thought about what I would do beyond the frantic running. I was never going to save my friends. The only thing I could do was buy them a few minutes, and even then, there were a million other bots out there, listening for human heartbeats to silence.

Maybe it was a few minutes they could use, I told myself. They could get away. There was something out there, waiting. There was somewhere safe. My brother had told me where to take them.

The vertigo made it hard for me to stay upright, and it was so dark, I kept tripping over branches and stumbling in holes. I would break my ankle in no time, and then the bot would kill the Ganger body. Scratch that. I was moving so slowly, the bot wouldn't even have to wait for me to fall. The only thing keeping me alive was the zigzagging, and at this point, most of it was purely accidental.

I was so weak. I had been wasting away just sitting in the car. What had I been thinking when I decided to go sprinting through a dense forest in the pitch-black darkness?

I had to focus. I had to believe I was strong enough. Just one more minute, I told myself. Give them one more minute.

And after that minute, I would give them one more.

I tried not to think about what would happen if—when—the bot caught me. The pulse would kill me; that much was certain, but this wasn't my body. If my mind were released, I could theoretically just wake up in my real body, probably with guards waiting to take me to a medical room, where my memory would be wiped. My friends would be left to die on Earth alone. I wouldn't even remember enough to know that I should grieve for them.

No, that wasn't an option! They would make it! They would be fine! This wasn't a Purge; this was a Cleansing. In the end, a portion of the human race would be left to start over—five million. I remembered that five million was the cut-off—the number of beings left to start the species over and rebuild from what was left of their civilization. Was three out of five million expecting too much?

A thin branch slapped my face in the dark. I felt the sting of it on my cheek.

But I hadn't told them *anything*. This stung worse than the small cut dripping red blood down my cheek.

They were in the dark. I had left the three people I loved most on Earth—the only ones I had left—alone in the midst of a disaster they didn't understand. They didn't know this would end. They didn't know they could be survivors. They didn't even understand how bots worked! The next time a bot appeared, what would they do? Throw a rock at it? Make themselves targets? Get themselves killed because, in my attempt to protect them, I had damned them by showing them *the wrong thing to do*? I gritted my teeth and pushed myself forward.

Fool! I had one job! All I had to do was protect them until it was over! How could I have screwed it up this badly?

I ran harder.

I was going to survive the machine behind me, and I was going to find my friends and protect them until this body failed. I promised myself—I promised my brother—that I would save the humans. In the past day, everything I had known had been ripped from me, but not them. When I got back to *Moga*, I knew my life would be over. Before they took my memories, I would go to sleep knowing that those I loved were safe.

A flash of light from behind me told me I was in more danger than I thought. I was right in assuming the bot would recognize me as an alien species, and now it was trying to beam me back to *Moga*. Thankfully, its aim with a transport beam was as bad as its aim with a pulse, because I was still running through the woods.

I had to think. I had to figure out how to escape the bot and get back to my friends. I thought of everything I had ever learned about them. It was true that their aim was terrible and they had force fields. Their purpose was to thin out the populations left outside the large cities. Once the population was down to a sustainable number, they

155

would be recalled. They were not bloodthirsty killing machines; their targets were entirely random. Unless, of course, you showed aggression. If you attacked one, it would single you out and eliminate you.

Apparently, they could also be used to hunt down fugitive aliens and beam them off the planet.

There was another flash of light. I tried to run harder, but it was getting so hard to breathe, and the coppery taste of blood in my mouth was sickening.

Bots were designed to work quickly. They sought out dense populations, eliminated them, and moved on. They would be done in only a matter of days. If you could survive the bots for that long, you would live. The population would be left to rebuild with the standard Peacemaker interferences.

You *could* survive a bot, I suddenly remembered. Bots were *fast*. I had had a head start on this bot, but it still beat me to that gas station, and it had been there for at least a little while. Yet, here it was, chasing me in my weakened state. Oh, sure, the trees were in its way, but how hard would it be to exert a burst of speed between turns? That, mixed with its bad aim …

Bots were designed to give you a chance, to let the strongest and most determined of the species survive. If you kept running and managed to evade it long enough, it *would* let a human live. But did the same theory apply to an alien fugitive? The bot knew now that I wasn't a human. At this point there was probably someone behind the controls, being given orders not to let me escape at any cost.

There was another flash. Of course they knew who I was now. There was certainly someone at the controls; the flash of light told me that. They could outlast me. They weren't going to let me go.

Still, I ran. It was the only thing I could do.

I don't know how long it chased me through the trees. I counted four more flashes. Each one made my heart leap, and I wondered if, when I opened my eyes, I would be running into the arms of something far worse than the bot. Every now and then, as I attempted to zigzag out of its reach, I would see its sleek metallic frame behind me. It was silent, so the flashes and brief glimpses were all that told me it was still in pursuit.

I felt a stabbing pain in my lungs, my throat tightening with an icy-hot sting. My breath was labored. My legs were moving as if I were dragging my body through boiling water; they screamed and burned with each step. My head was swimming, my vision going in and out. This was the end. I couldn't run anymore.

So I didn't.

I slid to a stop and spun around, facing my pursuer.

"*Enough!*" I yelled, though it came out more like a gasp.

The bot stopped not five feet from me, hovering at eye level. I could feel my heart hammering at my ribs, the blood pulsing in my ears. Fear grasped at my chest, suffocating me. I couldn't tear my eyes away from the bot. I knew this was it; there was no escape. This was the part where I was beamed back onto *Moga*. Injustice and imprisonment were waiting for me.

I said a silent apology to my friends, but I couldn't run anymore. I was weak, both physically and mentally. I had to surrender.

"I hope you can live with yourself," I whispered. "I know I couldn't."

The bot hovered there. Nothing happened. No flash came. Everything was still.

"*Come on!*" I shouted, never once averting my eyes. "Get it over with! *Don't you have more killing to do?* There are plenty of innocent people out there!"

My eyes never left it. I stood there, half slumped over, my legs barely strong enough to hold me up. I was shaking from exhaustion and fright, but somehow I stood my ground. I couldn't keep running; I stopped trying to get away because I was a spineless creature by nature, and I resented that truth more than anything, but I was brave enough to stand as I let them take me, so I performed one last act of defiance: I stared the bot down. Maybe that's not what it was. Maybe I was just frozen with terror and defeat, because that made more sense for someone like me, but either way, I was resigned to standing behind my mission with this final act. They would take me as a Peacemaker, devoted to the planet Earth and having given every last drop of life I could muster for its inhabitants.

"Take me," I whispered. "But if you go back for them, know that you can never wash the blood off your hands."

There was a spark. Not a flash of light—a spark. The bot jerked to one side. Then it fell, smashing into the Earth and breaking into pieces. Bots were made of ultra-light material. Without their force field, a single tap was enough to punch through the fragile exterior. Before my feet, this bot had been reduced to nothing more than shards.

I stood there, stunned.

Then I collapsed at the base of a tree, and I couldn't help it, I started laughing; a wild, hysterical sound mixed with spasms of coughing. I was alive, and my feet still had dirt beneath them! With the rate of decay of the Ganger body alone, I should have been dead, but for reasons I didn't understand, it was holding, and the bot …

I didn't understand what had just happened. Maybe I didn't need to. Whatever it was, it was a blessing.

I sat against the tree, gasping. Everything hurt. I couldn't catch my breath, my head was dizzy, my joints throbbed, my legs burned, and my skin was crawling. I leaned my head against the tree and looked up at the half moon. I had to get up, I told myself. I was a cowardly creature who didn't deserve this, but it was my second chance. I had to make things right. I had to get up and find my friends, but I didn't know how far I had run or which direction the gas station I had left my friends at was, and I was so tired.

It was the middle of October, and the air had a chill to it. I was wearing a short-sleeved shirt and a pair of shorts that went to my knees—not the kind of things you should be wearing for a night in the woods. I was caked with dirt and sweat. The worst thing, though, was the dark.

My planet had three suns. When one went down, the other two took its place. My planet was never dark—my people didn't know what dark was. We slept in the light, our dome-shaped homes open to the sky, with a warm breeze that came from the sea. When the three suns were at their highest, the gemstone-studded sands would shine a million different colors. My planet was so beautiful and bright. Earth was beautiful, too. Even as a child, I was mesmerized by its alien beauty, but it was also terrifying. I never truly knew the dark until my very first night on Earth, as a two-year-old child, sitting in the blackness. I had practiced living as a human for years, but in that tiny body, with its fragile, undeveloped mind, my alien fears took hold. I cried until the sun rose the next morning, clinging to my human parents, and I cried every night after for weeks. Even now I was afraid of the dark, but over the decades I had found ways to remedy my phobias—a candle, a TV, an alarm clock with glowing red numbers.

Out in the dark woods, my fears were mounting, because the one thing my people did dread more than anything was out there in the dark with me. Decades of being human had trained me to ignore it, but the humans were far away now. My race was terrified to be alone. We were raised in giant colonies, with mothers and fathers and brothers and sisters surrounding us at every moment. We slept in the same room—dozens of us curled up side by side in the light—ate together, played together, talked together, and swam in the giant ocean together. Even when Dorain and I visited home, we would fall asleep each night beside our brothers and sisters, nestled close to our parents. My kind did not know how to exist without others. It was something that had always confused me about humans, who put up walls in their own houses and locks on their doors. Like living without light, I had learned to adapt. As a small human child, I could demand attention from my parents, but as I got older, I had to learn how to meld my alien habits with a human lifestyle. In one cycle, I had a cat to keep me company; in another, a dog. After radios were invented, I learned that I could substitute human contact with the simplistic technology. Radios were almost as useful as TVs, which were a blessing, at least until everything turned to blood, sex, and horror. Even a book or opening a window kept me from feeling so alone.

But out here I was lost and alone, and I was scared. I felt defeated. I couldn't find the strength to get back up.

I felt *itchy*. I rubbed at my skin. I felt like something was crawling beneath my flesh. There were cuts all over my body, and each and every one of them was beginning to sting, as if someone had poured a disinfectant into the wounds. I held one of my hands up to the light of the moon. Nothing significant jumped out at me, but there was something so familiar about the itch that was spreading throughout my body. I could feel it in my lungs now, and the tickling drove me into a coughing fit. My hand went to my throat, and that was when I remembered the sting of the needle just below my chin.

Nanotechnology, I realized. My brother had injected me with nanotechnology. Emotion overcame me. How had he even come by such a thing? Nanotechnology was highly regulated, and the nanotechnology within my body, repairing the decay and damage to the Ganger, was all but impossible to obtain. I knew my brother didn't have access to it. I remembered the banging on the wall of the transport room.

Someone must have helped him. Someone helped my brother get me out, both out of the medical unit and off the ship. Then I recalled the twin doctors. I remembered their faces as the moons and stars carried me into the medical unit. I remembered them arguing as the gas took effect.

"*Thank you*," I whispered to the stars. I didn't understand what was going on, but there were people out there helping me, and that gave me strength. I forced myself to my feet. This was my second chance to do this right; I had to get to my friends. My brother did not send me back to sit in the dirt and feel sorry for myself. My colleagues had not risked themselves so that I could fail.

My determination was short-lived. My head started reeling and I felt faint. There was a sensation of being sucked into a whirling vortex the size of a straw, and I realized that it was much, *much* worse than that. Despite the enormous distance, and despite being awake, someone out there was trying to sever my mind's connection with the Ganger and force me back into my body. The bot was gone, for reasons I didn't understand, but someone out there could not stand to see me on this planet, and they were pulling me back *from the wrong end*. Someone was furiously trying to yank me back, and it hurt. It hurt so badly. I felt as if someone had punched through my skull and was ripping my brain out with their bare hands; only, they had knives for fingers.

I had always assumed that, had I ever been awake for this, it might be like getting lost in the dark, maybe even a little like going to sleep but still being aware of your surroundings. I assumed everything would go black, but it didn't. I had been naïve. Things only went black if you had a body. Outside of a body, the rules were different. It was loud, shrill, and bright, and I felt as if I were tumbling over and over again in a scalding hot sea, the relentless waves pounding me against a shore of glass. I had heard that it hurt. I had heard that some people who had done this awake had gone mad, but it was worse than I had ever imagined. All I could do was scream. It was the sound of unbridled anguish. I screamed for my brother, begging him to save me. I screamed for my parents back home, for my human parents on Earth—all five generations. I called out for faces that had been gone for years.

They couldn't do this to me! I would never find my way back in one piece, not with the distance and the pain. When I woke up, I would certainly be scattered. Only parts of me would find their way back, and I would be mad, or worse. No, I wouldn't be mad—I would just be a shell. It was a fate far worse than having your memories taken. It was worse than death. Who could possibly want to do this to me? How had I deserved *this*?

I wanted to die. I really, truly did.

I thought I heard voices over the shrieking noise, but I couldn't be sure. The sound was garbled. Was my mind slipping? Was I lying in a medical unit, surrounded by unfriendly faces waiting to put me back under and dissect my thoughts? I felt the sensation of being lifted off the Earth. They were tearing me away from my body. I was losing. I struggled, still screaming, begging them not to take me away, but the pain refused to lessen.

It went on for what felt like years, but it finally stopped. For whatever reason, they stopped, and I opened my eyes to see that I was no longer lying in the dirt in the cold, dark woods. It was morning. The sun was just coming up over the trees. Someone soft and warm had me pressed against her chest, cradling me in the back seat of a car.

"She's waking up," I heard someone say, though they sounded far away. But I would have recognized that voice under any circumstances.

Jillian.

Relief flooded me. I had never been so happy to hear her voice in my entire life. My friends were alive. They were safe. Against all odds, they had come back for me and saved me from that godforsaken nightmare.

"Ally?" I heard Jillian whisper, her voice raspy. "Can you hear me?"

161

I groaned. "When someone decides they're going to die for you, couldn't you at least have the decency to run away like they ask?"

I tried to manage a grin, but I didn't have the energy. The pain was gone, but I felt woozy and weak. I decided I would just lay there for the rest of eternity, listening to Jillian's heartbeat. It was the most comforting sound in the world.

"Sorry, Sleeper Cell," Tori said from the passenger's seat. "You try fighting that one," she said, pointing to Jillian, who sat there glaring at her, her eyes red around the edges and bloodshot. Tori didn't sound very concerned.

"We would never leave you," Marie added from the driver's seat.

"Well, there's that," Tori said sarcastically. "We're also *screwed* without you."

"Where are we?" I asked. We were moving fast, much to my surprise. Marie did not normally have a lead foot, but then, we were the only car on the road at that point, and normalcy had gone out the window long ago. I guess Marie had gotten with that program as well.

"We're heading toward Tennessee," Tori said. "You said there was somewhere safe we could go. By the way, you're the only one who knows about this safe place, yet *you* ditched us. Genius plan."

Tori scowled at me, her arms crossed.

"I couldn't think of anything else," I mumbled weakly.

"We appreciate it," Marie said meekly from the driver's seat.

"Don't be nice to her," Tori snapped, her eyes burning. "She's involved in this."

"Shut up, Tori! Stop saying that!" Jillian exploded. Tori looked startled for a second, but she recovered quickly.

"I'm sorry, but, first she drops dead, then she's undead. She kidnaps us before any of us have any idea what's going on, gets us out of the city just before the über bomb kills everyone, and has a safe haven tucked away in Tennessee. Oh, and let's not forget about the evil microwave. She seems to know a hell of a lot about it. And while I'm rambling, what about the *not* English she's been babbling in for the past few hours!"

I could tell this argument had been going on for a long time. Jillian was tense, her whole body shaking. From the look in her eyes, I thought she might hit Tori had I not been in the way. I had never seen her so enraged. Tori glared back, fists clenched, her body language just begging someone to try something. I didn't want this. They couldn't do this, not over me. I could taste the hostility in the air, and it was all over me.

Marie was watching me from the rearview mirror. My eyes met hers, so calm in spite of all the tension. She knew, I realized. She had known for a while, but she had kept it to herself. Sweet, innocent Marie. Everyone underestimated her, but the girl was smarter than all of us, and this entire time she had been doing me a favor I did not deserve. Out of what? Respect for me? Trust? I didn't deserve it. All I had done in the past day was cause animosity and fighting, driving two of the people I loved the most against each other. I had kept them in the dark, and all the while it was creatures like me who had done this to them. What gave me the right? Because I knew the rules, and they weren't allowed in on them? I wasn't better than them. No Peacemaker was; not after this.

"What language were you speaking?" Marie asked, holding my gaze. She was giving me a chance.

"Oh, my god, you nerd!" Tori shrieked.

I felt one of Jillian's tears splash against my cheek. I looked up at her and saw that she was looking at me with a look of hopelessness; that look behind her eyes that told me her trust was fading. She was thinking all those things too, but she was trying so hard to defend me and have faith in me. The look in her eyes begged me to prove Tori wrong, to prove to them that I was the Allyson they all knew.

But I wasn't, and I couldn't lie to them anymore.

I shouldn't have felt the utter disappointment and despair that I did. This had been coming since I had run to them in that hospital waiting room. I had wanted to play pretend and make believe that I could get through this. I had wanted to pretend that this wasn't different from my four other lifetimes as a Doppelganger, as if the rules that applied there could be used in this situation as well. I was wrong. We hadn't written any rules for this.

I just wanted to be Allyson Owens a little longer, but that life was over. I was Saira Ta'u, Peacemaker, and I couldn't do my job if I was anything else.

"It's called Dardi," I said.

The car was silent. Tori stared at me in disbelief. I couldn't meet Jillian's eyes. I took a deep, shaky breath.

I had to, I told myself. I had to.

That didn't make it any better.

"It was weird. It was really raspy and kind of—I don't know—halting," Marie said. She was picking her words carefully, encouraging me, allowing me to share my secret.

I pushed myself up, although I was still weak. The large bloodstain on Jillian's gray shirt helped explain why. I felt my face and discovered the blood around my nose and ears, some of it dry, some of it still wet. I realized how lucky I was. If they hadn't managed to sever me from the Ganger, they would have killed me, and not just this body. Whatever they had done to me, it was severe. I was not meant to be here. Someone was doing their best to make sure I wasn't.

I shuddered. Slowly, I took in the faces in the car. There was no turning back. I was determined to do this right, regardless of the consequences, regardless of who was trying to stop me.

"That's because your vocal cords are in your throat. Mine are in my chest. Darcii doesn't really sound like that. It's actually a beautiful language."

Marie's eyes watched me in the mirror, unsurprised. Tori grew more and more confused. She looked at me, then to Marie. Jillian was quiet and rigid beside me. I couldn't look at her yet.

"What's she saying?" Tori asked Marie, not quite getting it.

"Think about it," Marie said, watching me as she spoke, making sure she had gotten it right. She would have been fiddling with that cross necklace if both of her hands hadn't been on the wheel. "Where did the light come from? Who has technology advanced enough for that?"

"I don't get it. I'm right? She's an agent from … where? China? Russia? Europe? Does anybody even *have* red hair in China?"

"China and Russia are in the same boat right now. Every country on Earth is," I said.

"I don't—" Tori began, her face contorted.

"She's not human," Jillian said bluntly.

I closed my eyes and took a deep breath. There it was. The secret was out.

It was a strangely terrifying experience. I felt no liberation from it. I just wanted to go back to hiding behind my human guise.

When I opened my eyes, I saw Tori's expression. All of the color had drained out of her face.

"Shit!" she screamed. "Shit, shit, *shit!*"

She flailed her arms and tried to scramble away, but there was nowhere to go. Not quite the reaction I had hoped for, but then, Tori had a tendency to overreact. Except, she wasn't overreacting; I could see that the girl was genuinely terrified of me.

"She's a—you're a—!" Tori squealed.

"I'm a Thellessian," I said. "I'm from Maegora."

I felt the last nail go into the coffin as I said the words myself. There could be no mistake now. There was no undoing this.

"You look human," Marie said curiously. How was it that she could be so calm?

"I'm not," I said matter-of-factly. Everyone was quiet. They were barely breathing—and neither was I. I had done it. I had broken the biggest rule of all. What would come of it, I had no idea. I looked down at my hands, with the five strange fingers. I felt the heart beating in my chest. Twenty years I had had them, but now I felt like a stranger in my own body. I knew I was to the three humans in the car. I couldn't go back. I would never be Allyson Owens to them again.

Tori sat there, pale and trembling, staring at me, her eyes wide. I took a breath, bracing myself.

I looked at Jillian. She was just sitting there quietly. She stared at me, and I saw the look in her eyes. There was no warmth there. Her eyes were cold and hard, the trust gone. My heart shattered, but what had I expected? Did I really expect her to look at me and tell me it was okay, that she loved and accepted me anyway? I had lied to *her*— my best friend, my sister—for eighteen years. Who could forgive that? I wished I could undo what I had just done. I wished I could take the past few days away.

This was never supposed to happen. Not to her. How could I have hurt *her*?

"Jillian—" I whispered, my voice breaking.

"Don't," she said icily. "Just don't."

And with that, I saw the body of the red-headed girl in the morgue. I felt Allyson Owens die all over again.

CHAPTER 10

I stared out the window, watching the landscape go by. It had changed. Gone was the flat land of Florida, populated with green pine tree forests, palmettos, and canals filled with an assortment of water birds, tall and majestic, fishing among clusters of cattails. It was early afternoon now, and we had left Florida behind us hours ago. The flat land had given way to rolling hills and winding roads, beautiful stones and shelves of rock lining roads that had been carved out of mounds of earth that grew ever higher, the occasional stream below and an assortment of various trees I didn't recognize on each side. The leaves had changed for autumn. Red, orange, and yellow leaves clung to strong brown branches, shimmering in the sunlight as the breeze swept by. It was strange to see such vibrant beauty in a world that had grown so dark. Nature should have sensed what had happened to the world. The land should have been stark and ugly, devoid of the vitality that had been forcefully ripped from the earth.

But if nature sensed the darkness in the world, it was determined not to succumb to it.

As beautiful as the landscape was, that wasn't really what I was looking for. We hadn't seen a single bot since we fled that ill-fated gas station. It didn't make any sense. The planet was crawling with bots now—hundreds of thousands of them were roaming the planet, thinning out the population of humans. The chances of us avoiding all of them were nonexistent. Around every bend, I expected one to be waiting, but there was nothing. I had no idea what we would do when we ran into the next one. It had been dumb luck that we had survived the first one.

Well, most of us had. I thought about the poor boy, Chad, in the parking lot. I had wanted to save him, too. Death from a bot was painless, I reminded myself. It had stopped the biological signals to his heart and brain before he hit the ground. That knowledge didn't bring me any comfort, though. What had he done to deserve that? He had just run the wrong way. It could have just as easily been us. And what about the other man, Vince, who had heard the panicked sounds of people in trouble and had run straight for the danger? He was foolish to bring the gun. Bots targeted hostility. The sight of an identifiable weapon was so much worse, but he didn't know that. He was the kind of human who deserved to live. He was brave and selfless, unlike so many. But we didn't get to pick who lived and who died. Who were we to decide who was worthy of living and re-creating the planet and who was too much of a risk to live? That was why we had the bots. They didn't recognize any particular quality among individual humans, so long as they weren't hostile. Of those who survived, they survived by luck alone.

We had been too lucky, though. They should have come for us.

Little in my life was making sense. Why would the Elders lie to us? The technology scramble, the initial pulse, and the bots were all the work of the Peacemakers, as far as I could tell. I hadn't seen any signs that this wasn't planned and organized by us, and I had seen no signs to stop it. This had to be intentional.

And yet, what about before? What about the humans who had died before? That was typical pre-Cleansing procedure. We removed the sick and dying, ensuring that disease wouldn't eradicate the weakened, vulnerable race. But if it were planned, the Council of Traltix wouldn't have taken me prisoner. They wouldn't have found me guilty of galactic crimes.

Why had I been found guilty, I wondered. Why had our technology failed me? Why had it read false?

I had so many questions now. Why was this happening? Why to me? What could my brother want me to do down here? What did he know? Did he want me to save *all* the humans? I couldn't. He had to know that I couldn't. I couldn't even save two strangers at a gas station.

I closed my eyes and leaned my head back.

My name is Allyson Owens, I thought. My name is Saira Ta'u. I'm a human. I'm a Thellessian, the species that rose from the ashes, in a Ganger body. I am twenty-two years old. I have lived long enough to see human civilizations rise and fall. I was born in West Palm Beach, Florida, to John and Margaret Owens. I was born on Maegora, the Burned Planet. A twin brother followed me into life by mere seconds.

Who was I? Who did everyone think I was?

Who did I think I was?

"We have to stop for gas again," Marie said, startling me out of my stupor. The car had been unnaturally quiet since my revelation. I had thought they would have questions; that they would want to know more about the girl they thought they had known for so long, but they hadn't said a word. Marie had tried to start conversations, had asked a few questions here and there—but everything fell flat. They had just been frightened, angry, and silent, and it hurt.

I had just gone numb. Days of trauma, stress, and grief had left me an empty shell. My body was failing slowly, I had lost a lot of blood, and my head—they had done a number on it, and I didn't know if the nanotechnology could help me. My cuts and bruises were gone and the ache in my body was only bad enough to be constantly uncomfortable, but the damage done to my mind ... I perceived everything through a slow, hazy cloud.

We were still in danger. I knew death was waiting for us around every corner—except it wasn't. Hours had gone by without anything eventful occurring. In that time, I felt myself slipping into a state of lethargy. I knew I had been lulled into a false sense of security. I knew I had to be on alert.

But the reality of it was that I needed a break. I was drained. My entire body felt heavy. I just wanted to sleep. I think we all felt that way at that point. We had all just withdrawn into ourselves, finally giving ourselves time to process what had happened to us.

We could only feel fear for so long.

"Great," Tori mumbled from the back seat. "Another gas station. Because the other one went so well for us."

She didn't sound like the Tori I knew. She sounded ... deflated. My revelation had finally driven home that this was not a game. This was not something we would wake up from. Their world was over, and it was sinking in. There were no families left to go home to when this was over. Their friends were gone. Classes would not start back next week. Beings outside of their control had taken hold of a world they thought they had mastered long ago. They were helpless ants.

And beings like me were holding the magnifying glass on them.

We had no choice but to stop. No one had any desire to walk to Tennessee. We had been avoiding towns as much as possible in order to stay away from denser populations, but that had led us farther out into the middle of nowhere, where gas stations were fewer and farther between. Before we came across one, the gas light had been on for a while, and I was beginning to fear that walking was becoming our only option, at least until we came across another vehicle. I did not like the thought of all of us wandering around in the open, slow and vulnerable.

The vehicle came to a stop.

I admit that I was startled when Jillian threw the door open and jumped out, leaving the door ajar in her rush to get away. Tori and I had changed seats long ago. Marie had suggested that I move up front to help navigate, but the tension permeating from the back seat threatened to choke the life out of all of us. On the outside, Jillian looked calm, but eighteen years of friendship told me otherwise. I could feel the tension building, her emotions running rampant within her. I had hoped moving away would give her the space she needed to calm down.

Clearly, I was wrong. Of course, had I really expected moving seats to make up for the fact that her best friend was a liar from another planet?

"Jillian!" I called after her, scrambling to unclasp my seat belt. "Jillian, wait!"

She ignored me and began stalking across the parking lot.

"I'll go get her," Marie offered, unbuckling her seat belt and opening the door.

"No," I said, grabbing her shoulder before she could get out. "I want everyone near the car."

She nodded and gave me a look of encouragement. As I looked at the cross necklace dangling from her neck, I realized that I never would have pictured her as the one to defend the alien, but I found myself grateful for her trust and support, even if I didn't deserve it. They had every right to be upset.

"Good luck," Tori muttered under her breath sarcastically.

I sighed and looked in the direction Jillian had stormed off in, feeling my heart sink. She had stopped at the front entrance of another little convenience store and was sitting on the curb, her head in her hands, dark brown hair covering her face. I took a deep breath to steady my nerves; then I slid out the door. I stood up, and what was left of my blood rushed out of my head. It made me woozy, and

I had to lean against the car until my head cleared, taking in the cool autumn air in long, deep breaths. I was getting weaker. The nanotechnology in my blood was keeping me alive, repairing my Ganger as it failed, but it couldn't keep me alive forever. Even with millennia of technology and knowledge at our disposal, no higher species had ever been able to cheat death. No one could live forever. The nanotechnology would do its best to fix me, but at some point the rate of decay and damage would be more than it could handle, and the Ganger would fail.

I had outlived generations of humans. For decades I stood by and watched humans slip away, knowing full well that, no matter how bad things got for me, I would eventually wake up healthy and safe.

No matter how bad things got …

The white hospital beds flashed before my eyes. I tried to beat down the image, but then I could smell it—the scent of the sick and dying. I felt my stomach churn. My breathing quickened.

"Are you okay?" Marie asked. I opened my eyes to see the small girl looking at me with a concerned expression on her face.

"Fine," I said, and I let go of the car. I forced the past from my muddled mind, and walked across the parking lot as steadily as I could.

It was another lie, but they'd had enough shocks for now. They didn't need to know I was dying, on top of everything else.

I sat down beside Jillian on the curb and rested my head on my knees, watching her. She turned her head away, pretending to ignore me. The ache it caused in my chest was unbearable, and I swallowed hard.

Jillian had always run from her emotions, even as a child. She tried to come off tough and she tried to keep everything private—two things I could never do. Jillian had always been my opposite—Yin and Yang, my mother called us. It was what had ultimately inspired the half-heart necklaces—two halves that somehow made a whole that worked, like us.

Jillian's parents had divorced when she was eleven years old. She had been devastated. When she and her mom left and moved in with her aunt and uncle, Jillian became angry and inconsolable. After two days she vanished, prompting her mother to spend hours driving around in the middle of the night shouting her name. I found her in

170

the middle of the night, when she crept through my bedroom window and lay down next to me in bed, just like I knew she would. When the pattern kept repeating itself, Jillian's mother adopted her own pattern. She packed a suitcase every day, and at night, after dinner, Jillian stayed with me. She stayed with me for two months before she was ready to go back home.

Jillian had always run to me, but now I was the one she was running from.

"We need to stay together," I said softly. My eyes scanned the area, but I didn't see any immediate danger. Still, if a bot was within a quarter mile, it would know about us before we knew about it.

"Go away," Jillian muttered.

I reached out to put my hand on her shoulder. "Jilly—"

"Don't you dare touch me!" she snapped, her eyes blazing. I jerked my hand back, startled. I sat there, frozen.

She was on her feet, standing over me angrily before I knew what was happening.

"You lied to me!" she spat. "You told me you were my best friend, but you're not!"

I started, taken aback. "What?" I blurted, my mouth hanging open.

"You aren't Allyson," she said, voice dripping venom.

I stared at her. It never occurred to me that they'd take my revelation this way. It hadn't even occurred to me that they didn't see me as an alien playing human; they saw me as the alien playing *a* human. They didn't think I was the same girl who had roomed with them in college, who went to meet them for pizza and chocolate milkshakes what felt like a lifetime ago.

They thought I was an imposter.

"Jillian, I *am* Allyson," I said, in the most earnest voice I could muster.

"*Liar!*" Jillian shrieked. By now I was on my feet, too. I faced her. My heart was pounding in my chest. I couldn't breathe. Everything seemed small and far away. Somehow I knew this feeling, this overwhelming feeling of dread and despair, of denial. I felt as if I were watching disaster happen right before my eyes, but all I could do was stand there and watch it happen, powerless to stop it. I felt the terror rising. I felt as if I were watching someone die.

I couldn't do this again. I couldn't lose someone like this again, so close, within my reach but slipping from me by the second. I saw the white beds. They haunted me like ghosts.

The old memories came in a torrent, threatening to drown me. I forced them back. This wasn't the same thing, not even close. Those memories were not welcome here. They didn't fit the situation. I was being ridiculous.

"How can you say that?" I choked. I couldn't lose her. I wouldn't.

"You haven't been right since the hospital!" Jillian screamed. "Look at you! You don't even look right! You do things Allyson would never do! Allyson would never lie to us! She wouldn't—she wouldn't ..."

She stood there, fuming, so angry she couldn't even choke out the words. When she threw the pebble at me, it felt like she had slapped me. It was small, and it didn't even hurt, but Jillian was throwing things at me. She was trying to *hurt* me.

"Liar!" Jillian screamed, picking up another rock, this one bigger. "Liar, liar, *liar*!"

She flung rock after rock. There was nothing I could do but stand there and take her anger, shell-shocked, until finally she collapsed into the dirt, sobbing.

"I hate you," she wept, and that's when I dropped to my knees.

"Jillian," I blurted. "I met you when we were both four. Our mothers arranged a play date. Your family had just moved in next door. We went to kindergarten together. You pushed Eddie Johnson on the playground for me. In high school, I didn't want to play dodgeball because I thought it was mean. When that boy hit me in the face with the ball, I thought you were going to knock him out. Your first boyfriend was named Riley. You were fifteen. You cried when he dumped you right before the homecoming dance. When you were eighteen, you went to visit your cousins in Panama City Beach for spring break. You got a tattoo—an infinity symbol on your ribs. You didn't tell me for two weeks because you thought I'd be upset."

I choked back a sob. "Jillian," I pleaded. "It's *me*. It's Allyson."

She stared at me, her eyes hard. I held my breath, my eyes watching her, pleading.

"How *dare* you talk about my family," she hissed at me, holding my eyes. "*You* left them behind! *You don't care if they're alive or dead!*"

"Whatever you are," she said slowly, "you're horrible."

She meant for the words to wound me, and they did. I saw my nephews' faces staring at me, accusing. I had just let them die. I had left all of them behind as if they didn't matter, but they did. They mattered *so much*.

I heard the car start from behind me. Jillian stood, and with a look of pure disgust, she walked past me. "You aren't Allyson," she said. "We left her back at the hospital."

I sat there in the dirt until the sound of the car horn honking brought me back to the real world. My world was completely broken. I had been robbed of everything. Even if my family had survived, I didn't deserve them. I was a heartless monster.

"Let's go!" Tori was shouting. "Evil machines out to kill us, remember?"

I dragged myself to the car and got in the back with Tori. Jillian was in the front seat, her arms crossed and her head down, ignoring everything. Marie gave me a look, her eyes apologetic, and I averted my gaze. I couldn't handle her pity. I slumped into the back, wishing I could curl up into a ball and die. I wished this could be over, so I could hand myself in to the Council of Traltix and let them wipe away this horror. I just wanted it to stop. There was nothing left on this planet but pain and death.

"Has anyone told you lately that you look like shit?" Tori said as the car pulled away from the gas station. I couldn't help but laugh, but it was bitter. Why did Tori always have to show up to kick me while I was down?

"Thanks for the concern," I muttered irritably. "It means a lot."

"I'm serious," Tori said. I didn't need this. Why did she have to be so spiteful sometimes?

"Yeah, well, forgive me for not being designed to last this long," I said tersely.

Tori's eyes grew wide. "Oh, my god, you're a flipping robot!" she squealed.

I groaned. Why did I have to open my mouth? Being an alien was bad enough. I didn't need anyone thinking I was anything like the machines hunting us.

"*No*," I said, rubbing my temples. My head was throbbing now. I just needed everyone to be quiet for a minute, so I could pick up the pieces. "I'm a Doppelganger."

"A wha—"

"It means she looks identical to someone else," Jillian said, turning in her seat. Her eyes locked on me.

I shouldn't have said anything. I should have stuck with the robot.

"You look like someone else? Why?"

I sighed. "I'm a Peacemaker," I said, picking my words carefully, watching the girl in the passenger seat. "I'm supposed to go down to developing planets and act as an anthropologist—a historian, even. I'm supposed to live with humans, *be* a human—only, I can't do that without a human body, so I use a Doppelganger. "

"So you make your own human body?" Tori said.

"Yes," I said.

"You can do that?" Tori asked incredulously. I grinned slightly, nodding my head.

"Don't ask me how it's done," I said. "I'm just the anthropologist."

Tori looked me up and down, glancing to Marie and Jillian as if they might have a more plausible explanation. Marie, at least from what I could see of her expression from the rearview mirror, looked more curious than anything.

Jillian, on the other hand … I knew from the look in her eyes that I had said the wrong things.

"What happens to the double?" Jillian asked. Her gaze locked into mine and held it. I knew where this was going.

We left her back at the hospital …

Don't do this, I silently begged, but the look in her eyes told me that it was too late; I had already walked into it. How could I be surprised, though, when we had dropped a very real corpse right in front of them only yesterday? Had it really only been a day? Marie was looking at me. I met her eyes, begging for help, but she had figured it out, too.

She didn't move to defend the monster.

I was cornered. I felt myself bristling as they closed in on me. It wasn't my fault Allyson had died! She wasn't supposed to! I had wanted her to live! My mind flashed back to the morgue, to the limp body on the cold metal tray. She wasn't the first human I had impersonated who was sent back as a corpse, but that time had been different. I couldn't help what had happened then, but Allyson's death was a waste, no matter the circumstances. Where was the logic? Where was the mercy that was so characteristic of the Peacemakers? Forget the impending Cleansing; the girl should not have died.

"When we swap a Ganger with a human, the human is put into a partial stasis," I said, keeping my voice steady.

"So, what? You put them in a coma?" Tori asked.

"Sort of," I said. "We keep their body asleep, but their mind awake. We have technology capable of creating an alternate reality for their mind to exist in."

Show them the mercy, I thought. Show them we have mercy. Show them we care. That we aren't monsters.

It was becoming hard for me to convince even myself of that.

"Why would you do that?" Tori asked. "Wouldn't it be easier to just keep them in a coma?"

"Definitely," I said. "But it's cruel to take away someone's quality of life."

"So why did you kill the real Allyson Owens?" Jillian said, her voice cold.

"*What?*" Tori shrieked. She stared at me with her jaw open.

They all stared at me in abhorrence. I knew I had lost all three of them.

I sat there quietly. I realized I couldn't make them understand. They weren't Peacemakers. They could not comprehend the weight of our task. They couldn't understand how we thought, how we were willing to sacrifice for the greater good. They were still so young. I had never thought of them as such until now, as the three humans watched me, their minds only capable of accepting a world of black and white. Mercy and love fell in the gray.

"Well?" Jillian hissed. "If you're so benevolent, why did you give her back as a corpse?"

I realized then that I had never actually seen Allyson Owens, the girl I had spent twenty years living as. Dorain had told me a few things about her, but—when I ended up in that morgue, I hadn't even looked at her face. All of the people I loved had thought they were loving *her* all this time, and I didn't even *look* at her. I hoped that the world that had been created for her was incredibly happy. I hoped she had a great life.

Mercy was sometimes cruel.

"I don't know," I said, and I was crying, wondering how I could possibly make them understand. "She wasn't supposed to die. She was supposed to wake up in the hospital and live the rest of her life with you. That was the plan."

"So when you were done with us and your little research project, you were just going to give us back our friend, just like that?"

"You never knew *her*," I spat at her.

That made Jillian pause, and there was confusion in her eyes. She had thought she had cornered me. She had thought we'd taken Allyson days ago, not twenty years ago. This was the part where she realized that the alien *had* been her friend all this time.

Did that make things better?

"How was she supposed to come back?" Marie asked. "How could you give her all your memories? Does the fake life match yours? How do you do that?"

"She was going to wake up from a coma with no memories," I said. The words felt toxic as they slid out of my mouth. No, this did not make things better.

"In what way is that mercy?" Jillian snapped. "You wanted to take someone we thought we loved away and replace her with a shell? You're disgusting."

"I'm sorry!" I shrieked. I had finally had enough. *This wasn't my fault!* I didn't want to hurt them! I didn't want to hurt Allyson! I loved them, and all they could do was attack me! No wonder other races couldn't find anything to love about humans, when they attacked even the people who would give them everything!

"I'm sorry that I had to come back and ruin your lives!" I ranted. "I'm sorry that you ever had to find this out! I'm sorry that I have to be here! I'm sorry that I had to give up my life for yours! I'm sorry that your planet is so stupid that we decided to blow it up! *Aren't we all just sorry?*"

They were quiet—deadly quiet. I realized what I had just said. I had gone from a friend to an alien to a monster to a murderer in less than a day, and now I had just confessed to being part of the slaughter of the human race. I saw the horror in their eyes, the hatred. It was over. I had ruined everything. Any chance of them ever trusting me was gone. How could I have let this happen? What had happened to me, the kind-hearted alien who dreamed of humans? When had I learned to yell? When did I learn anger? When did I learn to be hostile toward people I loved?

But, then, I had never lost everything before. Maybe this really was me. Maybe I had to be stripped of everything before I could see who I really was.

I rushed to open my mouth, to take back what I said, to fix it, but that was when we hit something.

Thankfully, we hadn't been going very fast. Slow, careful Marie was at the wheel, and when the fighting started, I had noticed the car moving slower as things got more heated. Even so, the impact was jarring. It knocked the wind out of me. I saw stars dancing before my eyes, and for a brief moment, I feared that I would pass out.

"What'd we hit?" I heard Jillian shout from what seemed a million miles away.

"My head," Tori groaned. I felt an instant rush of clarity as the adrenaline kicked in at the sound of her voice. She hadn't been wearing a seat belt, which was so like her. She was clutching her forehead and wincing. I saw the red beneath her fingers.

"Are you woozy?" I asked, sliding across the seat beside her. I peeled her hand off and looked at the damage. There was a lot of blood.

"I must be, because I think we ran into an invisible wall," she said.

My head shot up, my senses on red alert. She was right. We hadn't hit anything. There was no damage to the front of the car. We had just stopped in the middle of the highway.

"Can you run?" I asked her. A familiar sensation rushed back to me, fully taking hold of my body: fear.

We didn't have a lot of time. I knew they were coming. Each heartbeat that crashed against my ribs called them closer.

"Run?" Tori asked, disoriented.

"We're in a net. Someone meant to catch us. We have to run," I said hastily. She nodded, and, grabbing her forehead tightly, I helped her scramble across the seat and out the door. We were all out of the car and running when the wind picked up suddenly, the trees swaying from the gusts.

"Run for the trees! Don't let them see you!" I shouted over the wind.

The gleaming silver hovercraft appeared above us, about the size of a small bus. It had been waiting beyond the trees, but now its trap had been triggered and it was moving in to secure its victims. I didn't know what it would do: beam the car on board, take us all out with one large, fatal pulse, or something else—I didn't intend to find out.

We bolted for the woods, throwing ourselves behind a wall of trees, but we didn't dare stop there. We ran, and didn't look back.

I should have known better than to tip off the bot at the gas station. Telling it that it was looking at a fugitive was not the cleverest thing to do. I should have known that someone would be able to trace its location once it sent the signal that it had found a non-human life form. I should have known that someone would be sent to find me. I should have known they wouldn't give up after they failed to pry me from the Ganger.

I looked behind me, but to my surprise, it wasn't pursuing. It must have known that it wasn't going to be able to reach us through the trees. It knew we were on foot. They would set the hovercraft down somewhere and they would send out a team to track us down. It wouldn't take them long.

"Stop!" I shouted to the three fleeing humans ahead of me. They skidded to a halt, looking confused and frantic at the same time.

"Where is it?" Marie asked, eyes wild.

"They're going to come after us on foot," I panted. I bent over, trying to catch my breath. I was already winded.

"Why are they after us?" Tori gasped, looking sick. Blood was running down her cheek and her face had taken on a shade of gray. That was hardly a good sign.

"Not you three," I said. "They're after me."

My mind was racing. I glanced up at the three humans and looked into the eyes of hatred. It made me freeze where I stood.

"So why shouldn't we give them you?" Jillian said. Her face was cold and impassive.

"Jillian!" Marie said. Horror didn't even begin to describe the look on her face.

I held Jillian's gaze. She didn't want me. None of them wanted me. I just inspired contempt when they looked at me. Everywhere I went—everything I did—I was just causing pain and anguish.

I had gotten them out of the city. Maybe that was all I was meant to do.

"She's right," I whispered.

I didn't belong with them anymore. It was time to end the agony. I closed my eyes and took a deep breath. My lungs screamed as the oxygen hit them.

I was damaged in more ways than one. What use could something so broken possibly be?

Branches were cracking behind us. The sound of heavy footsteps in dry leaves was unmistakable. They were moving quickly. They knew right where we were.

"Run!" I shouted.

To my surprise, all three of them hesitated. They looked at each other, conflict reflected in their eyes, though each of them was slowly inching backward.

"Do you want to die?" I snapped. "Go!"

Then they turned and ran. I watched them run. They didn't look back.

My pursuers wanted only me, and when they took me, all of this would be over. I was the one being hunted. Every bot and alien in the universe would be looking for me. Tennessee was close. They had a better chance of making it there without me.

They hated me.

I turned and ran in the opposite direction.

I heard them screaming.

I skidded to a halt. "No!"

My heart was pounding so hard, I thought it was going to explode from my chest. They couldn't have gotten to them first! I turned. Tori was on the ground, Marie and Jillian trying to get her to her feet. I could hear crashing through the trees. They were coming! They would see the humans! What would they do to them? Humans weren't allowed to know about alien life. What was about to come crashing through the trees, and if they saw it …

I ran back.

"She fell," Marie said, tears running down her cheeks. Her eyes were pleading for me to do something.

"Tori," I said. Her eyes were open, but she looked as if she were going to pass out. "Tori, get up. You have to run."

"I'm okay," she slurred. She wasn't. She had gone into shock.

"She can't!" Jillian shouted.

Marie's screams were terrifying. Jillian, petrified, fell to the ground when the shadow loomed over us.

It was a humanoid-looking figure in a white full-body suit, but its alien characteristics were unmistakable. The black face mask was impenetrable, reflecting only my shocked face. The hissing sound it made as the creature inside breathed only intensified the unnaturalness of an alien hovering over us in the middle of the earthly woods. There was a gun in its hand. I couldn't tell if it was a stun gun or a pulse gun—and there wasn't time to find out.

I shoved the creature hard, knocking it to the ground. For a brief moment, I was shocked at what I had done.

The feeling didn't last long. Soon I was standing over the creature, my face stony. I had put myself behind it. He had to turn away from my friends to confront me.

"You can't take me!" I yelled in Darcii. I didn't have to wait for its reaction; it was the one I was hoping for.

The creature scrambled to its feet, gun aimed right at me. I turned to run, but I only got a few feet. There was a flash of blue light, and I fell into the dirt. It was a stun gun. Of course it was, I thought bitterly, as dirt filled my mouth. A pulse gun would be too quick an end to this torment. I was surprised that I was actually hoping for a pulse gun. Did I even want to make it back in one piece anymore?

I couldn't see it, but I could hear it approaching. I heard it sling the stun gun across its back. Then it hefted me into its arms like a sack of potatoes. My arms fell at my sides like dead weight and my head lolled back and forth. If they were going to stun me, all I asked was that they also knock me out. Being awake as they carried me back as their prisoner would be torture.

As the alien carried me away from the woods, I caught a glimpse of the place where my friends had stood. They were gone. They had gotten away. I closed my eyes, and a small part of me found peace.

It was over. I had done all I could.

CHAPTER 11

The suit dumped me unceremoniously on the floor of the hovercraft, my body hitting the ground hard enough to knock the wind out of me. He slapped a pair of handcuffs on my wrists—two metal rings connected by slender chain-links. They were uncomfortable as I lay on them face-down on the cold, hard floor. They dug into my ribs and bit my wrists. He had put them on far too tight.

I was startled. The Higher Planets considered binding prisoners an outdated practice. We had evolved past barbaric things such as bars and chains, developing systems for handling criminal behavior that did not involve prisons or severe punishment. Even on board *Moga* as I was escorted to my trial, I was left unbound. Creatures, regardless of what they had done, could always be treated rationally and with humanity. We always moved toward rehabilitation before punishment. Yes, our rehabilitation methods could be harsh, as was my sentence on *Moga*, but to bind a creature, to take away its freedom and very quality of life? That was never the answer to a creature that was already so damaged that it would do something desperate. Not even animals were treated this way. Humans bound their prisoners as a regular practice. It was a sign of their youth. I was in trouble if I had been approved to be treated this way, if I was considered so dangerous that I was treated as less than an animal. I was already paralyzed. What did he think I was capable of doing?

The suit didn't even bother to hide his disgust toward me, leaving me to lay where I had been dropped.

I was starting to be able to move my limbs again, and I was able to lift my head off the floor and get a better look at the creature in the suit. The shoulders of his suit bore the moons and stars of the Council of Traltix. Why was the Council on Earth? Never before had any alien presence besides the Gangers and Impersonators of the Peacemakers been on this planet. As a Level Two planet, Earth had always been Peacemaker domain, and a Cleansing was the most delicate of Peacemaker matters. If it went wrong, the entire planet might be in jeopardy. How was it that the Council was on the planet, with their aliens in suits, bearing the mark of some unknown organization? This went beyond being against protocol. This broke galactic agreements.

"She is secured," I heard the suit say in Common Tongue. The voice that emanated from the suit was raspy, almost hissing. I racked my brain, trying to figure out which species I was dealing with.

Not that it mattered. Regardless of the species, I was paralyzed on the ground, and the creature in the suit would drag me off the planet in chains. Oddly, the thought didn't frighten me. This creature was taking me back to have my mind wiped, and all I could feel was ...

Relief. I felt relief. I was *glad* that it was over. The end was coming. Soon I wouldn't have to suffer.

I should have felt guilty for the thoughts that ran through my mind, but maybe it was for the best. Everything had been taken from me—my family, my friends, even the planet itself. There was nothing left for me on Earth. I was going home now. I was going home to my brother, my planet, and my family. And I would no longer have any memories.

I closed my eyes and just breathed. My grandfather—my mom's dad—had died after a two-year battle with lung cancer. I was eight when he died. I could still remember my grandmother's words after he passed: "I'm just glad it's over." I couldn't understand her then, but I could now.

I couldn't even feel as if I had given up. There was no way for me to do any more. There was no escaping my fate. This battle had come to its natural end, and I felt peace, knowing that I had done all I was capable of doing.

"She was with a group of humans," the suit said. The tone in his voice was hard. My eyes flew open with a start.

No! No, no, *no*! He had me! He got what he had come for! He didn't need to think about them!

"Humans aren't our mission," said another voice. The voice came from a familiar species, one I had been living intimately with for decades—one I had studied for even longer. I squirmed on the ground, trying to get a look at the Impersonator. The Council and Peacemakers were working together on this? The Peacemakers were allowing an alien species on the planet?

"They saw me," the suit said. "They're compromised."

"The bots will take care of them," the Impersonator said. He was a young man with handsome features: a square jaw, stubble, thick brown hair, and blue eyes. He was one of the most striking humans I had ever seen.

"The bots are still scrambled. We can't risk it," the suit said, sounding more than irritated.

Scrambled? What did that mean?

Whatever it meant, the suit didn't think it was anything good.

"They're moving toward us," the suit said, looking at a monitor on the wall of the ship. From where I was lying, I could see them too: three red spots moving across a pulsing radar. The side of the screen displayed vitals from the three isolated organisms picked up by sensitive alien technology, despite the distance. There was no mistaking the human readings. The suit walked up to the screen and tapped at it, pulling into focus an image of the trees outside the ship. In the distance, the technology had zeroed in on the images of my friends, slowly creeping toward the ship, ducking behind trees as they moved to conceal their location. Their attempts at stealth were useless. I could hear their heartbeats pulsating from the screen.

What were they doing? Could they not tell what this was? They could have been a mile away by now, buried deep in the woods. If they had just stayed hidden in the trees, the suit might have forgotten about them, but there they were, right in striking distance.

I wanted to yell at the suit to leave them alone, that they had who they were looking for, that my friends wouldn't pose a threat, but my jaw was paralyzed, and all that came out was a pathetic squeak.

The Impersonator sighed, then shook his head. "We can't let the Cleansing be a waste over three humans," he said. He shot me a glare as if it were my fault. My eyes burned back.

Traitor! How dare he ever call himself a Peacemaker! How dare he call himself the protector of lesser races! I gritted my teeth, seething. I still couldn't move, but that didn't stop me from trying, fighting against my restraints. All I got for my efforts was a headache as I managed to bang my head into the hard metal floor of the hovercraft. I didn't stop, though. The pain only made me more determined.

"Stay with her," the suit said, taking up the stun gun. I knew that if it were set high enough, it could kill. It would be incredibly painful, like suffering an intense electric shock. It could take minutes for anything to die that way. It was inhumane. The suit couldn't really be considering going after a group of humans in such a way, could he?

I felt bile rising in my throat. My friends would suffer terribly before they died.

"I can handle the humans," the Impersonator said. "They'll respond much better if they think they're looking at another human."

"Stay with her," the suit said. It wasn't a suggestion.

He made it a point to watch my face as he dialed the gun up as high as it would go.

This was a vile creature. I had never met a being so repulsive. His race may have made it to the ranks of the Higher Planets, but he was lost, left behind in development millions of years ago.

The suit stepped over me, making it a point to kick me in the spine as he passed. I clenched my fists, wincing in pain as he stepped out of the ship. I saw him on the screen, moving toward my friends. They saw him and ran.

Again I fought against the cuffs. I got further this time, managing to jerk against the chain, but it wasn't enough. I screamed in frustration, the sound deep and angry, unable to leave my paralyzed mouth.

He was going to kill them, and all I could do was lie on the ground! I was useless! I felt tears build behind my eyes as frustration choked me. They couldn't do this!

I had been such a fool to think that they would leave them alone. Why hadn't I fought harder? Why did I let him bind me, render me useless? I was supposed to protect them! *What had I done?*

I had never hated myself so much as I did then.

The Impersonator watched out the door for a minute. Then I heard movement around the hovercraft. I winced when the needle slid into my neck, and sensation suddenly rushed to all of my limbs.

I could move. Quickly, I sat up, staring at him in disbelief.

The feeling didn't last long. Soon my heart was pounding and I was on my feet, rushing toward the open door. I had to chase down the Council agent! He only had maybe a minute's head start. I still had enough time to catch up to him—to stop him. What I would do, I

185

didn't know. All I knew was that I had to stop him from harming my friends.

The hovercraft door slammed in my face, sealing me in with the Impersonator. I whirled around, staring at the man in incredulity.

"What are you doing? My friends—" I began.

"Are fine," the Impersonator said, cutting me off. He didn't look remotely concerned. In fact, he wasn't even looking at me. He was standing at the main console, tapping buttons and selecting things on the screen as they came up. It was so fast, I couldn't make any sense of what he was doing.

"The Council agent is after them! He's going to shoot them! Let me out!"

The Impersonator smirked as if I had said something funny. I didn't find it funny at all.

"If you do not let me out of here …" I nearly snarled at him. *"Do you want them to die?"*

I clenched my hands into fists, but I realized I was being ridiculous as soon as I made them. What could I do? Hit the Impersonator? Knock him unconscious and take over the ship? Even aside from the slim likelihood that I could bring myself to hurt the man, regardless of how angry and desperate I was, I didn't know how to operate a hovercraft!

I was completely at the Impersonator's mercy, and it enraged me. I felt my blood pulsing in my ears. I gritted my teeth, frustrated to the point of tears, if only they would fall. The Council agent was getting away, *and I just needed to get through the door!*

"I guess I should be glad they didn't ask me to hit you this time," the Impersonator said, suddenly adopting a thick Southern accent. He still wasn't looking at me.

"Jo'sha?" I asked, stunned. I was almost startled enough to forget that an armed animal was chasing down my friends as I stood there. Almost, but not quite.

"Relax, Saira. He isn't going to find them," Jo'sha said, as if he were reading my thoughts. "He isn't even close to them."

There was nothing in that ship that showed me that—that provided proof—but it was Jo'sha.

I started laughing. It was a hysterical, uncontrollable type of laughter. I clamped my hand over my mouth, but I just couldn't stop

186

it. It wasn't a happy laugh. Fear, grief, and anger suddenly erupted, and I laughed until I sobbed, my eyes transfixed on the first ray of hope I had seen in days.

Suddenly, I let go of everything I had been trying to contain. I knew I could trust Jo'sha. After centuries of working together, I considered him a friend, and I trusted him as one of the most devoted Peacemakers we had. He cared about the humans. I knew he would help us.

So I let go, and as the maniacal laughter quieted, a soothing relief flooded through me. We were going to be okay.

"Do you know how hard it has been for me to keep you on this planet?" Jo'sha grumbled. "And what happened with the bot? What could you have possibly been thinking?"

"I couldn't—*what are you doing here?*" I stuttered, too overcome with emotion to even think straight.

He had been watching me? How? There were seven billion people on the planet, and he had managed to keep watch over *me*?

"Do not do that again," Jo'sha said, still tapping a multitude of knobs and buttons, his eyebrows furrowed as he concentrated. New screens appeared. He tapped on more things that made no sense to me. He moved through one after another, faster than I could comprehend them. "Next time, just keep running. Someone is sitting in jail for saving your hide. Don't expect to get that lucky again."

"Someone is—*what*?"

"I just needed one more minute, girl," Jo'sha muttered under his breath. "One more minute and I would have sent him the other way."

Was he talking about the suit now? I couldn't keep up with his erratic thought process.

"Tori ..." I stuttered. "Jo'sha, what are you doing? *What is going on?*"

I moved to his side, watching his face as he continued to fiddle with the computer. My brother was the one who was good with technology. Computers, biology, chemistry, mathematics—my brother could make sense of all of it. He had once tried to explain to me how Gangers were built, but it had gone way over my head. He built the Gangers; I lived in them for a short time—that was about all I understood.

"I volunteered to help ... collect you," Jo'sha said, eyes transfixed on the screen. "It seems we are having problems beaming you back up, and the bots have suddenly decided to flee populations of high density. Last I checked, the middle of the Atlantic Ocean has become quite popular."

A smirk sneaked across his face; he seemed more than a little amused.

And I was more than confused. What would cause the bots to malfunction like that?

On the bright side, at least I knew why I hadn't seen any of them in the past day.

"Jo'sha, what's going on?" I asked again. "I don't know what to do! I have no idea what's happening!"

"It's not good upstairs, Saira. Things between the Council and the Peacemakers are tense," Jo'sha said. "Your little adventure down here is only making things worse."

"It's not good down here! Jo'sha, *why*? Why a Cleansing? What happened? What am I doing down here?"

Jo'sha didn't respond. His brow furrowed deeper as he tapped, tapped, *tapped* on the computer.

"*What are you doing*?" I asked, perhaps a bit too sharply. I couldn't help it, though. I was just so confused, and all he was doing was talking to the machine!

"Telling our suited friend to go play in the road," Jo'sha said, grinning slyly. He tapped the screen, pulling up a radar image. I could see three red dots not far from the center of the screen where the ship was, but the glowing blue dot...

"What do you think I've been doing?" he asked, smirking at me.

I took the man's face in my bound hands and kissed him on the cheek. He finally turned to look at me, stunned. I just smiled at him. He had sent the blue dot in the opposite direction, and it kept moving away. He would *never* find my friends!

"Next time, you start with that!" I said, still beaming at Jo'sha. I leaned against the hovercraft's walls and breathed. Finally, I was safe. My friends were safe.

"Jo'sha?" I asked, my mind racing. I could hear the desperation in my own voice, but I could also hear the hope. "Can you fly this thing? Could you get us to Tennessee? My brother said—it's a safe place, right? Do you know where I'm going? What's there?"

Jo'sha shook his head. He didn't take his eyes off the screen, but I could see the pained look on his face. "This isn't that kind of mission, Saira. All I can do is keep your feet on the ground."

"No! Jo'sha, please!" I begged. I felt the crushing weight of true desperation hit me square in the chest all over again. My breath came out in panicked gasps as I turned to face the Impersonator.

Jo'sha cast his eyes to the side shamefully. He couldn't look at me.

"*Please*," I begged. "I need help, Jo'sha! I can't do this! You can't leave us here!"

My bound hands grabbed his and he was forced to stop what he was doing. He closed his eyes and pursed his lips.

"I need you to stay strong," Jo'sha said. "You've got some people upstairs trying to help. I don't know for how much longer, though. They've tracked down most of us."

It all made sense then. Jo'sha was sabotaging this mission. He was interfering with the Council of Traltix, and thousands of miles from here, on board *Moga*, there were others helping me—and him. Peacemakers were working together to sabotage a Cleansing. But why?

The image of my brother flashed through my head. He had taken me from the medical unit and smuggled me to a transport unit, sirens blaring in the background. He had broken me out and sent me to Earth. He was part of this, too. My brother …

"Dorain?" I asked, panicked. What he did was surely illegal. They would find him. I hadn't even thought about what his fate might be, trying so hard myself to avoid the worst down here.

"Prisoner," Jo'sha said. "But don't worry about him. He's fine. You and your friends, on the other hand, are in a world of trouble, and I can't promise you that it's going to get better anytime soon."

My mind was reeling. My brother was a prisoner. The Council of Traltix was on Earth; they and the Peacemakers were at odds. Peacemakers were interrupting what, as far as I could tell, was a perfectly legal and organized Cleansing. *What was going on here?*

"I don't understand. Jo'sha—"

"We don't have time for you to understand," Jo'sha said, glancing at the screen.

All I felt was an empty despair crawling through me, gnawing at my nerves. My whole life was in shambles, and my one hope was telling me that I had to go back out there.

Alone.

"Get me out of here. Do *something*," I choked. *"Please.* I can't do this. I'm not brave. I'm not strong. Jo'sha—I've broken. Every time I need to be strong, I give up. I'm a coward. *I can't do this anymore.*"

He finally looked me in the eye, his face full of sympathy. I saw how deeply it hurt him; that he wanted to do more.

"I left my family, Jo'sha. *I left them.* And the virus—*I* did that. I brought it here! I'm a monster. I deserve whatever they have planned for me."

"You had best stop saying that," Jo'sha said somberly. "I'm afraid you might actually start to believe it."

"That virus was not *your* doing," Jo'sha said. "And as for your family, you have to know, that city was gone already. It was gone, girl. You have to forgive yourself. For all of it."

He took his hands from mine, and instead, he held them. I felt the warmth of his hands as he closed them around mine. They were soft and gentle. His thumb stroked my hands, an intimate, purely human, behavior. It was meant to be comforting, but I felt nothing but desperation.

"I don't *want* to do this anymore," I wept. "Don't you see? I'm worse than useless. I'm horrible! I just want to go home. I just want this to end. I don't even care what happens anymore!"

Jo'sha just watched me. I expected to see anger or disgust in his eyes. Instead, I saw compassion. He didn't despise me. In fact, I saw a small, sad smile creeping slowly across his face.

"They hate me, Jo'sha. They hate what I am. They don't want me. How can I be any good to them when they can't even stand being near me, and I just want to run away?"

The smile grew on his face. There was also pain, but I saw understanding in his eyes. "Do you think any one of us would feel any different in your place, Saira? You have done nothing wrong, and you are brave, girl. You are strong. I know you'll keep going."

"How?" I sobbed. "How do you know I can keep going when I'm just begging for the chance to give up? I was relieved when he took me, Jo'sha! *How can that be okay?*"

He let go of my hands and reached out, pulling something from beneath my shirt: the half-heart necklace. He held it in his hands, his eyes examining the silver letters pensively.

"Thellessians," he said, smiling. I could see tears building behind his eyes, though they would never fall. "Your race has been benign since you crawled out of your ocean and onto your scorched planet. Did you know that, for centuries, your race was a symbol to the Peacemakers, the species that rose from the ashes of our darkest moment?"

He looked me in the eye and I saw something in them that I could only interpret as hope. He saw *hope* in me. I had never seen someone look at me like that.

What could I possibly have done to deserve so much faith?

"You will keep going, Saira," he said, and there was no doubt in his voice. "You will keep running because you love them, and a Thellessian's second heart does not give up so easily."

He was right. I knew then that he was right. I would throw myself in front of an army of bots to protect them. I didn't have to be brave to do that; I just had to love them.

"Okay," I whispered. "But I need you to answer one question for me."

Jo'sha looked at me, uncertain. I saw a resistance in his eyes, an apprehension of yet another hope that he would have to deny me.

"What is this?" I asked him. "What is going on?"

The expression on his face was haunted. "If I told you the truth, Saira, I don't know that any of us could keep going."

What did that mean? I felt my heart sinking. Somehow I knew this was worse than even my darkest of nightmares.

But the time for questions had ended. Jo'sha reached under the computer, and when he pulled his hand out, it was full of wires and tubes. The screen went blank. I heard the door hiss open behind me.

It was time to run for my life again.

"Get the humans and run that way," he said, pointing in the opposite direction of the road. "There's a farm with food, water—whatever you will need. There's a car in the driveway. Take it. Turn left and follow the road back to the highway. You'll miss the net. Just don't take long. The bots will be back to finish the job. Once we scramble them, it doesn't take them long to unscramble them."

I stared out into the trees. More running. More bots. More danger. Did I really think I could keep going? This body was worn out, and mentally, I was exhausted. I had been relieved when the suit took me away. I was relieved when forces outside my control ended my misery before I could give up. I was weak, just as I had been all those months ago as I hid under the blankets and waited for my twenty-year mission to end. I was a cowardly creature, and I knew I couldn't change that.

"Please come with me," I pleaded to Jo'sha. He was stronger than I was. His race was brave and righteous. I knew that we had a chance with him at my side.

He shook his head. I saw the regret. He really did want to help me. "I can't keep your friends alive from here," he said. "You have to do that yourself."

I knew he wanted to do more than sit on an alien ship and force bots into chasing their tails. He didn't want to be hiding in an Impersonator body, quietly sabotaging the Council, hoping beyond hope that they wouldn't find him next. He was putting everything on the line, I realized. His mission was as dangerous as mine. I couldn't help but wonder *why*. Why do this? What could he possibly have to gain? If they found him, he could lose everything, and for what?

I took a deep breath, steadying myself for what I knew lay right outside the door. I held my chained hands out to him, but he shook his head.

"This can't look like I helped you," Jo'sha said.

I nodded. "What do we need to do?"

I felt nausea rising in my stomach as he lowered his head and pointed to a place at the back of his skull. "I guess you get to hit me this time. Make it count, girl. I don't want to wake up chained in a jail cell."

"What?" I asked, horrified. He wanted me to *hurt* him. "No! I can't! I *won't*!"

In my entire life, I had not caused harm to anything. I couldn't even eat the meat foods that the humans had already prepared for me, consumed by guilt from the knowledge that defenseless farm animals

192

had been caged and murdered for me to eat. I couldn't hit a friend, especially not one who was putting so much on the line for me. The thought of repaying that kind of sacrifice with violence was unthinkable.

I had pushed the suit, though. Where had that come from? I had stood over him and taunted him.

Jo'sha smiled at me, and his face, for a brief moment, looked as if it had found comfort, some ideal to cling to.

"A tip," Jo'sha said. "You have some very distinctive alien technology in your head. I'd be getting rid of that."

The chip! I had completely forgotten about the chip! No wonder they had known where to lay the net, knew where to wait. All they had to do was follow the signature of a technology far too advanced for this planet, and they could track me anywhere. I had been hiding a tracking device in my head for days, and I hadn't even realized it!

"But Saira," Jo'sha said, his voice somber. "If they can't find you, neither can I."

He was telling me that he couldn't protect me anymore. I had to run back out there without him to watch over me. I had barely survived this far, and that was with help! How could I expect to stay alive without him?

"He's an Aquir, if that helps," Jo'sha said. "But I must make a request of you."

I looked at him, confused.

"The *Allisandre* pulled him from the *Ninevier* as it broke apart in the midst of the war. Half the crew was lost. He was at the forefront of those who selflessly put their lives on the line to stop the violence. He is a broken creature, not cruel. Remember that."

I didn't understand. What did that mean? What did he want me to do?

In one quick movement, he was on the ground at my feet, a pool of blood forming around his head. He had known all along I couldn't do it, so he had forced his own soft skull into the glass screen of the computer, sending shards of glass flying and splitting his head wide open.

I stumbled back, fighting the urge to vomit. I had to cover my mouth not to scream. I looked at the body lying prone on the ground, the red puddle growing larger. He had to be dead. There was too much blood for him to still be alive.

It was too much. I turned and ran out of the hovercraft, gagging, forcing my stomach contents to stay down. I was a very squeamish creature. Red human blood didn't bother me too much—I was trained to get used to it over the centuries. Pain, on the other hand, I had no stomach for. I couldn't see violence and suffering right at my feet and not feel the urge to be physically sick. What Jo'sha had done—*why had he done that*?

He had said it couldn't look as if he helped me. He had said that things between the Peacemakers and the Council of Traltix were tense. If I escaped while under his watch, the Council would certainly blame him, and then, would they even trust the Peacemakers at all? The way he saw it, it must have been his only choice.

He did it so that he could continue to help me, so that the Council would still trust him as an ally. I hated it, but no matter how many ways I looked at it, his decision was right. Any other scenario left him suspect.

He was brave in ways I would never be. I would never be able to repay his sacrifice.

But what would this mean for me?

It didn't matter, I decided. No further punishment could be any worse than the fate that was already awaiting me.

I leaned against the outside of the hovercraft, my back against its sleek metal body, and forced my breathing to slow down. I closed my eyes, pushing the blood out of my mind.

Think! I had to think, I told myself. The alien in the suit was an Aquir, an amphibious race. He couldn't survive on Earth without the suit because, among other reasons, the atmosphere was too dry. The suit would be pumping extremely damp air to keep his gills from drying out. Without it, he would have maybe an hour before he suffocated.

His weakness was obvious—that was why Jo'sha had mentioned his race. I knew what he expected me to do, but it would hurt him. He would suffer and be frightened. I couldn't stand the thought of hurting the poor creature, despite my previous feelings toward him. They hadn't diminished much, but…

To see what he must have seen, to have had his experiences, and to think what he would come back to. They would all think I had succumbed to madness.

I couldn't do anything about it, though. Jo'sha was right then, and he was right now. I couldn't see another way.

I just hoped the Aquir had another helmet.

The problem was finding out where he had gone. Jo'sha had shattered the screen, but last I saw, my friends weren't too far from the ship, and the Aquir was approaching the highway. The highway was to the left, wasn't it? What if he had moved? Jo'sha was no longer telling him where to go. Was he walking around blind, or had he stumbled across my friends? What if they saw him and ran, the Aquir with the deadly stun gun pursuing them deeper into the trees? Every moment I stood there was a chance for the Aquir to find my friends, but if I ran in the wrong direction, my friends would die a horrible death.

What if they were already dead?

Which direction should I pick? I couldn't afford to be wrong.

I heard a bloodcurdling scream from behind me. My heart stopped before I realized it was a man's voice. It was Jo'sha. He wasn't dead! He was screaming, calling out to the Aquir in Common Tongue as if he were in extraordinary pain. Of course, remembering the pool of blood and how his skin had parted to reveal the bone beneath, I didn't think he was faking. Gangers and Impersonators felt pain just as humans did. I was surprised he was conscious at all, but then, I was realizing that Jo'sha was capable of far more than I had previously thought.

But the sound of him sobbing, pleading for help, nearly drove me back into the hovercraft to comfort him.

I fought back sobs as I heard my friend wailing in anguish, shoving my hand in my mouth and biting down just to keep quiet. It was almost the worst thing I had ever suffered through, listening to him scream while I just stood there, waiting to attack the creature that, hopefully, was running back to his colleague to help him.

All I could feel was an increasing hatred for myself. I had thought I had reached a low in the hovercraft, but I was quickly pushing past that point.

I knew Jo'sha would go back to his regular body and suffer nothing more than a nasty headache in the end. The Aquir would be okay. He would go back to the ship and the doctors would treat his gills and whatever foreign substances he may have picked up from exposure to the planet. I would be gentle with him, just as Jo'sha had asked. I would do my best not to leave him with emotional scars.

It would be okay. All that mattered was that Jo'sha was luring the Aquir away from my friends.

I stood there silently, my heart in my throat, praying that the Aquir would take the bait.

Just before I heard the crunching of leaves, the whisper of a thought crossed my mind, and I wondered if not letting him take me really was best. This could have ended. In fact, it wasn't even too late.

The crashing of someone running through the woods grew louder. From the weight and apparent clumsiness, I knew it was my target. I waited until I heard him scrambling inside the hovercraft.

"Where is she?" he asked frantically.

He didn't even ask if he was okay! He didn't even sound concerned for him! Jo'sha may have only been in an Impersonator body, his real body safe on a ship, but he still suffered!

I felt anger surge through my veins.

I gave him an answer by sweeping his legs out from under him. He crashed to the ground, his head bouncing off the floor. His suit protected him from the impact. He wasn't hurt, but he was about to be in trouble. He scrambled, trying to get back to his feet, but I was faster. I jumped on his back, pinning him, and slid my hands around the front of his helmet and released the clasp, pulling it off. A blast of warm, wet air hit me.

As I leapt off him, the Aquir gasped, and grasped at where his helmet had been. He clutched at the gills at his neck, his sleek olive-green skin glistening. His three round eyes were wide with shock. He blinked at me, two sets of eyelids sliding closed over his eyes, one after the other. Our eyes met. I saw the panic behind his.

The anger drained from me instantly.

What had I done?

"I'm so sorry," I whispered, and I truly was. I hated myself for being the cause of his fear, regardless of his character. He reached for the stun gun, but I ran, taking the helmet with me. I took one fleeting glance at Jo'sha. He was lying in a pool of blood, clearly in pain, but I could have sworn that he was grinning at me. He would be okay. They both would, and I could still save my friends.

I heard the hovercraft take off and held my breath as the sound faded. They had to leave. Jo'sha had smashed their tracking equipment, and the Aquir and Jo'sha would need a medic promptly.

Only after I heard a blissful silence did I release my grip on the helmet and let it fall to the ground.

I didn't pause to let the relief flow through me, though. I ran through the trees, calling for my friends. No one answered. I ran and screamed until my lungs hurt and my throat was raw, but still there was nothing. The landscape was hilly and filled with large stones, and I tripped with every step, my bound hands grasping for scrawny trees and branches to keep me from falling down the steep slopes.

I was too late. Somewhere in the trees their bodies were cooling in the dirt and dry, brown leaves. The thought of it just about drove me to madness. I could not lose them! Not after all I had been through.

"Jillian!" I screamed. I tripped and fell over a large stone, my face connecting with the earth. My vision hadn't completely come back after they had tried to pull me out of the Ganger. I was coherent, though slightly dazed, and everything in the distance was fuzzy. My peripheral vision was all but gone.

Small rocks skinned my cheek. I felt the pain, raw and throbbing, but I ignored it. I pushed myself upright as best I could and, panting and dizzy, crawled to a large boulder. I leaned against it, sobbing.

"Marie! Tori!" I shrieked.

A hand clamped down on my mouth. "Stop screaming!" Jillian hissed. She was standing over me from behind, half of her body shielded behind the large rock. My heart stopped racing when I saw Marie and Tori hidden behind a clump of trees in the distance, nervously canvassing the area as they slunk in our direction.

"God!" Jillian snapped. "Whales off the coast could hear you!"

"*Where were you?*" I said, as I pried Jillian's hand from my mouth and scrambled to my feet.

"You ran after us in the wrong direction, you idiot," Tori grumbled, as she trotted up behind Jillian. She was out of breath, but she was standing. The wound on her forehead was puckered and red, but it wasn't bleeding anymore. I counted it as a small blessing.

"We followed them," Marie explained. "When we saw the spaceship, we tried to sneak up on them to save you, but that guy came out with the gun and we had to run."

"The next thing we knew, there was all this screaming and Tall, Suited, and Creepy runs back, and then you're running around the woods screaming bloody friggin' murder," Tori muttered.

"Why didn't you respond?" I snapped.

Tori threw her hands up. "How were we supposed to know he was the only one?"

"Is that blood?" Marie squeaked, staring down at my feet with wide eyes. I looked down. My white sneakers, now much less white from running around in the wooded areas, glistened with speckles of wet, red blood, the soles saturated with crimson.

This time I couldn't stop the bile that rose in my throat. I leaned over and heaved. When what little I had in my stomach had come up, I slid back down to the ground and sobbed. My friends looked at me, completely at a loss, as I sat there and cried and cried and cried.

It was a while before anyone did anything.

Marie knelt down next to me and put a hand on my shoulder. The act of compassion surprised me. Wasn't I the monster? Didn't they hate me? Why did she care? Why had they bothered to approach the ship and try to save me? Why had they run toward my screams instead of leaving me behind in the trees?

"I'm sorry," I said, taking a deep breath. "He's okay. He'll be fine. I'll be fine."

It was more for me than for them. I still felt anger toward the Aquir. I still felt the horror of Jo'sha's blood spilling out on the ground. I still felt guilt and shame for my part in all of this and my behavior. Most importantly, I still felt the dull heartache of losing those I loved most and the sting of rejection from the only loved ones I had left.

"Someone you knew?" Marie asked.

I nodded. "They won't be coming back."

"You took them out? Way to go, Ally!" Tori said, grinning. I glared at her, my eyes burning. A deep, bitter anger flared in my chest, different from the anger I felt toward the Aquir. Such a childish human to be pleased by bloodshed in the wake of all the death and pain we had seen! How could she possibly make a joke out of this! How could she be so impenetrable as to not feel the grief and heartache from this experience, as I did? Did she have any humanity within her? Did any of them?

"I just had to leave a friend in a pool of his own blood! He was lying there, screaming in agony, and I did nothing! It's *nothing* to be proud of! And you know what? He did it for *you*, so show some respect for once in your life!" I snarled. Tori flinched, clearly taken aback. I could tell that I had hurt her, but I didn't care.

"If he was such a great friend, maybe you should have stayed with him," Jillian shot back defensively. My eyes met hers and I rose to my feet, facing her directly.

That was my limit. I had had enough of the humans and their yelling and petty anger. I was tired of their anger toward *me*. Did they even realize what was going on here? I could have so easily stayed behind and given up. I could have left them down here to fend for themselves in the midst of all this horror. Did they even understand what I was doing for them? Was this a game? I was giving them everything—no, I was giving them far more than I had—and all they could do was attack! My *friends*! I had risked danger for *them*!

"I'm sorry you're hurt, Jillian," I said, my voice dripping venom. "I really am, but we all are. We've all lost *everything*, including me. Get over yourself. There are people out there risking everything to save you, and, to be honest, I don't know why they would put their necks out for you. My own life is over once they catch me. Do you realize that? The last thing I can do before they haul me away and wipe my mind, then ship me off to my own planet for further punishment, is save *you*. The very last good thing I can do with what's left of me is to give *you* a chance. Show some respect. I'm not the monster you think I am."

She slunk back, wounded, all of the anger and pride drained from her.

I turned and stalked away, walking in the direction Jo'sha had told me was safe. Something changed in me there—no, it had started farther back, but I was too hurt to notice.

"Where are you going?" Tori called. "The car is the other way!"

"The car isn't safe," I called behind me, without pausing. "Jo'sha said there was a place not far from here, but we have to be quick."

I heard three sets of feet scampering behind me. Marie came up beside me, eyeing me with concern. Jillian and Tori silently took the rear.

"You hurt your friend for us?" Marie asked.

"He did it himself," I muttered irritably. Every bone in my body was begging to be alone, to process the emotions coursing through me, but there was no stopping, so I kept pushing forward, my eyes focused on nothing but what lay ahead.

"What happened? Why did your friends come after you?" Marie asked. I was quiet.

"What do you mean about your life being over? What did you do?" she questioned.

"Marie," I said. "Please, can I just have a minute to myself?"

Her face fell, hurt. I knew she just wanted to help, but at the moment I didn't feel like I could handle any of the humans, not even sweet Marie. I was so angry. I just needed a minute of not looking at them. She nodded, understanding.

"Thank you for coming back for us," she said. "And thank you to your friend."

She slipped back to join Tori and Jillian. All of us walked in tense silence. I kept my eyes forward. All I could focus on was getting to that house. Baby steps, I told myself. Get to the house, get to the highway, get to Tennessee, and don't die on the way. I could do this.

People were helping me, after all. I would just keep going for them—for people.

For my brother, who got locked up in a prison cell somewhere for me.

But what was I doing? My conversation with Jo'sha had only left me confused.

If I told you the truth, Saira, I don't know that any of us could keep going ...

This was a Cleansing, wasn't it? Why was the Council involved? Why were the Peacemakers sabotaging them? What was my role in all of this? What did they need me to do? Save three humans? What would that do?

200

I came to a screeching halt at the barbed-wire fence. It wasn't the fence that stopped me, though; rather, the hundreds upon hundreds of black bovine corpses scattered across the field. I hadn't noticed the large black birds circling overhead as we had approached, but at the fence, the taste of death in the air was unmistakable. As far as the eye could see, there was death.

"What the *hell*?" Tori said from behind.

"What happened to them?" Marie asked, coming up beside me.

I heard the sound of a forlorn animal nearby. I looked and there was a single black cow staring at us, tucked in the corner of the field, attempting to hide behind a few scraggly trees. It was frightened—the lone survivor. When it saw us, it took a few steps forward, attracted to the life amid the death.

"Here, cow," Marie called to it. "Come here, Mr. Cow."

"Don't call it over here, you idiot! It might be diseased!" Tori hissed.

The cow took another step, then fell mid-stride. It was dead before it hit the ground.

"Oh, my god!" Marie sobbed. "Oh, my god! We have to get out of here!"

"It's okay," I said, staring at the corpse. "We're safe."

"What is this?" Marie said, hysterical. She was pacing the fence, beside herself. She had grown up on a farm. I wondered if this looked like home to her.

"Mercy," I said bitterly.

Carefully, I climbed over the fence. It was more than difficult with my wrists bound, but I managed to crawl over it without tumbling into the pasture. I proceeded across the field with a brisk pace. I stepped across and around corpses, trying to avoid looking at them, lest I be sick again. Buzzards and black crows dotted the field, picking at the fresh meat. Their shrill cries frayed my nerves.

I recognized all of this: the diseased falling over dead, herds of livestock being wiped out—this was a strategy for a carefully planned Cleansing. People had to be sent back to Earth with these specific viruses, and they had to be given time to spread across the planet. Even the fastest virus would take a week or two to spread, assuming that Gangers were placed strategically across the globe. Then the viruses wouldn't be triggered until an agent entered the body, usually something released into the water. The diseased were eliminated first, ensuring that all survivors would be healthy and the race wouldn't accidentally be wiped out by transmitted illnesses. The idea behind the livestock was similar. Large herds of animals were filthy, and without humans to keep their populations in check, their population would swell and consume everything, until finally, everything would start to die from disease and starvation. The planet would become one large, decaying petri dish.

Now I knew what the virus—or at least one of them—in my blood was really meant for, but why had its true nature been concealed from me? Why had I been forced to harbor it in secret? The Elders sent us all back with a virus in our blood; that much I had known. That wasn't unusual. Peacemakers preferred to control viruses and natural disasters as a way to manipulate the development of lower species. It was certainly kinder than engineering wars or genocides, even if the results weren't as direct, and the Peacemakers who came back from those were never the same. We did it because it was best and necessary, but the effects such things had on us ...

Old memories still haunted me: white sheets and doctors, the sick lying in rows of beds, nurses with masks, the coughing and sickness that never seemed to end.

One of the many horrors we had created in the name of creating a better world. I still had those memories, though the emotions attached to that lifetime had been removed and stored. I could access them again if I wanted to, but I knew I never would. I stepped over another body and forced the memories back into the dark, where I would forever keep them.

I couldn't deny it. The Elders had ordered a Cleansing, as was their right alone, and it was proceeding flawlessly. I hadn't known, but they had no need to justify their actions to the likes of me. The only thing wrong here was me, the coup, the creature who was threatening the peaceful resurrection of the human race. The Cleansing wasn't the disaster: I was. I had been used.

No, I thought, thinking of my brother and Jo'sha. They wouldn't use me. They had no hatred for this planet. Despite all the signs that this was right, something told me what I was seeing was just the opposite. This *couldn't* be right.

But what was this? Everything was perfect. This Cleansing followed every protocol to the letter. Except for the coup. Except for the Council of Traltix. My mind flashed back to my trial, where I was found guilty of galactic crimes. How had that technology failed me?

No.

Why? *Why* had that technology failed me?

Finally, I understood. I was part of a coup all right, but not the one I thought I was.

The Elders didn't order a Cleansing. It had been forced. Someone had tricked us all, and they had been on the inside. Peacemakers had done this, but not the right ones. Someone *made* this happen, and they made it look as if I had been involved, only their plans were backfiring. Someone had known what was happening—they got me out. The Peacemakers were battling themselves, and now the Council was involved.

No, that didn't make sense either. I had been screened before I left. If there was something in my blood that wasn't right, *someone* would have caught it! Our technology was too advanced to just trick! No, we couldn't have just let this happen. How many would have to be involved for that to happen?

My mind was reeling when we reached the house—a little yellow ranch with blue shutters and a wraparound porch. It was too much to process, and I had too few details. I had to let it go or I would be madder than I already was. I had been given a mission and I had to focus on it now. I went straight for the kitchen and started digging through the drawers.

I found a long, sharp kitchen knife.

"Weapons!" Tori shouted. "Now we're talking!"

"No," I said, my hands shaking as I held the angry-looking piece of metal. I saw my eyes looking back at me in the silver metal; yellowed, bloodshot, and terrified. "Absolutely no weapons."

"No weapons?" Tori asked, incredulous. "Have you *seen* what's out there? I think we need to be thinking about how to defend ourselves!"

"No weapons," I whispered. "We can't defend ourselves. All we can do is run."

I slammed the drawer shut and turned to them. My hands shook. I couldn't take my eyes off the knife.

I was not going to like what was coming.

"Then what is that for?" Jillian asked warily.

"There's a chip in my head," I whispered, my voice so low it was barely audible. "They can track us with it. It has to come out."

I tore my eyes away from the piece of metal and looked at Jillian. Our eyes locked. My heart was racing.

Her gray eyes grew wide. "*No.*"

"Tori just suffered a head wound, and Marie goes into shock at the sight of blood," I said, forcing myself to sound like I knew what I was doing. "Besides, we both know you've been having daydreams about stabbing me with a sharp object. Here's your chance."

That comment was unnecessary, but strangely enough, it made me feel better.

I thrust the handle of the knife into her hand, forced her fingers around it, and put my head down on the counter. She stood there, incapable of processing what I was asking her to do.

"Well, come on!" I shouted, my fists clenched so tightly that my knuckles were white. I couldn't do it myself—I didn't have the nerve. They had to do it before I lost all courage and was reduced to a blubbering heap on the floor.

"Wait," Tori said, digging around in the drawers. She pulled out a metal meat tenderizer.

"First things first," she said. She struck the cuffs around my wrists, each time aiming at what must have been the weakest point, where the chain met the bracelet. When the chain finally snapped, my wrists were bruised, but I was free.

"Now, your turn," I told Jillian. My tone of voice told her she did not have a choice.

I saw the hesitation in her eyes, but she didn't fight me. We all knew it had to be done.

She took a deep breath. "You two hold her still," she said.

Marie and Tori both nodded, but I was pretty sure Marie was going to faint, and Tori looked as if she were considering it, too. There was still some dry blood on her forehead and the gash looked angrier than before.

I pressed my right cheek against the table. I grabbed Jillian's hand and placed her fingers behind my left ear, right on the flat, smooth surface between the ear and the arc of the human skull. "Do you feel it?"

Her hand resisted me as I held it to my soft flesh.

"If you don't do this," I said, "they'll find us."

"I feel it," she squeaked. I felt her commit. Her fingers pressed down on my skull firmly, right where the chip was.

She took a deep breath and I saw the knife coming down. I clenched my eyes shut. The kiss of the knife bit into my skin and I cried out. It was a cold, raw pain. I felt Marie and Tori's grip tighten, fighting to keep me still as I squirmed under the knife, gasping from the pain. Any minute now it would be too much and I would start fighting to pull away.

"I see it," Jillian said. I felt her trying to dig it out with her fingers, which only took the already unbearable pain to a new level. She cursed.

"The damn thing is embedded!" she said.

"Cut it out," I managed to squeak, when all I really wanted to do was shove the humans off me and find somewhere to hide until the pain was gone.

"I—" Jillian began. She backed away.

"Do you want to die?" I snapped at her. She took a deep breath, and the knife dug in harder.

Blood ran down my neck and into my eyes. The pain was unbearable, a raw, screaming throb. I felt the tip of the knife slide under the chip, gnashing and tearing my skin as Jillian did her best to pry it from the tissue. I had endured this five times before with an anesthetic. Never had I realized just how rooted the chip was to my body.

Just when I thought I was going to pass out, I felt Jillian pull the small silver chip from my flesh, and the pain subsided.

"Thank God," Tori said. I carefully brushed blood out of my eyes and opened them as she sank to the ground. Marie ran to the sink and threw up, sobbing between heaves. All three girls were trembling.

Jillian grabbed a hand towel off the stove and pressed it against my head, though it only made the wound protest more.

"Smash it," I told them, too woozy to lift up my head and look. "When it's a million tiny pieces, throw it in the oven. Make it as hot as it will get."

Each loud thud that meant the meat tenderizer had once again smashed into the tiny chip gave me enormous relief. I heard the buttons on the stove beeping, followed by tiny clinks as Marie opened the door and tossed the fragments in. It was gone. They couldn't find us now.

I took the towel from Jillian and sank to the floor next to Tori, too shaky to keep standing. Tori sat there, cradling her head between her knees. Marie and Jillian shuffled around near me, but my mind had blocked them out.

"How's your head?" I whispered weakly, eyeing the gash above Tori's right eye. I held the towel against my own head and leaned back, deciding it would be best if I just closed my eyes.

"It's fine," she muttered. "Damn thing just bled a lot. It was over pretty quick."

"I found car keys," Jillian said. At least, that's what it sounded like. "I'm going to go find us a car."

"Stay inside," I mumbled, as I heard her legs go past. If I had been standing, I would have stopped her. Outside was dangerous. As things went, I was impressed that I could make myself sit up.

She disappeared, ignoring my comment, but I realized that maybe she wasn't just going to look for the car. She was upset, and Jillian wasn't about to show us to what extent, if she could help it.

"They might have a first-aid kit in the bathroom. I'll go look," Marie said shakily. She flitted out of the kitchen before we could say anything. The counters were still red and the poor girl needed to get away from all the blood.

I sat there and prayed that the throbbing would end. I hoped the nanotechnology would heal the wound soon, though the thought made me feel guilty. Poor Tori didn't have nanotechnology, and her gash looked like it hurt considerably.

"I'm sorry," Tori said. My eyes snapped open.

"What?" I asked, confused.

"I screwed things up in the woods. You got caught. I screwed things up at the gas station, too."

"That wasn't your fault," I told her. She stared at me, and I was startled when I saw tears forming in her eyes.

"At the gas station, why did you tell me to take the car? You looked right at me, and you told *me* to make them leave."

"Tori—"

"It's because I'm selfish," she said. I saw the first tear fall. "You knew I would run away. You knew I would leave you there. And you know what? I tried, but I couldn't make them run."

"Tori, you're not—"

"I am, Allyson," she said. "I did exactly what you knew I would do. Don't try to defend me."

I stared at the girl with the spiky black hair, her brown eyes staring up at the ceiling, lost in thought.

"I know it's you," she said.

"What?" I said. My brain was so muddled from blood loss and a sea of emotions that it was all I could manage.

"I know it's you," she repeated. "The real Allyson. Not the other real one—you know what I mean. You've always watched over us and taken care of us. You've always cared for me in a way that no other person has. No alien impersonation could live up to that."

She chuckled feebly. I saw a smile tug at her lips, but it didn't quite make it.

I smiled weakly. "You don't sound too happy about it."

"You're one of the nicest people I've ever met," she said, meeting my eyes. "You may be the best person I know, and you're not even human. What does that say about us?"

"I haven't been very nice lately," I whispered, remembering the scene out in the woods. Guilt consumed me. How could I have done that to them?

"You're selfless, Allyson. You're saving our lives. Look at what you just did *for us*."

She chuckled, though it didn't sound happy. "Just don't tell me Marie is also an alien. Let the humans have one naturally good one."

"You're all good," I whispered. "Some of you just have a hard time showing it."

Tori started to say something, but she was cut off by the sound of Marie's terrified screams carrying down the hall.

CHAPTER 12

It was cold. Dorain had never imagined that it could be so cold anywhere in existence. He pressed himself farther into the corner of his cell, huddled where the light from the small slit of a window, which gave off the only light in his dark, confining prison, hit, but it offered no relief. He had long since exhausted his energy maintaining his own internal temperature, and even then, he could feel his core temperature slowly dropping.

He didn't shudder. Thellessians didn't shake when they were cold. Why would they, when, in all of evolution, they had been blessed to never experience such a thing? He knew he was cold, he knew he was suffering, but his body knew of no response but to quietly slow down.

Of course, it was more than just misery from the biting cold that had taken control of his sluggish thoughts. Overwhelming grief and pain had given way to a shock that numbed him, but he still felt the whispers of thoughts and fears that had run wild in his mind for what seemed like weeks.

Dorain didn't even know how long he had been in that cell. Had it been hours? Days? *Weeks?*

He didn't know. Dorain kept his eyes focused on the tiny, thin window. He held on to the sight of the small blue planet beyond it, his eyes locked onto its glimmering, radiant form as if it were the last thing holding him to the world.

He hadn't seen anyone in days. Eyes appeared behind the slit in the door from time to time—Council agents checking in on him, he assumed—but no one spoke to him. No one came in.

He had never been enclosed in walls before—not like this. He didn't know what it was like to be isolated any more than he knew what it was like to be cold or hungry. He had no idea how to react, so he didn't. He simply sat there, holding on to the blue planet and all it stood for—all that it held. At least, there were things he hoped the planet still held.

He was starving. His normally royal-blue skin was a shade of pale blue now, the white flecks on his skin a shade of deep gray, and the silver flecks were swollen. They rose off his chapped skin, making it feel rough and lumpy. If it were not for the fact that the ship rotated with the planet below, there would be no light at all for him to even attempt to sustain himself. He knew it would not be anywhere near enough in the end.

He heard footsteps coming down the hall and he raised his head. It was a delayed motion, and the footsteps had already stopped at the door by the time he had fully turned to look. It was normally only one set of feet that caught his attention, but today he heard many. He stirred, his body daring to come to life for the first time in ages, when, instead of the slit in the door sliding open for the eyes to peer through at him again, keys rattled, and he heard them slide into the door. He was on his feet when it swung open and the tiny figure was thrust inside.

"You'll pay for this, you dishonorable beast!" Pask cried as the door slammed closed, sending a metallic echo throughout the cell. Pashka spat at the door, the green slime landing on the sliding window just before it opened.

"Will you two calm down? This helps nothing!" a voice hissed as Pashka arched his head back, preparing to spit again. Dorain recognized the voice.

"Jo'sha?" he asked. Slowly, with movements that were cramped and appeared painful, Dorain carried himself to the door. Grudgingly, Pask and Pashka stepped out of the way. He knelt down enough for his eyes to look through the slit, and he saw the eyes on the other side widen in shock.

Jo'sha cursed.

"Those fools," he muttered. "I told them to get a lamp down here. Are they trying to kill you?"

Dorain watched him. His cold, muddled brain attempted to wake up at the sight of him. He felt it trying to form the words he had longed to ask for so long. He could almost remember them now— had it been that long ago that he had been curled against the door, crying them out at the sound of footsteps passing by?

Did he really want to ask them anymore, he wondered? Did he want to know the answer? It seemed more and more likely that his fate—his punishment for his senseless crimes—would be met down here. Perhaps it was best that he did not know before then.

"My sister?"

His own voice startled him. He didn't realize he had the strength to utter the words.

Despite his imprisonment, he was not ignorant to what had happened to the planet below. He had seen the giant glinting cannons surround the planet, punctuating its surface among a sea of serene stars. He had watched as they hovered there, so calm and quiet. They looked so harmless out there in the black. Everything had been so still and silent that Dorain almost did not register the dread settling into his second heart. It was like watching a dream.

And then the clouds swirled and parted everywhere he looked as pulses raced down to the surface. The planet lit up. It was light so bright that Dorain had to look away. So many cannons went off that the planet's surface vanished in a golden glow.

When he opened his eyes again, it was over. The cannons returned to *Moga*. The clouds re-formed, seemingly healing the gaping holes that had been left in the planet. It was almost as if nothing had ever happened, but Dorain knew better.

The shock came later. The true realization of what they had done sank in after the planet disappeared in blinding light for the thousandth time behind his eyelids.

The planet ... the human race ... his sister.

Saira was gone. There was no way she could have escaped. There was no way her mind could make it home.

"She's alive, Dorain," Jo'sha said reassuringly. "I've seen her."

Dorain felt relief wash over him. Jo'sha spoke words he had never imagined he would hear. A weight lifted off his second heart. A numbing blackness drifted from the depths of his mind and he relaxed, sliding down the door to rest at its base. He had never known what true exhaustion felt like, but as it took hold of him then, he also knew what redemption felt like. He had carried the loss of his sister in his second heart for so long.

But he hadn't sent Saira to her death. His sister was still alive.

"Is she safe?"

"She is almost where she needs to be. I have made certain she will get there."

"And her humans?"

There was a tense silence from beyond the door.

"Jo'sha, what of the humans?" Dorain asked again, an almost urgent tone rising in his voice. He felt the despair settling into his second heart again. The weight of it seemed to pull down his depleted body. He wondered how much more his Thellessian body could take. He knew it would not be too long before the weight of it was too much to bear, and he would no longer have the strength or desire to move.

"She has lost much," Jo'sha said quietly.

"Then she is suffering greatly," Dorain responded, his voice hushed.

He closed his eyes and behind them he saw the figure of a young girl. Her hair and eyes were dark. She was screaming as nearly half a dozen Peacemakers held her down against a white floor. He saw the tears that could not fall right before they managed to get the needle in her neck.

It was a memory that still haunted him. Why had he not promised himself that day that he would never let his sister know pain like that ever again?

"She's scared," Jo'sha said. "But your sister is unbelievably strong. I do not think I have ever encountered a being such as her in all my years of existence."

Dorain leaned his head against the door, only partially listening. Why had he not stopped her from returning to the Earth for her fifth lifetime, knowing what the fourth had done to her? Why had he encouraged her to return again to complete the Elders' request? Almost one hundred years ago, he could have taken his sister back home, and she would have been safe. If he had asked, he knew she would have left with him then, and she would not have to run for her life now.

What had stopped him?

"Please, Jo'sha ..." Dorain started, but he could not find the words.

There was a patient pause beyond the door.

"The thought of her suffering weighs heavily on my soul."

Still, there was no response beyond the door.

"The day she came back—the day the child died ..."

Dorain couldn't even stand to see it in his mind, though it had happened so long ago.

"Don't let her go through that again. Protect her. Don't let her suffer."

Dorain heard Jo'sha shift behind the door. There was a defeated sigh.

"Suffering cannot always be prevented," Jo'sha said slowly. "And sometimes it is necessary."

"For what?" Dorain asked. "I cannot believe that a creature's suffering can ever serve the purpose of good. Jo'sha, *do not let my sister suffer.* I beg of you."

Again there was a stagnant, almost painful silence. Then footsteps echoed outside the door, approaching them from down the hall.

"I'm sorry, Dorain," Jo'sha said, and he was gone.

Dorain was still, listening as the sounds outside drifted away. It was only after the still, cold silence had returned for some time that he turned his head to look at his companions, who had remained tensely quiet since Dorain had begun speaking.

Two faces were watching him intently. One had an eye that didn't open all the way. The other's hands wouldn't stop shaking, and a thin trail of drool leaked out of his mouth, which hung partially open.

"I have feared for your well-being for many days, my friends. I am thankful to see you."

Both faces stared at him, watching him closely.

"Are you badly injured?" Dorain asked. Once, he would have rushed to them to measure their well-being, but he felt the chill settling into the depths of his body, and he didn't have the strength to move.

"No worse than we shall be," Pask said quietly. Dorain did not miss the hostile tone that lurked beneath her breath.

"Have they handed down your fate?" Dorain asked.

Pask nodded slowly. "For our crimes, we are to be separated."

Dorain could not stop the surprise from leaping onto his face.

"That is not within their right to dictate!"

"Does any of this fall within the rights of the Council?" Pask asked harshly.

"You are not both strong enough for such a procedure."

212

"No," Pask said quietly. "Without the proper recovery time, Pashka will certainly perish during the procedure. And it is sad to say that I will most likely encounter some misfortune—some medical complication from my nefarious acts that does not manifest itself until it is too late for them to save me."

Dorain's eyes narrowed. "What are you saying?"

"I wonder if the Council would find it convenient if there were no one among the Peacemakers to question their guidance in these horrible events. How nice it shall be to be applauded as the heroes in this tragedy—the darkest days of the Peacemakers."

Dorain watched him, his mouth agape. "You don't mean to say—"

"But we do."

"The Elders will not—"

"The Elders were gone before your sister and her ill-fated companions were dragged kicking and screaming from the surface of that planet to be tortured and put down like animals," Pask spat, her eyes glinting. "They are still punishing them, even now."

"What do you mean?"

Pask shook her head, her eyes cast down to the floor. "You would weep to know how many we have lost. We have sacrificed much and gained nothing."

"Jo'sha will not—"

"Jo'sha walks around freely. He no longer hides behind a suit. He has been welcomed into the ranks of the Council and serves as one of their agents."

"He is in disguise as one of them, but he does not serve them. I saw it when we rescued my sister. He is fighting to protect her. He is taking a huge risk and fighting for all of us."

"A convincing act, isn't it?" Pask said darkly. "But, tell us, how long has he left you down here, slowly starving to death?"

Dorain found that he had neither the desire nor the will to reason with them. Whether or not he admitted it to himself, he had known the truth for some time.

They were still for a time. Dorain looked at the thin window and let his eyes linger on the blue planet beyond. In his mind, he saw the face of the red-headed girl as he turned and left her on the floor of the transport room.

"Why did you do it?" Dorain whispered.

"Do what?" Pask asked.

"You would have died had I not pulled you out of that room. Why sever the gas line, knowing you would die? Why risk everything for my sister?"

Dorain turned to look at the doctors, and he caught a look in their eyes that he could not fully understand.

"Your sister is among one of the most beautiful creatures we have ever come across."

"Why?" Dorain whispered.

"She gives us hope."

"How?"

The doctors examined him, and for all the knowledge he had of the universe, he could not presume what was going through their minds.

"It is not something we should share," they said quietly.

Dorain nodded, but he did not look away from their penetrating eyes.

"I am blind," he said. "And your sacrifice was for nothing because of me."

They watched him, waiting.

"I held on to my ideals so tightly, and now ..."

Pask's eyes were sympathetic. Slowly, the doctors settled beside Dorain, and he felt a rush of relief as they pressed their body against his, and the warmth stirred something inside of him.

"And do you regret that?" Pask asked. "What do you believe now?"

Dorain lowered his head in shame. "There is a blackness consuming me. I can feel it in my second heart now. I do not know what it is."

"Fear," Pask said quietly. "Grief. Anger. Rage. Hatred."

"What is it doing to me?"

Dorain closed his eyes, but all he could see was the face of the red-headed girl as he abandoned her to her fate.

"I have thoughts in my head now. I think things that I never would have considered before. I used to have such hope for the future. What has happened?"

"This ship is rank with grief," Pask replied. "It has found a home in all of us."

"Is that what all of this is?" Dorain asked.

Pask nodded. "Somewhere in our universe, ships drift in pieces and there are loved ones who will never be recovered from the wreckage. Planets will burn now for them."

"All I can think about is my sister," Dorain said. "I wish nothing more than to have stopped her."

"We know," Pask replied.

"You know that you will never see your sister again?" she said gently.

"Yes, I know now," Dorain whispered.

"And tell us," Pask asked. "What shall you do?"

Dorain sighed, his body cold and heavy.

"I will grieve for my sister," he said. "But for the love I have for her and everything we worked for and believed in, I will not be like them. It is the last thing I can do for her."

Chapter 13

I don't know where Jillian came from, but she had bolted through the kitchen, leaping over our legs, before Tori and I could get to our feet and race down the hall to where Marie was still screaming. I attempted to follow, my heart racing at the thought of what horrible thing had found Marie, only to find that the sudden movement made the world spin around me. I collapsed shakily back onto the ground, too weak to get up on my own.

How much blood had I lost in the past few days? That, mixed with the fact that I couldn't remember the last time any of us had eaten.

Oh, and of course, I was still slowly dying. When had my mouth gone so dry? I could feel my lips cracking as I asked Tori to help me to my feet. My mouth was so parched that swallowing was becoming a pointless task.

I ignored it. Dehydration was the least of my concerns.

I had to brace myself against Tori as we both stumbled down the hall. It surprised me how gentle she was with me, one arm behind my back and the other clutching one of my wrists, my arm behind her neck, slowly matching my stride as I moved toward the now silent Marie and Jillian as quickly as I could.

We found Marie on the floor, curled up against the wall, sobbing. Jillian was collapsed against a door, clutching the doorknob with pale knuckles. Her face was stark white and haunted.

"We need to go," Jillian said, her eyes wild and her voice hysterical. "I want to go! *Now!*"

"What's in there?" Tori asked.

"A guy," Jillian whispered. Marie sobbed harder.

Tori hesitated, eyeing the door. "Is he okay?"

I looked at the floor, and that's when I noticed the thick dust under our feet. Jo'sha's voice rang in my head: *The bots will be back to finish the job.*

The hair on the back of my neck stood on end. Jillian was right. It was time to go.

"He's everywhere," Jillian said, growing ever paler. "He had a gun. His head …"

"Why is this happening to us?" Marie wept, clinging to the wall. "What did we do?"

I saw the family photos on the wall: a smiling mother and father with three cheerful boys. They all looked to be under the age of ten. The smallest child, maybe a year old, had long brown hair and a bottom tooth that stuck out too far. The mother had long, curly dark locks and glasses. The father had kind blue eyes and a thick brown beard.

It was a beautiful family. The portrait reminded me of the family picture hanging on the wall at my parents' house. I remembered going back to hug them before I walked out the door. I had thought I would come back. I didn't know that that was the last time I was ever going to see them. I didn't know they would die that day. And if I had, what would I have done?

I should have saved them. I should have gone looking for them. *I had left them.*

I looked back at Jillian, Marie, and Tori. But at what cost did trying to save my family come? I couldn't have saved them all.

I chased the thoughts from my mind. I never could have saved them. Jo'sha told me there was no chance. I knew I had to forgive myself.

I also knew I would never be able to.

Jillian was watching me, her eyes begging me to tell her *why* our families had to die. *Why* we had to grieve for them while fighting for our lives against a seemingly insurmountable adversary. The look of sheer helplessness on her face was heartbreaking.

I just wanted my family to know how very sorry I was, and if I couldn't tell them I was sorry, could I just say goodbye? Was that so much to ask of the world?

"Not nearly enough to deserve this," I whispered, swallowing back the emotions.

There was nothing I could do for the family in the picture. There was nothing I could do for my parents and my sister's family. I had to focus on the small family I had left.

Tori released me and moved toward the door.

"What are you doing?" Jillian said, clutching the doorknob tighter, the look on her face just daring Tori to try to pry it back open and expose the horror within.

"We could use a gun," she said.

"No guns!" I shouted, grabbing her shoulder and pulling her away from the door.

"*No guns?*" Tori snapped at me, turning on her heel to face me. "In case you haven't noticed, the only thing we've got going for us is you, and I don't know if you've looked in a mirror lately, but I've seen corpses that look better than you. When your fake body finally kicks it, we're sitting ducks. I think we're entitled to a little self-defense!"

"If a bot finds you with a weapon—if you use a weapon on a bot, it *will* single you out," I snapped. We had just gone through this! Did the girl *ever* listen?

"What about other people? Looters. People who would hurt us. What if we run into people like that? I've seen the news! The world ends and all the crazies come out to play!"

"It's sad that you think the next person you come across only wants to hurt you," I said to her, my voice grave.

"I'm realistic," she shouted. "I've seen it on TV! When supplies run out, people will be at each other's throats! They'll all turn into a bunch of animals!"

I stared at her, eyes hard. "Other beings saw you and thought the same thing."

I turned to Marie, indicating that the gun discussion was over. "Go get supplies, okay?"

She nodded and got to her feet, sniffling and wiping her nose with the sleeve of her shirt. She brushed the dust from her pants.

She paused. "What is it?"

"What is what?" I asked, though I knew all too well what she was thinking. I felt repulsion as she looked at the dust covering her hands, her brows furrowed.

The last thing in the world I wanted to do right then was tell her the truth of what we were all standing in.

"The dust," she said. "It's too thick to be house dust."

"It's left behind by bots," I told her, and she nodded, accepting my explanation, much to my relief. There were some things the humans were better off not knowing.

She wandered down the hall and disappeared into a bedroom. I could hear her stripping sheets off a bed. She walked out the door, shaking dust off a child's comforter. It scattered in the air, covering me. I had to fight the urge to gag. She wadded the blue checkered comforter in her arms, then walked into the kitchen. I could hear her rummaging through the counters and drawers.

"Where's the wife's body?" Jillian whispered, though I could tell from her voice that she was figuring it out. Perhaps my face had given it away. "Where are the children? If the bots were here, why don't we see their bodies?"

I pursed my lips. I couldn't do it. I couldn't bring myself to tell her. We had seen people fall to the ground and die at our feet, but I just couldn't admit to them what would come next. It always seemed to me that it was the rational next step, *but actually seeing it* ...

"I guess they weren't here," I said, avoiding her gaze. Again I looked at the family portraits on the wall. The eyes of the family of five watched me, smiling from their frame. I would do them a favor and remember them that way. It was the only kindness I could show them.

We were wrong, I realized. Whatever logic we found in the bots, whatever mercy we thought we were so compassionately delivering— we were wrong. The father in the bathroom was more than enough proof that we were wrong. Yes, the deaths we gave them were painless, but what about before? What about the running and the terror before they fell? We were wrong.

It left a bitter taste in my mouth.

"How do they kill you?" Jillian asked. She finally released her grip on the door handle, looking at me with hollow eyes. "I want to know, in case I ever get caught by one. Does it hurt?"

"They aren't going to catch you," I said, and I meant it. They weren't going to touch her.

"But in case they do," she said.

I started to argue, but her eyes were begging. I felt the family on the wall staring at me. She wasn't just asking for herself.

"Please?" she whispered.

"It doesn't hurt," I said slowly. "The pulse stops your brain and heart instantly. It has something to do with the way your cells signal to each other. Honestly, I don't really know how it all works. I just know that everything stops. You're dead before you can feel the ground shake."

"Why?" Tori asked bitterly. "Why not just blow us up? Wouldn't dropping a bunch of bombs be faster?"

"It would be cruel," I whispered.

Not that I believed that anymore, but what else could I say but the words that had been branded into my mind over the centuries? I had believed them for so long. Without them, I had no explanation to give them.

"Cruel? If you're so worried about being humane to the poor little humans, why not just blow up the whole planet? Why make those stupid things hunt us down?" Tori challenged.

"We don't want a Purge. This is a Cleansing. We're letting the human race start over," I said. I left out the part that we hadn't meant to. We hadn't, right? I wouldn't be here if we had. At least that's what I was trying very hard to convince myself.

"So why not just use your lasers or satellites or whatever and just blast us?" Tori asked.

"It's a kind of natural selection," I said.

"It looks more like slaughter," Tori said, indignant.

"Most people never see them. Those who do don't usually get far."

Why was I arguing this? Why was I just spitting out memorized lines that I knew weren't true? If I couldn't even convince myself that they were true, how could I expect two suffering humans to believe me? Was it because I was embarrassed?

That was it, I realized. I was ashamed. I didn't want them to look at us—at me—like heartless monsters. We were good creatures, and this was all just a very bad ...

Mistake? Error? I couldn't call this anything like that. "Good people make bad choices, too" was not the kind of logic to be used in this situation. "Good people" did not commit genocide.

So, when all this ended, were we still good and benign? Was I?

I didn't feel like such a good person as I stood there in the dust and fed my loved ones lies.

"And that's humane?" Jillian asked, looking up at me from where she sat on the floor, still guarding the door. She looked so frail sitting there, so broken.

"It's the best that we can do," I said, but my voice was weak. I didn't know what to believe. We were supposed to be Peacemakers, the protectors of young planets, entrusted with their fragile development and well-being, and this is what we came up with when things went wrong? This was our fail-safe? This was the best mercy we could show the truly wicked?

"Go in there and tell him that," Jillian said coldly, her eyes boring holes in me.

Her words stung. I felt their icy, sharp edges gnawing at me. Did she really think I was okay with this? Almost twenty years of friendship and she acted as if she thought I was truly heartless. How could I not feel for the poor father, who was driven mad as a machine burst into his home and robbed him of his wife and tiny sons?

"You think we wanted this?" I yelled at her.

Again I felt the anger burning in my chest, the same anger I felt out in the trees after I was forced to leave Jo'sha lying in his own blood. It flared in my chest. I felt it spreading out through my veins. It was the kind of anger that would run wild if left unchecked, and at the moment, I wasn't in the mood to fight it back.

There was something about the burning that finally made me feel like I had some control in this world.

"This is your fault!" I screamed. I was tired of taking the blame for this! I was tired of being guilty and hated! They did this, the humans, with their wars and violence, with their inability to learn! They would blame everyone before they blamed themselves! No more!

"Our fault? I'm sorry! Did we send a signal out into space that said 'Hey! Come kill us?'" Jillian snarled.

"YES!" I yelled, my voice shrill. My head throbbed in protest. I winced and held my head, still wet and oozing red blood down my neck. I hadn't bothered to take the towel with me. The nanotechnology wasn't healing me. My guess was that they were overwhelmed with other tasks, like keeping me alive. I pulled my palm away and stared down at the glistening red.

And, was it just me or did everything feel like it was floating away?

The family was still watching me, smiling. I felt myself losing it. The anger was raging, taking hold. All I wanted to do was yell at them until I was hoarse. This was their fault! Why was I the one paying for what they had brought on themselves? Why was I the one bleeding all over the place? Why was I the one who had had her rights stripped away? Why did it have to be my entire life that ended after all of this?

"Guys!" I heard Marie yell from the back of the house. "Can you come out here?"

Her little voice snapped me out of it. I was standing there, fists clenched and nostrils flaring, glaring at two of my best friends. I felt the anger like poison, and I was ashamed.

"What is it, Marie?" I asked, trying to sound calm, though I could still hear the biting tone in my shaky voice. Jillian and Tori were glaring at me, but Jillian was on her feet now and Tori was moving toward the kitchen, leaving me to maneuver the house myself.

They were all angry at the bloodlusting alien all over again.

I started to follow. My legs felt heavy and wobbly, but I told myself to ignore it. I would just add it to the list of things wrong with my failing body.

"Please come here!" Marie shouted. The sound of it caused the three of us to rush out the back door of the house, where Marie stood on the back porch looking out into the distance.

I was the last to join the small girl at the door. Marie turned and looked at me, clutching the blue blanket to her chest. "Where did the cows go?"

I looked up. The field was clean. There were no corpses in sight. Even the birds were gone.

The bots will be back to finish the job...

"Run for the car," I whispered, but I knew we were too late; they had already seen us.

The car—a small red vehicle so old that the window tinting had turned purple— was in sight when we saw the first bot coming at us from the field. The girls had gotten to the car when two more appeared around the corner of the house. My dying body made me slow; I was still several feet behind them. The girls got in the car, but waiting for me would cost them time they didn't have. The bots were too fast. Without hesitation, I picked up a rock and flung it toward the first one. I missed, but all three turned their attention toward me, ignoring the three humans in the car.

"Allyson!" Marie called, panicked. The bots were moving toward me, coming between me and the car. I would never make it past them.

"Now would be a good time to start driving!" I shouted. I ran, darting toward the house and through the back door. The bots pursued, following me through the door one at a time. It slowed them down just enough for me to race through the house and out the front door, slamming it closed behind me before I felt the pulse.

Not dead.

The girls were waiting for me only a few feet away, car door open, Marie and Jillian waving me on. I jumped in, and Tori hit the gas before I had closed the door. I looked out the back window in time to see the bots bursting out the front windows of the house, force fields activating as the glass shattered around them.

"Left out of the driveway!" I shouted, remembering what Jo'sha had told me. Tori turned sharp, throwing me into Jillian, Jillian into Marie, and Marie into the window with a grunt. My head wound throbbed from all the running and roughness, but it was a dim whisper compared to the panic I felt as I watched the bots racing across the front yard toward us.

"What should I do?" Tori shouted, watching the bots catch up to us in the rearview mirror.

"Their aim sucks! Keep far ahead of them and swerve!" I shouted, as I watched the metal killing machines move closer.

That was easier said than done, though. The small dirt road was narrow and bumpy. The occasional pothole made my chest clench as the car hit it and lurched violently. The vanilla-scented tree hanging from the rearview mirror swung around as if possessed. I felt my brain rattling around in my head, the wound behind my ear reacting to every bump and bang. There was another pulse, and we got to live.

"This isn't working!" Tori shouted.

"Just get us to the road!" I shouted back.

The bots were closer—close enough for the next pulse to kill at least those in the back seat. We had only seconds to live, if that. I couldn't breathe. I couldn't take my eyes off them as I waited for the end to come. There was absolutely no escape that I could think of this time.

The lead bot flickered, a brief flash of its gray force field. It happened so quickly that I thought I'd imagined it, but then the other two did it. It was just a brief glint, but ...

You've got some people upstairs trying to help.

Bots didn't flicker.

I held my breath and prayed.

"Hit the brakes!" I shouted.

"*Are you mad?*" was Tori's response.

"Tori, hit the brakes! STOP!" I screamed. It had to be *now*. This was the only chance we would have before they killed us.

"Are you—" Jillian started to shout, panicking, but she was interrupted as Tori slammed on the brakes and we were thrown forward.

I felt the first impact, then the second, then the third. The car lurched and the back windshield cracked, but to my relief, it didn't shatter. Two bots went tumbling violently in different directions, their force fields flickering but failing to activate completely. When they hit the ground, they shattered into pieces. The third bot was nowhere to be found. My guess was that it was in pieces at the base of the car. Tori hit the gas, and we raced down the dirt road toward the highway.

"I will yell at you for being risky and stupid after I get done kissing you," Jillian said breathlessly, throwing her arms around me in a tight hug.

"How did you know that would happen?" Marie asked, staring at me.

"Bots don't flicker," I whispered as I leaned back in the seat, breathing a deep sigh of relief. Jillian and Marie collapsed beside me, shaken. I closed my eyes and repeated silent prayers for those who had saved our lives yet again. I didn't know how they did it or at what cost, but I knew I would never be able to repay them.

Somehow, though, I knew we wouldn't get this lucky again. You didn't get to outlive bots a third time. My friends upstairs knew I was in this area. They probably guessed when they sabotaged those bots. Now we were leaving my last-known location and the chip was gone. I knew that my guardian angels had disappeared with it.

The knowledge that my protection was gone left a sickening feeling in the pit of my stomach. No more bots dropping out of the air. No more failing force fields. The next set of bots would come at us full force.

I curled up in the corner of the seat and prayed that it wouldn't happen. It was all my throbbing head, trembling limbs, bleeding, cracked lips, and raspy lungs would let me do. As I sank into the seat, I let everything drift away, and felt lighter.

"Hey, look at that!" I heard Tori say after what felt like an eternity. I heard her, but I didn't open my eyes to see her.

"Tennessee!" I heard Marie squeal. I felt her move past me to crawl into the passenger's seat. Again, I didn't open my eyes. I wanted to, but I didn't.

"Hey, Allyson! How far are we now?" Tori called.

I wanted to respond, I really did, but I felt so tired. It seemed like too much effort to speak, so I just sat there quietly, my eyes closed, and felt myself drifting farther away. I was falling into the dark …

"ALLYSON!" Jillian shouted. My eyes slowly fluttered open as she shook my shoulders, but I realized that I couldn't feel her hands on me. She was blurry and quickly slipping away from me.

"Allyson, look at me!" Jillian said, grabbing me by the jaw and forcing my eyes to meet hers.

I didn't see her anymore.

"*Shit*," I heard Jillian shout. "I think she's in shock!"

Everything fell away.

When I opened my eyes again, I was lying on a tile floor, looking up at a stark white ceiling with fluorescent lighting that was much too bright.

"She's up!" I heard Marie say. I looked over and saw the curly-haired girl sitting cross-legged beside me, watching me intently. We were in a bathroom somewhere—I didn't know where. It was small and cramped. Marie was leaning against a wall. I could make out Jillian and Tori at my feet, Jillian pressed up against the bathroom door and Tori sitting in the handicapped stall. I felt something cold on my forehead and reached up to feel a pile of wet napkins on my forehead.

"What happened?" I slurred. I coughed. My throat felt dry and raw. My tongue stuck to the roof of my mouth as I spoke, and my saliva was so thick, it was hard to swallow.

"Get the water," Marie said, as she slid behind me and dragged me into her lap, trying to pull me into an upright position. She wasn't a strong girl, and though I tried to help her, I was too weak and incoherent to help anyone, and the end result was me half-propped in Marie's lap while Jillian held a bottle of water to my lips.

I swallowed, suddenly realizing just how thirsty I was, but I ended up coughing up the water on myself, Jillian, and Marie. They didn't seem to mind.

"Slower," I heard Jillian say, and when she put the bottle to my lips again, I obliged, taking a tiny sip from the water bottle.

We sat like that until the bottle was empty. Tori opened another one and handed it to Jillian, but by then I was strong enough to sit up. Jillian handed me the water bottle and I sat with my head in my hand, wishing the throbbing headache would go away.

"What happened?" I asked again.

"What do you think?" Tori said.

"We didn't realize you were bleeding so badly," Marie said. Her tone of voice sounded ashamed. "You passed out."

My hand went to the back of my head. I felt two butterfly strips covering the wound, but I didn't feel any blood. The wound was clean, albeit still very angry.

"It stopped about two hours ago," Tori said. "But ..."

"You don't look well," Marie whispered.

I nodded, understanding. The nanotechnology had finally had its limit. Over the past few days, I had felt the ups and downs. Sometimes I didn't really feel that bad. Other times I was sure I would fall over dead at any minute. I sensed that this was different. I had gone over the edge and would spiral downward until the end.

I hadn't really thought it would go this way. We had been running from bots, the Council of Traltix, and pulse cannons. I hadn't thought my own body would be the thing that would end this journey for me.

I had felt relief when the Aquir in the woods took me. Now, I felt bitter. I had done it. We were in Tennessee. The caves were only a few miles away.

But it was time for me to die. I didn't know how long I had. Maybe a few hours? I certainly didn't have any longer than a day. I could feel death. I didn't feel pain, but I felt ... a lack of life. Things were stopping, giving up. I felt my systems ebbing away.

I felt betrayed by them. I had committed to this madness. I had fought tooth and nail, summoning all the courage and willpower I had and more, and now my own body was dying.

It was one of the cruelest jokes life had ever played on me.

"Allyson?" Jillian asked, watching me carefully.

"The water is making me feel better," I lied. "I should probably eat something."

"There's plenty of stuff here," Marie said.

"I'll go find something," Tori said, rising to her feet.

"Don't go alone," I said, looking toward Jillian. I saw the conflicted look in her eyes.

"Go with her," I said. "I've got Marie."

Reluctantly, she got to her feet, and they both walked out the door, leaving me sitting on the floor next to Marie.

I felt the sweet girl staring at me. I felt the tension in the air as she tried to think of something to say.

"Allyson—" she started, but I cut her off.

"I drank a lot of water," I said.

I couldn't stand to hear words of sympathy or pity right now. She closed her mouth and lowered her eyes, wounded, but I knew that she understood. She nodded and stood up, offering me her hands.

Getting up was painful. As I pushed myself up, my right leg went out from under me, nearly sending me crashing to the ground on my bottom. Marie caught me, and together we slowly got me to my feet. My knees felt nonexistent. I was certain my shaky legs would give out again at any second, but I pretended as if they wouldn't, and shuffled my way into the nearest bathroom stall and locked the door behind me.

"I'm going to find you some clean clothes to wear," Marie called, as a door squeaked open.

"Thank you, Marie," I said gratefully, and I heard her leave.

The brown urine told me that this body wasn't going to need to relieve itself much longer.

When I stumbled to the mirror, I looked at the yellow skin and eyes, blue veins bulging in my neck, slightly blue lips and haggard face, and wondered how my friends were able to look at me. I looked like a walking corpse.

I didn't feel pain anymore, which I considered a blessing and a curse. Everything was becoming numb. I could barely feel the cold water running over my hands and face. The dangling metal chain from the handcuffs around my wrists made scraping sounds against the porcelain sink.

I made eye contact with the girl in the mirror. "One more day," I whispered to her. "Please, I just need you to hang on for one more day."

I couldn't die now. My friends weren't safe yet, but we were so close!

I slammed my fists on the sink. This wasn't fair!

Someone pounded on the door. "Ally!" I heard Jillian whisper. Her voice sounded urgent.

She threw the door open and I saw the alarm in her eyes as she looked at me.

"What?" I asked.

"That ship just went by!"

Oh, god! Not that! Of all the things in the world, that was the last thing we could handle! I couldn't run anymore, and I knew Jo'sha wouldn't be on this ship.

As fate would have it, this was the moment all of my luck ran out at once.

I panicked. Jillian helped pull me toward the window at the front of the store, but I dropped to my hands and knees before I could get there, approaching it at a shaky crawl, just barely peeking my head above the window sill. I looked just in time to see the hovercraft disappear behind a building down the street.

"It knows we're here!" Tori whispered. She and Marie had taken cover behind a display only a few feet away.

I looked back out the window, arching my neck to get a better look. I saw a brief ripple in the road, like looking at one of those puddle mirages on black pavement in the middle of a Florida summer, and I blinked my eyes, confused by the trick of the light. Then it was gone.

"They just put up a net!" I whispered. They were blocking all escapes, making sure we couldn't get away this time.

228

It hit me with full force that we were not going to escape this time. I looked back at my friends, so small and helpless, and felt the tears building up behind my eyes.

"A net? They don't need a net!" Jillian hissed, bobbing her head above the bottom of the window. "We're right here! We're sitting ducks!"

"We need to run!" Tori said as loudly as she dared.

"*Net!*" I said in return.

A car rushed past—a blue SUV of some kind—heading right for where I had seen the net. It was going to get caught! I started to stand, to try to wave them down and warn them, but Jillian grabbed my arm. I looked at her, completely at a loss as to what to do. We couldn't just let them drive into the net!

"There's nothing we can do," she said, and I could see that it hurt her to do nothing, too.

I looked up. The car was caught. A woman ran from the driver's side. She had long brown hair and looked to be in her early twenties. A man and a woman of similar age ran from the back seat.

My heart leapt into my throat. I pictured an audience of Gangers, all standing still, watching a crowd of alien beings.

"I know her!" I said. Even with the distance and my failing eyesight, I recognized the woman I had stood next to at the meeting with the Elders. "She's from my unit! She's a Ganger!"

I watched with horror as two humanoid creatures in suits emerged from behind the buildings. These two had obviously learned from past mistakes. They had themselves perfectly in place when the Ganger and two humans ran right toward them. The Ganger fell in a blast of light. The earth shook once, signaling the pulse that took out the humans. I closed my eyes and sat back against the wall, sickened.

"They killed them!" Marie squealed.

"Shut *up*," Tori whispered, "or they'll come kill us too!"

But even if they sensed we were here, they had no intention of coming after us. There was a flash of light. When I looked again, the humans' bodies were gone. The wind kicked up ash. It twirled and spun through the air where the two ill-fated humans had fallen. The two suits carried the Ganger woman away and disappeared, their ship vanishing into the sky.

I was too stunned to move. I didn't recognize my colleague in her human form, but it was someone from my unit. I *knew* her. Of all the Gangers I worked with, there wasn't one I didn't feel a sense of kinship toward. Gangers were good. They had devoted their lives to helping lesser races, and that one had come back to this nightmare and chosen those two humans to protect. They were probably all she had left.

And the Council of Traltix had come down here and killed them right in front of her. They didn't even hesitate. The kind of pain she had to be experiencing—my heart broke for her. I felt anger at the heartless creatures that had caused her that pain. How could they go through with it? Did they even have consciences?

Marie was the first to rise. She rushed out of the building, slapping at her head, sending a small cloud of dust into the air. She wiped at her face and spat repeatedly.

"People!" she shrieked. "Oh, my god! They're all over me!"

"Marie!" I shouted, somehow managing to clamber to my feet and rush out to her. I grabbed her and pulled her close. "It's okay. It's okay."

She put her head in my chest and sobbed, grabbing my shirt in tight fists.

"Why?" she cried, her voice muffled.

"I wish I knew," I said, staring down the street as the wind scattered what was left of the two humans my colleague had so desperately tried to save. I closed my eyes and held Marie close as she cried.

We all got back into the car quietly. Marie cried for the longest time, but finally fell asleep, with her head tucked in my lap. Tears had created wet streaks on her dusty face.

"You should sleep, too," Jillian said beside me. "It might help."

"I'm fine," I said, as I brushed a strand of curly hair out of Marie's face. I gently slipped her glasses off and tucked them into my shirt.

"Tori and I can get us the rest of the way," she said. "We found some maps back at the store. The caves aren't far."

I shook my head vehemently—after what we had just seen, I refused to close my eyes and wake up to piles of ash.

"Really," Tori said from the driver's seat. "Microwaves will or will not attack us whether or not you're awake. Scary suited men will or will not fry us to bits. Please, get some sleep. It can only improve your condition."

For all her sarcasm, Tori sounded genuinely compassionate—she may have even been making an attempt at being gentle.

"What if I don't wake up?" I whispered, meeting Jillian's eyes. That scared me more than aliens with pulse guns, and it was more of a reality than the Council of Traltix sweeping down to smite us. This body was far gone. The only thing keeping it going was willpower. If that disappeared—if I relented, even for just a second, what would happen?

"I'll make sure you do," Jillian said.

There was a genuine softness about her face that made me trust her. Tori eyed me from the rearview mirror with a look of real concern. I was exhausted. Every fiber of my being told me to keep my eyes open. I only needed to be alert for a few more hours. I could give up when we reached the caves, but I was just *so tired*.

I looked down at Marie, sleeping peacefully in my lap. Finally, she wasn't crying. She wasn't scared.

I just needed a minute to not be scared, too.

I nodded, and Jillian let me lean against her.

As I closed my eyes, I saw piles of ash blowing in the wind.

CHAPTER 14

I dreamed of my dad. He was sitting at a picnic table under a pavilion by the beach we used to go to all the time when my sister and I were kids. I was barefoot. I felt the warm, white sand between my toes and the sun beaming down at me, and I smiled. The sea-grape trees rustled in the wind. There was a big one not far from the pavilion, I remembered. Growing up, Jillian and I loved to climb high up into its branches. Halfway up, there were two forked limbs. Jillian and I would take our lunches up there and watch the ocean. She sat in the higher branch and I sat in the lower. We carved our names up there when we were eleven with a pocket knife she had stolen from her stepdad. I scolded her for stealing it, but she just rolled her eyes. Our names were still up there. I wondered who would see them next, the names of two little girls who lived before the world ended.

My mom, sister, and nephews sat down at the picnic table. My sister's husband, Ethan, came up behind them. I never saw much of him. He was always away on business trips, but he was a good man. He loved my sister, and he doted on those boys, taking them fishing every weekend he was home. I thought it was a barbaric practice, but Michael and Aidan loved to go out on the boat. Michael was the fisher, always trying to reel in the biggest fish to please his dad. Aidan was scared of them. He would never come close enough to touch one, but if you held it out to him, he would stand there and watch it, a big grin plastered across his face. He was my partner in crime when I went with them, helping me put the "pretty fishies" back into the ocean, waving as they swam away.

Dad placed on the table a box of chicken strips from a fast-food place down the street. I laughed. It was the same kind he used to bring when he would surprise me at school on Fridays, right down to my favorite honey mustard sauce. Truth was, I never really ate them. I just picked at them to make it look like I ate them and devoured the French fries on the side. It didn't take Dad long to catch on, and over time, my parents learned that my vegetarianism was a permanent thing. Still, there were certain things that always had a place in my memories.

I watched my family for the longest time, but they didn't see me. They laughed and joked. Michael and Aidan built a castle in the sand, complete with stick and leaf flags and decorative seashells—even a bridge and a moat. Dad and Ethan sat out in the sun, talking and enjoying the warmth, while Mom and Meredith walked in the surf together. They were all happy. They were okay. They didn't blame me.

"Ally, wake up!" Marie shouted, shaking me vigorously. I woke with a start and nearly head-butted Jillian.

"Mom? Dad?" I muttered sleepily, still partially within my dream world. It only took me a minute to realize where I was, and fear gripped me. I propped myself in Jillian's lap and stretched to see out the window, looking for the bot or hovercraft that was chasing us, my heart racing. Seeing nothing that warranted panic, I glanced around, confused.

"Sorry," Marie said, looking guilty. "You stopped breathing."

"Oh," I said, not quite sure how to take the information. I was groggy. I could still hear the ocean waves crashing in the background. I tried to rub the sleep from my eyes, but it didn't help. Everything felt heavy. I just wanted to go back to sleep.

"Just for a second," Marie said. "But it kind of freaked us out."

"No kidding," I muttered. I sat up and stretched, feeling stiff. My head throbbed where the wound was, pulsing as blood went to my head, but I didn't feel any pain. I tried to ignore the twitch in both of my hands. I rubbed at my wrists where the metal cuffs had dug into my skin. There hadn't been anything at the general store that could get the cuffs off, so I was stuck with them.

"How much longer do you have?" Jillian asked quietly, avoiding my gaze.

"I don't know," I said, shrugging. "A few hours? A day? Two?"

Jillian was quiet, chewing her fingernails in the corner, pretending to look out the window. The reality of my limited time had finally set in for all of us. I had never really talked to them about leaving, about a time when they would have to go on without me, but the truth was, my end in this story would play out one of two ways: either I would die or the Council of Traltix would take me. Either way, I would end up back in my alien body to serve out my punishment.

At least I hoped that would be the case.

Maybe I should have prepared them better. Maybe I should have prepared myself better. Looking back, I hadn't really thought about what would happen after all this. I tried to imagine what life would be like for them once this was all over. The world would be reduced to five million humans, a far cry from the over seven billion that inhabited it before the bots. People would have to band together to survive. Their race wouldn't have to start from scratch, though. All of their knowledge—volumes of books, scientific advancements, medicines, technology—was still there; they would just have to relearn it, what with most of their advanced minds destroyed with the big cities. There would be no governments to tell them what to do; they would have to build them again, using knowledge from the past to choose the best leaders and representative bodies. Most people would have to go into farming for the race to survive, as slowly but surely the preserved foods on grocery store shelves expired or ran out. It would be decades before their species could move forward again as they struggled year after year to learn how to adapt to this life, but they would. I had seen it before. The human race would come back. I found comfort in that. I wondered if the Peacemakers would rebound as well. I knew that, high above the Earth, we were descending into chaos. Would we still be around to help the humans?

Did I even want us to be?

"Look on the bright side," Tori piped in, snapping me out of my stupor. "You'll make it long enough to get to the caves."

She pointed to a sign that said we had forty miles to go. I sat back, feeling as if a great weight had been taken off my shoulders. I let out a breath. It felt like I had been holding it for days. We weren't out of the woods yet, but I knew we were going to make it. We couldn't come this far only to fail. I closed my eyes and silently thanked those who had helped us: my brother, Jo'sha—everyone.

"What's there?" Marie asked.

"I have no idea," I said. "No one told me. They just said I had to get you there."

"Maybe it's a resistance!" Tori said. "You know, people or aliens or whatever who have figured out how to take out the bad guys!"

"I don't think so, Tori," I said, sighing.

"Why not? They have to have a weakness. I'm sure someone can figure it out."

"Of course they have a weakness," I said. "But you have to understand that they aren't bad guys."

"Excuse me?" Tori said incredulously. "They're killing us. They're going to kill us all and take our planet or something, like in the movies. They've used up all their resources, and they've come to the Earth to harvest what they need. Oh, my god! What if they've come to harvest *us*?"

"Which is why they've vaporized everyone," Jillian muttered. "Genius, Tori, you figured them out."

I leaned back in the seat and prepared myself for yet another argument, but I was too exhausted and relieved to be irritated. At that moment, nothing could darken my mood. Everything was going to be okay—at least for them, and with that in mind, life seemed a little brighter.

They were just children, I reminded myself. Children didn't learn if you didn't have patience, so I sat back and was calm. What would my race have thought millennia ago?

"Any race with the kind of technology you've seen is smart enough to fix its own problems without your planet," I explained. "Your planet is suited for you, not us. Most species wouldn't be able to digest your food or drink your water. Some of us wouldn't be able to handle even the most basic of bacterium. Your planet is useless to us—even deadly."

"Well, what about raw minerals, like gold or coal or something?" Tori argued, not giving up on the they-want-to-steal-our-planet idea.

"Those are easy to make," I said. "And they aren't really all that valuable."

"Overpopulation. They need more space."

"I just told you that this planet isn't suited for them."

"They can wear suits or terraform—"

I shook my head, immediately derailing her argument.

"Then why the hell are they killing us?" Tori exploded. "Is it fun? What? They have their own reality TV show: *Let's Kill the Humans*? 'On this episode, let's see how the humans handle evil microwaves!'"

I looked at Tori, fuming in the driver's seat. She had a quick temper and the mouth of a sailor. She didn't make the best life choices, sometimes stumbling into the apartment drunk and belligerent in the middle of the night. Those nights had become rare, but they had happened. Now she mostly stayed in the apartment and drank by herself. She was dark in more ways than one. Her wardrobe was comprised of blacks, reds, and grays, silver spikes and skulls on all her jewelry. She didn't like bright colors. She liked horror movies. She played violent video games.

She wasn't the only one with dark qualities, though. Even sweet Marie had her moments. And wasn't it Jillian who, as a small child, had gotten angry enough to push a little boy off a jungle gym? Even human children, the most innocent of them, could hurt one another.

"We're scared of you," I said quietly. "You're the bad guys. At least, you could be."

"Us?" Marie squeaked.

I looked at the three young, naïve human faces. They had fiery tempers and were prone to attack and destroy things they didn't understand. They were arrogant and rude. They thought they were invincible, and all the while they had no idea what was really out there. They had no notion that there were creatures millennia old and capable of technological feats that they could only dream of. They were blind to so many things. And yet, they had so many wonderful qualities. I had seen Tori sit through an afternoon of Marie's favorite TV show, which we all knew she absolutely hated, because Marie's mom had called to tell her that her old cat had died while she was at school. Marie volunteered at a soup kitchen with her church almost every weekend she went home, and as part of the education program at school, she tutored kids at a nearby elementary school at least once a week. She never said a mean word. She was always respectful. She was sweet and meek and kind, and she would do anything for you— not because she had been raised to be religious and thought it was some sort of requirement, but because that was just Marie. She was just that good.

Jillian had been by my side for almost this entire cycle. She was my best friend. She was in the nursing program because she wanted to help people. She wanted to save lives. She had been a lifeguard in high school. I remembered the day I heard she had jumped in a pool and saved a toddler. We were seven when she found a stray dog and snuck it home. Her dad had been furious, but that little girl found that dog's owners and returned it to its rightful owner. She could come off cold if you didn't know her. You never really knew what she was thinking; her face never revealed what she was feeling unless she wanted you to know. She sometimes had a quick temper and could be bullheaded, but Jillian was good. She was brave and selfless. Most of this life was memories of her. And my mom and dad? My sister and nephews? They were beautiful people. I loved them dearly. I missed them terribly.

Hadn't I seen wonderful things on this planet? Hadn't I seen miracles? Hadn't I seen things that, despite living for centuries and seeing countless worlds, still astounded me and left me in admiration of this race?

"I've kept you in the dark, haven't I?" I whispered. It was my fault that they didn't understand, I realized. They were good. They were capable. They deserved more than this.

They deserved the chance to grow up and thrive.

"You know some of the things that bother me?" I asked.

"You mean, like eating meat, slaves making our clothes, deforestation, animal cruelty? Vaguely," Jillian said sarcastically.

"We don't have slaves," Tori said. "There's an amendment."

"Check the back of your shirt," I said.

"What?" Tori said, clearly confused.

"Where was your shirt made?"

"Hell if I know," Tori said. "And so what? Some other country with slaves made it? That's not my fault."

"It is your fault," I said. "Your species is guilty of it."

"So you decided to kill us over where our shirts are made?" Tori said. "That's freaking ridiculous!"

"No," I said. "We didn't want you to die. We wanted to help."

"Well, you did a great job," Jillian muttered.

"I don't think it was us," I whispered, feeling the weight of the metal bonds on my wrists.

"But you just said—" Marie started to say, but I cut her short.

"Peacemakers have the sole ability to order a Cleansing or Purge. We did it, but I think someone forced it."

"Why would they do that?" Marie asked.

237

"There was a war," I said slowly, and as I spoke, more of the pieces were coming together. "It scared us. I think it scared some people so much that they would do anything to prevent another."

"A *war*?" Tori said. "Someone out there had a war, so they decided to blow us up? Who the hell cares? War happens! It sucks, but it happens!"

"On this planet," I said, shaking my head. "Not among the Higher Planets."

Tori opened her mouth to argue again, but I held up my hand, begging her to listen.

"You have to understand; it's not just us. Peacemakers aren't the only ones who know about humans. Other planets watch you, too. Even children study your species in their earliest educations. I was a child when I first learned about you—first saw you and your planet. Your lives are not secret. You even beam your television into space for us to see."

"Wait," Marie said, suddenly looking horrified. She understood. "You can watch our television? All of it?"

"*Yes*," I said, and the look on my face told the humans that I was less than pleased with that fact. Human television was, for the most part, disgusting.

"All the movies with the alien dissections and invasions and stuff?" Marie asked, looking me up and down. She was blushing. She was actually embarrassed. Jillian was biting her nails again, looking disturbed.

"The first time I saw one of those, I cried," I said. "I was a child Ganger. I thought your government was going to come get me and cut me open."

"I remember that," Jillian whispered, eyes focused on her lap. "We were twelve. My stepdad let us watch it. I thought it was just too scary. I called you a baby."

Her eyes met mine, and I saw the shame. "I didn't know."

"Oh, get over it! It was just a movie!" Tori said, rolling her eyes. "You know, entertainment?"

"That's what's so horrifying!" I exclaimed, my voice earnest. "Don't you get it? That *entertains* you. You daydream about blowing us out of the sky and ripping us apart with your bare hands, and it *entertains* you. You make movies about torturing your own kind, and

238

people pay money to watch them. Your children play games where they shoot people, and it's *fun* for them. We see your wars, your school shootings, your domestic violence, your kidnappings, your rapes and murders. *We see all of it.*"

"You can't have a perfect world," Tori said. "There's always darkness; we just—"

"No," I said. "Don't defend this. You're right. The world can't be perfect, but don't you dare try to justify how you can sit there and laugh while someone on your TV set screams as their internal organs get spilled onto the ground by some psychotic killer. *Don't you dare.*"

Tori stared at me. Her neck turned bright red and she sat there fuming, gripping the steering wheel with white knuckles. She had never been able to handle being told she was wrong, and I had hurt her pride.

"They don't understand," I explained. "I'm a Ganger. I've lived with you. I love you, even with your flaws. You're just children having trouble growing up. Peacemakers know that. We've been trying to help you learn, but you've pushed them too far."

Everyone was quiet for a while, Jillian biting her fingernails and Marie squirming in her seat, chewing on her necklace. Tori clutched the steering wheel, but I watched as her face got redder and redder. I was surprised when I saw a tear rolling down her cheek.

"You know what TV show we should have?" Tori finally said.

"*My Roommate is an Alien*," she said, grinning, but there were tears sliding freely down her cheeks. "That would be a good one. Three human girls and one little green Martian in a dorm room. The Martian is always asking us if we have homework or want help doing the dishes."

I couldn't help but laugh at the absurdity of it, but at least she was trying. At least she had heard me. I wasn't sure if they were really comprehending. You could shame a child into behaving and make him apologize for his actions, but you can never know if the child truly understands or just doesn't want to feel bad again.

Still, they were at least listening to me.

"I'm blue," I said softly. "And I'm not little. You're thinking of a Xiaxia."

Laughter erupted from Tori's throat. She slapped a hand over her mouth, but she couldn't stop the giggles. "You're shitting me! You're *blue*?"

Marie looked thoughtful. "If there's no resistance—if there's no stopping this—why are you here? Aren't you fighting against them? Didn't you fight the aliens in that ship?"

I smiled, but it was a weak smile. "It's already almost over. A few more days and we'll be done. I don't know what I'm doing," I said. "I'm just as helpless as you are."

"But you've been fighting," Tori said. "You have a mission, don't you? Someone sent you as covert ops or something?"

"I've just been protecting you," I said. "That's it."

"Why?" Jillian asked. "What makes us so important?"

"I think," I said, slowly working it out in my head. "I think we know that, one day, history will look back on us, and it will be in horror. This will be the shame of the Peacemakers, that we ever let this happen, regardless of the reason. I don't think some of us can live with that—I can't. I think this is our only chance to redeem ourselves; to let history know that there were those of us who refused to just sit there and watch it happen. That there were some of us who were not afraid to fight what we knew was wrong."

"What will happen to you?" Jillian asked.

"Nothing I'm not okay with," I said, and I felt peace for the first time in what felt like a very long time. Whatever punishment they had waiting for me, I regretted nothing. If I had known my fate before this—if they had told me what the consequences of my actions would be—I'd do it again.

"Has this happened before?" Marie asked.

I nodded somberly. "It's not something we are proud of."

"Have you ever totally killed a planet off?" Tori asked. "You know, no one gets to live?"

"Once," I whispered.

"What did they do?" Marie asked.

"They were a terrible race. They lived deep underground. They never went to the surface of the planet—they never saw the sun. They were extraordinarily intelligent, but with their intelligence came an unnatural lust for blood and destruction. They destroyed and polluted everything, and when there was nothing left, they turned on

240

each other. The Peacemakers tried to help, but we couldn't adapt. We couldn't fit in. They rooted out each of our Gangers and Impersonators, and slaughtered them. When we lost all hope for them and finally realized that somehow nature had gone awry, that they had been designed to be monsters, we turned our technology on them. We caused mass volcanic eruptions that flooded their underground world with magma. We melted the planet alive."

They stared at me, their eyes wide with horror.

"*You can do that?*" Tori said, nearly hysterical. "You can freaking play with nature and *melt us?*"

"Yes," I whispered. Sometimes, the power the Peacemakers possessed overwhelmed even me.

"Who were they?" Marie asked.

"The Maedrogans, the burned people of Maegora, the planet that burned," I said.

"Maegora?" Marie said, "Isn't that—"

"My home planet?" I said, smiling gently as I remembered my faraway home. "Yes."

"How?" Jillian asked. "You told us you're a Thellessian. You're not a Maedrogan."

"I can't even pronounce what we call ourselves in this body," I told her. "But in the Common Tongue, *Thellessian* translates as 'the species that rose from the ashes,' only, that isn't quite right. My ancestors came from the ocean."

I thought about my home planet. I had always thought it beautiful, but for those who knew its history, just the sight of it could inspire dread. The land was white, stripped of life long ago and left to bleach under the three sun-like stars. Precious minerals had been unearthed as magma burst from underneath the ground and carried them to the surface, the planet's way of showing the eyes that watched it that, one day, beauty would return. Black, petrified trees, as large as houses, with twisted, knotted limbs that reached toward the sky, blanketed the planet in thick forests. When the volcanoes erupted and belched sulfur into the sky, the entire ecosystem of the planet changed. The ocean, left relatively untouched by the seas of molten rock, experienced a mass die-off, but red algae appeared as the primary ocean dweller, turning the oceans blood red. For centuries, it was said to represent the blood on the Peacemakers' hands for what they had done, but when the first Thellessian emerged from the waters, they realized what had really happened. My race, derived from a deep-sea organism, had evolved to be one of the most peaceful species the universe had ever known. Out of blood, something good was born.

I wondered if, millennia from now, people might look to Earth and think the same thing.

They asked questions for a while. Well, Marie and Tori did. Jillian was mostly quiet. They asked what my planet looked like, where it was, how many alien planets were nearby, what exactly a Peacemaker was, how long I had been one. Even when we stopped at yet another dreaded gas station, they clung to their seats, eyes bright with curiosity, one question followed quickly by another. I smiled the entire time, each question easing the dread off my heart. I should have told them from the beginning. I loved the wonder in their eyes. I loved finally being honest with them.

For the first time since I had been sent back to the planet, I felt calm and still.

"Five miles!" Tori finally shouted from the driver's seat, pointing to the sign that told us that we were almost at our destination. When we had stopped at the gas station, the girls had made off with half the candy in the store. We had been passing around candy bars and chocolate for miles. It was the first thing I had eaten in days. My weak body didn't respond to the food, but I could see the humans slipping into sugar comas. Tori was practically bouncing in the driver's seat. It was nice to see them in a state other than distress.

"What's under it?" Marie asked from the passenger's seat, pressing against the window to get a better look.

"What?" I asked. I craned my neck, trying to get a look at the lurking bot that was waiting to kill us, but I couldn't see anything.

"It's a person!" Marie squealed, practically crawling up the window in excitement. "I see a person!"

Tori hit the brakes. Sure enough, there was someone crouched beneath the sign, mostly hidden beneath a bush. Slowly, she stood up and waved her arms at us. Based on the supply of water bottles hidden in the tall grass beside the road, she had been camped there awhile.

"Ganger?" Jillian asked. She looked to me, waiting to see if I would give the signal to run.

"It could be," I said. I felt my heart pounding as the woman slowly made her way toward us.

"Bad Ganger?" Tori asked.

"Keep the doors locked and your foot near the gas pedal" was my response.

She walked toward us. She was Hispanic, guessing by her skin tone, and her long black hair was pulled back in a ponytail. Her jeans and shirt were stained with what looked like dirt and blood. She was wearing sunglasses, so I couldn't see her eyes. It made me nervous that I couldn't see part of her face. I couldn't get a read on her, gauge if she was friend or foe, but as she got closer, I could see that some of her skin was an unnatural shade of yellow, she walked with a slight limp, and her movements were painfully slow, as if she were sick or in pain or hadn't slept in days.

"She's part of my assignment," I said, sighing. "She's safe."

As she got closer, I realized I was giddy with excitement to see her. I rolled the window down as she approached, and she leaned in, looking everyone over, her arms crossed and expression nonchalant, as if she survived an apocalypse every day.

"I was beginning to think we'd seen the last Ganger," she said, grinning. Her voice was slightly masculine. "I haven't seen anyone else in over twenty-four hours."

"What are you doing out here?" I asked her. She looked tired and hungry. She had to have been waiting under that sign for hours. I was surprised she hadn't collapsed, but that was probably because she had braced all her body weight against the car. She looked together enough, perhaps even strong, but there were tell-tale signs that she was doing just as poorly as I was.

"I'll show you mine if you show me yours," she said. She turned her head to the side and pulled back a gauze patch, revealing a long, deep, angry cut. It had to be at least four inches long and an inch wide, as if someone had sliced part of her skull off. I held back the nausea and returned the favor. I turned my head and pulled my hair back so she could see the carnage behind my ear.

"Name's Roxana," she said, flashing her teeth. "Call me Rocky. Sorry to scare you. We just don't want anyone leading any Council goons or bots out here."

She opened up the back door beside Jillian. "Make room, tiny human!" she said, laughing as heartily as her failing lungs would let her, and slid in. She laid her legs against Jillian's lap, which caused Jillian to stare at me, confused as to how to handle the zealous Ganger. Even for a sick girl, she had a personality and a half.

"Hey, they know we're all tentacle-ly and stuff, right?" she said, still grinning with her teeth exposed.

I nodded while Jillian, Marie, and Tori tried to process our guest.

"Good," she said, crossing her arms and leaning back, looking completely relaxed in the back seat of the car. "Some people weren't told. You wouldn't *believe* the problems it's caused."

She looked back and forth between Marie, Tori, and Jillian.

"You got three," she said, looking grim. "That's better than most of us. I woke up in a morgue. By the time someone let me out, the emergency signal had been going off for a while. I managed to grab one guy—didn't even get his name. We got out of Memphis just before it was gone. Lost him at the first gas station I stopped at—didn't even see the bot behind the dumpster."

She looked at my wrists. "Nice jewelry. I imagine the Council gave you those. They chased me back and forth for a while before I realized they were following the chip. Had to cut it out myself. Passed out from the blood loss in the kitchen of some fast-food place."

I looked at the Ganger in the back seat: no personal boundaries, confident stature, the way she was so laid-back, even though we were sitting out in the open. Not to mention the fact that she had to flash her teeth every time she smiled.

"Talyn?" I asked. She looked at me and beamed, white teeth gleaming. It was always easy to spot a carnivorous species. They weren't very good at imitating species that evolved from prey animals, and humans were rarely so boisterous. If I recalled, Talyn's species was one of the few four-legged species to be able to adapt to a bipedal Ganger. I had always looked up to her. She was intimidating in her other form, to say the least, but she was a leader and she was strong in her convictions. If I could pick only one person to survive this disaster with, she'd make the shortlist. I smiled in return, glad to have her.

"What gave me away?" she asked. "Oh, hey, we're in the road. Drive, girl!"

"Are you a Thellessian?" Marie squeaked, eyeing her from behind the safety of the passenger's seat. Tori eyed her from the rearview mirror, and Jillian just sat there, too startled to move with a strange alien *sitting in her lap*.

"Thellessian?" she said, grinning, and her eyes fixed on me. "*Saira?*"

"You gave me away, Marie," I said, chuckling. I was ecstatic to have another Ganger around.

"Wait. Your name isn't Allyson?" Tori asked, confused.

Rocky threw her head back, laughing deep and loud, as if she hadn't heard anything that amusing in a while. I couldn't help but grin. She reached forward and slapped Tori on the arm, shaking her head as the poor girl eyed the two of us back and forth, wondering if what she had said was really that funny.

"I'm a Rux," she said, ignoring Tori's comment. "Think of a big lizard."

"A big lizard?" Tori asked. From the sound of her voice, I think she expected Rocky to start cackling again as soon as she opened her mouth.

"You know," Rocky said, shrugging. "Claws, teeth, scales, beady little eyes. I'm not very cute; even I'll admit that."

"Teeth?" Marie squeaked. Rocky winked at her, smirking.

"Don't worry, little human. We've evolved past eating little morsels like you, though I bet my ancestors took on food bigger than you. You'd barely be a bite."

Marie stared at me, the look on her face begging me to tell her she wasn't serious. I just shrugged.

"Stop at the campground. It's not too far of a walk through the woods to get to the caves," Rocky said, leaning forward to hover over my shoulder. "Your three will make twenty-six humans—haven't caught your names, by the way. You'll be the eleventh Ganger. We don't expect any more. Those of us who got off the ship ended up mostly in morgues. We've got one dude who woke up with some doctor hovering over him with a scalpel. Most of us just barely got away, then barely escaped the bots and the Council. We don't expect that the rest of us were as lucky."

"What's at the caves?" I asked.

It was the question we were all too afraid to ask.

"Us," she said, but her tone was grim. "If there's any particular significance to the caves, we haven't found it. It certainly won't protect the humans from the bots. The only reason they haven't found us yet is because of our little friends upstairs, but we don't expect that to last."

My heart fell. Part of me hoped that Tori had been right, that there had been a resistance. I had hoped for the fairytale ending, too, but I knew that the happiest outcome for my three humans would be that they would live through this to fight for survival for the rest of their lives. It was a grim future, but it was all I could give them.

"We're sending the humans off in a convoy tomorrow morning," Rocky continued. "They'll head for the coast and take some boats out into the ocean for a few days. The bots won't go into the ocean—no population density there. By the time they get back, it'll be over."

"*Boats?*" Tori erupted. "We're from *Florida*. We had an ocean right there!"

"I don't know what to tell you, little human," Rocky said. "We all hoped for better, but we got nothing. Our friends may have had plans for us, but they didn't have time to tell us, and they aren't going to. We've all assumed that they ran into problems of their own. Whatever it was, it never happened."

"So what was the point?" Tori shouted. "We've crossed two states and risked death for nothing!"

Rocky held up her hand. "No," she said. "You've got a group. Those of us who got out with enough information and had clear enough heads to figure out what was going on grabbed people we knew would be important. We've got three nurses, and we found two park rangers at the caves. You're going to need these people long after the bots are gone. Sure, you might have been able to survive the bots where you were, but what about when all the food is gone and you have no idea where to get clean water? What if you get sick? You've gone from three little girls to twenty people who will watch out for you."

"There were people in Florida! You have to do something!" Tori shouted. "You have to stop them! You were our only hope!"

"There's not that kind of hope here," Rocky said somberly. "We aren't saving the world. We just gave a few good humans another chance."

"You said the humans are going to the coast," Jillian piped in. "Where are the Gangers going?"

"We're dying," Rocky said in her gravelly voice, giving a small, nonchalant shrug. She made it sound like more of a nuisance than a crisis. "Our bodies are far away; that's why they stopped trying to pull us back. If these bodies fail here, our minds won't find their way back. Not all of them, anyway. We're sending you on your way tomorrow, then we're turning ourselves in before we find ourselves scattered and mad. We've done as much as we can."

"You can't do that!" Marie said.

"We have to," Rocky said matter-of-factly. Her eyes met mine in the rearview mirror, and I nodded. "There's always been only one end for us, and it's overdue."

I was quiet the rest of the way. I had known the end was near, but hearing Rocky say it made it that much more real. And tomorrow morning? I was having a hard time processing it, though I knew she was right. It had to be soon, and there was no use putting it off any longer. I looked at my three humans in the mirror and I felt true heartbreak. They were quiet, watching out the windows as Rocky tapped her finger on the window, humming as if all were right with the world.

Tori parked the car at the campsite, and we shoved as much food as we could into our pockets. Then we began the hike to the caves.

It was just a quarter mile from the campsite through the woods, but it was all uphill, and it had rained recently. The path had rivets in it; the wet, red clay was slick, and large stones and roots poked out to trip me at every step. Rocky and I did not do so well with the climb. Marie took my hand and pulled me along in the front, while Rocky, weak and weary from being out in the elements all day, had to be led up by Jillian, with Tori behind her to catch her in case she fell backward. We both stumbled quite a bit, but in the end, the trees parted and we were standing on a walkway paved with bleached red bricks. I looked up. Beyond the cottage-like convenience store, the mountains rose up in the distance. Trees as thick as weeds grew up their sides, and gray clouds, heavy with moisture and spitting the occasional fat drop of water at us, churned low at their peaks.

"I'm glad someone thought to grab chocolate bars," Rocky said breathlessly, as we all just stood there and stared, grateful that we had actually made it. "We've got a four-year-old who loves them."

Marie's face lit up. "I love kids."

"Good," Rocky said. "Someone's going to have to teach her how to read."

"I don't see the cave," Tori interrupted petulantly, gazing around at the dense woods and sheer rock walls that surrounded us.

Rocky pointed her finger at the convenience store, its windows completely blocked out by newspapers, magazines, and other paper articles. I realized that that was not an accident.

"Doesn't look like the entrance to a cave, does it?" Rocky said, grinning. "We're hoping everyone else thinks the same thing."

At the corner of one window, where the glass was left uncovered, something flashed. A pair of eyes was there and gone in an instant.

Then I heard a bell ding, and someone was running at us.

"Rocky!" I heard a small voice cry.

Rocky smiled and looked at us.

"Welcome home," she said, and with that, she took a step toward the end of our journey.

CHAPTER 15

A little girl with a mess of bouncy blonde curls ran across the bricks, scrambling down the slope leading to the cabin-like store, her tiny feet carrying her as fast as they could. Both shoes were untied, and the tangled laces were discolored by dirt and other elements of the earth. Keeping them tied was a chore for some poor soul. Her face was filthy and her hair was unkempt, with a single pink barrette just barely clinging to strands of knotted gold. There was red clay beneath her nails, and she had a radiant smile.

Her eyes were blue. The sight of them reminded me of everything I had lost.

Aidan, my nephew, had the same blue eyes, so bright and full of wonder. This little girl was his age, and there was no mistaking the childlike curiosity for the world that she possessed. The aura of innocence around her seemed such a contrast against the dark backdrop of the world that, for just a minute, I didn't know what to make of her. Her eyes, despite all she must have seen, had hope behind them, a naïve sense that life was still well and good and the world would always be a place of warmth and happiness.

Despite all that was wrong with the world, there before me stood one tiny beaming ray of light that still saw wonder and magic. Amid my grief, I couldn't help but feel hope.

"Rocky!" the child squealed, flinging herself at Rocky's legs. Rocky, despite her fatigue, scooped the child up and spun her around, the little girl kicking and laughing in her arms.

When the squealing stopped, those blue eyes were staring at me. They were inquisitive and slightly apprehensive. She looked at Rocky, her childish face scrunched as she tried to decide if she liked the four strangers in front of her. She liked Rocky, and she wanted to like Rocky's friends, but it was hard for a small creature to feel comfortable around four dearly traumatized intruders in a world where a lot of bad surprises were waiting for you.

"Guess what?" Rocky said as the little girl looked at us bashfully from over her shoulder.

"You found new people," the little girl said matter-of-factly.

Rocky gasped dramatically, feigning surprise. "Did I?" she said, giving us a wink. She pulled the child closer to her and whispered into her ear. "And guess what they brought you?"

The little girl eyed us curiously. She looked from Rocky to us with her innocent little face and thought really hard about what the tired, dirty strangers had brought her.

"I don't know," she sighed in her tiny voice, throwing her small hands into the air and giving a big shrug.

"They have *chocolate bars*," Rocky whispered into her ear. The little girl's eyes grew wide.

She squealed and wriggled out of Rocky's arms, ungracefully dropping to the ground on her bottom. Rocky laughed as she scrambled to her feet and leapt before us. Marie held a melted chocolate bar out to her, and she snatched it with a squeal of delight.

Rocky grabbed her by the shirt collar before she could disappear with it. "Say thank you, Kaitlin."

Kaitlin scurried back to Marie and threw her arms around her legs. The tension in Marie's face lessened as the little girl looked at her—an instant bond. Clouds of ashes disappeared from behind her eyes and were replaced by little golden curls. Marie looked at me and grinned slightly.

For a moment, seeing Marie relax made up for the fact that the entire trip here had been fruitless. It wasn't a resistance or a miracle, but there were finally smiles.

"Now, quick, before your aunt sees you with it," Rocky said, grinning.

Kaitlin ran back toward the store, just as a flustered woman with blonde curls came running out, panting. One look told me that she was a Ganger.

"Katie, what did I tell you about running away!" she cried. She looked so tired. She couldn't have been any older than I was, but her face was worn and her eyes were haunted—she had seen too much. She knew she was on the verge of losing everything. She was fighting a long, impossible battle, and the look in her eyes told me that she was trying desperately not to concede out of sheer exhaustion.

I knew the look. I understood.

Her bloodshot eyes met mine, and I felt us connect. Then her eyes wandered to the three women beside me, and she took in the face of each one. Her gaze moved to the little girl, and the sense of sacrifice and disregard for anything else in the world but that one child was palpable.

Yes, this woman and I understood each other perfectly. A void filled somewhere deep within me that I hadn't even known was there. It had been just me battling the bots and the Council of Traltix, but before me stood two other women who had also stepped into hell and had chosen to keep walking through the flames, knowing that there was no happy ending for them when they finally emerged. Knowing that I was not alone gave me some comfort.

The little girl darted past the blonde woman, who threw her hands up. "Katie, tie your shoes! You're going to trip!"

She kept going until she disappeared through the door, ignoring her flustered aunt. The child took something with her. The outside world grew noticeably darker.

The child's aunt sighed heavily, her hand on her forehead. Then, letting go of her frustration, she turned to Rocky. A look of tired relief spread across her face. I couldn't help but think again how old she looked. Had I grown to look the same, a haunted look etched into my face?

"You've been gone since before the sun came up," she said. "We were all worried."

"Found a few stragglers," Rocky said, shrugging, looking down at the ground. There was tension in her neck and shoulders. She moved even slower now. She had been strong for the little girl, but something had happened to her, and her carefree attitude had diminished.

Something had taken all the strength from her, and I wondered what kind of darkness the caves held within them. *Something* made sitting under a sign before the sun came up more appealing than this place.

"Emilee, this is Allyson and her humans—still didn't get your names," she said.

Emilee smiled at me, but it was a sad smile. "My niece was the only one I could get out."

I nodded, not knowing what to say, though I knew how she felt. My family was gone, too. I felt the hole their loss left with every heartbeat.

We all stood there silently, trying to look anywhere but at each other. I felt the coldness—we all did. Any comfort I had felt was being stripped from me. Yes, I had found people who shared my plight, but the weight of their despair was pressing down on me too. We *were* the same, and that meant solidarity as much as it meant shared pain.

This was supposed to be our place of hope. This was the place my brother had sent me. This was where, I prayed, the answers would lie.

But there was nothing here.

With the bubbly child gone, it felt as if we had happened upon a tomb—a cold, empty tomb. If I stood there any longer, it would suffocate me.

"Come on," Rocky said. "Let's introduce you to everyone."

With every step closer to the dark, the atmosphere changed, shifting toward something sinister.

We entered the convenience store, the bell signaling our arrival with a *ding*! The sound of it tugged at my frayed nerves, but I tried to ignore it. Inside, a refrigerator hummed. It had once been filled with beverages to sell, but they were all gone, most likely down in the caves where the survivors were. Trinkets and gifts sparkled and glinted around me: geodes and rocks of various colors, carved bears, deer, butterflies and other animals, jewelry boxes and necklaces, shirts, hats, and ceramic plates—souvenirs advertising the caves. There was a storeroom to my left, but it had been cleaned out. Whatever was stored inside had been taken down into the cave as well.

I took in all of the beautiful things that were once sold to happy tourists who came to our salvation as a day adventure or a family trip. I couldn't process it. I couldn't remember a world where people bought shiny trinkets and went to caves for the fun of it.

"This way," Rocky said, leading us through the main part of the store. We passed the bathrooms, and in the very back, an old, simple door—which had clearly been painted and repainted over the years—stood before us. It didn't look like much, but then, what did I expect?

Was the entrance supposed to be barred and bolted shut? In a world before this one, this was a tourist attraction, not the last stronghold of the human race.

Rocky knocked on the door and I held my breath as we waited. I'm not sure what I was hoping to see, but I prayed for something more than *this*.

"This place's strength is also its weakness," Rocky said. "This is the only way in or out, but ..."

She didn't have to finish. If a bot or the Council found us, there was no way out. We would either keep the enemy out or we would die inside with them.

"There are some holes that the bats come in and out of, but I can't tell you where they are, or if any of them are big enough for a bot to get through."

The first part was bad enough. I wished she hadn't said the last part.

The door swung open and a man appeared before us. His almond-colored eyes looked kind. He was large, with dark hair and skin, and he was definitely another Ganger. I didn't know who he was, but I liked him immediately.

"Rocky," the man said, smiling.

"Derek," Rocky responded.

"I've got the door for a bit longer," Derek said, "but you lot are just in time for dinner. Glad to see some new faces."

We slipped past the man. He smiled warmly at each of us. As I walked past him, our eyes met.

"Welcome home," he said to me, but I heard something else. With two words, he was telling me that my journey was over. He was telling me that my friends and I had survived, and they were going to make certain that my friends would be taken care of after I was gone.

It was the most beautiful thing I had ever heard. It was almost enough to drive away the feeling of dread that was crawling underneath my skin.

Almost.

Inside, the cave was cool and wet. I had never been in a cave before—not in this lifetime or in any of the others. Cracks ran through the ceiling like veins. Soda straws had formed around them where water had come through the earth. On all sides, even above, walls of strong beige rock encircled me. Lights had been strung up around us, and though they did make it possible to see, their biggest effect was to change the sea of beige to pink or orange where the lights struck the rock, with the occasional splotch of green where some sort of rudimentary plant life had chosen to take advantage of the artificial light. Far off in the corners where the light could not touch, everything was darker than black. The farthest crevices of the caves were so dark that they reminded me of the most remote expanses of space. The blackness could have gone on forever, twisting and turning in the earth, or the wall of the cave could have been only inches away. I would never know. The lights, despite the humans' best attempts, didn't eliminate the dark. They made it retreat into the corners, but it was waiting to creep back and reclaim the cave. It was only a matter of time.

That was just the main entrance. The ceiling was only a few feet away, the sides not that much farther.

"Come on," Rocky said. "We have everyone camped inside."

I took a step forward, but when the water splashed between my eyes, I gasped.

"You got a cave kiss!" Kaitlin squealed. I hadn't heard her approaching, but here she was, the little ray of sunshine.

"Mr. Scott, he gives people tours down here. He says they're good luck!" the little girl rambled. "He showed me lizards and crickets with long, funny legs! You've got to see them too!"

Then she was off, giggling, around a wall of solid rock.

"Kaitlin, don't run! You'll slip!" Emilee called after her.

We followed, though at a much slower pace. The path was slick, and there were patches of loose pebbles that would leave you sliding across the path if you stepped carelessly. The path went up and down, and I could no longer tell how far below the surface we were. We climbed stairs and made our way gingerly down slippery slopes, and still the ceiling always seemed to be just as far away, though I had to duck to avoid a nasty bump on the head in a few places.

We passed a pool of clear and sparkling water, the artificial lights reflecting off its surface, making it glimmer.

"At least we don't have to worry about water," Marie said meekly.

Rocky laughed.

"Whatever you do, don't drink that," she said. Marie was quiet.

When I didn't think we could walk any more, the path opened, and there before me stood a wide cavern, probably two hundred feet from the bottom to the top. I stared in awe. Stalagmites rose from the floor, great pillars of rock reaching upward toward the ceiling. Stalactites reached down in return, and where pillars of rock embraced, great columns spanned from floor to ceiling. Its magnitude took my breath away.

In the middle, where the floor was smooth and the walls on either side opened up to provide pockets of out-of-the-way shelter, sat the camp.

The makeshift camp was comprised of sleeping bags and supplies. Dim lanterns lit the claustrophobic space the survivors had chosen to call home. Now that we weren't moving, it hit me all at once. The air felt stale and damp, threatening to choke me as it crept its way down my throat and into my lungs. There was a wet, mildewing, earthy smell in the air. Normally, the smell of nature was soothing to me, reminding me of the free air of my home planet. This smell reminded me of things that hid and grew in the damp dark, away from the light of the sun. It smelled eerie and foreign, and made me want to run outside into the sunlight.

I hated the dark. I hated the damp cold. I wished we had never come here. I wished my brother had sent us somewhere—anywhere—else but this terrible place.

I choked down the hysteria. I couldn't give up now, not after we had come all this way and had gone through so much. There was something here. There had to be. I had faith in my brother. I had faith in the people who were fighting to protect us. I had to believe that we were here for a reason.

"This place was a tourist attraction when the world wasn't ending. A party of overnight cavers had just started a tour when the pulse cannon went off," Rocky said, distracting me somewhat. "The visitors took off to check on their homes, but the guides had already set up camp down here and stocked up on food. A few of them stayed behind. It would have been harder without them."

There were people heating canned soup over burners in the center of the largest living area, surrounded by a few meager boxes of supplies and sleeping bags. The people who occupied the sleeping bags didn't sleep; instead, quietly staring up into the dark recesses of the cave.

"Adam!" Rocky shouted at the fire. A man with red-brown hair stuck his head up. "We've got a few more mouths to feed!"

The Ganger smiled. His face was tired, but it was also kind. "I'll consider that good news."

He was a gentle person, but his young face was weary, the edges of his brown eyes shriveled with premature age. It gave him a hardness. He had a strong jaw, covered in stubble, as could be expected of a man who'd been on the run for days. It made him look even older. I knew with one look that he was a leader. If anyone had the answers, it would be him. The idea made me feel slightly better, and my limbs and body relaxed.

Kaitlin ran up to Marie, breathless. There was chocolate in the corners of her mouth. Emilee saw it too and frowned ever so slightly. I saw her glance at Rocky, who just stood there and tried not to grin.

"I drew the aliens!" she said excitedly, forcing white sheets of paper into Marie's hands. Marie stared down at them, her eyes not really comprehending. My humans were shocked by what they were seeing, and not in a good way. They stood there, staring into the cave with hollow expressions, not sure what to think. A look of despair was creeping into their eyes. It was the same look that was etched into Emilee's face.

There was no hope here. We were here for nothing. There was no safety. There was no end to this.

I shook my head, trying to shake the defeat away. I would not think that. I refused. I trusted.

The child looked at me, her eyes so very innocent. "Are you an alien? Can I draw you? Are you weird? Do you have lots of arms and eyeballs? Aunt Emilee says she has four arms and antennas!"

I looked at Kaitlin, but this time I *really* looked at her. She stared at me, unafraid, bouncing up and down in her uncontainable excitement and chocolate-induced sugar buzz. She wasn't scared of me. She didn't hate me. She had just met me and already she trusted me.

I looked from Kaitlin to Emilee. It finally occurred to me that this was not a normal child. This child should have been screaming in tears, not smiling at me. This child had been raised by a Ganger, and the imprint it left on her suddenly became glaringly obvious.

In all the world, there was still innocence. There was one human left who hadn't succumbed to desolation. She was tiny, but even I could feel her power. This child's world was more complex than most. She still found wonder and magic in the universe, despite everything.

I was wrong. There *was* hope here, and looking into its blue eyes, I knew that I had no choice but to be strong. I looked up and saw the same blue eyes, though these were older. Emilee stared at me, her lips pursed. I met Rocky's eyes. They all looked so human, but there was something else behind all of them, too.

I knew why we were here. We were Peacemakers, and all around me was the peace we had created. I just needed to cast off the dark to see it.

"I'm blue," I said to the child, smiling at her.

She gasped. "I have to go find my blue crayon!"

She spun on her heel and was off again.

"I don't think she understands," Emilee whispered, watching the girl dart away. "I was supposed to be watching her while my sister was at work. My sister is—was—a single mom. She left Katie with me a lot. Lindsey had just started her shift when they beamed me back. By the time I got back on the planet, all I had time to do was grab Katie and run. I couldn't save my sister. I couldn't even warn her."

She paused for a minute as she fought back the sorrow. "When I got back, Katie was trying to make macaroni and cheese in the microwave, and the real Emilee was dead in my bedroom."

"When I walked out, she asked me how my nap was," Emilee said. Her eyes were focused on something far away. "I still don't know how much she saw or how much she understands."

Her voice broke and her face contorted into sobs, but, like me, the tears never fell.

"I think she understands more than we know," I said. "But maybe not about the things you fear."

She turned her face away, trying to stifle the sobs with her hand.

"I'm going to go look around," Tori muttered. I almost jumped. My friends had been so quiet since we had arrived. I nodded, and as they slipped away together, I fought the urge to call them back to my side. I had fought for so long to keep them with me, it was hard to let them walk off by themselves in that tiny camp.

But the day had come, and it was time to let them go. I wouldn't be around much longer. It was time for them to start living without me.

Someone was moaning in the corner. This time the sound really startled me. I jumped and spun around, on the defense for bots or Council agents, waiting for the chaos to ensue. It didn't. It had already come and gone. Lying on a cot was the blond man I had stood next to at the meeting with the Elders. His empty brown eyes wandered around the cavern slowly, looking past everything, seeing nothing. Every now and then he moaned, clutching at the empty air, only for his hand to drop at his side, and then he would be silent again.

"Who is that? What happened to him?" I asked, appalled. I knew full well what had happened to him but refused to accept it. No power in the universe could be so cruel. They couldn't have done this.

"They scattered him," Rocky whispered, and her voice dripped with venom. I heard her heavy footsteps as she rushed away.

"His brother and father got him here. They lost his mother to a bot," Emilee explained. "Rocky found them a few miles from here. That was two days ago."

"He hasn't …?"

"No. He isn't going to come back," she said. I stood there as she quietly slipped away, leaving me alone with the moaning shell.

I don't know how long I stood there, my feet frozen to the earth. I felt my single heart pounding in my chest, the blood pulsing in my ears and drowning out the world, until there was nothing left but me and the man groaning on the cot. Cold chills crept up my spine and my hair stood on end. The world started to give way beneath my feet. I remembered. I didn't want to remember, but I couldn't stop the memories. Not this time, with the prone body lying there before me, just like so many others had.

"You okay?" I heard someone ask from behind. The world snapped back into focus.

"Who is it?" I whispered in a hoarse voice. I realized then that I had been silently crying.

"Dami'na, as far as we can tell," Adam said, walking past me with a steaming bowl of soup. It smelled like tomato, which had always been my favorite, but now I couldn't find any comfort in the sweet, familiar smell. It made me feel sick; as a matter of fact, the thought that anyone could think of food right now made me sick.

"*Why?*"

"They had to try to get us back somehow," he said.

I knew they wouldn't have just released us. Somehow I knew why they gave up ripping us back from our Gangers. I hadn't wanted to believe it. How many of us had been sacrificed before the rest of us were released? How many of us were fragmented, lying in the dirt somewhere as shells? How many of us would never be whole again?

There was no fixing this. The man who groaned before me was worse than dead. Only a small fraction of him existed in the Ganger body. The rest of his consciousness had leaked out into oblivion, never to find its way back. I didn't know where the rest of him was. Was the other half of him back in his own body, groaning and staring into the eyes of the monsters who had done this to him? Part of me, and I was disgusted to realize it, hoped that he was. Or perhaps he was just gone, dissipating across the universe. I didn't know. Where did souls go when they weren't contained in a mortal form?

I was going to be sick. Bile rose in my stomach, burning my insides as it came up.

"Can you help me?" Adam asked, calling me back to reality again. He was kneeling in the dirt, soup in hand. He watched me patiently, analyzing me.

"*I can't,*" I blurted out before my mind had time to digest what he was saying.

"I just need you to hold the bowl," Adam said. "Dirt will get in it if I set it down."

I nodded abruptly. Then I dropped to the ground beside him, refusing to look at the groaning man again. I didn't want to do it. I wanted to run away screaming, but this was my colleague. He had given everything he had. The least I could do was hold a bowl of soup for him.

"You're afraid of sick people," Adam said. He put his hand on the broken man's shoulder, and the man stared up at the ceiling and was still. Adam spooned tomato soup out of the bowl and tried to gently ease it down the Ganger's throat, but his mouth wouldn't open, and the soup ran down his face. He was still frozen, only blinking.

"Yes," I whispered.

"What did you live through?" he asked. I pursed my lips and clenched my eyes shut.

"Why are you doing this? He can't eat," I said, perhaps more forcibly than I meant to. Adam looked at me, eyebrows raised, but he didn't get defensive.

"Why do we ever do anything for the dead?" Adam said.

"It's not for him," he explained. "It's for them. It lessens their grief. It's not going to help him, but it makes them feel better if they think that we have the power to do something, to show that we care."

We sat there quietly as he continued to pretend to spoon-feed the empty being. My legs began to cramp beneath me, the blood leaving them as I sat on them, but still I didn't move. I watched Adam as he patiently played his part.

When we were dying, there was a nurse who came and sat at the foot of our beds. She would hum and talk to us as if nothing were wrong. She would play with our hair and tell us how pretty we were. It always made us feel better when she came by each day.

At least, until she didn't. She died too.

Adam reminded me of her.

"1918. Influenza," I said. "I was fifteen."

"What was your name?"

"Lucy."

"Who did you lose?" he asked, his voice gentle.

"How do you—?" I began.

"It's the way of young planets. It's unavoidable if you live enough lives here. In time, war, famine, disease, or some other tragedy will take someone from us."

"Lizzie," I whispered. "She was seven."

"She had blonde hair and bright blue eyes," I said, remembering the little girl's face. "She was—"

"She was your sister," he said. I looked at him, startled.

"How did you know that?" I said, my voice breaking from the emotions brought forth from a life lived long ago. As he watched me, I could have sworn I saw anger in his eyes, but I couldn't be sure; I was too busy sobbing, almost one hundred years' worth of pain engulfing me.

"I was holding her hand when she died. She was so scared, but I promised her—I promised that she wouldn't die. I swore that she would be okay, but she wasn't, and she died. I was sick, too, but when it was my turn to die, they didn't let me. They pulled me out. When I begged them to let me die, they knocked me out as I fought, and I woke up okay, but she died. She didn't get to wake up again, *but I did.*"

Adam watched me as I sobbed, my head hung low.

"Do you wish they would let you love her?" he whispered. I stopped and looked at him. My mouth opened and closed, but there was nothing to say.

Because he was right.

"It's like watching a movie," he said. "We see it—we *almost* feel it—but it's from a distance. We remember the pain and watch the memories where it's safe, and it isn't real anymore. It's just a reflex, like your heart tugging at you when you look at an old, wrinkled photograph from too long ago. You should feel something, but time has washed it away, and where the emotions were, you just feel hollow. You wake up and discover that you've forgotten the emotion entirely."

He was staring past me now and I turned to follow his gaze. Tori was in the corner, sitting against a stack of boxes. I didn't recognize the man she was talking to. He was older. He looked nice. She smiled at something he said.

"Do you wish you could love your sister like you love her?" Adam asked, motioning to Tori.

Did I? For the first time in hundreds of years, it hit me. I had never wished to love them again. But I had, hadn't I? I did love them, right? All of them?

I must have, but how could you remember how much you loved someone? How could you measure love?

"Tell me, Saira," Adam asked, and I was surprised to hear him say my name. "When you look at him, what are you really afraid of?"

His eyes met mine. I was afraid the anger behind them would burn me.

"Dinner is getting cold," Rocky called from behind us. I stood straight up, the bowl of soup dumping on the ground.

"Shoot," I muttered, feeling unsteady. "I'm sorry."

"It's okay," Adam said. "I think we were done."

His eyes met mine as he walked away, and he knew. He knew what I was really afraid of, even if I hadn't for so long.

It was at least a minute before the world stopped spinning and I could move.

I sat between two men. One was a black Ganger with strong, handsome features and kind eyes—Derek—and the other had steel-gray eyes and curly black hair that hadn't been cut in a while. I heard someone call him Davis. Jillian and Marie sat across from me, beside Emilee. Kaitlin was in Emilee's lap, showing Marie her pictures. Tori sat, deep in conversation, next to someone I assumed was one of the park rangers. He was the same man I had seen earlier. She was still smiling. I felt my lips twitch.

Tori was smiling.

I watched all three of them. Utensils were scarce, so dinner was lukewarm soup in a plastic cup. I dutifully put my mouth to the cup and pretended to drink every now and then. All of the Gangers were doing the same. Our bodies were past the point where food was useful, but it was like Adam said: it made the humans feel better. They didn't need to know how bad off we were. If they noticed what we were doing, they didn't say anything.

After a while I set the cup down and looked from face to face. Everyone sat in the dirt, making conversation, as the small flames from the fire in the center of our tight circle crackled, giving off the only light we had. We had turned off the lanterns in case the humans needed them later. As a result, grotesque shadows danced on the wall. I looked at the Gangers, who stood out now against the sea of humans. Our end was coming soon. You could see it in our faces; the gaunt, yellowing skin, cracking lips, and bloodshot eyes, but more importantly, you could feel it. With each passing moment, each of us was preparing ourselves for the end of our journey.

"Does anybody know anything?" I tried to whisper, but my voice cut like a knife, and everyone fell silent. The Gangers looked back and forth at one another with grim faces.

"Oh, we know things," one of the men said. "Not that it helps us. Or them."

"It was the war," another man said. "When the Quintatinks and the Sebicans went to war, the Council sent dozens of races to intervene. Avinox ships led them."

That made sense. The Avinox had always been vocal champions for peace. They were an old race, slightly rigid in their behavior, but they had always been a just, kind species. It did not surprise me that they would risk themselves in— even put themselves at the front of—a battle that they did not have to fight.

"Before they could drive the Quintatinks and Sebicans apart and secure their battleships, the Avinox lost three ships of their own. About two thousand of their people died."

"Since then, the Avinox have led the talks imploring the Peacemakers to be more rigid in their methods."

"They blame us?" I asked. "It's been ten thousand years since we left Xarus! The Council of Traltix themselves voted to allow the Quintatinks to join them as a Higher Planet only two thousand years ago!"

"They are afraid," Adam explained. "As Peacemakers, we do not aim to control the most fundamental aspects of the species we monitor. After they are beyond our control, those parts of them evolve with them. The Avinox fear that violence and bloodlust are an integral part of human nature. After talks of reclassification and a Cleansing failed, they asked the Elders if they would consider selectively monitoring the human gene pool."

"They asked if we would engage in eugenics?" I asked.

"They asked if we could eliminate the most violent of the humans, making sure only the most passive and benign were allowed to endure."

"That is against everything we believe in! That is against our entire purpose! You cannot make a race what you want it to be! The consequences—"

"Which is why the Elders told the Council no."

"That's all we know," Adam said, staring down into his cup, his brows pulled tight in concentration.

I knew what he was thinking. For all the "no's" we had heard about, someone must have said "yes" to something, or this wouldn't have happened.

I was quiet for a minute. I played with my soup, but I could barely hold the cup anymore.

"We have Avinox on board *Moga*," I said. I don't know why I said it. I shouldn't have; it was mean-spirited and so incredibly stereotypical.

"We thought the same thing," Derek said beside me. "They've always been ... intense in their beliefs."

"We have an Avinox here," Rocky said, her gaze holding fast, staring into the flames of the fire, which would go out soon if we didn't throw more wood on it.

"Who?" I heard Marie squeak, looking around fearfully, as if she expected them to jump up and get her.

We all looked up, staring grimly into the dark, where the prone figure on the cot was finally quiet. He had drifted to sleep maybe thirty minutes before. I considered it a blessing.

Davis chuckled beside me. "That explains my brother."

I was mildly startled. It had been difficult to discern whether or not Davis was a Ganger or a human. He looked haggard and grief-stricken. He was pale. His face was gaunt, and his eyes were swollen and bloodshot. His hands constantly shook. I had mistakenly assumed that he didn't speak because he was too exhausted to, not that he was too bereft to. It was insensitive of me to assume that the Gangers would be the worst off. The humans had suffered, too. I couldn't imagine what it had been like for Davis and his father to get to the caves after losing his mother to the bot, but to have his brother struck down and lobotomized right in front of them? I knew how helpless Jillian had looked when I opened my eyes and found myself clutched desperately to her chest. They had gone further than that with the Avinox. Davis and his father had watched helplessly while their loved one was tortured, completely at a loss as to what was going on. He probably lay in their arms while they begged him to fight and hold on as they realized he was slipping away. The mental image was gut-wrenching.

"Brandon was always a righteous bugger," Davis continued, "He used to drive me crazy. I would tell him to screw up a little so I'd have less to live up to."

A smile tugged at the corner of his mouth and he chuckled.

"He was studying to be a lawyer," he said, and he let the smile spread across his face. "Not prosecution, though. Not-for-profit-type stuff. He was all about giving back and making the world a better place."

"And what about you?" Adam asked.

"Me? I was going to be a social worker. All because of that goody-two-shoes," Davis said, nodding in the direction of the fallen Ganger.

"Why's that?" Derek asked.

"I used to get bullied in elementary school. So, one day, I told my big brother, thinking he'd protect me. You want to know what Brandon did?"

We nodded, encouraging him to keep talking.

"He invited him over for dinner," Davis chuckled. "He invited that kid over, and wouldn't you know it, he became my best friend. What Brandon knew that I didn't at the time is that his mother had just moved out and left him with his father. His father wasn't the nicest guy. Nate was angry. That's all it was. He just needed someone to be there for him. Ever since then, I've always wanted to be a social worker, to protect kids like Nate who didn't have annoyingly noble kids to look out for them."

His lips trembled and the tears started rolling down his cheeks.

I shouldn't have said anything. I felt guilt consuming me.

Everyone was quiet after that. No one touched their food again. When the silence finally became too much and I felt the walls pressing in on me, I found my way out of the cave and sat in the grass. It probably wasn't the safest thing to do, but then, what did it matter if something happened to me now? I sat down and took a deep breath, filling my lungs with the smell of damp earth. Out in the open, the smell of grass, leaves, and tree bark was almost soothing.

Almost, but not quite. The smell of the cave, cold and closed off from the world, still lingered. I knew what resided in the dark. I saw him when I closed my eyes. I saw her.

I could see all of them now.

"My name is Allyson," I whispered to myself, my eyes clenched tight. "My name is Lucy. My name is Mila. My name is Yelizaveta. My name is Anastasia."

I opened my eyes and looked up. The stars twinkled above me, oblivious to everything. "Allyson, Lucy, Mila, Yelizaveta, Anastasia …"

"Jillian, Tori, Marie, Meredith, Aidan, Michael, Ethan, Mom, Dad …" My voice broke.

Who was I?

"Sarah?" I heard a voice call. I heard them walking up behind me, the grass giving way softly beneath their feet.

I sat there listening as the person wandered closer, looking for their friend.

"Allyson?"

It was Marie, I realized. I turned my head and watched her, not sure what I was feeling as the girl wandered around in the dark and called me by two names.

"Over here, Marie," I said quietly, as if I were afraid of disturbing the world around me. Only, I was pretty sure there was nothing left to be disturbed.

"I'm sorry," she said as she approached, and then whispered, "I'm not sure how to pronounce your name."

Allyson, Lucy, Mila, Yelizaveta, Anastasia … I realized what I had done. I had left one out.

But then, I hadn't been Saira in a very long time, had I? I had barely recognized the name when Adam said it.

Adam. Who was Adam?

No one was going by their real name.

"It's Allyson, Marie," I whispered. Saira was gone. I had lost her, just as I had lost my other identities. I wasn't sure if I would ever see her again.

Marie nodded and sat down beside me. I was surprised when she scooted up against me.

"It's cold out here," she said, pulling her knees to her chest.

I wrapped my arms around her. Together, we found ourselves staring at the sky.

"It's strange," Marie whispered. "I keep expecting to see a plane or something, but it's just so … quiet."

I didn't say anything. I kept staring up and up and up. Somewhere beyond what my eyes could perceive, there was a spaceship. I wondered what they were seeing. I wondered what they were thinking. Did they feel bad about killing us?

I shook my head. I couldn't think that way. That was anger talking. Of course they felt badly about the situation. How could anyone want this? How could anyone *really* want this?

"My brother, Nick ..." Marie said.

"The one in the Air Force?" I asked, and I felt my heart sink. I already knew where she was going with this.

"His base was really remote. Do you think—?"

I looked at her with sympathetic eyes. She nodded and looked away.

"I figured," she said. "I guess it's kind of silly, but I've been looking for him. Like, maybe he got a plane and got away, and he's working on a way to rescue all of us, and we'll all be okay and together again. Is that stupid of me?"

I felt her start to cry against me, and I pulled her closer. She put her head against my chest, and I let her sit there and cry for a long time. Both of us just sat there under the stars.

The cave made everything feel too real. It stripped away all of the illusions we had been holding on to.

We had been quiet for a while, just sitting there, holding each other. "I've been wondering," Marie finally said. "How many planets are there? With life, I mean. Is there one for every star?"

"I don't think we've found them all," I said. "There are over twelve thousand Higher Planets."

"That's ..." Marie paused, trying to find the words. "That's overwhelming."

I looked at her. It was hard to see her clearly in the dark, but I knew she was clutching at something at her neck, and I knew without seeing it that it was the tiny silver cross necklace. She told me once that it had belonged to her great-grandmother.

Jillian and I had known each other for years, but we happened upon Marie and Tori by chance. Jillian and I roomed with each other for the first two years of college, and when it came time for roommate selection for our junior year, we naturally asked for each other. Tori, with her spiky hair dyed jet black and—what was the number again?—twelve piercings ... well, Tori and her rebellious attitude had a hard time getting along with anyone. No one wanted to room with her. Marie was Tori's polar opposite. Marie was the daughter of a pastor; she was raised in a small town in the middle of nowhere, where *everyone* went to church on Sunday; and she was a straight-A student. People saw her as boring—not to mention that they thought she would turn them in for hiding alcohol in their closets. But Marie wasn't like that. Marie was sweet and shy, and she never forced her beliefs on anyone—not even the wild, mischievous Tori, who did not always act responsibly. When junior year came, they put the four of us in an apartment-style dorm on campus, and the strangest thing happened: we got along. By the time roommate selection for senior year came along, we were inseparable.

"I think I judged you, and I'm sorry," I whispered to Marie. She looked at me curiously.

"I have to admit that I didn't expect you to handle all of this so well," I said, and I was grinning ever so slightly.

"Why do you say that?" she asked.

"How did you know what I am?" I asked. "You knew long before I told Jilly and Tori."

Marie sat up straight. She was still fiddling with the necklace, and the look on her face was strange. She flipped the necklace over, looking at it from all angles, giving it considerable thought.

"When I saw that light come out of the clouds, I thought it was God," she said. "I thought Judgment Day had finally come, and we were all being punished for our sins. I was even deluded enough to think that you might be an angel. But when I saw that machine, I knew it didn't come from God."

She sat there, still examining the necklace.

"I guess I immediately jumped to one spectacular conclusion because I was so open to seeing it. I've always been looking for it. When I saw evidence of what it really was, it wasn't so hard to jump to the next irrational idea. I guess it even made more sense."

"What do you think I am now, Marie?" I asked.

She looked at me funny. "You're Allyson," she blurted out, as if it were the most obvious thing in the world.

"Am I really?" I whispered.

Marie shrugged and picked a blade of grass. She began twirling it like she did the necklace. "I can't see you as anyone else."

As the weight of her words sank in, I felt even more confused. Was I Saira the Peacemaker, or was I Allyson the ... something else? I wasn't human, but then, I felt more human than anything.

"Do you believe in God, Ally?" she asked. Her question caught me off guard. For all her beliefs, it was one she had never asked me. It was something that wasn't discussed in our little apartment.

"No," I said slowly. She nodded, not surprised.

"I don't think I do either," she said. I must admit, that surprised me.

Slowly, and without ceremony, she took the necklace off and dropped it in the grass.

"Don't do that," I scolded gently, picking the necklace up and brushing the dirt off.

She looked startled. "But you—"

"I don't know everything," I said matter-of-factly.

"I can't believe in something that's wrong," Marie said, and the tears were starting again. "All my life, my father told me that we were special. He said we were made in the image of God. He was wrong, wasn't he? There are twelve thousand planets, and some fantastic being thinks we're the only one that matters? All his talks, lectures, and sermons never told me about *you*. How could God have spoken to people but not told us about you? We missed that information because there is no God to speak to us."

"So maybe a few things are wrong," I said. "That doesn't mean that all of it is."

I held the necklace out, but she didn't reach for it. I sighed and held the necklace in my palm, feeling the warmth infused in it from Marie's little body. It had always been such a part of her. I had never seen her without it.

"Would you like to know a little bit about how I was raised?" I asked.

Her face lit up.

"Yes," she said, and she was genuinely excited. I don't know why I volunteered the information. I don't know why I thought she needed to hear it, but it felt right.

"Family life for Thellessians is a little different from humans. My race is polyamorous, though we mate for life. One person can have three or four partners, male or female. I was raised by thirty-two parents."

"*Thirty-two?*" Marie gasped.

"I have fifty-seven siblings. What we call a family—a colony—is different from what you would call a family. My parents planned their children together, one at a time per female. My race is long-lived, so mothers have one child, wait until it's an adult, then have another if they choose. I was raised with twelve brothers and sisters. I even have an identical twin brother."

"Identical?" Marie began. "But male and female twins—"

"Are fraternal for humans," I said. "But my race isn't exactly like yours, is it?"

I gave her a wink as her mouth fell open.

Marie stared at me in disbelief. "Your guys and girls look the same? How?"

I couldn't help it; I giggled.

"Close your mouth, Marie," I teased. "It's not that weird."

"What's his name?" she asked excitedly.

"Dorain," I said, smiling, but my smile turned into a frown as I thought about him. "He risked everything so I could help you. He didn't have to. They didn't suspect him of being guilty of anything."

I was quiet for a minute.

"When we were kids," I whispered, "we were inseparable. At night we would curl up next to each other. We slept next to a different parent each night, but we always slept beside each other. He followed me into the Peacemakers when I followed my daydreams of seeing new worlds and strange races."

"He must really love you," Marie said.

"On my planet, family is everything. I love my family. I love *all* of my families, including my human ones."

"How many have you had?" Marie asked.

"Five human families," I said, smiling as I remembered the faces of loved ones from long ago. "It was in the 1500s when I first set foot on this planet. My name was Ana back then."

Marie gasped and choked, trying to speak. "*How old are you?*"

"Somewhere around two thousand, based on human years," I said. I laughed at Marie's facial expressions as she tried to keep her composure.

"Is it strange being put into a young human's body? Being forced to be raised by humans and treated like a child?"

"When they put me in a Ganger, I am a child. I have my memories, but they are stored in a human brain, and I am at its mercy. I *am* a human."

"What's it like?" she asked.

I looked at her, trying to figure out how I could possibly put something so complex into words.

"Do you want to know why this is my favorite scar?" I finally asked, pointing to the scar by my nose. She nodded.

"Human parents know when their child is gone. I don't know what Allyson Owens was like, but I'm sure we were different babies. Mom and Dad noticed the first morning they walked up to my crib. I saw it written all over their faces. We had the hardest time bonding, I to them and them to me. They hated themselves for rejecting me, although they never admitted that they did, even to themselves. I blamed myself for their inner turmoil. We struggled for years, all of us just playing our respective parts. When I was five, I fell off a swing set and landed face-first in the dirt. I hit a rock. The first thing I did, without even thinking about it, was to scream for my mom at the top of my lungs. This little scar marks the first day I was able to connect to my parents."

Marie looked thoughtful, and I could tell she had something unpleasant to ask. She opened and closed her mouth several times before she finally found the courage to blurt out her question, though she couldn't look me in the eye. "Why did the Peacemakers take Allyson? Why did you replace her, of all the other children in the world?"

"Allyson Owens was born with a genetic defect. She would have developed leukemia. Our models say she wouldn't have lived past her tenth birthday."

Marie stared at me, her eyes conflicted. "You ... saved her?"

I sighed. "I really don't know."

With that, I opened her hand and pressed the cross necklace into it. I closed her fist around it, then sat there, my hand encircling hers. I got up and walked away without another word. I didn't really understand what I had said, but I hoped that it helped her. Maybe it was just something I needed to talk about before I was gone. Maybe it was just the last real conversation two friends got to have before they said their goodbyes.

Maybe that was goodbye.

"Allyson!" Marie called back to me. I turned. She looked so small sitting there in the dark.

"It's nice to know *you*," she said. "I wish we could have sooner. I'm going to really miss you," she whispered.

Yes, this was our goodbye.

I walked back to the girl and knelt beside her, wrapping my arms around her.

"Not as much as I'm going to miss you," I whispered. Her hair tickled my nose.

"Thank you for what you've done for us," she said.

I squeezed her tight, then I stood up and rushed away, sniffling. It was all I could take. I didn't want to say goodbye. I didn't want to leave them.

I stopped when I saw Jillian. She had been listening, standing there rigidly in the dark, gripping a sapling at the edge of the tree line as if it were her lifeline. I couldn't understand the look on her face as she stared at me through the darkness. I started to say something, but then she was gone, the swaying sapling the only indication that my eyes hadn't played a trick on me.

I stood there, trying to feel harmony with the world again. I couldn't. I felt loss and discord. I had left this planet five times in the past, not wanting to go any of those times. But this time it was more than just not wanting to leave. This time, it felt *wrong* to go.

"Are we done now, Dorain?" I whispered. "Is this really the end?"

If my brother were here, he would know. I wished with all my heart that he was safe, not alone and frightened. The one good thing about goodbye would be seeing his face. It was the only comfort I had.

I heard footsteps rushing toward me, and strong hands gripped me by the arms. I almost stumbled back, surprised by Tori's excited face pressed so closely to mine.

"Tori?" I blurted out, trying to figure out where she had come from.

"Ally!" Tori shouted breathlessly. "The ranger guy has a plan!"

"A plan?" I asked, still shocked to have her nose so close to mine.

"He says he has guns. He says we can fight back and—"

Guns? *That* was what she was excited about? Was that what she was smiling about all this time? I felt the fury building, blood rushing in my ears. I couldn't stop it. We had run from bots and the Council of Traltix for days. We had seen people die in front of us. I was leaving in the morning, and this was how I was leaving her? I had told her that she couldn't fight! I thought she had finally listened to me!

I would leave in the morning, and when I did, some park ranger who had yet to even see a bot was going to be Tori's closest ally. He would get her killed.

"*Tori!*" I snapped. "No!"

"But—"

I pushed her hands away and threw my hands up. My breath came out in a frustrated hiss. I stumbled to the sapling Jillian had been holding and pressed my forehead against it, feeling the blood rushing in my ears. I could have sworn I felt tears of frustration behind my eyes.

I turned and looked at her sternly.

"No!" I scolded. "Have you learned nothing? *You can't fight!* I need you to listen to me! I need you to live! After all we've seen and been through, why do you continue to fight me? Why do you have to be so stubborn, Tori? *Would it kill you to listen to me for once?*"

I was tired and near hysterics. I shouldn't have been so harsh, but time was running out, and she *just wouldn't learn*. It was always Tori, the headstrong one—the one who couldn't be told no without a fight for the sake of a good fight, who had to argue and have an opinion on everything. It made me so angry!

"I'm leaving, Tori. I'm not going to be here to be your babysitter anymore. I need you to grow up."

I realized as soon as I said it that it was the wrong thing to say. I was such an idiot. I should never have gotten so angry. She was only human.

She glared at me.

"You're a coward," she spat. "If you really cared about us, you would do something."

I reached out for her, but she slapped my hand away. "Tori—"

"No!" she shouted, and there were tears in her eyes. "You're stupid! All of you are! If you're so wise and powerful, you should be able to help us, but you're not! You're leaving us to go back to your stinking ship! You're running away! You made me think there was hope, that you could do something, but you're nothing! You're weak and afraid, and you're leaving us here to rot! *I hate aliens—and I hate you!*"

She spun around and marched away, fists clenched.

"Tori!" I called after her. "Stop! Come back here and talk to me! I didn't mean it!"

"*Stop treating me like I'm a child!*" she shrieked, and she disappeared out of sight.

I should have gone after her, but I didn't.

I leaned my head against the tree, wondering how I could have let myself say all those things. It was Tori, after all. How had I let myself lose control?

In under a minute, I had ruined my relationship with someone I loved. Again. This time, I was sure it was permanent. I'd never have time to fix it. It had happened so fast. What if that was my goodbye to Tori?

"We're all tired," Derek said from behind me. I opened my eyes and turned around to stare at him, but it had gotten too dark. He was just a silhouette.

"That's not an excuse," I said. "There's no excuse for what I just did."

I could sense his smile in the dark. "You're only human."

I giggled, allowing myself to laugh at the irony. "How can I expect her to learn when I can't be the model? I don't even know where that came from! It's not like me!"

"How can you expect her to learn if she can't see herself in you? If none of us ever made mistakes, how would they ever trust us?"

I stared at him, mouth agape, not sure if there were words for the emotions he was eliciting in me.

And here I thought I had all the lessons to teach.

"The girl will come around."

"I don't have time to wait," I said. "It's over tomorrow. I can't leave us like this."

Again I felt Derek's smile in the dark. "You have all the time you need. Right now, you need to worry more about sleep. Tomorrow is a big day for all of us."

I scoffed. "I won't sleep—not for what tomorrow brings. I already spent part of today unconscious. Sleep is a waste of my hours."

"Permit yourself the luxury of a few hours of nothing," Derek said. "Forget everything for a while. It's the last piece of mercy those like you and me will get for a very long time."

"Mercy," I said, and the word tasted bitter in my mouth. "We like to use that word, but I think we've forgotten what it means. We always thought we were so peaceful and compassionate, but what kind of peaceful creature has to show *mercy*?"

Derek walked over to me and placed his hands on my shoulders, looking down at me with warm brown eyes.

"Don't argue with me, girl, I'm older than you are." I still didn't know who he was, but it didn't matter.

I sighed. "How can you be so calm?"

"It's better than the anger," he said.

I relented under his gaze. I was too tired to be stubborn, and I had already known that I wouldn't last the night without some sleep. The only reason I was standing was because of the sapling. I nodded, and we slowly made our way to the cave together.

I cast a longing look to the stars before we walked through the door of the gift shop. Then the cave swallowed us whole.

There was a sleeping bag for me against the wall, and I dropped down into it gratefully. I was even more drained than I had thought. Everything ached, and my eyes burned from exhaustion, both physical and emotional. I stretched out on my back and closed my eyes. Derek was right. These were my last hours of serenity.

I heard my human heart beating.

I would never have another. The realization was oppressive. Tomorrow, I would go to my fate. Tomorrow, I wouldn't even have the memories of this night.

I wanted those hours of peace more than ever. I ached for them.

"Ally Cat?" I heard Jillian whisper.

My eyes slowly opened.

"Hey, Jilly Bean," I whispered. I took it back. Sleep was not the thing I wanted right now. I hadn't even realized how much I missed her until I heard her voice.

I hadn't liked Jillian when I first met her. As a four-year-old, she had been physical, aggressive, loud, and obnoxious, and had more than a wild streak in her. Her tantrums involved throwing things and screaming. The first time we played together, she hit me for touching her favorite toy—a worn-out stuffed dog named Woof who still sat on Jillian's bed to this day. As an adult, Jillian was still physical, but in a different way. She was one of Florida Eastern's star softball players. Her skills as a soccer player were almost as impressive. It was yet another area where we couldn't have been more different.

And, yet, it was that four-year-old, who loudly bulldozed her way through life, whom I had first connected to in this cycle. Her parents had asked my parents to watch her when they went out of town. It was the same night an awful storm hit, and I, in my tiny toddler body, was still so afraid of the dark. I had been terrified that night, sitting up in bed as thunder rattled the house, leaning over the railing of my bed, trying to get out to ... who did I go to? Meredith would have yelled at me for waking her, and despite my efforts, I still had no connection to my human parents. With not one person to run to, I felt alone and desperate as I sobbed in the dark. And then there was a little girl touching my shoulder. I thought she'd be mad at me for waking her up. I thought she would hit me, like she had when I touched her toy. She didn't. She patted the bed, and when I crawled next to her, she wrapped her arms around me and just went to sleep. I had found my best friend that night.

It was too dark to see her, but I could feel her warm breath on my face. She was on her hands and knees, cautiously feeling around in the dark. I felt for her hand, grasping it when I felt her smooth, warm skin beneath my fingers.

We were both still for a while.

"Is this spot taken?" she finally whispered.

I smiled, though she couldn't see it. Gently, I pulled her down and wrapped my arms around her, like she had eighteen years ago. She curled up against my chest, and when I felt her heart beating against me, strong and healthy, I pulled her tighter and buried my face in her hair.

"I'm so sorry," she whispered

She was crying and I was crying too, her wet cheek against my chest in stark contrast to my dry eyes.

Tomorrow, I wouldn't even remember her.

This was my sister. This was the girl I had spent eighteen years of my life with—my other half. I knew I would never feel whole without her.

"You have nothing to be sorry about," I murmured into her hair.

"No," she wept. I felt her tears slide down my neck. "You're my best friend. I've lost everyone, and now I'm losing you too. You've given up everything for me, and I—"

I felt along her neck and pulled out the half-heart necklace. I held it out to where she could see it, then I pulled mine out of my shirt. I could barely see the outline of them in the dark, but they were there.

"I shouldn't have taken everything out on you. I was just so angry. I don't know what I'll do without you. My family is gone, and I'm so scared, Ally. I'm so scared."

I shushed her and stroked her hair, like a mother would for a weeping child, as she cried openly. She didn't seem to mind. When her tears finally ran out, I brushed them off her cheek. She watched me in the dark, eyes still glistening.

"You're going to live, Jilly," I said. "You're going to be happy. You're going to have a beautiful life."

"How?" she whispered back. Her voice sounded so small and scared. "How can life ever be beautiful after this?"

"Because there are people like you left in this world. You're still here. Marie is still here. Tori is still here. There are good people all around you. They're going to take care of you."

"I don't want them, Ally! I want you!"

"If I could," I whispered, "I would stay with you forever. I would never leave."

"But you can't," Jillian whispered back, her voice breaking.

"No, I have to go."

"I can't go with you?"

"No, Jilly Bean, you have to stay here. They need you to make this world better. Make it better than it was, Jilly. Show them what humans are capable of."

I heard a melodic sound not far from us: singing. It took me a few moments to recognize the voice as Emilee's. She was singing something in another language. I realized that the language wasn't one from Earth, nor was it Common Tongue. I didn't recognize it at all—it must have been her native language.

The child was whimpering beneath her words.

"It's okay, sweetie," I heard Emilee coo. "It's okay. You can cry."

"I want to go home. I want Mommy," the little girl sobbed.

I had no doubt that the tiny child was the strongest among us—the most innocent, but in the dark, not even she was impervious to the horror that had befallen the world. Even she knew fear and grief, and I was certain she felt anger, maybe even hatred, toward those who had caused it.

Emilee picked up the song again, but when Emilee stopped and the child's voice continued where she left off, I was startled. It was completely against protocol, but Emilee had taught the little girl an alien lullaby, and she knew the song by heart.

Jillian was quiet while I listened. From the sound of her peaceful breathing, I thought she had drifted off to sleep, but she stirred after a few minutes and lifted up her face. She was looking at me in the dark.

"We're not normal," she said. "The way we behave with each other—I heard you talk to Marie. You treat people differently, and I treat you differently."

I nodded. Just as the little girl had picked up Emilee's alien song, Jillian, even if she hadn't noticed it, had bonded to me like a Thellessian. I had never noticed it before either; it had always felt normal to me.

"I'm not like them," she said, her voice firm. "You made me different from the rest of them. I don't know how yet, but I know you did."

"Yes," I said.

"I never noticed until after the car accident, after I had to live my life without you by my side. For eighteen years, I had you, and then … It was like being a stranger, Ally. It was like watching my interactions with people through a glass wall. I can't tell you how I'm different, *but I feel it.*"

Her voice trailed off.

"I was four years old when I met you, and you had already lived for thousands of years. Whatever I am, you created me. I never stood a chance, did I?"

I smiled, chuckling slightly. "No."

"You made me better."

"You were already better," I said. "You all are. I just taught you how to show it."

The alien lullaby ended and everything was quiet again. People had drifted off to sleep all around us.

"What am I supposed to do now?" Jillian asked.

"Just don't forget," I whispered. "Don't forget how to show it."

CHAPTER 16

It was dark and cold. As I stepped into the light from the burning torches, which were mounted into stone walls that dripped icy-cold water slowly as if they were weeping, I couldn't help but feel as if the walls were closing in on me, reaching for me like skeletal hands. I felt trapped and alone. The light from the torches was too dim to see by, only bright enough to cast grotesque shadows against the gray walls. They were coming for me. I didn't know why I thought that, but somehow I knew. They twisted and danced on the walls and took the shapes of things so strikingly familiar, yet I couldn't place them. I could hear them speaking, whispering unintelligibly, their garbled voices trapped in stone. I knew they were calling to me, but I couldn't hear the words. I felt them moving behind me, the presence of them pressed against my back, but when I looked for them out of the corner of my eye, all I saw was the pale glow of torchlight.

Then, something did move. It was behind me. It was alive.

I was surprisingly calm as I turned. I guess I had known she was behind me the entire time. My eyes focused on the figure in the center of the room, bound and gagged, struggling and sobbing, her wrists chafed and bleeding from being tied to the chair. I surmised that she had been there for a while, based on the amount of filth that had collected beneath her. The room stank with it.

I didn't move toward her. She couldn't have been more than a few feet away, yet it was like watching her through a sea of water. She seemed so far away. Something told me that I should help her—remove the ropes and set her free—but my limbs felt too heavy to move, so I just stood there, watching. I shouldn't have felt so calm. Was I numb? Was it the cold?

Did I even feel anything?

She was only a teenager, maybe fifteen or sixteen years old, with straight brown hair that went down to her shoulders, deep brown eyes, and a field of freckles against her pale skin. I knew her face, though I couldn't place her in my memory. Despite her anguish, her face looked sweet and innocent. I thought I liked her. Yes, I'm sure I liked her. I'm sure we were friends. If only I could remember who she was.

"Lucy?" I heard a small voice say. My eyes followed the meek sound, and I tried to focus on the small figure standing in the doorway. The light from beyond the room was so bright that I was forced to look away.

When I heard the door close, I looked back toward the figure. Slowly, the younger girl was walking into the room, taking a few anxious steps toward the helpless girl. The ribbon in her hair was blue. I was enamored by it.

I wondered where Teddy was. Teddy was supposed to stay with the blue ribbon.

Why did I wonder where Teddy was?

Who was Teddy?

"Lucy?" she asked, her voice trembling. "Get up, Lucy. I want to play."

She stopped only a few feet from the girl in the chair, her auburn curls bouncing around her face, her gray eyes puzzled. Her bed of freckles matched the girl's. Her brows were scrunched up in concern, her little face contorted as she tried to understand. Her skin looked like porcelain. She practically glowed in the soft light of the torches.

She'd be upset with me if I told her she would get wrinkles on her nose if she kept making that face.

But she didn't notice me, and I never said a word.

"Please, Lucy," the little girl begged again. "Please, why won't you play with me?"

The girl in the chair didn't notice her. She didn't even look at her. She sat there, moaning and fighting. The red blood was dripping freely from her wrists now as she fought harder and harder against the shackles.

There were no tears.

"Lucy!" the little girl shrieked, but the girl didn't respond. Her struggling was becoming more frantic. The gag came loose and suddenly the room was filled with an unearthly howl as a scream erupted from the depth of her lungs. She screamed and screamed and screamed, and I didn't think she would ever stop.

The little girl clamped her hands over her ears and stumbled back, terrified. Her eyes were wide and confused, but there was something else hidden in them. She felt heartbroken. She felt betrayed.

"Lucy, I just want you to play with me!" she sobbed. "You promised me you'd always play with me! You promised!"

"She can't play, Lizzie," Jillian said from behind me. I just stood there, unfeeling and unmoving, as she walked past. I should have been startled, but I guess I had felt her behind me, watching.

"Why?" the little girl cried, her hands still clamped to her ears as her sister screamed like a wild animal in the chair. The sound that came from her throat was tortured, as if every breath of life—every heartbeat—was more than she could possibly bear.

"She doesn't remember how," Jillian said, taking the little girl by the hand. Reluctantly, she nodded and turned away. She gave the wailing girl a fleeting look.

"Wait!" I managed to cry as they walked to the door. I tried to move, but I was still frozen. That is, my limbs were still frozen, but I could feel the even colder chill of grief creeping up my throat.

I was afraid. The shadows were moving again, but this time they looked at me angrily. Their movements were violent, as if they were trying to crawl out of the stone, to claw their way out to get to me. They wanted me.

"Jillian!" I cried. I felt a cold terror permeating through my chest. The icy cold of the room was penetrating me. I felt it clutching at my hearts, threatening to wrap around them and crush them in its grasp.

The door was open. The light was blinding again. Jillian turned and looked at me, with pitying eyes. "Just let her play," she said.

I turned away, and when the blinding light had disappeared, so had Jillian and the little girl. I could move. I pounded on the door, screaming for them to come back. I kicked and punched it, tried desperately to pry it open, pushed and shoved all I could, but it wouldn't budge. I was trapped in the dark with the shadows and the prisoner.

The screaming behind me stopped all at once and the room was suddenly silent. I turned slowly, trembling, to see the hollow eyes locked onto me. My vulnerable hearts were racing and I felt the cold creeping closer. It was going to get me.

"Stop," I whispered, my voice barely audible. She didn't even blink.

"Stop!" I shouted at her, but she still didn't move.

"Stop it!" I shrieked. "What do you want from me? Leave me alone!"

Her eyes moved. Slowly, they focused downward. My gaze followed.

I hadn't even noticed the rope in my hand—the same rope that bound the girl to the chair.

"No," I whispered. I tried to drop it, but my hand wouldn't unclench. I felt the cold pierce my heart as my hand began to pull the rope tighter, completely of its own accord. I looked up and saw that the girl was choking, the rope wrapped around her neck.

"No!" I shouted, but I couldn't stop myself. I pulled tighter and tighter, the rope constricting around her neck even more.

Her eyes didn't waver. She just stared at me as the rope choked the life out of her, and as her eyes went dark, her expression never changed: she was hollow. There was nothing left—nothing but a tortured animal. There was no fear or hope or even hatred or anger. There was only the primal hunger to exist and the mind-

282

numbing madness of an entire existence bound. The girl had been gone for years, only her husk left behind to rot in the dark, comforted only by the sounds of her own carnal pain. All she had was pain.

"No!" I screamed as, finally, my hand released the rope. I ran to her.

"Wake up," I begged, clutching at her face. "Please, wake up. Wake up, wake up, wake up!"

The eyes just stared at me. They weren't even accusing. How could she not blame me?

"Please!" I shrieked at the lifeless shell, but she didn't move.

She had to come back! I couldn't have done this! Not me! I couldn't—I would never do something like this! I—

I heard footsteps approaching from behind me, and I leapt up.

"I didn't mean to!" I shrieked, as the red-headed girl calmly looked up at me.

She was pale and gray. Her lips were blue. They were smiling.

How could she be smiling at me? I had left her in a morgue.

"Of course you did, Saira," she said. She calmly walked past me to the lifeless girl and caressed the bonds, which dropped to the floor. She scooped her up into her arms, the smile never leaving her face. She started humming. I reached out for her as she walked past, and she stopped.

"I didn't mean to," I whispered. "I didn't want to."

Her smile fell. Suddenly, she looked sad. She leaned into me, encouraging me to kneel down, and she pressed her lips against my ear. "I wish I could save you."

She felt so warm.

She kissed my blue cheek and turned away.

"It goes faster if you pull harder," she said as she walked out the door, and she disappeared into the blinding light.

I heard a whimper from the corner. I saw the figure huddled in the dark. The rope in my hand led into the shadows.

"NO!" I shrieked, but it was too late. I was already pulling, dragging the girl out of the dark as she kicked and gasped and clawed frantically at the rope around her neck.

She had red hair. She had a half-heart necklace.

Both of my hearts had turned to ice long before she stopped breathing.

"Allyson! Wake up!" Jillian shouted, shaking me awake. I sat up abruptly and hacked violently, clutching my throat as Marie patted my back. As the oxygen began to flow through my body, the first few breaths gave me a strange rush, like being born again.

"You need to stay awake, dummy," Jillian muttered groggily, nudging me with her foot, trying to be playful. She tried to fake a smile but failed. The smile fell. She looked exhausted and was on the verge of tears. Most of the humans had spent all night shaking awake Gangers who had stopped breathing.

Well, all but one of us.

I looked into the dark where the empty cot sat. Its occupant had been removed quietly in the night, and his brother and father had done their mourning in the trees. I saw them at the edge of the cave, quiet. Their loss permeated the air, but I could also feel the immense relief that radiated from them. It was the kindest thing we could do for him. Waking him to breathe would have only prolonged the suffering.

We had all taken our turns paying our respects in the quiet dark, and that was all that could be done.

At least for one of us, it was over. He was free.

I considered him the lucky one.

I looked around. Jillian and Marie flanked me on both sides, but we had company as well. Emilee sat beside Marie, humming the alien lullaby under her breath as she brushed Kaitlin's hair. Kaitlin sat in Marie's lap, aggressively scribbling on a piece of paper with a blue crayon. She was sadder than she was yesterday, of that I had no doubt. And, yet, it was as if she knew but refused to succumb. She was four years old and was trying her best to be cheerful. Rocky whispered to her as she leaned over the picture and pointed to various parts. I heard laughing, and I saw Adam and Derek sitting across from us, nudging each other as they cackled at the joke I had missed.

"What'd I miss?" I asked. My voice sounded so weak. It was barely audible above Emilee's humming. I wondered if I could lie back down, just for five minutes, but I saw the look on Jillian's face as she watched me out of the corner of her eye, and I knew better. I tucked my knees against my chest and rested my chin on them, willing my eyelids to stay open. It felt like all of my willpower was going into that one task.

I felt guilty being the weakest among us.

"Talking about this idiot taking on an ixraz as a kid," Derek snickered, referring to the ill-tempered, swamp-dwelling amphibian of his home planet, Imma. I had never seen an ixraz, but I knew enough about life on other planets to know that it was a foul-smelling blob of a creature with a bad habit of spitting mucus in the face of anyone who risked looking its way, let alone coming near its prized territory in the mud.

"You dared me, you giant flat-faced lizard!" Adam chuckled, miraculously matching his brother's liveliness. I knew they both felt awful, but they refused to let it show.

"You were dumb enough to do it, Snout Boy!" Derek howled, slapping his knee.

"See, they don't tell you this," Derek said to Marie and Jillian, "but my species is just a wee bit smarter than his."

Adam rolled his eyes. "Keep telling yourself that, but we both know that Mom always liked me better."

Jillian and Marie giggled, and I couldn't help but grin myself. I appreciated the effort Adam and Derek made to distract my friends. The brothers looked as sickly as I felt, and yet, there they were, using the last of their energy to try to put smiles on Jillian and Marie's faces.

"I don't get it," Marie said. "How can you two be different species but still be brothers?"

"Ever heard of adoption?" Derek said, smirking.

"Is it common for two different species to live on the same planet together?" Jillian asked. I was surprised by the look of genuine interest on her face.

"Not really," Adam said, shrugging lazily. "Our ancestors were just really bad at killing each other off, so they decided that living in peace was easier. I guess we got used to it."

"And I got stuck being raised with this joker," Derek said. Everyone laughed. It was a nice feeling.

"Is it common for families to join the Peacemakers together? Allyson, didn't your brother join with you?" Marie asked. I quietly nodded, though it took a lot of energy.

"Being a Peacemaker takes a certain kind of being," Rocky said, glancing up from Katie's picture. "It's not an easy task."

"So why did you join?" Jillian asked.

Rocky smiled, her teeth flashing briefly. "Did you know that my father named me in your language? He was a Peacemaker too, long before I was born."

"So you joined because of your father?" Marie asked. Rocky sat up straight and stretched. I could see her thinking as she pressed her tongue against her teeth.

"In a sense," Rocky said. "My father called me Talyn, after the great birds of prey on your planet. We have nothing like them on my planet, so, seeing them, my father felt a sort of kinship to them. He never could describe to me exactly what it was about them, though. When I grew up, I wanted to understand how such a simple creature could inspire someone so much more powerful."

"You were named after a bird?" Jillian said.

"It sounds ridiculous, doesn't it?" Rocky said.

"Did you? I mean, do you understand now?" Marie asked.

Rocky sat quietly for a minute, running her tongue over her teeth, playing with another thought.

"What I have seen—what I have felt and experienced is different. Your planet has changed so much since my father's time."

"How?" Marie asked.

Rocky sighed, letting the air out forcefully all at once. I saw the memory forming in her eyes, growing ever more real and vivid in her mind. Seeing the deep look on her face, I wondered who and when she was seeing.

"I didn't start as a Doppelganger. This is actually my first cycle as one," she said. "My sixth time on Earth was in Europe in the 1940s. It was the last time I served as an Impersonator."

This piqued Marie's interest. "World War II?" she asked excitedly.

Rocky nodded. Her eyes looked very far away now, as if she were watching something in the distance. I understood that look. I knew what it was like to look back and see a full life that was lived so long ago, to remember its sorrows and delights.

From the severity in Rocky's eyes, I wasn't too sure that experience saw any joys. Her face was growing haunted. She was remembering things that usually visited her only in the dark.

"There were Peacemakers in Europe during the World Wars?" Marie squeaked. "What did you do? What side were you on? Did you guys end the war?"

Marie looked at me, giddy, but when Rocky met her eyes, her grin fell. She looked confused.

"I was a Nazi," Rocky said slowly, as if it hurt to speak the words.

Marie looked between the Gangers, not understanding. "What? Why? Were you sabotage? Like a secret agent or something?"

"Our job wasn't to make it better," Rocky said, and her eyes reflected something tragic behind them. Even with the emotions taken away from her, the memories still lingered, and I saw that, despite the strength of her predatory nature, there were things left behind that would torture her forever.

None of us escaped the pain of a young planet. It was the price we all accepted, though none of us ever truly understood the implications until it was much too late.

"What did you do?" Jillian asked.

"It started simply," Rocky whispered, and she didn't meet anyone's eyes. She was looking far off into the distance, seeing a land decades away. "I impersonated some higher-up—I don't even remember his name. I spoke to those around me in confidence, planting ideas in their heads individually, waiting until, one by one, the thought became their own, and finally, the collective's. It wasn't just me, of course. There were hundreds of us placed strategically, all whispering the same idea. When it took hold, I became a doctor. I sat behind a desk and presented logic and reason. I used my authority and played into fears and hopes until people became comfortable with the idea of atrocity and welcomed it into their lives. When the atrocity mutated and grew into an abomination, I stood in a train yard as a soldier and listened to the voices of thousands of souls, and when the other soldiers hesitated to approach them, I stepped forward with confidence and waited for them to follow."

"You organized a genocide," Jillian whispered.

"Yes," Rocky said.

"You *killed* people."

"No," Rocky said. "Humans killed other humans. I only whispered to them."

Rocky looked up into the eyes of my humans. "It's easy to manipulate people when they are alone. When you present them with their fears and share in them, they listen. They get validation that their beliefs are justified and that others share them. They feel empowered knowing that they aren't alone. Slowly, they talk about it to others.

The fear is shared in groups. They stop hiding it and talk openly. Then they get angry, and they start acting."

"That's not fair!" Jillian snapped. "You can't plant ideas in people's heads and then be disgusted when you push them to act on it! You *made* them act because you wouldn't stop pushing! You didn't give them another option!"

"Peacemakers never act unless you give us something to work with. You gave us a reason to go down and start whispering. Don't think there weren't others fighting for the other option—for peace. Don't think that wasn't the decision we were praying you would make. For every Impersonator who pushed for fear, there was one who urged for peace. Humanity made its choice. The vast majority did not say no to fear. The work required to quell it and create tolerance was too much. When you made your decision, we pushed. We made you go as far as the human race could."

"But w*hy*?" Marie cried. "How could you ever encourage something like that? *Millions* of people died!"

Rocky met her eyes. What stared at Marie through them … We all felt the weight of dark moments in human history. We all had been given our demons to battle. I saw Rocky's demon then, lurking behind her eyes, just as Adam had seen mine when the white hospital beds of 1918 surfaced from the depths of my own memory.

"You aren't going to do that again, are you?"

Her voice sounded numb. "Well, that was the idea, at least. You humans are remarkably unwilling to learn."

"You *made* us …" Jillian began. There was an urgency to her voice that told me that she was looking for something—anything—that could shift the blame, to place it back on us.

"'No' was always an option. I never did anything but talk. All it would have taken was enough people to tell me not to."

Jillian stared at Rocky, her eyes burning, her jaw clenched, tears of frustration in her eyes. Rocky looked past her. At that moment, Rocky wasn't there. I felt for her. I really did.

"Did you find any happiness here?" Marie asked. "It seems like all you found was bad. Is there anything good here at all? Ally says everyone thinks we're evil."

"Did *you* ever do anything good?" Jillian whispered.

Slowly, I saw a smile creep onto Rocky's face. "I caught fireflies with my dad and brothers once. You should have seen the field light up with them."

"I had a sister who danced ballet," Derek said.

"My older brother played the saxophone," Adams added. "The first time I heard one …"

Adam shook his head, smiling. "Don't be confused, little human," he said. "Our scars might be large, but this planet *and* its people are beautiful. We would not put ourselves in the middle of wars and diseases if they were not. The stories we share—we have no hatred or anger for you or the trials we have endured. Our stories reflect the extent of our love for you."

"So you're telling us that you can suffer through the worst experiences we have to offer—that you can see things so bad that they hurt decades later, and you aren't the least bit angry with us? Even though you'd never have to experience them if it weren't for us?" Jillian asked.

"Yes," I whispered, and it was the truth. I had said things to my friends before. I had been angry and hurt then, but it had never really been their fault, had it? For all the mistakes this world made, it also had so much beauty—so much I would miss.

"I don't understand that," Jillian said.

"Maybe one day you will," Derek said.

I came to this planet to protect people—to make peace out of the chaos that came with being young. Could I ever consider the human race wicked, knowing full well what they were up against? No, I couldn't.

So what did that mean for us, I wondered. As we orchestrated the worst catastrophe this planet had ever seen, what was our excuse?

"Aunt Emilee," Kaitlin said. "Will I get to see you when you're small and have lots of arms?"

We all jumped, startled by the sound of the child's small voice.

"I don't think so, baby," Emilee whispered.

"Why not?" Katie said innocently, still focused on the picture. Emilee looked up at all of us, her mouth opening and closing, but her eyes, full of questions, focused on me.

"Let me see that picture, Katie," I told the little girl. She held up the picture of the blue figure, speckled with white and gray, limbs over-exaggerated.

"Perfect," I told her. "Why don't you give it to Mr. Derek and he'll make sure it gets put somewhere safe."

"C'mon, kiddo," Derek said, standing up and brushing off his pants. The little girl jumped up and ran past him, giggling.

"Lindsey was sixteen when Kaitlin was born," Emilee said, watching the child dart away. "Kaitlin's father didn't want the responsibility of a child. Our parents did the best they could to help, but we had three younger brothers, and we'd never had much money."

Emilee fiddled with a pebble in the dirt, rolling it back and forth beneath her hand.

"I was eighteen. I could have gone to college, but ... she was my sister, and they both needed me. After a while, I kind of got used to thinking of her as both of ours."

Gangers weren't allowed to have children during their time on Earth. We were discouraged from dating—marriage was out of the question. We could not start our own families. Our bodies were even created sterile to make certain we didn't bring human children into the world. There would be nothing wrong with a child born to a Ganger, but the emotional implications of having a human child that you would be forced to leave would be devastating.

"You taught her a song from your planet," I said. "I heard you singing it to her."

"I shouldn't have," Emilee said. "I know I shouldn't have, but— when we're at home, Lindsey just thinks—thought—we made up a language together. She thought it was cute."

"Katie can speak your language?" Marie asked, eyebrows raised.

Emilee nodded, eyes downcast. "I really shouldn't have, but I knew I'd be ... well, I knew she would forget by the time she was older. It would all just be a childhood memory—a little game she played with her silly aunt."

"Maybe it won't be," Derek said, shrugging. "This kid is different."

"She has to forget about me—about all of it," Emilee whispered, and her face looked haunted. "They'll find out. She isn't allowed to know. I don't know what I was thinking."

"The Elders didn't take her after you came back—after they got the memory chip. It can't be that bad a thing," Derek said, shrugging.

"It's because you did the right thing. Finally, somebody did the right thing," Rocky muttered. "I only wish I had done it first."

Emilee stared at her, mouth agape. Rocky didn't say any more, and as the weight of the silence set in, Emilee broke down.

The tears never fell, though. Only humans cried. Ganger tear ducts worked for physical pain. Tears would fall if I stubbed my toe on the corner of a doorframe or cut an onion, but I had never once cried tears. None of us ever had. Crying tears was a uniquely human attribute, and though we fully understood it biologically, it was something we had never been able to replicate, making a Ganger an almost flawless human copy at best.

"I can't leave her. I don't want her to forget me!" Emilee cried. "I can't! *I can't!* I'd rather die!"

Rocky put her arms around her and stroked her hair. None of us said anything. What could we say? That everything would be okay? When the sun came up, the humans would leave to struggle and maybe die without us, left to survive in the waste of a wounded planet, and we would go ...

We would go to forget—to have everything taken from us. It hit me then, and I looked up. I met Adam's eyes. He had been watching me, his eyes burning. I had noticed that he hadn't said a word since the little girl left, but I hadn't felt the heat radiating off of him until now.

We held each other's gaze for the longest time. I looked over and saw the same fierce look in Rocky's eyes.

"They were my first family," Emilee sobbed. "She's all I have left, and I—and I ..."

"She's going to be fine," Jillian said, trying hard for a genuine smile. Of course, she couldn't. "Marie and that kid are already joined at the hip."

"I have to go make sure they got Teddy. She can't sleep without him," Emilee said, scrambling to her feet, though, when she walked away, she walked to the pillars. I saw her lean against one, her shoulders shaking.

I felt a pang go through my chest. It startled me, the way it stabbed with the force of a thousand knives. I felt the grief rising, though I had no idea where it was coming from, clawing up from my chest like a rabid animal, ripping and tearing as it went. Hysteria was rising; I felt it threatening to erupt. I had to get up. I had to run.

"I'll be right back," I whispered, and forced myself to get up and walk away calmly. I stumbled out of the cave and out into the trees. It was dark. I couldn't see where I was going. I didn't care. I plodded along before I finally tripped and went to my knees in the dirt. I didn't even realize I had fallen.

I was choking. I was in pain. Why was I in pain? What was this?

She had carried that teddy bear with her everywhere she went until she was six. The ribbon around his neck always matched the ribbon Mother put in her hair. She had asked for him when she got sick. He had been sitting on the bed, blue ribbon around his neck, tucked under the covers right beside her when she died.

The full brunt of the memory hit me with a blinding force. I was choking—no, I was drowning in it. It was everywhere. It was all around me, screaming at me, claws outstretched. It had been trying to break free all this time, but I hadn't remembered.

"Allyson," Adam asked from behind me, his voice steady and calm. I leapt to my feet and stared at him, gasping.

"She wasn't blonde," I whispered.

"I forgot!" I suddenly screamed. "I forgot her! How could I ever forget her? I couldn't even remember what she looked like until now! *She was my baby sister!*"

"It's amazing," Adam murmured. "Look at what our mind lets go of when we have no reason to remember."

I stared at him. I felt so weak. I didn't have the willpower to stand. I sat down in the dirt, empty. I had lost so much. How had I never realized it?

"My name is Allyson," I whispered. "My name is Lucy. My name is Mila. My name is Yelizaveta. My name is Anastasia."

I stared at him. He waited.

"But what are their names?" I sobbed. "I can't remember their faces, Adam."

"I know," Adam said.

I shook my head, refusing to accept it. So many families. So many parents, brothers, and sisters. So many friends. How many could I put names and faces to? How many had faded away altogether?

I had done this before, I realized. This entire story had been on repeat, and I hadn't even noticed. I had been going through the pages and had failed to notice that the author had only changed the names. I had once watched death walk around me, taking everyone I loved. I had fought so hard to keep them all alive, praying with every ounce of my being that I would save them.

I had failed.

I had thought that I understood my story. I lived as a human until, twenty years later, I left, and when enough time had passed, I came back. I haunted the Earth like a phantom—that was my fate. It had never been about me living, though. That was only half the story. What about those who were left to die and be forgotten? Why had I let them start the story over? Why did I come back to live and just watch as those I loved around me died ... again?

When the other realization hit me, I felt panic. *Who had faded away indeed ...*

I had been so distracted. I had thought it was over, that my job was done. I guess that was why I never noticed her absence.

"Adam?" I whispered.

"What?" he asked, realizing that something was awry.

"Where's Tori?" I whispered.

We were both up and running through the trees as fast as our weak Ganger legs would carry us. We didn't hesitate. We burst through the main camp in the cave, nearly knocking over humans and Gangers alike, all of whom stared at us wide-eyed, wondering where the immediate danger was waiting for them.

"Tori!" I shrieked. "Tori! *Where are you?*"

I should have listened when she came to me. She was just a child seeking guidance, and I had snapped at her. I had pushed her away, and now she was really gone, out there somewhere in the dark doing the wrong thing because I was a fool. If anything happened to her ...

"*Tori!*" I screamed hysterically.

"She's not here," Jillian said, running up to me breathlessly. "We've been looking, but we can't find her."

Marie was with her. They looked terrified. I felt like I was going to throw up, but not while my friends were staring at me like that, looking to me for answers. I had to *do* something! I had to find her!

"Who's missing?" I heard Derek say as he slid to a halt beside me. Rocky and Emilee were with him. I felt a strength in them; the need to protect, to fight and die for those they loved. They were Peacemakers who felt their calling beckoning.

"Tori," I whispered. "I don't know who—the ranger. Where's the park ranger? Where's his car or cabin or whatever? *Where would he keep his guns?*"

Rocky sprang into action. "Adam. Derek. The cabin is a quarter of a mile away over the ridge. Emilee, get the humans packed up and ready to go. They're leaving now. Allyson, let's go."

We heard the gun blasts in the distance.

"Emilee!" Rocky shouted. "Get the humans out of here!"

"Run!" I shouted at Jillian and Marie. "Go with Emilee!"

I didn't look back, though I heard them shouting for me.

We ran hard, the other Gangers and me. We pushed ourselves as hard as we could, perhaps even harder. We were all dying, but for that brief moment we called on strength we didn't know we had. We ran through the trees, running for the gun blasts, leaping over fallen trees and tearing through brush and thorny vines. I didn't even feel the pain as they cut my legs. My heart pounded. Every beat pushed me forward, toward Tori.

I slid to a halt when I saw them: nearly a dozen bots, all of them circling a group of about half a dozen humans. Everything moved in slow motion. I could hear my single heart pounding in my ears, each beat growing louder than the next, counting down the moments. I inhaled, taking in the scent of the earth.

There were so many.

Rocky was not far from me, watching the same scene. Adam and Derek were with her. The look in their eyes …

My insides twisted and the world fell away. We all knew it; there was nothing we could do.

But it was Tori, and I would never accept that. *I would not lose her.*

I ran for her. Each step I took dug into the dirt, thrusting me forward, but I couldn't move fast enough.

There was no way they could escape. The park ranger raised the gun and fired, but the shield easily deflected the bullet from the bot. There was no glitch, no wavering of the force field. Not this time. It turned to face them dead-on, its targets firmly in its sights.

Tori saw me. I will always remember the look on her face.

"*I'm sorry*," she mouthed, tears streaming down her face. She turned her face away and closed her eyes.

The stillness was eerie.

"*NO!*" I howled, and the trees echoed with my anguish.

I felt the pulse in the ground as the humans fell.

I watched Tori fall, her body twisting hideously as her legs gave way. She never hit the ground, though. There was a flash of light, and where she had been, there was only ash. It scattered as the bots raced past, coming right at us.

I didn't notice them, though. I was too busy screaming.

"Tori!" I shrieked as the bots flew past me. I didn't even see them—didn't even realize that they had let me live. I didn't care. I just kept running, my eyes trained on the last place Tori had stood—the place she died.

"Allyson! No!" Rocky shouted. She grabbed me and dragged me back, away from Tori.

"Let me go!" I shrieked, clawing at her arms. "I have to get to her! I have to—"

"She's gone! There's nothing you can do!"

I don't know how, but I broke free. I only got a few feet before Rocky had me by the waist, and this time, I tripped. We both fell to the dirt. I didn't even feel the impact. I was sobbing so hard, I could barely breathe.

"Allyson! Stop this! Stop! She's gone! You can't save her!" Rocky screamed, but she was sobbing too.

I clawed at the dirt. I wanted to turn the clock back. I wanted to get to Tori. I had to fix this. I had failed her.

Then Rocky had my shoulders. She was in my face, screaming. She was shaking me. It didn't make sense. It wasn't fair. Why, after all we had been through? I wanted to lie down in the dirt and be done. I *was* done. I couldn't find the strength to move anymore, and I didn't want to.

"I'm sorry!" I sobbed. "I'm so sorry! She needs to know that I'm sorry! She can't die! She can't just die when I—she can't—"

The last time I had ever spoken to one of my best friends—to one of the people I loved most on this earth—I had yelled at her. We had fought, and she had told me she hated me.

That was it. We would never have the chance to make it right.

How could I just accept that?

It was time to give up. It was time to die, too. I just lay there and prayed for it, me for her, as I watched what was left of Tori settle into the dirt. She deserved so much more. I would do anything for it to be me instead of her. I begged that, finally, someone *would just let me die instead.*

Why did I always get to live?

"Allyson! I'm so sorry, Allyson, but you have to run!" Rocky shouted, the words coming out between sobs. "Run to Jillian! Run to Marie! For God's sake, RUN! Don't let them die too!"

I blinked. The world snapped back. It was just us. The other Gangers had vanished. Everything else was still. The bots were gone.

But where?

I turned and looked behind me. I could think of dozens of reasons why the bots had moved on, and every one of them was a reason for me to move. I swallowed the sobs. Still gasping, I pushed the pain away. My job wasn't finished. I had two reasons left to live. I forced myself to my feet, and somehow I managed to turn my back on the ash. Somehow I forced myself to run, and I left her.

I left Tori behind. I never got the chance to say goodbye.

When we burst through the trees, the bots were on them. Two humans fell as I approached. The others ran in all directions, screaming, desperate looks across their faces. Death had come for them and they knew there was nowhere to turn.

We would all die here. I knew that, but that didn't stop my heart from beating as it did, willing me to fight to live. It had refused to quit, even after all it had endured. So long as it was still fighting, I had to, too.

Human hearts were remarkable.

So long as they weren't silenced by bots.

Marie and Jillian ran toward me, darting from side to side to make themselves a more difficult target, but I didn't know what use it would be with a dozen bots chasing us.

It didn't matter. The bots would have to go through me before they could take them. My corpse would serve as their shield. It wouldn't stop them, but I would send a message to those upstairs that they could not take the lives of those I loved.

I clenched my fists and gritted my teeth. If it was a fight they wanted, then fine, but it was they who had done this.

"Don't stop!" I shouted as they ran past me. I picked up a rock and flung it at the pursuing bot, but it had no effect. It raced at me and I put myself firmly in its path. We were on a collision course. There was a branch at my feet. Without hesitation, I picked it up.

My insides were on fire.

"Come on!" I screamed at the bot. For some reason, it hadn't fired. It didn't even seem to see me. As it raced past me, I raised the branch and brought it down over the bot as hard as I could. The force field went up and the branch splintered into a million pieces. I stumbled backward as the bot continued forward, unfazed.

It didn't see the Gangers, only the humans.

"*No!*" I hissed. I knew I wouldn't have any effect on it. I knew I would lose.

But then, this bot had never encountered a Ganger with only two things in the world left to lose.

The flashes of light startled me. A Ganger vanished to my left, but there wasn't a bot in close proximity.

The transport beam came directly from the ship.

This wasn't an accident—a group of bots stumbling upon a cluster of humans. The bots were singling the humans out, distinguishing them from the Gangers. The Council had found our hiding place. Our friends were gone. Our protectors weren't here to watch out for us anymore.

This was their way of cleaning up.

Another Ganger disappeared to my right. Another human fell. The screams filled my ears.

"Allyson!" Jillian cried. They were running at me, but they were growing tired. Another bot was behind them. It would catch them soon. They ran past, and this time, when the bot came at me, I didn't move. Another branch would be of little use. This time, I would make sure the bot stayed on the ground.

It wasn't programmed to see me. It plowed into me and I wrapped my arms around it, digging my nails in, trying to grasp it. It hit me hard; it was like being hit in the chest with a baseball bat. I thought I heard something crack over the sounds of human cries.

The shield went up as it hit me.

My breath was knocked out of me. My balance was lost. Still, when I went tumbling, so did the bot.

Shields weren't made of solid matter. I couldn't even feel it under my hands. When I hit the ground, I lost my grip, and the bot was gone. I had lost it.

When I rolled over, I coughed up blood. Everything was spinning. I tried to stand, but I couldn't. I collapsed, my face pressed into the dirt as blood ran past my lips. I couldn't breathe.

"Allyson!" Jillian sobbed. She was beside me. "Get up! *Get up!*"

Marie had my arms. She was trying to pull me up, but my feet gave way and I ended up back in the dirt.

With the last little bit of strength I had, I pushed them behind me. The bot was coming.

In the distance, directly in front of me, my eyes locked onto the forms of Emilee and Rocky, their arms around Kaitlin, her face hidden in her aunt's neck as she clutched at her shirt collar. They weren't running. They were just standing there.

"Run!" I tried to shout, but nothing came out, except the blood that was dripping from my mouth.

There was a flash of light. They disappeared.

All three of them.

Marie sobbed as the bot came at us, but she didn't run. Jillian was begging me to get up. I felt her pulling at my shoulder. I reached behind me with one hand. It hurt so much to move, but I did it.

"Take my hand," I managed to say. I looked behind me and met their eyes. Their instincts were telling them to run and never look back, but they stayed planted where they were. They wouldn't leave me.

"Trust me," I said, my breath coming out in gasps.

They grabbed hold of me. I felt both of their hands; one in mine, the other clutching my wrist. I saw the look in their eyes as they

298

watched the bot. It was almost on us. I closed my eyes and held my breath.

There was a flash of light.

I heard Marie screaming uncontrollably. Jillian cried out. They both pulled away from me—I felt their hands slip away. I reached out but felt only air.

"No," I tried to say, but the word never came out. They couldn't leave me. They had to stay close. I had to keep them safe.

The surface beneath me was not leaves and dirt; instead, I felt a cold metal floor. We were on a ship, but I was certain it wasn't *Moga*. *Moga* didn't have cold, dark cells like these. Everywhere I looked, there was callous metal, encircling us like a tomb. The only light came from a slit in the farthest wall, and it was barely enough to make the outlines of my frantic humans visible.

We were on a Council ship. I had dragged my friends on board a Council ship. I had saved them from the bot, but now their death was even more certain, and I was not sure I had given them the better one.

If it had just been *Moga*...

Marie screamed as she backed away from the two—make that three—aliens huddled in the corner of the cell, closest to the window. Jillian pressed her back against the wall and slumped down, quiet, but pale and terrified. The signal to her brain to tell her to start screaming had not made it there yet.

Pask, Pashka, and Dorain looked almost as startled.

"Saira?" I heard the voice of my brother. He was the wrong shade of blue. When he realized it was me, he rushed out from the shadowy corner, threw himself to his knees, and sat beside me.

"What did they do?" he whispered. He pressed his fingers into the pool of red forming beneath me. When he pulled them back up, I saw something break inside him.

"I'm okay," I whispered, reaching a hand up to him. He took it and grasped it tightly with both hands, staring at me with a doleful look in his eyes.

"Saira Ta'u, what have you done to yourself?" Pask said, hovering over me as Pask and Pashka's arms gently felt my broken human body. Pask had one eye that she held almost closed. Pashka's hands were shaking, the pressure he applied on my body with them feeble. His bottom jaw dangled limply. I didn't think he could speak.

"Couldn't let the bot get them," I whispered, and somehow I managed to grin. "I think I taught it a lesson."

"Saira Ta'u, you will stop talking. You have internal bleeding and broken bones," Pask snapped. They fiddled anxiously, powerless to help me.

"It's okay. Time's up," I whispered. I coughed and tasted warm metal.

All of a sudden, I felt calm. Maybe it was my brother's touch. Maybe it was the blood loss. Everything was turning gray and fuzzy. The world was going quiet. I felt it slipping away, as if I were falling.

"Allyson?" I heard Jillian whisper. "You're really hurt."

I could tell from the sound of her voice that she was trying to be strong, but she sounded so scared and uncertain. I hadn't noticed, but Marie had crawled over to her and was huddled against her side, no longer crying but visibly shaking.

"It's okay," I said, my voice barely stronger than a whisper. "This is Pask and Pashka. They're friends. This is my brother."

My friends were quiet, staring, trying to comprehend.

"Katie's drawing was pretty good," Marie squeaked.

I managed the twitch of a smile. "He's taller."

"Are you hurt?" Pask asked my humans. They shook their heads.

"To think that we would get to see real humans," she said sweetly, and though their lips couldn't curl into a smile, I could tell from her voice that they were.

"Are you a doctor?" Marie asked. Pask and Pashka both nodded.

"Can you help her?" Jillian asked, her voice shaking.

"Nothing to help, Jilly," I choked out. "I'm going to wake up s-s-soon. It will b-be okay. They w-w—"

My tongue was getting heavy and it was hard to move my mouth.

Jillian looked around, searching. She was looking for someone now, but she wouldn't find her. I felt the pang of the loss as my heart clenched, even as it was failing. I felt the anger ignite. It felt like fire as it rushed through my numb limbs. She should have been here!

Jillian's eyes met mine and I held them, apologizing, begging for her forgiveness with that one despairing look. Marie's face changed as she realized it, too. The grief took hold in her chest and begin

300

squeezing, twisting at her heart, sinking in its gnarled nails. Her breath caught and her eyes fill with tears. Jillian just stared, her eyes distant and hollow, angry.

"Where's Tori?" she whispered

"I t-t-tried," I choked. It was all I could bring myself to say.

Everyone was still. It was so dark and cold in that cell. Even with the numbness and burning anger, I felt the icy chill creeping into my bones. My brother must have been freezing to death and half-starved, trapped in this horrible place. All I could feel was cold.

It was getting darker, but it had nothing to do with the light coming through the window.

"Idiot," Jillian whispered, her voice enraged.

"Jillian ..." I mumbled. I tried reaching out for her, but I couldn't move. My hand gave a feeble twitch before it was still again.

"*Idiot!*" she screamed. She smashed her fist into the wall. She hit it, then again, then again and again and again. She was screaming. Marie was sobbing, huddled in a ball against the wall, her face pressed into her knees. It felt like it went on forever, but then it was over, and they were both quiet. Jillian sat there, panting, her face streaked with tears, while Marie crawled into her lap and laid her head down, sniffling. They both looked as if they had given up and accepted their fate. They realized there was no escape from this. They knew they were next.

And I hated myself. There were seven billion people on that planet, and I couldn't even save three! One was dead, her ashes scattering in the wind, and the other two were stuck in an alien jail cell, waiting for the executioner to come walking down the corridor. I had failed them.

Jillian looked me in the eye. "You're going to die now, aren't you?"

I tried to shake my head, but I didn't have the energy.

"I n-n-need y-you to be s-s-s-trong for me, okay? They're g-going to c-c-c-ome for us n-now."

I was right. At that moment, I heard footsteps echoing down the hall.

"Saira!" Dorain gasped. I met his gaze. I somehow managed to pull my hand free and push his hands away. I couldn't speak, but he understood.

"Come here, girls," he said to Jillian and Marie. "Get behind us."

"What are you going to do?" Jillian asked, pressing herself against the wall, keeping as far from the doctors and my brother as she could. Marie grabbed her arm, watching us, trembling.

"I'll be r-r-right b-back," I said.

"You can't leave us," Jillian whispered. They were pressed up against the door. The footsteps were growing louder. They were almost here.

"They c-can't m-make m-m-me," I said, my voice hard.

She nodded, and with fists clenched, she pulled Marie up, and they both walked into the arms of the aliens. My brother pulled them behind him, and he backed them up against the wall, using himself as a barrier. Pask and Pashka followed his lead, placing themselves in front of him.

"Take c-c-care of them for m-me," I whispered. "I'll be b-back for you."

"What are you going to do?" my brother asked.

It took courage and strength, but I forced myself onto my hands and knees, and crawled to the door. I couldn't take a breath. The pain from moving was too much. My ears were ringing. The world was going black, but the fire under my skin told me I had to stay up. I gritted my teeth. I couldn't stand, but I would not be on the ground when they came for me.

I heard the footsteps stop outside. The door to the jail cell slid open with a hiss.

The very last thing I did as Allyson Owens was raise my head and look them in the eye. I never felt the ground pulse.

CHAPTER 17

The world had been turned upside down and inverted. I was being ripped through a vortex, unnaturally bright, cold, and screaming with ear-shattering noise. I was tumbling over and over again. I tried to reach out and grasp something—anything—but I was being pummeled, collapsing in on myself, suffocating. It hurt. I felt icy-hot knives of agony stabbing inward, twisting and tearing at me like the jaws of a rabid animal. I was being ripped apart from all sides. I writhed and screamed, trying to push away the attacks that came from everywhere, but I couldn't escape. I was being destroyed.

Slowly, my eyes fluttered open. The pain was gone—disappeared. It seemed like just some distant memory—not even a memory. I had awoken from a dream that was already forgotten. In its wake, I felt warm and calm, as if I had just woken from a deep, restful sleep. There was no shrieking noise, only a low humming sound. It was so soothing. I knew it meant me no harm. It was bright, but I liked the light that surrounded me. It made me feel strong and healthy. I could feel it on my skin, gentle and nourishing. I heard the two hearts beating, fast and strong. I felt the long, strong limbs flexing, remembering what it felt like to move.

I blinked. The movement was sedated. Where was I? I tried to think, but my mind was much too slow. I wasn't fully awake yet. My eyes had opened, but I was barely aware of the outside world. I shook my head languidly, trying to clear away the fuzzy blanket of confusion that had wrapped itself around my mind.

I clenched my eyes shut, trying to focus—to force comprehension on myself. There was something I had to remember … I needed to wake up. I needed to move, but I couldn't remember why. Everything felt so soft and gentle, lulling me softly back to sleep. Time didn't exist; I just floated in light, independent of everything.

I felt as if nothing could hurt me in the light. It was just me and the gentle warmth. I wanted to stay there forever.

I opened my eyes. I became aware of the small window in front of me. Curiously, I leaned forward ever so slightly, intrigued by the sudden appearance of the rectangle in my world of light.

As I peered out, another pair of eyes was looking back. No, not a pair of eyes—three eyes. There were three eyes, white with pitch-black irises, watching me. They were waiting for me.

Why were they waiting for me?

A sudden memory flashed before my eyes.

My eyes. They had reflected in the black mask of the suit as he raised the pulse gun at me.

The force of the memory hit me, violent and angry. The sense of calm and comfort I had was obliterated in an instant.

They had shot me! They had just walked in and killed the Ganger body! The last thing I had expected was a warm reception from the Council agents, but what kind of beast simply walks up to and shoots another being in a cage? What kind of creature has a cage to put me in in the first place? And who in their right mind would ever extract a Ganger in that manner? I was lucky that the distance was short, or they would have risked insanity! Was that what they were hoping for? Was that what the three eyes were checking for as they appeared in the window again? Were they doing the same thing to the others? Were they okay?

And if they had shot me, what had they done to Marie and Jillian? Even as a criminal, I would still be viewed as higher than them. Would they be put down like the animals the Council so clearly believed them to be?

There was a clanking sound. My brain registered the sound as chains dropping. They had chained the door closed on me, but they were opening it now.

They had *chained* me inside a box! The realization made my blood boil. They had expected me to come back insane and locked inside a metal canister. If I were mad, would they have bothered letting me out, or would they simply have counted me as lost and dead, and let the box serve as my coffin? As I stood there in the tiny cylinder, its walls pressing in on me, I was suddenly reminded of the final resting place of Allyson Owens. They had abandoned her inside a box, too.

The door hissed, then opened slightly. They were coming for me, but they were doing it slowly, hoping that I was still disoriented and they could get the upper hand before I came to.

But I vowed to myself that they couldn't have me. They couldn't have my friends. They couldn't have my memories. I was done letting them take things from me.

It was my turn to take. It was my turn to destroy.

They were foolish to shoot me, and not simply because of the moral implications. They should have followed the procedure, because, for the first time ever, I woke up in my body *feeling something*.

For the first time in my life, I felt blind rage. I felt injustice. I felt the need for revenge. For once, I had come back to my Thellessian body with more, but I had also come back with less. Some integral part of me had been left on the wounded planet below. It left me the moment they took someone I loved right before my eyes. They had killed her as if she meant nothing, and now they had come for the only two I had left. They had come for the memories that were all I had of those I loved—five generations of families that I had lost and would never see again.

I wished mercy on the beings outside the door, because what was missing from me now—it had been something virtuous and loving, and I feared that it was entirely gone.

It didn't stand in my way now. It wouldn't protect them.

My race was passive. The aggression response within us was almost nonexistent. It was close to impossible to even force one of us into an act of belligerence. Because of that, what was probably unknown to the two aliens waiting outside with their stun guns was that my race was unbelievably strong.

The two aliens didn't know what hit them.

The door erupted outward, dented from the force of my kick, and it took the three-eyed alien with it. He collapsed against the wall. I didn't get a good look at the second Council agent. From the corner of my eye, I saw the gun go up, and then he was flying down the hall, crying out in shock.

The sound of him connecting with the wall didn't even register.

I wondered how long I had been out. Seconds? Minutes? Hours? Where were Marie and Jillian? Could Dorain, Pask, and Pashka protect them? How could they? Even if they could, where would they take them? Where could *I* take them? Would the Council's agents shoot my brother and the kind doctors, too, if they got in the way? Were they expendable traitors, too?

I knew they hadn't meant for me to return to my body in one piece. It would be such an inconvenience for them if I came back with my mental facilities fully intact. How sad it would be if their little scapegoat was too far gone to stand a proper trial.

I realized then that that was all I had ever been to the Council. This was their fault. I knew this was their fault. The guards, the jail, the cold-blooded murder—all of it told me that this was and had always been the Council's fault, and they expected me to take the fall. I didn't know what I had done to deserve such a fate, but it hardly mattered now. The damage was done. My life was over.

I was over. They had destroyed me just as completely as they had destroyed the planet below. I had been a loving creature once, but that girl wasn't the one who woke up this time.

I heard human screams coming from down the hall, echoing against the cold metal. The desperate cries pierced the still silence of the dark hallway, and I felt them find their way into my second heart. I felt it shattering. The sound of their distressed cries drove me into a rage I had never felt before.

The Council would take responsibility for their actions, not me. I would make sure of it.

I ran. I was fast. I don't know how my weakened legs, unused to movement after over twenty years in stasis, moved so quickly, but they carried me down the darkened hall, lined with stasis chambers, all of which were wrapped in chains, and into the light of catacombs of jail cells. They had imprisoned all of us in one section of the ship, and it was easy for me to follow the sounds of my humans' frightened cries and come behind the savages in suits. I moved too quietly for them to hear me.

It was a trait often attributed to the gentleness of my race—we hardly made a sound when we moved.

I was fast and quiet enough that the two beings at the cell door—one by the doorframe and one only a few steps inside—didn't realize I was on them until it was too late.

They both turned and raised their guns at the appearance of my shadow, but I grabbed the closest alien by the scruff of the neck and tossed him out of the cell like a ragdoll. I kicked the other one's feet out from under him, then grabbed him by the ankles and threw him behind me. I heard the distinct thud of each one hitting the wall and collapsing down in a heap, but I didn't look back.

I hoped they never got back up.

Jillian was screaming. It was the sound of pure terror and anguish, and it drove me into a blind panic. She was by the door. Her nose was bloody and her lip was split. I couldn't think. All I could hear was the sound of her terror rattling around inside my head. All I could see was the blood dripping off her chin and splashing on the ground in a tiny red puddle.

They had hurt her. *They had hurt her!* I came at her, my arms outstretched to snatch her up and protect her, but she backed away, still screaming, her eyes wide with unbridled fright.

She didn't recognize me.

The Ganger body that used to be me was lying on the floor not far from me, eyes still open. The incineration mechanism in the pulse gun used to kill her was too dangerous to fire into the small jail cell, so the suits just pushed passed her as they came in. She had been flung aside and piled into a heap beside the door. She was watching me. I felt sick. If I had been a human, I might have vomited, but as it was, I just wanted to weep. The cold, blank eyes stared at me. The body was slowly turning a shade of gray as I watched it.

I couldn't take my eyes off my old body. It seemed so much more familiar to me than the one I currently inhabited. My real body felt ... wrong. No, my real body was growing cold on the floor. Try as I might, my mind would not let go of the thought that the girl on the floor was still me. I didn't feel like an alien. I still felt human—I *was* human.

I met the eyes of the terrified human girl bleeding on the floor. She didn't see me as Allyson anymore. I was as alien to her as I was to myself.

This was a cruel fate. I had spent twenty years living and growing up. I had changed. Now I had woken up and that change hadn't been removed from me. The girl I had changed into couldn't fit in this body.

"Allyson?" I heard Marie whisper. Her eyes peered out from behind Dorain, Pask, and Pashka. She moved toward me.

But my brother threw his hand up and stopped her, pressing her back further, where it was safe. His eyes were locked on me. My brother knew I would never hurt my friends, but in his alarm over seeing my violence, he failed to truly recognize me.

How strange I looked to us all, the broken, enraged human-monster who had been forced into an old ghost's shell.

I hadn't been Saira in a very long time, and now we could all finally see it.

But who was I?

I knelt down on my knees and closed my eyes. I couldn't let myself be a monster. No one recognized the blue alien in the jail cell, but we were all attached to some memory of her. I clung to that knowledge. Whoever I was, whatever patchwork creature I had become, there was some piece of her that my loved ones needed, and I tried to call her back, if only for a little while. I loved them enough to do that. I forced a feeling of calm through my limbs. My hands, once curled into weapons ready to attack, relaxed, and I reached out to Jillian with a gentle blue hand—the strange, mild-mannered creature that they remembered in one form or another.

"Hey, Jilly Bean," I said. The human language sounded strange coming from my Thellessian body, but the words were clear enough.

What could I possibly say to wipe the terror from her eyes and replace the image of her friend as the lifeless body to her left as the image of her friend, tall and blue, with one hand reaching to her in comfort. How could I remind her of eighteen years of friendship?

I blurted the first thing that came to mind.

"Do you remember that goldfish of yours? You had him for two weeks before he died. I wanted you to name him Spot because he had gold and black spots, but you named him Killer. I whined that he wasn't a killer, he was just a little goldfish."

Her expression changed, as recognition flashed through her eyes. She looked directly at me, her eyes meeting mine. She held them. I could see that she was still afraid, but not enough to look away.

"I wanted to give him a funeral. You dug a hole in your backyard, which I still found barbaric, but it was better than flushing him. I wouldn't let you read from the Bible, because I said that probably wasn't his religion, since he was a fish. We read from a children's book instead. I don't remember which one it was."

Jillian looked over at the body of Allyson, her expression conflicted. She stared at her for a good while, but when she finally looked back at me, the relief in her glistening eyes was obvious. There were tears running down her cheeks, but a smile was trying to form. I saw the corners of her lips twitch as emotions ran rampant through her. She held out a half-heart necklace, spattered with red blood and dirt, before she broke down in sobs, covering her face with one hand.

"You were always a little odd," she choked. I gently took the necklace from her and tied it around my wrist. My neck was too large to wear it now. I pulled her toward me, scooped her up, and cradled her in my arms. She buried her head into my chest and wrapped her arms around my neck, sniffling.

"Marie?" I asked the small human who stood unsure and fearful behind my brother and the two doctors.

"I'm okay," she whispered, staring at me with wide eyes.

My gaze became fixed on my brother. Silver blood ran from a gash on his face. He was staring at me, and there was something in his eyes that made my second heart skip a beat—something sad, as if something precious had been stolen from him, but I also saw pity. He was pitying me, but I didn't know why. Was it because I had lost myself? Was it because I was a monster? Or was it because this situation we had all found ourselves in was so terribly sad?

"Are you okay?" I asked gently in Darcii, watching a droplet of the silver blood slide down his cheek and drop, hitting the ground with a tiny splash. The ground was speckled with red and silver. The Council agents hadn't discriminated in whom they hurt. My brother had selflessly put himself in harm's way to protect my friends, and the price looked like it was painful. My brother was stronger than he seemed, though, and if he was in any discomfort, he wasn't showing it.

Dorain nodded slowly, though his eyes remained transfixed on me. His expression didn't change. There was a time when I would have gone to him. I would have touched his face and pressed my forehead against his. I would have whispered to him that everything would be okay, and we would hold each other like we used to as children.

But neither of us moved. We just stood there and looked at each other, and I realized that we had become strangers to each other at some point in this gruesome journey.

It was a heartbreaking realization. It affected me less than it probably should have, but then, that was just another example of how broken I really was.

We heard footsteps echoing down the hall. They were running. There were a lot of them.

"Dorain, get Marie!" I shouted. I was on my feet, Jillian in my arms, facing the hall.

There were other cells. I heard voices crying out, pounding on the doors to be released, though the walls were so dense that it was hard to figure out which cells the voices were coming from. The walls were smooth, outwardly seamless, but I could still see the outline of the doors. I approached the closest one and raised a fist, Jillian cradled under the other arm. I punched once, twice, and after the third time, I had buckled the door enough to be able to force one hand into the ridge that formed between the wall and door, and pry it open. It was empty. I moved to the next one, but then the Council agents were on us.

One was a humanoid alien with tentacles erupting from its head and face. Its beady black eyes stared at me, challenging me to make another move toward the cell door, its stun gun raised. At least it was a stun gun ... The second alien had white, see-through skin, and I could see the red heart in the middle of his chest beating steadily. He hissed at me, sharp teeth exposed and forked tongue flicking in and out, testing the air.

The third alien was an Avinox. I had always found the Avinox to be an intensely beautiful race. Humans might call them angelic in appearance. They had long white hair, tinted a silvery blue. Their skin was pale and flawless, and their features were elegant and angular. Their eyes were probably their most striking feature. Whereas the creature with the tentacles –a Thrusk, I recalled—had black voids, the Avinox had pure, soft, baby-blue eyes. They were beautiful.

When I saw the Avinox, all I could think was that I would love to break his pretty face. I felt my second heart racing. My eyes narrowed, glaring revulsion at him. For the first time, I felt true hatred for someone, that horrible Avinox with his self-righteous ways and the torment he had caused. It was illogical, but right at that moment I held him, and him alone, responsible for every grisly experience I had ever endured on the planet below, every bad thing those poor humans had been forced to suffer through.

All of the evidence had pointed to him, hadn't it? And there he stood, the Avinox in the Council agent's uniform. I wanted to make him pay.

The Avinox opened the jail cell beside us. "In," he commanded in Common Tongue. "We do not wish to harm you, but we will fire."

I took a threatening step toward him, my free hand clenched in a fist, and I saw a brief moment of shock flash across his eyes. He held his composure well, though. He raised his gun directly at me, his face calm.

I saw that this would not end well, but I hardly cared. I would make sure it was not my side that suffered. I took another step closer, looking for the opportunity to disarm my opponent.

My second heart pounded harder. I had not fought this hard just to be stopped by that one awful Avinox.

A frightened sound from Jillian in my arms was the only thing that stopped me.

A roar erupted from down the hall. The force of it echoed in my head and vibrated down the halls. It was a disturbing sound, the force of it threatening blood and violence. Not even the most vicious of animals on Earth could produce a sound matching it. The Avinox's face betrayed his fear then, and I saw terror flash through the eyes of the other two. It gave me an odd sense of satisfaction.

"Rocky is very angry," I snarled, my face callous. Everything about me now was as cold as stone.

The three aliens stared at me. Warily, the Avinox lowered his gun and set it on the ground. He raised his hands to show that he meant no harm, and slowly stepped backward into the cell. His two accomplices eyed him, their guns still pointed at us, but there was no mistaking that they did not hold them with confidence.

Another roar hit us with the force of a jet engine. It was angrier. The halls were vibrating. Rocky was coming, and she was moving quickly. Every step she took toward us shook the very floor we stood on.

"I do not wish for bloodshed," the Avinox said. When he spoke, it almost sounded like he was singing.

Slowly, the three aliens set down their weapons and stepped inside, but at the last second, the Avinox slipped out and slammed the cell door closed. I heard the two agents inside shouting angrily, pounding on the door, demanding that he let them out and explain his heinous betrayal.

"Boys, that was too easy," Jo'sha cackled, feigning his favorite Southern accent.

He turned, and his eyes directly met mine. He stood there, facing me with only a few inches between us, and I could see the loyalty burning brightly in his face. I could see the dedication and sacrifice in his very being.

The rage drained out of me, replaced by shame, and I was momentarily unable to speak. He grinned at me, leaning against the wall lazily, his arms crossed, the cocky little imp.

"So, are you going to rip my head from my shoulders, Thellessian, or are you going to give your old friend a hug?"

I set Jillian down and rushed to him, throwing my arms around him.

"You snake!" I whispered, pressing my forehead against his. "I thought you had turned on us!"

The Avinox's body felt much cooler to the touch than a human's or Thellessian's, but the slight chill against my skin was refreshing. Even if the change was only slight, I felt some tiny part of me snapping back. I had my loyal friend, who had fought and sacrificed for me this entire time, finally at my side.

"Keep it together, girl. You've made it this far. We'll get them through this," he whispered to me, and he sounded so strong and confident, I couldn't doubt him.

He stepped back and held my gaze. He didn't see me as damaged. He didn't see me as a monster. He understood me because he had been in my position so very many times before as an Impersonator.

The hallway shook. Scales and talons came into view, caving in the wall as the monstrous beast heaved herself into the hall with a thrust, landing before the Avinox dressed in the guise of a Council agent. She lowered her head, six red eyes holding him in her sights, her lip curled, exposing teeth the size of steak knives.

When Rocky said "giant lizard," she should have said miniature dinosaur. The Rux species was larger than I was, though their faces resembled scaly, barbed bats more than any lizard I had ever seen, with wide, flat noses and square skulls. Rocky turned her head and stared at me with three of her red eyes, her flat black tongue flicking in and out between three rows of teeth, tasting the air. Her two tails twitched back and forth in agitation, the barbs on the end of each poised to strike. She snapped at Jo'sha, threatening him.

Jo'sha simply took a step toward her, laughing heartily.

"Do you plan on devouring me, Talyn?" Jo'sha asked, grinning, not the least bit intimidated by the mammoth creature.

A fuzzy little tan alien slid off Rocky's back. It was quite a drop for her, but she landed gracefully on the ground, springing lightly as she landed, much like a doe might. She would barely reach an adult human's knee, and she walked on her tiptoes. Her four tiny arms—two little fingers each—reminded me of a *Tyrannosaurus rex* I had seen at a museum years ago. Her beady black eyes and antennae made me feel like I was looking at a grub, her little two-toed feet like I saw watching an insect-like deer prance about.

"Where is Kaitlin? Have you released her?" Emilee, whom I now recognized as Aya, chirped. She sounded like a cricket, if a cricket could speak.

"I can't tell which cells are occupied," I told her. Without hesitation, she danced past me, prancing up to the nearest door. Her antennae twitched as she listened for sounds. She must not have heard anything of interest, because she quickly moved to the next door, focused on her mission.

I turned my attention back to the giant beast.

"How did you get out?" I asked Rocky.

If I had to be shot to get free ... I had only seen agents in my cell. They came for me first.

"Carefully. Wasn't expecting the chains. Was expecting the guards," Rocky grumbled in her guttural voice. "Neither of those should be a problem anymore."

I nodded. Maybe I didn't want to know. Willpower and desperation, especially with the sounds of screaming and death outside your door, were powerful things, after all.

"We need to get the rest of the cells open," I told her.

"Start with this one!" Emilee chirped, standing in front of a door a few cells down.

I turned toward the cell, but one powerful claw stopped me. Rocky looked me in the eye and I nodded. She slid past me to the cell, and with one mighty thrust, her black claws sank into the door. She ripped it from the wall with a definitive jerk. Jo'sha whistled, his comma-shaped, white-blue eyebrows arched.

A small blonde child rushed out. She saw the sandy-colored grub and smiled.

"Aunt Emilee!" she squealed. She rushed up to the alien, who was only three-quarters her height, and wrapped her arms around her.

"Are you okay, sweetie?" Emilee chirped, looking the child over. Her tiny face was streaked with tears.

"I kept my eyes closed, just like you said," the little girl replied. It seemed to me that she was the bravest of all of us.

I couldn't help but notice what looked to be the shadow of a hand lying at the doorway. I looked down at Emilee, who looked up at me with her beady black eyes, past the curly blonde locks of the little girl.

I knew how they got out, looking into her eyes. I could only guess what the small alien let Rocky do to her so that she could be reunited with her niece, let alone what Rocky had to do to herself to leave the human body behind for the enormous, scaled creature that lumbered down the hall.

I would never ask.

Rocky moved down the hall, ripping doors off the wall. Nearly half were empty, but we ended up with eleven humans and five more Gangers; so few, compared to what we had started with.

"We need to get the humans off this ship," Jo'sha said, as the last door was pried from the wall and Derek and Adam walked out, looking exhausted and nearing the point of collapse. No humans followed them out. Rocky was panting, obviously strained, but she stood resolute. She was prepared for what was to come. We all knew that we weren't done yet.

"We won't be of much use like this," Adam said, holding out his trembling human hands. A few of the Gangers had settled onto the floor, spent. Adam looked to Rocky. She was tired, her gigantic chest heaving inward, her mouth partially open as she panted, but her eyes showed resolve. She bowed her head, and I felt one of my hearts skip a beat as I realized the gist of their conversation.

"I will be kind," she growled.

I scooped Jillian into the crook of one arm and picked Marie off the ground with the other, holding her by the waist and hoisting her onto my back. She wrapped her arms and legs around me and squeezed tightly. Following my lead, Dorain scooped up the tiny Kaitlin without a word, Emilee wrapped up in her small arms. I turned away, leading my brother and Jo'sha down the hall, a small pack of frightened people trailing behind us, taking in the alien ship with stunned eyes.

We didn't need to be around for the next part. This was finally the end of the Gangers—all of us. I knew they would all be back again shortly, albeit in different forms, but still, I didn't want to watch. I had seen enough of human forms falling at my feet, even if these went willingly and peacefully.

I ran, Dorain matching me stride for stride, little Kaitlin in his arms. She held Emilee tight, the way some children clutch a small dog or cat, but if Emilee was uncomfortable in the child's grasp, she didn't show it. Marie's face was pressed against my neck, warm and smooth. I could feel Jillian's heart against my own chest, its beat alien compared to the fast trill of both of mine. Jo'sha sailed past me, his stride smooth and flawless, his long, beautiful hair flowing behind him, and took the lead.

I heard sharp bangs behind us. There was only one short cry from a male voice. Then the floor was trembling, and I moved aside to let Rocky's massive body through as she raced past, moving to the front of our group with Jo'sha. She was so large that her body took up three-quarters of the hall, her head threatening to touch the ceiling with each lumbering leap forward. She was hardly graceful, but she was fast.

315

I heard numerous beings coming up from behind. Then, two aliens ran up beside me. The one that looked like a bipedal, tailless alligator with eyes protruding from its head on foot-long tentacles plucked Marie from my back, nodding at me. I gave a quick jerk of my head toward Adam, grateful I could move a bit more agilely without the added weight. Derek, whose face resembled a flattened, spiky, yellowed version of Adam's, had his own human in his arms. All around me, former Gangers were joining the pack, taking on their own human charges and moving with great speed. The pack of us raced through the ship, strong for once.

It gave me hope that our story might actually end well. Perhaps not for us, but for the humans we had devoted ourselves to.

That is, until Rocky came to a sliding halt ahead of us, roaring in distress. I stopped behind her and felt the dread rising as I saw what was in our way. Ahead of us, a line of Council agents had formed, stun guns ready. Rocky rose up on her hind legs, using her gigantic body as a shield so they could not shoot the humans behind her. She raised her barbed tails, stabbing at the air, threatening to harm anyone who came near. Her lips peeled back in a snarl, exposing row after row of serrated teeth. Little Kaitlin gasped, and even I was frightened.

"We just need to get around that corner and down the hall!" Jo'sha shouted in frustration. "The transport room is right there!"

Rocky looked back at us, her red eyes fierce. She made eye contact with Jo'sha and me, and though the facial expressions of the Rux were often hard to read, there was no mistaking the look in her eyes.

"Go," she snapped.

I tried to shout at her, but she dropped down before I could think of another way. The floor quaked under her weight, knocking some of us off balance. She ran at the line of Council agents full blast, each leap rattling the halls. The agents weren't expecting that. Some of them raised their guns, but others backed up, preparing to run. I saw one trip and scramble backward, flailing in fright.

I prayed that they would all just run away, but we weren't that lucky.

Rocky fell when the blasts hit, her legs collapsing beneath her as she crumbled into a heap, but I think that had been her plan all along. Self-sacrifice had been her only option. She tumbled down the hall, sliding like a limp doll, colliding with the line of agents with her massive body. Then she came to a rest.

"Rocky!" Kaitlin called, reaching out for her in distress.

"It was just a stun gun, sweetie," I heard Emilee chirp, attempting to console the child. "She's okay. She'll get up soon."

Stunned or not, though, we all knew that was a lie. Rocky wasn't coming back, and now that the Council had her, her fate was sealed.

"Take him," I heard Derek say behind me. I turned to see him handing his charge—I recognized him as the fallen Avinox's brother, Davis—to Adam. Then he was rushing past me. All around me, former Gangers were handing off their charges and moving forward, toward Rocky.

"Derek!" Adam called out to his brother.

"Sorry, brother," Derek called back, "but you know you don't need all of us! We'll hold them back for as long as we can!"

There were flashes of light and sounds of struggle as the Peacemakers met the Council agents.

"We can't stay here! Go!" Jo'sha shouted, as Derek and another Peacemaker fell in a blast of blue light.

I forced myself to turn away and run. Jo'sha was right. There were only minutes before all the Peacemakers fell, so we ran and didn't look back. At least, we tried not to.

Jo'sha slid to a halt in front of a silver door. It opened at his command, and we urged the humans in—as many as the door would let through at once—without a second thought, glancing over our shoulders at the hall behind us, waiting, using our own bodies as barricades until they were all safely inside. I urged my own two friends in before me. The rest of us backed in slowly, checking to make certain the danger hadn't followed us. To my relief, the Council hadn't caught up.

Yet.

"Come on," I called to Adam and another Ganger, a green Xiaxia, as I put one leg through the door. They glanced at each other, then looked back at me.

"You know those Council agents are only a few minutes behind us," Adam said.

"You won't stop them," I argued back.

"No," Adam said, "but I'll settle for slowing them down."

I wanted to keep arguing, to convince them to come inside and not choose the fate of getting shot, but I knew there was no other way. They were right. Council agents would come running down that hall sooner rather than later, and we needed every precious second that we could get.

I stepped inside and pulled the door closed behind us before I could give it another thought, my second heart clenching with regret. The lock clicked, sealing us in. More importantly, it sealed everyone else out, including Adam and the other Peacemaker.

The room looked much like the transport room on *Moga*, only this one was cold and metallic. It had a dark, ominous presence. We were in the main control room, the transport room itself located adjacent to us. The large computer console, with its various buttons and switches, was a mystery to me, but much to my relief, my brother and Jo'sha approached it undaunted. They pressed various buttons and the holographic screen popped up, reading off various commands and statuses in Common Tongue as my brother and Jo'sha tapped at the translucent images.

The lights in the transport room came on. I heard machinery humming, powering up and charging.

The lights above us flickered. Jo'sha muttered something in his native language.

"What?" I asked, watching Dorain and Jo'sha cringe, their hands moving in a flurry of activity. The screen was flashing words across in seemingly urgent strings.

"The Council was anticipating us," Jo'sha muttered. "They've already started draining power to this room."

"We need to divert all power to the transport beam, or it'll never finish charging," Dorain said, focused on the console.

Suddenly, the lights in the main room went out, casting us in shadows. Light from the transport room provided the only light for us to see by. It made everything feel sinister and all the more urgent.

"Two at a time! Get them in the room now!" Jo'sha called to the former Gangers in the room. Besides Emilee and I, there were only two others.

"Two?" I asked, incredulous. "We don't have time for that! The Council already knows we're here!"

"Jo'sha's right," Dorain said, pressing buttons in a determined manner beside the Avinox. "We're not going to be able to get the beam fully charged. Any more and we risk sending them back in pieces."

I looked back at the almost dozen humans. How long would it take to get them all on Earth with the power deteriorating? The transport beam would have to charge after each time it discharged, a process that, from my experience, normally took about half a minute. How long would it take now? What would happen when two humans became too much, and we were sending them down one at a time? They already knew where we were. They were certainly coming for us. Adam and Derek could only hold them off for so long. Did we even have a few minutes?

"It's our only option!" Jo'sha said. "The child goes first! Get her in there!"

He was right. This *was* our only option, and the more time we wasted trying to argue against it, the less time we would have to send our loved ones to safety. Shakily, I knelt down to Kaitlin, who stood there quietly, with wide eyes, by my tall, strong legs, clutching her alien relative in her arms. I touched her arm gently and looked her in the eye. "You have to let Aunt Emilee go now. You have to be brave."

"I know," the little girl whispered meekly.

She took a deep breath and set Emilee down. She took my hand.

"Marie goes with her," Emilee squeaked. Even with her insect-like voice, I could hear her heart breaking.

Marie was standing by my brother in a transfixed state, watching him and the Avinox work, but she started at the sound of her name. Her eyes met mine, glazed over and in shock, but she registered the situation quickly. She nodded and came forward, reaching for my outstretched hand.

"I love you," Kaitlin called back to the tiny alien as I pulled them hastily into the room. Emilee reached out, two tiny fingers outstretched, but she didn't move toward the little girl.

I felt a sudden emptiness in my palms as I let the two warm human hands go and slid the transport room door closed. The door clicked as it sealed them in.

All of the transport rooms in *Moga* were just white walls. They had no windows. It made the leaving process easier for those of us who were saying our goodbyes for the next twenty years. Council ships did not send their people away for years at a time, so there was no need to remove the windows. I moved to the side and looked through the one that revealed the inside of the transport room, and I saw Marie standing there with the little girl, both of them watching me. I placed my hand on the glass, trying to think of words I could say.

"Goodbye, Allyson," Marie whispered, taking the child by the hand.

The flash of light took them both away.

It was so quick. I stumbled back, numb. That was it. She was gone. I would never see Marie again.

"Where did you send them?" I asked Dorain, stepping away from the door, the room reeling.

Behind me, the two other former Gangers ushered two more humans through the door as the transport beam recharged. Emilee sank down to the ground, her antennae drooping. She sat there, staring into the distance with glossy eyes.

"A coastal town in Canada," Dorain said, focused on his work, pressing buttons with great determination, working as fast as he could. "No bots in the area. They'll be safe."

I felt something small and warm press up against me. I looked down, startled.

Jillian's hand grabbed hold of my considerably larger one, clenching it tightly. A memory flooded my mind. I was six years old and my mom was trying to drop me off for my first day of kindergarten. I wouldn't go. I was terrified, begging my mom not to leave me with the strange teacher, in a classroom full of children I didn't know. It wasn't until Jillian and her mother arrived that I could be cajoled into letting go of my mother's jeans. Jillian had taken me by the hand and walked me to the classroom. She had held my hand for most of the day, until finally I didn't feel scared anymore and I let go.

I felt realization sinking in, and it felt heavy and cold as it nestled into my chest and sat there. I had let go of Marie in the heat of the moment. She had been there and gone in an instant—so fast, I hadn't even had time to think about it. I hadn't even said goodbye to her. Did I even realize what I was doing when I shoved her into that room?

But now I had one more human to let go of, and she was looking me dead in the eyes. I took in her expression. It was aggrieved. It was terrified. Bitter tears slid down her cheeks. She knew what this was and what it meant, and she didn't want to go.

I held her hand tighter and squeezed my eyes shut, praying for strength. It was time to say goodbye. I had only a few minutes— maybe only seconds—and a lifetime's worth of words to say. I realized then that, even after five cycles on the planet below, I didn't know how to say goodbye when it was forever.

"You're next," I whispered to Jillian.

"I'll go when it's my turn," she said, and her grip on my hand grew tighter. She was holding my hand so tensely that her knuckles were white, but in my real body, I hardly registered all the pressure.

There was a flash of light. I was out of time. A lifetime of words would have to go unspoken. I pulled Jillian toward the door, but she dug her heels into the ground, resisting me. "Wait!" she cried. "I'll go after them, just—*please*, not yet!"

Her gray eyes were desperate and the look on her face was beyond grief.

"You two, go!" Jo'sha shouted at two other humans. I looked over my shoulder, torn, as the two aliens ushered them into the transport room and closed the door.

"The power is falling faster," I heard my brother say. I felt both of my hearts racing. I was running out of time to get Jillian to safety.

"I'll go, I swear," Jillian whispered. "I just—"

She clutched my hand, staring at me as her world came crumbling down.

I knelt down and wrapped both arms around her, feeling her hair tickle my face.

"Find Marie," I whispered. "You two stay together—always."

I felt her nod weakly.

Jo'sha was looking down at us. He gave me a sad smile, his eyes apologizing. I squeezed my eyes closed and held Jillian closer, pretending that time wasn't flying by much too quickly.

"You remember what I said, okay?" I whispered.

I felt her nodding. "Ally," she whispered. "I—"

She never got to finish.

"The power's critical!" Dorain shouted. "They all have to go now! We have to risk it!"

His words—his panic—cut through me. There were only three humans left: Jillian, Davis, and a young woman whose name I did not know.

"Divert more power!" I shouted. I was standing now. I had Jillian clutched in my arms.

"We are, but this is it!" Jo'sha shouted, pressing buttons frantically. "There's nothing left to divert, and they're still draining the transport beam! They've got to go!"

I rushed toward the door, but I hadn't expected Jillian to fight me. She kicked and screamed in my arms, trying to force her way free. I almost lost my grasp on her, I was so startled.

"No!" she screamed. "I'm not leaving you! They're going to—"

In this form, I was stronger than she was. She couldn't get free. The other two humans were already in the room. I got to the doorframe, but Jillian grabbed it, holding on with all of her strength.

"I'm staying!" she screamed. "They can't take you away!"

"Get the girl in there!" Jo'sha shouted. "We can't maintain the power level any longer!"

I pulled Jillian forcefully from the doorframe and nearly tossed her inside the room. She stumbled and fell, landing on her knees. I slammed the door closed before she could get up.

The door clicked, locking her inside, away from me. She kicked and screamed on the other side.

"NO!" she shrieked. "I'm not leaving you! Allyson, open the door! I don't care what they do to me! *Open the door!*"

I knew it wouldn't open, but I braced the door, ensuring that it stayed tightly sealed. Jillian appeared at the viewing window, pounding on the glass, tears streaming down her face.

"Ally, let me out! I can't leave you!" she sobbed.

I clenched my eyes closed. I couldn't look at her.

As I held the door closed, listening to her pleas, I felt myself dying. Losing her was more painful than any sickness.

And it felt as if I had stood here so many times before.

"Ally, *please!* Don't do this!"

322

"Do it!" I screamed. It had already taken much too long.

The flash of light never came. Instead, the room went black. The power was gone. I heard the door pop as the lock slid open. I heard the sounds of struggle coming from outside the room.

"Grab the humans!" Jo'sha said. "There's another room! Hurry!"

He hadn't heard them yet. He didn't know it was too late.

The door burst open.

There were flashes of light. I fell before I even saw them come through the door, landing hard on the ground. It was dark, but I could hear footsteps all around me. I felt someone grab me, but then their hands were gone. There was screaming. There were pulses in the floor. I heard falling. I heard dying.

They were killing the humans.

Although it felt like an entire lifetime, it only took a few seconds before we were all down. Dorain was beside me, unable to move. He had fallen with his hand reaching out, but he wasn't reaching for me. My eyes followed his arms. I saw Jillian lying a few feet away, facing away from me. I couldn't see her chest moving.

She wasn't stunned.

She was at Jo'sha's feet. He was still standing, looking perfectly at ease amid the line of Council agents.

He nudged Jillian with his foot. "I don't think this one will be a problem," he said. "I took care of her myself."

Something truly broke in me then, even more so than when Tori had died in front of me. That had destroyed part of me, but now, I felt myself die. Whoever I had been, she gave one quiet gasp, and the light went out—she was gone without even putting up a fight.

I wanted Jo'sha to die. I wanted to kill him. If I got the chance, I would rip his pretty little body apart with my bare hands, and I would feel nothing. I wouldn't feel regret. I wouldn't even feel satisfaction, because I knew I could never feel happy again. I had been robbed of even feeling justice at his death, but he had robbed me of my final purpose in life, and I would make him pay that debt with his last breath.

How could I ever have trusted him? How could I ever have let him trick me into feeling hope? Why had I been so *stupid?*

I had cost Jillian her life.

CHAPTER 18

J o'sha rushed down the hall, the walls closing in with each step that he dared to take. He felt them watching him; their silent shouts seemed to echo down the hall. They were against him, part of the ship that so desperately wanted to tear him and all he stood for apart. Every shift in the air currents sounded like someone calling out to him, ordering him to stop. The hum of the lights above would drive him to madness. They were whispering to the others, calling his executioners to come put an end to his mission.

He knew they would. He had played them for far too long. He felt his time—his absurd luck—running out.

His eyes hardly ever faced forward, watching behind him, lest someone should decide to follow. He had waited hours for the opportunity to escape, waiting for the perfect moment when he knew someone would not see him slip away, but the sinking feeling in his chest told him that he was missing something. Something was out there waiting for him and it was going to destroy everything he had sacrificed for.

His heart rate accelerated faster and faster for every miraculous second that the alarm did not sound. Only when he felt the tightening in his throat did he remember to breathe. He could still remember the sound of his breath echoing in his ears when he wore the mask of the Council agent, as if to remind him that each breath he took only fed the lie that was his existence.

There was a sort of poetry in it.

No one had noticed his absence—yet. He knew it would only be a matter of time before the Council's agents realized that members were missing from their ranks—members they barely trusted as it was. Jo'sha had not failed to notice how they watched him out of the corner of their eyes. No matter where he went within the great Council ship, *Allisandre*, he felt their eyes boring into his back. He had begun to see their stares even when he laid his head down to rest.

Not that he had had the time to do so. He could not tell what he wanted more—to lie down and surrender to the fatigue that had plagued him for days—or had it been years now?— or to run from the perdition he had endured for so long until his body collapsed far away from this wretched place.

Then there was the other part of him, the part that forced him to march down the hall with the body of Jillian Carter slung over his shoulder, moving forward toward his destination. He was almost there. The alarms had not sounded, and this part of the ship remained clear.

He had almost made it. He was almost done.

He heard a crackling sound, and with a speed that surprised even him, he ducked behind a corner and paused. His chest heaved as he tried to catch his breath for a brief moment.

The corpse was heavy, dead weight dangling over his shoulder. He shifted her yet again, feeling his spine protest with stabbing needles of pain and his neck burning with a dull, creeping agony that he knew was only going to get worse. He had been carrying her for what felt like days, but he dared not set her down. She had been his salvation when the Council agents had broken into the transport room. Her sacrifice had been enough for them to forgive his actions when the prisoners escaped, but he was not done with her yet.

Jo'sha closed his eyes and raised the crackling watch to his face. Careful not to drop the girl, he somehow managed to balance her while activating the communication system in the watch with his other hand.

"This is Jo'sha," he said. His voice was strong and commanding when he spoke. If centuries as an Impersonator had taught him anything, it was how to hide the perturbation in his voice. He had people following him. How could they stay strong if they saw his fear?

"Sir, where are you?" an agitated voice said in Common Tongue.

"I'm almost there. Did the others make it to the rendezvous point?"

"They made it, sir. They've gone to complete their final objectives."

Jo'sha leaned his head against the wall and breathed a sigh of relief. No one had been captured. The alarm had not been raised. They were going to make it.

"How are they?" Jo'sha asked, but this time he was not inquiring about his fellow Peacemakers.

There was a long pause.

"We got them back under before they fully regained consciousness," the man said hesitantly.

"What happened?" Jo'sha asked, reading into the man's tone.

"One of the females did not wake up," he replied.

"Keep an eye on her vitals until I get there," Jo'sha responded.

"Sir," the man said quietly. "There are no vitals. She's cold."

Jo'sha leaned his head back and closed his eyes. He felt a crushing sadness in his heart. Suddenly, the body felt even heavier.

"Which one?" he whispered.

"She has short hair."

Jo'sha glanced back at the girl over his shoulder. He let out a sigh of relief, realizing that it wasn't her. He should not have felt relief; he knew that. It was not his intention to lose even one. Still, he could not stand the thought of losing *her*.

Jo'sha shook his head. There was nothing he could do. They had known the risks, and there had been no other way.

"What about the chips?"

"We have them. They're all intact," the man said. "Yours will be the last."

Jo'sha counted his blessings. At least one good thing would come from all this.

"Good," he said. "I need you to wake them now."

"Sir?"

"I'm almost there, Ravaan. I need you to wake them. Start with the remaining girl."

Jo'sha could sense the unease beyond the watch.

"They won't awaken before I reach you," Jo'sha said. "We can't send them back to that planet unconscious. I need them up and talking—screaming and fighting against us, if that's how it's going to be—and I need it soon."

"As you say, sir," Ravaan said.

"What's the status on that transport room?"

"No one suspects that we are in control of it."

"Keep it that way," Jo'sha said.

With that, the watch static ceased. The hall was silent again.

Jo'sha shifted the girl from one aching shoulder to the other, though it hardly lessened the fire in his spine. Then he slipped out from behind the wall and rushed down the hall as quickly as his exhausted legs could carry him.

He knew something was wrong when he reached the door.

"Ravaan?" he said loudly, rapping on the door for the third time. He pressed the watch for the fourth time. "Ravaan, it's me! Open the door!"

He was met with a deafening silence.

He cursed under his breath. He had just spoken to the man not even five minutes ago! He wanted to weep as he stood there on the wrong side of their final hope.

The door hissed as the pressure system failed. It drifted open a few inches. A jolt went down his spine and dread crept through his veins.

Jo'sha glanced over his shoulder. The dead girl was looking at him, her eyes murky. It disturbed him to see the same look of betrayal she had given him just before he had grabbed her by the shirt collar and pressed the stun gun, which he had set to full strength, into the back of her head. She died instantly, thankfully. He tried to feel some comfort in the fact that she never felt it, but he couldn't. He felt the bile rise in his stomach, and he was forced to look away.

Against his better judgment, he pushed the door open. He knew no friend waited for him inside. He could run now—possibly evade capture—but he knew that had never been an option. He had known all along that there would be nowhere to hide in the end.

He closed his eyes and took a moment to steady his racing heart. Cloudy eyes looked back at him behind his closed eyelids. The guilt twisted in his stomach, hot and nauseating.

There was only one way he could escape it. He stepped inside.

The room was pitch-black. He didn't see the prone figure lying at the base of the door. When he tripped over him, he went crashing to the ground, dropping the body as he fell. She landed in front of him in such a way that her dead eyes watched him as he stared at her on his hands and knees. He tasted the bile in his mouth and forced it back down.

When he raised his head, his eyes found the figure of her still-breathing double, prone and unconscious on the metal table only a few feet away from him. The light from the open door hit her face, and Jo'sha let out a sigh of relief as he realized she was still unharmed.

The same could not be said for the girl beside her. She was petite, with brunette hair cropped in a pixie cut, and could not have been more than twenty years old. Jo'sha could see that she was turning the same shades of blue and gray as the body on the floor. The young man with black curls, however, was breathing and looked healthy.

Jo'sha rose to his feet and rushed forward to aid the two vulnerable humans, but that was when the others in the room chose to step out of the shadows.

"We admit, we thought we had you figured out," a voice hissed. A stun gun came between him and the girl, the barrel pointed directly at his head. Beyond that, the blazing eyes of the doctors held him in their gaze.

"Pask? Pashka?" Jo'sha asked, stunned. "How—why?"

He looked back at Ravaan. The Sebican was piled at the front of the door. His long, nimble legs, which ended at two dainty hooves, had collapsed beneath him. He had landed face first, his equally slender arms, three dull claws on each, sprawled around him. The nostrils flared on his doe-like face and one of his large oval ears twitched. Jo'sha felt relief. It was an unfortunate fate for the poor creature, who had been trying so hard to undo an offense he felt was created by his own race. The indentation in the fur on his head indicated that Ravaan would be unconscious for some time, but he was breathing.

Jo'sha looked back at the doctors, who watched him with unbridled rage.

"You sent the Doppelgangers to a fate worse than death! You imprisoned countless Peacemakers! The Elders of this ship have not been seen nor heard from! You have brought an end to millennia of peace and a way of life! You have caused pain and suffering. You have maimed, tortured, and killed. You are a disgrace to this world and all the good that is in it, and you should be removed from it for your crimes!" Pask shrieked.

"Pask, *please!*" Jo'sha whispered. "You must lower your voice and drop the weapon!"

"Why should I do anything you say?" Pask hissed. "You were there when they passed our sentence. You could have spoken in our defense! You could have protected Dorain, but you shot him in the back and threw him in a cage to starve to death! And his poor sister! You sent Saira to Earth, knowing full well that the pulse cannons would kill her or her Ganger would fail! Did you see her when those bots of yours dropped her on that prison floor? Do you have any idea what you have done to her? To *all* of them?"

Jo'sha watched as Pask turned up the power on the stun gun. He did not have the will to speak.

Pask turned her head toward Pashka. There was an exchange he could not hear, and then she was watching him again. This time, the burning wrath was mixed with confusion.

"And yet," she said, lowering the gun, "it would have been so easy to leave them all to the bots. It all could have ended there—a few rogue Peacemakers caught in the crossfire as the bots served their natural purpose. Tragic, yes, but whom could anyone blame?"

"You didn't, though. You pulled them and their human charges from that planet and dropped them at the feet of those who would defend them."

Pask raised the gun again. "And then murdered the humans right in front of them as they were on the verge of safety and delivered them straight to the Council in chains! What game are you playing?"

Slowly, Jo'sha rose to his feet. He raised his hands above his head, watching the irate doctors with unwavering focus, lest they should decide to pull the trigger on the stun gun.

Their eyes were wild and their hands shook unsteadily.

"You aren't well," Jo'sha said slowly. "The gas caused neurological damage. You're experiencing mood swings. Your impulse control has been damaged. That's all this is. You don't really want to do this. Put the gun down, and I promise that I will find you help."

"We've seen how you help," Pask snapped. "We want none of it! Give us a reason not to do to you what you did to that poor girl!"

"It was the only way to get them on this ship," Jo'sha said slowly.

"Surely you could have come up with a less treacherous way! You had them beamed up here amidst a slaughter!"

"It had to be at the right time," Jo'sha said, trying not to make any sudden movements. "Too soon, and the Council wipes them out and hides any evidence that anything ever happened. Too late, and nothing can be done."

"So hide them in ampules of aether, like the boy tried with his sister! Beam the Gangers over and awaken them in the pods following established methods! Do not beam them down to a hostile planet, only to shoot them awake on an enemy ship later! Do you understand how fortunate it was that their bodies weren't far?"

Jo'sha held the doctors' eyes. "I did not mean the Peacemakers."

Pask and Pashka's eyes widened. Jo'sha watched them slowly reach behind themselves. He cursed when he saw the vial in their hands, two chips glinting as they caught the light from the door.

"Give those to me!" he snapped. "You don't know what you're doing!"

"These do not belong to Peacemakers," Pask said slowly, eyeing them. "They're the wrong design."

"No, they aren't from Peacemakers," Jo'sha whispered. "And you *must* give them to me."

"How long have we been putting chips in humans?" Pask whispered.

Jo'sha kept his eyes on the chips, afraid to speak, to move, lest something should cause the doctors to bring harm to them.

"That is where these come from, is it not?" Pask asked, shaking the vial. Jo'sha felt his heart leap in his chest. "And I'm guessing that their unusual design is what kept us from detecting them? How you managed to put them in humans without us ever noticing?"

"Until too many got close together," Jo'sha whispered. "We didn't mean—we didn't know that would happen. We didn't know the Council would send the bots to investigate. We were supposed to beam them up at the right time and—"

"You brought the humans up to our ship and put chips in their heads?" Pask shouted. "That is illegal! That is depraved! How *dare* you harvest the memories of creatures who do not give them willingly."

"We did not put the chips in their bodies," Jo'sha whispered.

Pask and Pashka's face changed, repulsed, as realization set in. Slowly, Pashka turned to look at the human girl lying on the table, Pask holding Jo'sha in her sights. Pashka brushed aside the hair

330

behind the living girl's ear. Then he checked the other side. When he did not see what he was looking for, his gaze turned to the dead girl on the floor.

Again, there was a silent exchange between them.

"Who is this?" Pask asked, pointing at the breathing girl on the table.

"Jillian Carter," Jo'sha whispered.

"No," Pask said. "Jillian Carter was injured. We saw the Council agent strike her. *That* is Saira's friend."

They pointed to the dead girl on the floor, her lip split where the Council agent had struck her across the face when she pushed past them to pull the necklace off the empty shell that had once been her best friend.

"No," Jo'sha said. "That is the copy the girl has lived in since she was a child. Jillian Carter has been her own Doppelganger for most of her life."

"You didn't—" Pask whispered.

"We knew we had failed long ago; not with Earth, but with ourselves. We knew what would happen," Jo'sha said. "We were desperate."

"The humans ..." Pask said, abhorrence in her voice. "You turned them into their own Gangers! You stole their bodies, stripped their minds from them, and inserted them into our own artificial copies!"

"We were careful!" Jo'sha said. "We put the chips in the artificial bodies to protect them from any side effects. Their real bodies were always kept safe in case something went wrong. There was never any risk to them."

"Their minds are underdeveloped!" Pask snapped. "How did you plan on putting them back into their real bodies? A Transference is risky on a higher species, let alone a human being! Look at that girl! She's dead! And you can only hope that she's dead and not scattered as well! Is that the fate you would force on these people?"

Pask pointed her quivering finger at the short-haired girl. Jo'sha couldn't bring himself to look at her.

"This should not have been possible!" Pask said. "I saw Jillian Carter cry tears! Doppelgangers can *never* cry tears! What did you do

331

to their bodies? What other unnatural and dangerous acts did you force on them to fit your own agenda?"

"It did not take us long to figure out how to fix that, once the need was there. We kept it to ourselves, of course. If the Doppelgangers ever knew we could correct the flaws in their artificial bodies, they might pressure us to correct the twenty-year limit on their viability. You and I both know we need that flaw for the system to work. It's hard enough getting them to leave the planet, even when they know that staying there means death."

They both stared at him. "You stole innocents from their beds? You took them from their bodies? What was the purpose of this? What could possibly be gained?"

"It is the last testament humanity can give to save itself," Jo'sha whispered. "It's their only hope."

"Against centuries of Peacemaker memories and recordings of human nature? The Council and the Peacemakers have already seen the testimonies of the human race, and it did not save them! What makes these memories different?"

"These three are humans raised by Gangers. They were introduced to Gangers early in their lives. They grew up alongside them, inundated with their behaviors and thought processes. They are what humanity becomes when Peacemakers are inserted into every aspect of their lives. They are the evolution of humanity. Jillian Carter was introduced to Saira at the age of four. That man is the younger brother of a Doppelganger. He was exposed to our kind from the moment he was born, as was the woman beside him. We tried for more, but ..."

Pask stared at him blankly. Then laughter erupted from her throat and rose to a hysterical pitch.

"People are dead! They died for *this*. You're telling me that this was the grand plan all along? This is how we're going to save the human race? With three memory chips from creatures they already hate and fear? *Are you mad?*"

"This is how we're going to save ourselves!" Jo'sha said. "This is how we're going to save *everything*. You think this is the only planet the Council is striking? You're wrong. It was simply the first one they reached. Once they have finished here, they will move on to the next planet. Then the next. They have a *list* of planets to Cleanse. And, what's worse, is there are ships heading to *this* planet—Peacemaker and intergalactic governments of all kinds. What do you think will happen when they get here? What if they intervene? What if they don't?"

"What if this escalates? What if Cleansing planets is not enough? They've gone mad, Pask! They can't see past their blinding fear! What happens if that fear goes so far as to destroy our entire way of life— and I don't mean just the Peacemakers. The Higher Planets are at risk, too. All we know is failing. What happens when everything we believe in is ruined?"

"You are mad if you think *this* is enough to stop anything," Pask snapped, rattling the chips in their vial. Jo'sha winced as he heard them connect with the glass with a sharp *clink*!

"I trust the Elders," Jo'sha whispered. "They know more than we do. They said this was the way."

"They are bound in chains. Their wisdom has brought them nothing. It has brought *us* nothing but dead bodies and a wasted planet," Pask spat.

"They told me what to do—"

"They may have told you at the start, but they are gone now! You're making this up as you go and hoping you're getting it right! You're blind *and* insane!"

Behind them, there was a groan. Jo'sha jumped as the girl stirred. He saw her hand twitch, and her eyes fluttered for just a moment before she was still again.

"We were wondering when she would wake up," Pask muttered. "Lucky we stopped him before he woke the boy up."

"We have to get her to a transport room!" Jo'sha said. "They're all supposed to wake up with the others on the planet!"

"That's thoughtful of you," Pask said. "Wake them up before you beam them to the planet. That way, they have the chance to run when the bots come after them."

"Gangers have given their lives and freedom for these people. If you have any love for any of them, then *please* give me those chips and help me get these people to a transport room. Do not let the hatred caused by what you have suffered let this all be in vain!" Jo'sha begged.

Pask blinked, surprised. Jo'sha watched as she involuntarily lowered the gun.

"You at least love Saira, don't you?" Jo'sha asked, taking advantage of the moment. "Look at what you did to yourself to protect her! You're standing over the one human she loves most in this world. Help me get her off this godforsaken ship!"

Conflicted, Pask lowered the gun to the floor. She looked back at the human girl, eyeing her thoughtfully. Jo'sha was relieved to see that the sedative was wearing off slowly. She continued to be still.

"You love the girl, too, don't you?" Pask whispered.

"What?" Jo'sha asked, taken aback.

"Of all the Gangers, she's the one you always went to first. You went looking for her specifically when her brother took her. You went down to the planet yourself to keep that Council agent from getting to her. Why Saira?"

"I could ask you the same thing," Jo'sha whispered.

Pask was silent, watching him with narrowed eyes.

"They say the reason no one is allowed in the room during a Transference is that the process is too gruesome, but that's not it, is it? There's more to it than that. The Gangers go back to their bodies with their emotions stripped from them, but not their memories. That sounds like quite the process. I've always wondered ... when you dig around in their heads to strip them of everything they ever felt on that planet, what do you see?"

Pask and Pashka both narrowed their eyes at him. "That is not for you to know!"

"I'm right, aren't I?" Jo'sha said, ignoring the outburst. "You do see things. What was it that you saw in Saira's head? What is it about her that you'd sacrifice yourself for her?"

Pask and Pashka stared at him, resolute. Their jaws clenched shut and their eyes burned holes into him.

"It was the little girl," Jo'sha said. Slowly, making movements that would not startle the doctors, Jo'sha reached his hand into his suit. When it emerged, it was clasped around a faded blue ribbon.

Pask and Pashka gasped. "*Where did you get that?*"

"So you do know what it is?"

Pask stared at the ribbon, her mouth agape.

"I had been on that planet over nine hundred times before I was sent to retrieve Lucy," Jo'sha said. "By that time, I was so numb to my work. I had done so many things as an Impersonator—retrieving Doppelgangers, mimicking humans, causing accidents, averting tragedies, playing an enemy or an ally, sabotaging their technology or planting some of ours—that it was just another order, just another thing to do in the name of helping a young race evolve. I had retrieved the girl before. I couldn't remember it then—she was just another face, nothing special—and I thought it would be insignificant. Go in, get the girl, job done. Another mission accomplished for the Peacemakers."

"I didn't know the influenza had gotten Lucy until just before we left. I thought we were going in to rescue her—that she'd be happy."

Jo'sha paused, his eyes focused on the ribbon. "I went in as a nurse. I saw the sister—Lizzie—first. I got there just in time to watch the child die. There was nothing that could be done for her. Lucy had her by the hand …"

"I knelt down beside her as she sobbed and told her I was there to take her home."

"And she said no," Pask finished.

Jo'sha nodded.

"She fought me. It took half a dozen of us to get her into seclusion so that we could beam her up without anyone seeing. The entire time, she begged us to leave her there. She begged us to leave her with her parents and sister, knowing it was a death sentence. I didn't understand for so long …"

Jo'sha shook his head. "We have all been making the same grave mistake this entire time, and only she and those like her knew it."

"The sister adored her," Pask whispered. "They were inseparable. Such a sweet, gentle little thing."

She looked back at the human girl. Jo'sha saw something in her eyes. It was the look of someone who was keeping a secret they did not want anyone to know. Jo'sha had triggered it somehow. He felt the weight of it from where he stood.

"The Doppelgangers are not the only ones who know how wrong we are," Pask said.

They watched him, tumultuous emotions churning in their eyes. Jo'sha dared not speak, lest he elicit another outburst from the doctors. He waited, tense.

"We ... did something," Pask said slowly, as if the words hurt as she spoke them. "Except, it wasn't just us. It started small and innocent, but over time ... All of the doctors do it now. It's our secret, and we're all in it so deep. We can never stop, do you understand?"

Jo'sha was silent, waiting— unsure of what they were trying to say.

"The Elders do not know. Nor do the Gangers," Pask said, her eyes locked onto Jo'sha's.

"What did you do?" Jo'sha said, his voice barely above a whisper.

"What do you know about the Transference?"

"You pull the Gangers out of their human shells. You contain them in an ampule while you strip the emotions from them. Then you put their consciousness back into their true forms."

"What do you know about the contents of the ampule? What do you know about aether?"

Jo'sha struggled to remember. "I don't know what it is. I don't even know where it comes from," he finally admitted.

"It came with the first Peacemakers from a planet that has since followed the natural course of life. Its history has been lost to time as well," Pask said. "No one remembers that planet's name anymore, nor does anyone know how a physical element has the capability to bind an immortal consciousness—a soul, if you will—and, despite all our technology and understanding, we never will."

"The Transference is unpleasant to watch; that much is true. No matter how deeply you put a Ganger under, when that needle slides into the back of their head, they always shudder a bit before they're still. Then the aether seeps in, and when we pull it out, the Ganger's mind comes with it. Aether has a strange property. There are thousands upon thousands of different hues—perhaps minuscule changes in its makeup that allow it to so fully bind a consciousness. Again, we'll never know. We use this to our advantage, though. Memories always look the same. The images of memories—the pictures and faces we see when we look back on an event that has long since passed—those are always darker. Emotions are lighter, and the newest emotions, the ones formed as a Ganger—those are always the purest of white. Pulling off those fractions takes no effort at all."

Pask's eyes grew distant for a moment, as if she were looking at something far away. "It's not that simple, though. As in our minds, the emotion is tied to the image, and a deeper gray always comes entangled in them. It has to be severed from the emotion and returned."

"When you reach in and touch them, you can feel the memories," Pask whispered. "You can see them. You can feel *her*. I've seen the day the sister died. I've felt it. We've shared in so many moments of that girl's life. Can you imagine how it feels, standing there, being her for one brief instant, and then realizing you are about to take away all she is?"

Jo'sha's sat there, mesmerized.

"I know how much she loved that little girl. She was there when she was born. We've seen and felt the births and deaths of four of her families. Do you have any idea how much she loved them all?"

Pask's face grew distraught and her fists clenched as she spoke. "And we're supposed to take that from her? All of that love and happiness? *What gives us the right?*"

"Would you be able to do it? Could you look the girl in the eyes after she woke up, knowing what you had stolen from her?"

Pask shook her head. "It started simply for all of us. One sliver of white returned within a sea of gray. One little bit of love and happiness that they can hold on to. Over time, though, we figure out how we can tuck the emotions away in such a manner that they'll never know they're there. A sliver of white goes back with a blue ribbon, a teddy bear, a song sung as a child—little things. We give them little things to hold on to."

"You have to understand," Pask said. "We can't just take it all away from them. We all know what it is that we're doing, what we're taking from them, and we just *can't*. We can't have that on our conscience."

"They feel," Jo'sha whispered.

Pashka turned to look at the human on the table. His face became thoughtful. Jo'sha watched as something was silently said between the conjoined twins, and then, Pask's face changed. She dropped her defenses.

Pask dropped the gun at their feet. "Call your people. We cannot add the human girl to the list of our regrets."

Without hesitation, Pask leaned over the corpse and held the vial out to him.

Jo'sha saw their eyes as he reached forward and, slowly, took the chips from them. There was something behind their eyes that he could not place. As alien as the expression was, it was familiar. How many times had he seen it flash behind the eyes of a Ganger?

A Ganger who felt too much.

"You have one more to collect," Pask said, holding his gaze. His skin crawled. Gangers should never feel their previous lives. They had in the past, with disastrous consequences. It was not, however, the revelation that the Gangers could feel that made Jo'sha tense. He knew it should have. He could only imagine the implications, both for the Gangers and for Peacemaker protocol.

But it was how the doctors watched him that made him realize what he had missed.

Jo'sha pulled the knife from within his suit. He felt his stomach tighten for a moment, but he forced himself to swallow the apprehension. Then, he turned his back on the doctors.

He paused, staring down at the cadaver. Ravaan was the doctor. He knew how to remove the chips without damaging them. The doctors behind him knew as well, but he dared not ask them to do it, lest they become suspicious that he was setting them up in a vulnerable position.

"It'll be embedded," Pask said, seeming to read his mind. "Slide the knife under the chip and ease it out."

He bent down and slid the blade under the blue skin of the dead shell, digging just behind her ear until he saw the metallic glint. He swallowed hard, forcing his stomach contents to stay down as he tore at the skin and slid the knife beneath. He pulled the fragile silver sliver from the tissue and slid it into the vial with the others. He breathed a sigh of relief once all three chips were safely contained.

He had to move quickly, though. He knew what had happened with the bots when too many chips got together. The Council would not be able to ignore the presence of the strange technology for long.

He pressed the watch to his face. "I have chips that need to get out of this room and humans who need to be woken up. Someone get here!"

It amazed him how strong his voice could sound, even if he felt anything but.

"Where's Ravaan?" a voice answered.

"There was a complication. Get here! We don't have much time!"

Jo'sha's head was spinning. Half of it he blamed on the blow to the head he had taken in his false human form. He hadn't felt right since. The other part of it was sheer exhaustion and a general feeling of disgust. And then there was the whisper in his mind, growing louder and louder, that told him that he had yet to avert disaster. He told himself to be strong, that it would end soon, though he was not sure what the outcome would be.

"Why did you stun the brother?" Pask asked.

"Dorain?" Jo'sha said, trying to shake the uneasiness that slithered under his skin.

"You didn't have to shoot him. You didn't have to wait until his back was turned and betray him."

"I sacrificed his sister. If there had been any other way, I wouldn't have—I didn't want her to get hurt. He was standing there in the transport room, and he reminded me so much of her. His selflessness and gentle naiveté—I wanted to spare him from all of this."

"So you shot him."

"And then they transferred you into his cell, and I knew you would keep them from coming after him. You wouldn't let them hurt him anymore."

"Saira is destroyed," Pask said. "She won't be the same after this. You understand that?"

"I saw," Jo'sha whispered. "I don't know that I'll ever forgive myself for the role I played in that. The one comfort I have is that there is one Thellessian left who may still continue her legacy."

There was a knock on the door, and when Jo'sha saw the Peacemaker on the other side, a great weight lifted from him.

"Get these on the screen," Jo'sha said, exchanging with him the chips for vials filled with amber liquid. The Peacemaker nodded uneasily and quickly slipped from sight.

"We can't wait here any longer," Jo'sha said, steeling himself. "The humans have to go home."

He started to turn, but that was when another Peacemaker appeared at the door.

"Sir!" the man cried.

The Peacemaker stood before him, the body beneath his suit edgy.

Something had gone wrong. The realization made Jo'sha's heart stop.

"What's happened?" he asked breathlessly, though he tried to hide his fear.

"The Thellessian! She—they've taken her before the Council!"

"Are our agents still in place in the medical units?"

"Yes, sir," the Peacemaker said.

"Then what's the problem? Grab her when they bring her in and get her to safety."

"Sir, I don't think she'll be going to the medical chamber."

Jo'sha's eyes widened. "Get those chips on the Council's screen *now!*"

The Peacemaker vanished, and Jo'sha spun on his heel.

The doctors had the stun gun pointed directly at him.

"She changed her name and her face," Pask said, "but she's still Lucy. What did you think she was going to do?"

"What are you doing?" Jo'sha asked, his heart racing.

"Nothing, as long as you toss me that watch," Pask said.

Jo'sha hesitated, but the sight of Pask moving her finger toward the trigger changed his mind. Quickly, he unclasped the watch and tossed it to the doctors, who caught it and turned to the girl lying on the table behind them. He watched with bewilderment as they put it on Jillian's wrist.

"Jillian, you need to get up now," Pask said in English.

"She's unconscious!" Jo'sha objected.

"We both know it only takes minutes once the injection has been delivered," Pask said. "She's been fully awake for some time now. We made sure she had time to be."

"You—" Jo'sha said, "you were never going to shoot me! You were keeping me away from her!"

They ignored him and focused on the human girl lying on the table.

"Jillian Carter, you must get up! Saira's life is in danger!" Pask said urgently.

Jo'sha's jaw dropped in shock as the human girl bolted upright.

Then his heart dropped when Pask placed the gun in her hands.

"What are you doing?" he whispered.

"Jillian, you must run! They've taken Saira! You must stop them from harming her! I'll guide you, but you must go now!"

Jo'sha saw the matching watch on Pask's wrist. He looked over, and the absence of Ravaan's watch was not lost on him.

He looked back. The scene had already changed. Jillian was moving at him, fast. He stepped in front of her to block her.

"Jillian, no!" he cried.

He was on the floor before he knew what had happened, and the girl was gone.

"She hit me!" Jo'sha cried.

"You shot her," Pask replied matter-of-factly.

"What have you done? She is ours to protect!"

"You think a few memories are enough to stop the Council? They've lost their minds!" Pask snapped.

"The girl attacked me, and you're guiding her to the Council with a weapon you set to kill! You must stop her! She is frightened and angry! This will not end well!"

"Then it won't!" Pask shouted. "But I will not let more people die for your contrived plans!"

"You think this will save people? She will attack! She and others will die! If you send her in there, this is the end to the only chance of peace we have! You said the girl must not be one of our regrets!"

"There was *never* a chance," Pask whispered. "The only regret I would have about that poor child is making decisions about her life *or* death for her. I refuse to abandon her on that planet and hope that she is not another tragedy! I refuse to stand by and be used to facilitate the agendas of soulless cowards any longer! I will not stand aside and let us ignore the weak and helpless again!"

"What are you doing?" Jo'sha said, his voice pleading.

"You would let the last testament of the human race play out on a screen?" Pask snapped. "You took a girl from her bed to use her as a tool. You stole a chip from her head and would send her back to that planet to live out her life as best she can, while we stay up here where it's safe and comfortable and decide her fate? How like a Peacemaker you are! Remove the emotions! Let the memories play out where it's safe! We need never get our hands dirty, *do we*?"

Jo'sha backed away toward the door.

"No more!" Pask snapped. "Let the girl make her own decisions. Let the human race stand up for itself! You think this will end badly, then so be it, but we will not let those in power hide from her or her race any longer! If they want to destroy her world, they cannot do it from here, where they see not so much as a human face! Let them face *her*!"

Jo'sha turned, scrambling out the door. He ran as the doctors whispered into their watch, praying that he was fast enough.

He wasn't.

CHAPTER 19

They picked us up and carried us away. Jo'sha carried Jillian's limp body in the opposite direction. I knew it would be the last time I ever saw her.

They placed us all in a holding cell, bound in shackles. Rocky, Derek, Adam, and the other Peacemakers were already there. Rocky's mouth was covered in a metal muzzle, a bit between her teeth, threatening to crack them if she so much as even snarled. Her feet and tails were tied together. She lay there on her side, unable to move. A harness around her neck tethered her to the wall. She was a pitiful sight. She looked at me, her eyes pained as she lay there, not fighting, her spirit broken.

I saw the same expression on Derek's and Adam's faces. They were tethered to the ground by their bound wrists and ankles, a collar around their necks keeping them chained to the wall the same way that Rocky was.

I knew the indescribable agony they felt. They had robbed us of everything.

When Tori died, I had nearly gone mad with grief. I had screamed and cried for her. I had begged for it to be me instead. But with Jillian ... It was like suffering a mortal wound. A vital part of me had been ripped away, and without it, the unspeakable trauma was so severe that my body had no conditioned response.

I was silent. I appeared calm, but the reality was that my shock was so deep and intense that it went beyond a physical response. The very core of my being was suffering.

They kept us in the dark, cramped cell for hours, chained to the walls like animals, though I didn't even feel the collar around my neck or the chains around my wrists and feet. Dorain was chained across from me and Emilee was beside me, her tiny arms tied together and bound to the wall. None of us looked frightened, but then, frightened meant you had something worth losing. Some of us had gotten our people out, but others had lost them. Either way, we had lost them. This was the part where our punishment—the forgetting—came.

It seemed strange to me that I had once been a girl who welcomed the chance to forget her pain. As I sat there feeling the worst agony any being could dare endure, I realized that I didn't want to hide from suffering and loss anymore. I didn't want to be safe and sheltered from grief anymore.

I had had enough of being forced to forget.

And I was *angry*. I felt it trickling out of me, burning under my skin. I let it. I *wanted* to be angry. I *deserved* to be angry, and I was realizing it for the first time. I had defended my own alien people through this entire tragedy. I had called this a mistake. I had begged my friends to understand and had made excuses. Finally, at the end, it occurred to me that none of this had been a mistake. My own people were the bloodthirsty murderers I had prayed they couldn't be. They had taken me prisoner and hurt me. They had chased me across the planet they had brutalized. They had robbed me of my friends and family.

They had killed them in cold blood. Their lives meant nothing to them.

"I'm sorry we couldn't save her," Emilee whispered to me after what seemed like years of silence.

I didn't say anything, but I didn't think she expected me to. What was left to say? My family was dead. I had failed Jillian. I had failed Tori. They had both died with me standing only feet away. Was Marie okay? I would never know.

We had saved only eight humans out of seven billion. Eleven had made it on board the ship that now held me captive. I could only assume that the others who were left on the planet had succumbed to the bots. Of the eleven we had put in that transport room, three had died there.

How useless we truly were.

It just enraged me more.

Dorain started singing, his voice strong but filled with grief. He always sang when he knew others were sad. It was a trait he had picked up from one of our mothers. It was one of our favorite songs from our childhood, about a child who loved to dance in a magical village. It was not a song with a happy ending, depending on how you interpreted the story, but somehow Dorain had always managed to hold on to the light within the dark. Even now, my beautiful brother remained hopeful.

I looked at him, but he wasn't familiar to me anymore. It wasn't that he had changed. I had. I used to look at him and see my reflection. Now when I looked at him, I saw a ghost. I was dead, and something abominable had taken my place. I saw it in Dorain's eyes when he looked at me.

The reflection in his eyes held a monster. It sat still and quiet, but it was terrifying nonetheless. I was grotesque and twisted on the inside, a perverted, hateful creature in the shell of a gentle being, and we could all see it.

But he kept singing. I didn't know how he could.

I leaned my head back, trying to understand how I had ended up where I was—how I had turned into this depraved creature.

I had been born a Thellessian named Saira over two thousand years ago. I had been curious, loving, and full of life. I saw wonder and excitement in everything. Then I was made a two-year-old girl. Her name was Anastasia. I was made Yelizaveta. I was made Mila. I was made Lucy. As those human girls, I was good and gentle.

I had been made so many people. They, and those they loved, had all died so many decades ago.

Each one of them let themselves be used, and I knew that now.

Dead eyes stared out at me in the darkness that was my own mind. I saw the red-headed girl covered in a white sheet on a cold metal table. I saw the red-headed girl lying on the floor of a cold metal ship. I saw the red-headed girl choking, grasping at the rope at her neck as a blue Thellessian dragged her out of the dark.

I had finally been made Allyson, and it was as that human girl that I realized what my nightmares meant.

Jillian had been horrified that we took children. She had been appalled that I replaced children. Perhaps some could accuse me of robbing them of their lives, but I knew the truth now. At the end of each lifetime, it was not just friends, family, or even stolen children who suffered: it was also me. It was every higher creature that thought this was the right way.

Because each time I left them and agreed to forget them, a piece of my own humanity died with them. Loved ones were not meant to be forgotten.

The footsteps approached us. We were almost thankful that the Council had finally come.

"The Council of Traltix has voted to see you individually, to judge you and pass sentences fairly in the context of the crimes you have each committed," one of them said.

No one acknowledged them.

Then they came for us one by one, until my name was called. I didn't fight them as they undid my chains from the wall and used them to drag me away. I wanted to. The anger beneath my skin was boiling now, but my wrath was not directed at the two Council agents, so I was quiet. As I willingly got up and followed them, I saw the other faces staring at me: Dorain, Rocky, Emilee, Adam ... Their turns were coming. Some of them almost looked envious.

I stopped at the doorway and looked back at my brother. He watched me with woeful eyes, wishing to walk by my side. We had done so many things in life together, but now we had to face our fates alone. I saw how badly he wished for my comfort through this and how badly he wished to be there for me.

"You said once that our work was not done," I said to him.

He watched me, quiet, listening.

"I know now what I have to do."

The Council agents were pulling me through the door before he could respond.

"I know you're better than I am. You're the one who's going to make the world better," I whispered to him. "Goodbye."

I saw that he didn't understand my words, but there was no time to explain. The guards tugged at my chains, and I walked forward, leaving my brother behind.

I didn't pay attention to the path we took, and it seemed like only seconds before they led me through large double doors into a stadium-sized room where over twelve thousand species were present, with representatives of each of them sitting in endless pews. There must have been over twenty thousand beings housed in this room alone. They were talking in low whispers, but all of their thousands of voices were deafening.

When they saw me, the room fell to complete silence. I felt the weight of thousands of eyes boring into me.

Below them, just over my head, sat the Elders. They stared at me silently.

I paused when I saw them. The Elders never left that chamber on *Moga*. They couldn't …

They appeared free enough, as if they were present by their own will. Still, when I looked closer, I saw the occasional bandage and wrapping that must have hidden the gaping holes where wires and tubes had once been connected. How long had it been since they had been out of that room? How long had it been since they had been disconnected from that great machine? They were still connected to each other through their artificial tubes, but gone was their connection to the device that fed them their purpose.

I hardly believed that they would have undergone the process it took to remove themselves from that room just so they could look down on me.

I didn't care about their plight. I didn't care to know how they came to sit above me. What good had they done, anyway? They had all the power, and still this had happened. Had they even tried? Did they even care? Perhaps they were just tired of the machines and their piteous lives, and gave up. Maybe they wanted to be here. Maybe they did this.

As they stared at me, I realized that I truly hated them. I was glad to see them on display, torn from their purpose just as ruthlessly as I had been.

The guards pulled me forward. They chained me to the floor before them all, shackled in an awkward kneeling position, with my neck and arms fastened to the ground with short chains.

The metallic floor beneath me shimmered, like ripples in a pond. With a brief flash, metallic silver vanished, and in its wake was a sea of endless stars, stretching beyond sight in all directions. It was beyond anything that could be seen from any planet. Without light pollution, clouds, or other aspects of an atmosphere to obscure them, the stars glimmered, suspended in black gossamer, by the billions. My breath caught in my throat as I saw them, a once familiar sight as I stood from one of the many viewing windows aboard *Moga*.

But it was not the glimmer of radiant balls of light dancing across all of space that caught my attention. It was the planet below me slowly rotating on its axis that was the sole captor of my focus.

347

I knew the rumors that the Council of Traltix's caucus met in a chamber that had a view of the entire universe. It was said that any member of the Council could look out beyond the stars and find his home planet. It was meant to put into perspective the vastly important job they had of keeping order among the Higher Planets, with each member holding dear the gleam of their distant home world. It worked similar to the technology we used to cloak our ships from lesser planets, though on a far more complex and massive scale. While the outer hulls of our ships could reflect light, so that any creature looking up saw past us into space, this room bent reality so that the floor, walls, and even the ceiling vanished before your eyes. Instead, we all hung suspended among the stars.

Instead of looking out, searching for my home planet of Maegora, I pressed my palm to the hidden floor. Three blue fingers reached out to the planet below. It looked unfamiliar. As Europe drifted past, dark from the shadow of the moon hovering above me, there were no lights. Once, the Earth had been alive with light, cities stretching across its surface like golden veins. The planet was all but dead now. It was just dark; a cold, lifeless speck of dust in an incomprehensible universe.

I raised my eyes to face the Council. There was fire in them.

It was then that I saw the single Avinox standing before me. I recognized him immediately: the Grand Chancellor of the Avinox. I looked into his pale blue eyes and instantly detested him. I knew without a doubt that this was his doing. The dead planet and people below were because of him. He smiled at me, his white teeth flashing.

"Saira Ta'u," he spoke, and his voice was beautiful. "Do you know what you have done?"

Again I felt thousands of eyes staring at me. I looked up, and all I could see was so many living souls seated above me. So many, and yet, had anyone spoken up to defend the tiny planet below? How could so many fail to see the tragedy?

"Saira Ta'u," the Chancellor said. "You have betrayed the confidence of thousands of worlds. You have betrayed the trust of one of the most benevolent organizations in existence. Do you understand the gravity of your deception? Millennia of good has been undone. You have killed almost an entire species."

All of a sudden, the room came to life. All around me, images flashed across the walls, dancing sporadically amongst the stars. There was no sound, but that didn't make the death and ruination that danced before my eyes any better. I closed my eyes, blocking them out, but when I did, my own horrors surfaced, jeering at me.

I couldn't stand them. I felt the rage boil under my skin, so hot that I thought it might burn my flesh from my bones. I could taste the raw venom of hatred in my mouth. The images were meant to subdue me—to paralyze me. Any other Thellessian would have wept and whimpered at the sight of all the pain, but my kind, empathetic nature had been annihilated.

What I wanted more than anything was to make them pay for what they had done. I wanted them to know how warped we all were. I was done being timid. I was done being kind and understanding. If they wanted compassion, they shouldn't have killed my family. They shouldn't have put my pain on display. It was as if they were gloating at what they had done. Something in me snapped as I watched the worst few days of my life play out on their screen, and not one of them looked at the beings on it. Not one of them showed any signs of remorse.

Slowly, I opened my eyes and met the Chancellor's.

"You're lying," I said coldly.

His brows furrowed and his stance went rigid, his eyes penetrating into me.

Had he expected that I would cower before him and simply accept my fate? Is that what the others had done? Or were they too defeated to care what lies this terrible creature spoke about them?

"Saira Ta'u, do you have the audacity to—"

"Yes," I snapped, my eyes not leaving his gaze.

I wanted to hurt him. I wanted to make certain he knew what it felt like to have part of himself destroyed right before his eyes.

"You are all liars," I hissed. "You are all monsters. Your very existence is an insult. Do not sit there and look down at me as if you are better than I am. You have murdered beings far better than you will ever be!"

"Saira Ta'u, the destruction of the human race is your fault. It is you who must take responsibility for—"

"*My fault!*" I burst. The chains around my wrists tensed as I clenched my hands into fists and attempted to rise to my feet. The chains pulled me back down, but it was then that I realized that they weren't strong enough to hold me. "Do not dare stand there and blame me for your crimes. You are a sad, frightened excuse for a living creature, and it was your own wickedness that caused this!"

He stared at me, his eyes hard, challenging me.

"We both know who did this," I snapped.

"Admit your guilt, Saira," the Chancellor said, ignoring my outburst. "Let us move on from this tragedy. We may still be able to help you. There is still hope."

I laughed, but it was a cold, hard sound. "Hope for any of us ran out a long time ago. We just didn't see it."

The Chancellor's eyes didn't waver as they held mine. They matched my burning hatred.

My opponent was just as heinous as I was.

"Would you like to know what I am guilty of?" I said. I heard murmurs floating around the room.

"I am guilty of believing I was different. We looked down on those we deemed lesser than ourselves and thought we were better. Look down now! Look below your feet! We're worse! We thought we knew how to reconcile our greatest sins, but we just got good at hiding them. What we call wisdom—we're just fooling ourselves. We hide from pain—remove it. We think we have the answers to all the problems, but we just got so good at running away from them that they didn't have time to catch up. Well, they have now, and we didn't know how to deal with them, did we?

"And do you want to know the saddest thing of all?" I said. "I believed that we had the answers. I believed I was doing good. But if I am so benevolent, why can't I remember my own sister's face? Why can't I remember my mothers and fathers? I've forgotten them all, and I can't even feel guilt! How can I ever be good when I don't know what pain is? How can I ever really love anything if I can't experience loss?"

The Chancellor looked at me, and if he felt anything but pure contempt, he didn't show it. His eyes were hard. He was as far gone—if not further gone—than I was. I could see behind his eyes, and it was the same darkness that I saw when I closed mine.

"Saira Ta'u," he said sternly. "You do not have the right to speak here. You were brought here to be punished for your crimes. Do you understand?"

"I was brought here to be your scapegoat! I was brought here so that you can hide behind me!"

I saw the Chancellor's eyes flash just for a moment. Still, he kept his calm. So long as he did not react to my words, he kept control. He only needed to maintain the act for a few moments longer, and we both knew it.

I wouldn't let him. He wasn't going to win.

"Saira Ta'u, for your crimes you have been deemed irrevocably degenerate," the Chancellor said slowly. "Your actions are evidence of ingrained defects that are inherent to your being. We fear that these defects cannot be fixed or removed. Do you understand what I am saying?"

"Yes," I said.

It was too late for any of us. We were all too far gone to be saved from the hell we had descended into. He was committed to his act. Perhaps he had been putting it on for so long that he no longer realized he was pretending.

"The Council has deliberated, and we have devised a punishment we deem appropriate. We are creatures of mercy, Saira. You are still young. We would like to see you have a chance. As such, your entire memory will be erased, stopping before the end of your childhood years. You will then be moved to a rehabilitation facility on your own planet, where we hope your life can begin again."

I looked up at the rows upon rows of beings, all staring down at me.

"Tell me," I said. "Does that sentence give you comfort? Do you justify it? Do you tell yourself that in the long run I'll come out okay, and life as we know it will continue?"

"You do not have the right to speak!" the Chancellor said, his voice booming.

"Is there something you do not wish for me to say?" I said, not backing down.

"This is your sentence, Saira," the Chancellor said, his eyes holding me. I saw something behind them—just a flicker. It was fear. I was not playing my part, and it frightened him.

Good. I was done pretending. I was done playing the roles that others designed for me.

"I reject it," I said.

The room erupted in thousands of voices.

"Saira Ta'u!" the Chancellor snapped, his face aghast. "As a criminal guilty of galactic crimes, it is not your right to deliberate your fate! The Council of Traltix has passed your sentence!"

"No," I said. "You have not listened to me."

"Escort her from this room," the Chancellor spat. "Take her to the medical chambers."

Guards with stun guns moved toward me. The Chancellor turned his back on me.

"No!" I screamed. I stood then. The chains that held me broke midway. I barely felt their resistance before they snapped. As they fell and hit the floor, all that could be heard was the harsh sound of metal connecting with metal. The room was silent. The guards hesitated, unsure of what to do.

The Chancellor turned to stare me down, his eyes burning. And yet, I saw the dismay lingering behind them.

"Do not threaten us with hostile actions, Saira Ta'u. Are your sins not great enough?"

"More than you know," I nearly whispered. "I am guilty of sins that I cannot live with. This existence we have created is disgraceful. I have watched those I love disappear from existence, and I can't even remember them enough to miss them. I am a monster of the worst kind. We are *all* monsters, and I refuse to stand by and let it continue."

"You think you get the right to decide—" the Chancellor started, but I didn't give him the chance to finish.

"I will be forced to forget!" I shrieked at him. "I will forget those I have loved—every memory I have from the planet below us; the planet you haven't even had the decency to look down at to see what you've done. I will forget mothers, fathers, sisters, brothers, grandparents, and friends. Countless faces I have seen and loved. I will forget birthdays and deaths. I will forget all of their flaws and defects, but I will also forget every beautiful thing I ever saw them do. I will not let this cycle continue. It must stop here!"

I glared at him, my voice full of vitriol. "And do not think that I will forget everything you did to them. I will not forget the dying, the fear, and the pain. I will not forget that you were so frightened of a helpless species that you chose to kill them all, and you framed me for it. No! I will not forget. I will take my memories to my grave, and I will hold you responsible for the loss of everything I have loved. This time, I will forget no one."

"Saira Ta'u," the Chancellor said. I heard the slightest tremble of rage in his voice now. His composure was failing, "It was you—"

"It was me?" I retorted. I laughed, and it was a cold, pained laugh. "I risked everything to save three humans, and it was because of you that I lost two. I had a family. I had a mother and a father. I had a sister and nephews. I *loved* them, and you ripped them all from me as if they meant nothing!"

I didn't know where this was going. I didn't know how I could win, but I didn't stop yelling. I just knew that I would do everything in my power to keep them from taking me.

"Their names were Jillian and Tori. My mother's and father's names were Marg—"

"Enough, Saira Ta'u!" the Chancellor bellowed over me.

"My sister's name was Meredith! Her sons were Michael and Aidan! They were six and four years old!" I shouted in response. "I hope you at least have the decency to remember their names until you die, and I hope you live a *long* time," I snapped.

I took a step toward him, my fists clenched. The Chancellor stepped back, staring at me with wide eyes. The entire room had gone silent, waiting to see what I would do. I doubted that even one of them had seen an enraged Thellessian in their entire lives. The guards didn't move to stop me. It occurred to me that they were all too cowardly to directly deal with a hostile threat.

They preferred to let pulse cannons and bots do it from thousands of miles away.

"I was better as a human being than I ever was as one of your precious 'higher species.' The human race is better than you will ever be because they at least recognize their flaws. They do not deny them, and though they may fall victim to them more often than not, they fight the darkness. Do you even know how twisted you are? Do you even realize what you've become?" I hissed at him.

"I found my purpose as a human being. For the first time, I'm going to do the right thing. I will not run here at the end and take the safer fate. Do not think I will leave this room willingly to have you take away everything I have!"

The Chancellor watched me, his jaw rigid and his fists clenched in outrage. I could feel the wrath rolling off him.

"Guards!" he snapped. "*Get her out of my chamber!*"

They moved toward me. I felt the chains dangling limply around my wrist, thick and heavy. I wrapped both hands around them and clenched them tightly.

I was going to hurt them. If I couldn't yell my way out of this, I was going to hurt them, just as I had hurt the other Council agents in the jail cell, and I didn't care. I *wanted* to hurt them. They would see all of the desolation they had caused me, and I didn't care what that meant. I just wanted someone to pay for what had been done to me and those I loved.

I saw Jo'sha slip in from a side door.

I would hurt him, too.

"Saira Ta'u!" the Chancellor screamed at me. "Do not make this worse for yourself than it already is! There are harsher fates for you, if that is what you wish!"

I saw Jo'sha's face then. His nose was bloody. He ran toward me, but a guard at the side of the room grabbed him. Still, he struggled, reaching out for me.

Begging me to stop.

But I wouldn't. There was nothing left in the world that could quench the seething hatred I felt.

"Allyson!" I heard a child's voice giggling.

The entire room seemed to jolt as a small, red-headed human girl appeared on the walls, smiling as she sat on the steps of a pool. She swam forward, moving toward the person whose eyes we were seeing through. She splashed the person, and that's when I heard Jillian's childish giggle again.

"Ally, stop it!" she laughed.

The memory blinked, and it was me again. I couldn't have been more than six years old, standing on a playground with my hands on my hips.

"You hurt him!" I accused.

354

"He deserved it!" I heard Jillian snap in response. "He was mean to you! He made you cry!"

"You can't hurt people just because they're mean to you," I countered. "It's *wrong*, Jilly Bean!"

A hand appeared. It scooped up a handful of playground sand and threw it at me angrily.

"What do you know about it?" Jillian yelled. "You don't know anything, because you're stupid!"

She blinked, and I was in her face, looking into her eyes. Mine were full of childish compassion. Jillian gasped.

"I-I'm sorry. I didn't mean—" Jillian's six-year-old self started to say, but she broke down into sobs before she could finish. I saw myself lean in and hug her.

Then the screen took us somewhere else, and there were two boys walking down a sidewalk. All around us, leaves were changing for autumn. I recognized the red-headed boy looking down at me. I met Brandon as an adult in the cave. At least, I met what was left of him.

"Come on, Davy."

"I don't want to! Please don't make me!"

The boy speaking looked ahead to another boy sitting on the curb, his head of short, dark brown hair facing downward as he picked blades of grass from the ground and shredded them.

"We're just going to invite him for dinner."

"I don't want to—"

"Hey, Nate!" the older boy called, interrupting his little brother's protests.

Another memory flashed by: it was me again. I was eight years old, fastening the silver chain of a necklace behind my neck. I grabbed the gaudy hot-pink half-heart pendant and held it out so I could see it better.

The smile spread across my face until my teeth showed between my lips. Then I threw my arms around Jillian.

"Thank you," I whispered to her. My red hair was in her face, but she didn't seem to mind. "I'll keep it forever."

How was this happening? These were clearly memories, but ...

There was a little girl. Her blonde hair was in pigtails and she wore denim overalls. She couldn't have been older than seven. I didn't recognize her, but the way she watched the person from whom we saw the scene told me she hadn't been born human.

"No, Shannon," the little girl said calmly, with a tone far too mature for a seven-year-old. "You have to ask for the toy. You have to be *nice*."

"It's *mine*," an even younger girl snapped. She couldn't have been more than a toddler. The perspective changed, and we were looking down at tiny hands gripping a worn-out plastic doll. Its hair had been cut off, and a child had drawn all over its face with black marker.

"I was playing with it," the older girl said. "I would have given it to you if you had asked. You just have to ask."

"Shan, I know you can be sweet. Don't you want to be nice?" the older girl added.

The smaller girl looked up from the doll slowly. "Please?"

We only had access to memories through chips, and only Gangers had chips. Every one of the memories playing on the walls was from the wrong perspective.

The scene changed again. It was dark, and the person whose perspective we saw it from was lying in bed, clutching a green and purple pillow close. She was crying. The door creaked open, casting more light in the room.

"Jill?" Jodie Davis, Jillian's mother, whispered. The crying stopped. She held her breath. Everything was still as the sound of blankets rustling signaled Jillian's mother settling on the bed.

"Talk to me, baby. Don't shut me out."

The weeping started again. Jillian rolled over and wrapped her arms around Jodie.

"She has to wake up, Mom! I need her to wake up!"

"Shh, baby. She will. I promise you, she will."

The memories I saw were impossible.

"Leave her alone!" I heard Jillian shriek; only this time, I wasn't hearing a memory.

I looked over. Jillian was standing at the edge of the room, opposite Jo'sha.

She had a stun gun.

It wasn't me he had been trying to stop.

"Jillian!" I screamed. The chains dropped from my hands. I barely heard them as they connected with the metal floor with a shrill, deafening sound. I was frozen in place. The room erupted into a roar. Jillian ran toward the Council agents with the stun guns, undeterred by the missing floor. She didn't even look down. The guards stepped away from me, startled.

Jillian approached the center of the room and slowed, clearly frightened but holding her ground. She kept moving, but when the agents with the stun guns turned toward her, still clearly confused, she stopped. She stood there, eyes locked on me, but she didn't back away.

The gun was raised. It was pointed right at the guards, though her eyes never left me.

"Jillian, no!" I screamed at her. "Go!"

The rage drained out of me; it bled from my veins, hemorrhaging from my body. What was left behind was a sharp terror that left me shaking.

I didn't understand why I couldn't make myself move. I didn't understand why I couldn't go to her.

"I told you I wouldn't leave you," she said. She took a step toward me, but the Council agents raised their guns higher. She stepped back, but she didn't back down. She turned her gaze and stared at them, challenging them to act.

"They're going to kill you!"

What had I done? This was my fault. This was all my fault! Every creature in the room was enraged. Raw hostility was rampaging beneath their veins. I had goaded them. I had screamed and shouted and threatened violence. If I had known …

I was savage and imprudent. I should have let them take me. None of it had been worth it.

Jillian wasn't listening to me. The Council was quiet. They were all staring at the first human they had ever seen up close.

"Jillian," the Chancellor said in English.

I hadn't watched him to see how he had reacted. He stood there, watching my best friend, and I knew then that he was experiencing true fear. He had lost control and he had no idea how to regain it.

Jillian looked over her shoulder at him, and I couldn't believe my eyes when she turned to face him, putting her back to the agents with guns, and pointing her own at the Chancellor.

"Jillian!" I cried as she turned to face our mortal enemy, the same enemy who undoubtedly wanted to see me suffer unbearably for the fierce verbal attack I had just unleashed on him.

"Are you the creature that didn't give me a chance?" she asked quietly, but her voice was dripping poison. I had never in my entire life heard her speak like that, not even when I was certain that she hated me.

"Our Council has its rules and the reasons behind them," the Chancellor said firmly. Only Jillian and I could see his eyes, though, and I knew he felt anything but in control. "We do not expect that you understand."

"Oh, I understand. I'm the big, scary human," Jillian said, her voice scathing. "Well, take a look! Am I as terrifying as you hoped?"

I was helpless. The guards were right beside me with stun guns. They were pointed at Jillian's back. If I moved to protect her, would I startle them into shooting her before I could reach her? I had already lost her once today, and I couldn't bear the thought of losing her again. I couldn't imagine what they would do to Jillian if they subdued her. Would they restrain her, or were they moments away from turning their guns to full strength?

I looked up. The eyeless Elder was watching me intently. I held his face in my gaze, then the Elder beside him, then the next. I silently begged them to help me—to save her—but not one of them moved. They just stared down at me.

"Stop this!" I cried out to them, but they did nothing. They just watched me with their empty eyes.

For the first time, Jillian looked down and saw the Earth, black and barren, beneath her feet.

"On my planet," Jillian said, "we tell stories like this. This is the part where the hero barges in with a gun and shoots you, and by some miracle, he gets away. This is the part where I rescue my friend, and have somehow managed to rig your ship to explode, and you all die. It's a happy ending. The human race gets to live. I get my friend back, and my life is happy."

She looked up and took a step forward. I saw the guards with their guns flinch, but they didn't fire. "But that won't happen here, will it? I'm not a heroine. There is no happy ending for me. I can't defend myself against you. You've killed my family, you've taken away

358

my future, my planet is full of corpses, and that alien behind me is all I have left, and you're going to take her away, too."

Another memory appeared on the wall. It was me. I was four years old, standing behind my mother's legs.

"Ally, do you want to go play at Jillian's house?" she said, trying to introduce me to the little girl who had just moved in next door.

Then Jillian was moving toward me, her hand outstretched. I remembered that day. She had been beaming at me. She had been so happy to meet me, and she was so full of life and energy.

I saw my four-year-old self grin shyly and take the other child's hand.

Jillian was watching the wall, too. The expression on her face changed from rage to what I could only interpret as a mixture of defeat and mourning. It was a look of longing for something that was gone. She turned back to the Avinox and looked him in the eyes. "I could shoot you. I could kill you. I could do it right now, and maybe I'd feel like I brought justice to the people you took from me: my mother, my father, my little brother, and my friends. Because of you, I will *never* see them again."

"I won't, though. I don't want to be like you," she said.

With more courage than I had, she dropped the stun gun down at her feet and kicked it away.

The sound of the gun skittering across the floor echoed through the chamber. Jillian turned her back on the Chancellor and walked to me, pressing past the two agents with stun guns. They just let her through, too astonished to act. She collapsed to her knees in front of me. I knelt down, weeping, and she threw herself into my arms. I wrapped my arms around her and pressed my face into her hair. I never thought I'd see her alive again, let alone feel her heart beating against me.

She looked up at me. There were tears streaming down her face. "I told you that I wouldn't leave. Whatever your fate is, it's mine too."

She buried her face into my chest, sobbing and shaking, as we waited for what would happen next.

The Chancellor didn't say anything. No one did. The room was silent and still for what felt like the longest time. He walked to the center of the room and knelt down. With shaking hands, he undid the restraints on my wrists. I listened as they hit the ground, giving off a loud clanking sound in the midst of the deathly quiet chamber. He never once looked at me, but slowly reached out, and I will never be able to explain what I felt when he brushed Jillian's hair aside and looked at her face. She flinched when he touched her, and when she turned her head to look at him, I saw their eyes meet. I saw the exchange between them.

The last of the Chancellor's rage melted from his eyes. Genuine contrition replaced it.

And then it was over. The Chancellor turned away, his head in his hands. Everyone was still silent, but I could hear his sobs.

I picked up Jillian without a word and walked toward Jo'sha, cradling her in my arms.

The memory that always lingered with me from that moment was the half-heart necklace around Jillian's neck, its sister wrapped around my wrist.

CHAPTER 20

I walked into the white chamber, and the antiseptic smell, mixed with hot rubber and metal, hit my nose. Even after so many decades, the room smelled exactly as I remembered it back when I had stood there long ago as a frightened, red-headed Doppelganger.

I looked up and met the eyes of some of the Elders. A few held my golden eyes, and others, though they looked down at me, did not appear to see me. Still others stared straight into oblivion, while others' eyes wandered the room aimlessly. Most of them were lost in the pictures that whirled by on the walls, feeling through memories, emotions, and images from surveillance, immersed so absolutely that it was as if they were actually living the experiences.

I didn't look at the walls. I didn't want to see what they saw.

"We thank you for meeting with us," said the eyeless Elder, though I heard the voices of dozens speak through him. He appeared to be watching me, the tubes and wires protruding from his head making him appear malformed, though I didn't recoil from the sight of him. I had seen him in my mind, over and over, for decades now.

"It is not often that the Elders call upon me," I said, and I left it at that. I didn't ask why they had called for me. I knew that the Elders only revealed their intentions when they wanted you to know them, and so I waited patiently.

I didn't know why I had responded. I had once sworn that I would never stand in their presence again. In all the times they had begged my audience before, I had never acknowledged them. In time, they left me alone. It had been decades since they had last attempted to bring me back to *Moga*. Time had almost turned them into ghosts—just whispers of bad memories that lingered in the back of my mind.

Almost, but not quite. Those whispers transformed into nightmares each time I closed my eyes, and every night, I remembered. Time could never make me forget what we did.

The eyeless Elder just sat there, looking down at me. The room blinked various colors and intensities of light as images appeared on the walls and disappeared as quickly as they formed.

"How is Dorain?" the Elder asked.

"Well," I said, and there was the hint of a smile in my voice. "His children are a few decades old. He tells me they can walk now. They can even speak a little."

"We imagine that they are growing quickly," the Elder said, his voice taking on a tone of mirth, though it was hard to tell with all of the voices speaking together.

"I imagine they are," I said. I waited, my arms crossed against my chest, a strangely human thing to do. It was an awkward position to hold my Thellessian body in, but it was a habit that I had stopped trying to break decades ago. I was no longer just a Thellessian, and I had accepted it.

The eyeless Elder moved his head back and forth, perhaps in thought. He was reading me, trying to process my body language. I had come to the conclusion long ago that he saw me through the eyes of the others, and as he blindly watched me, I wasn't awed or even startled by this phenomenon, just patient.

"It has been long since you have seen your family," the Elder said. "You make no attempt to go to them. You make no attempt to create your own, though you are at the appropriate age. What holds you back, Saira Ta'u?"

"I have survived five families," I said. "I have lived and died half a dozen lives. Why should I begin again when my existence is already so full?"

And it was. Pask and Pashka had begged me not to do it—they had said my mind would not be able to handle taking everything back at once, but my dutiful friends had done as I requested. Emotions could not be destroyed. Energy of that magnitude could only be moved and stored, so when the doctors took my emotions from me, they stored them in aether in the depths of *Moga,* to be kept safe and forgotten. Everything was meant to be forgotten.

But I had had enough of forgetting, so I took everything back. The process had nearly driven me mad. I wanted to be awake for the procedure, and each lifetime that came back to me, one at a time, nearly drowned me. Pask and Pashka told me each time that I would not be able to handle the next one—or the next one—but I begged them not to stop. In the end, I took the four other lifetimes back, and the weight of every emotion and memory that came back to me all at once left me screaming in a darkened room for three days. The doctors thought they would never get me back, but slowly my mind quieted. The creature who left that room was one I had never been before.

And now, I never forgot them. I felt them with me every day.

"Is that why you stay in the dark, Saira? Do you float on the edges of space so that the remainder of your existence cannot be filled? Do you aim to keep the rest of your life empty?"

"You know what we do out there," I said.

"You are looking for other worlds," the Elder said.

"Worlds untouched by you—by the Council of Traltix. We're looking for worlds that have grown up without you there to intervene."

"And what do you expect to find there?" the Elder asked.

"Nothing," I said. "We're not looking for other worlds for us. We're doing it for them."

"So that when you find them, you can keep them from us," the Elder said.

"Yes," I answered.

"Do you find us that reproachable?"

My eyes traveled to each member of the Council, holding the gaze of each one. Once, I had loathed them, but my anger left me the day I took my four human lifetimes back and became someone else. Who I was now, she was … tranquil. I spent most of my days in silence, remembering.

I chose not to answer. Truthfully, there were no words in any language that could describe the role the Elders continued to play in my life, nor how I felt about them.

"That is only half the truth, is it not?" the Elder asked.

I let out a pensive breath. It was yet another human trait that I had adopted. "What do you think the truth is?" I asked.

"Guilt," the Elders responded. "You still hold yourself accountable. You keep yourself away from other life forms to punish yourself for what you believe you did."

"I am guilty," I responded. "And I have every reason to feel responsible. Five billion people died, and I have never stopped wondering how many of them died because of me."

"You did nothing," the Elders responded.

"That is true," I said. "I did nothing. I didn't think. I never questioned. I was so consumed by a sense of righteous duty, of thinking that I was one of the virtuous saviors of the human race, that I let you put their death in my blood without hesitation. People died because I let you think for me."

"There was nothing you could have done."

"Perhaps not," I said. "But you could have."

I wasn't accusing. My voice was neutral, not hostile. I knew what they had done, but it had been long ago and in another life. It was as if it had happened to someone else in the distant past. To live, who I was now had to let it go.

"Yes," the Elders said.

Truthfully, that startled me. I had known for nearly a century that the Elders had let the Council of Traltix destroy the Earth—we all did, though no one could prove it. I never thought I would hear them admit to it.

"Why?" I asked. "Why let five billion people die? You never pulled back the three thousand Gangers and Impersonators living with them. They were your own people. Why sacrifice so many lives when you could have stopped it?"

"Stopping it was the wrong thing to do."

"I will never believe that," I said.

"There are twelve thousand Higher Planets," the Elder responded. "There are trillions of beings who live on them. If we had stopped the Council, what would have happened to them?"

"I do not understand how stopping a tragedy endangers the lives of trillions."

As I said that, a brief memory flashed before my eyes and was gone. A Doppelganger sat by a fire, telling my friends about a person she had been once before. I didn't want to admit to myself—to them—that I saw reason in the words they spoke, that I had understood it once before as an undoubting Doppelganger who accepted a genocide as a necessary lesson.

I didn't let my face betray my thoughts.

"Fear," the Elder said. "Fear of the chance that another war and more suffering would ensue. It would corrupt them and cause animosity until, one at a time, they turned on one another. Once they did, it would permeate like a ripple effect, and all we know would be lost."

"So you sacrificed what you saw as one lowly planet to save the rest?"

"They had to be made to feel shame for their acts of violence before fear and anger made them impassive toward it."

I shook my head. I would never understand. I would never let myself try to. They knew that, and so they did not press their point.

After a long silence, I finally spoke. "When did you take Jillian?"

It was a question I had been waiting decades to ask.

"When it became necessary," the Elders said.

I stood there, patiently waiting.

"Jillian Carter was five years old when she became her own Ganger."

"Why her? Why then? And for what purpose? She was a child. She barely knew me."

"We saw the bond growing between you. You may not have known it then, but we saw the patterns that would lead to a deep relationship. We acted so that we might have access to the knowledge of how a Ganger impacted her development."

"Did you care what would happen to her? She had no training. She didn't know what to do. No one knew what would happen to a human Ganger."

The Elders didn't respond.

I sighed slowly, thinking. No matter how many times I tried to understand this part of the tragedy that had unfolded, the actions of the Elders made no sense.

"You thought you had control, didn't you?" I asked. "You thought you knew everything—could predict how the Council would behave. You saw the day they fell. You saw how the Chancellor broke when he watched two thousand of his innocent people torn apart in a battle they selflessly sacrificed themselves to stop. You watched how his devastation corrupted the others. You thought you could teach them as if they were one of your 'lesser species.'"

I scoffed. For a brief moment, an old anger flared in my chest as I remembered the feel of cold steel chains kissing my wrists as I knelt in the Council's chamber. I remembered the eyes of the Elders as they sat there, helpless as the world fell apart around us.

"I imagine you were quite surprised when the Council tore you from your perches high above us all," I said, the hint of a bite in my voice.

Again the Elders were silent, watching me. The distress dissipated, and I was quiet inside again. The old memory from another girl drifted away.

"It was always in your power to stop it," I repeated, my voice calm once more. "You don't know what the Higher Planets would have done. No one had to suffer."

"It would have been an abuse of power," the Elder finally said.

"An abuse?" I asked. "Abuse was knowing that the Council was compromised and doing nothing to protect us. Abuse was knowing that they had used their fear and hatred to corrupt and recruit Peacemakers into helping them turn against the human race. Abuse was knowing that we had been betrayed, but instead of working to stop them, you worked *with* them. You knew they had switched the cattle virus with the Cleansing viruses before I left this ship. You let them inject them into my blood. You let the Council have our ship, and they took our pulse cannons and wiped cities off the face of the planet. You could have saved an entire planet, but instead you permitted the actions of madmen. And it was just to teach us all a lesson?"

"Do not think that we did not try, Saira Ta'u. We spoke reason, but others spoke madness. In the end, they made their own choice. It was our decision to allow them to follow it through."

"Did it play out the way you hoped? I can tell you that it won't," I said. "Because, in all your wisdom, you could not recognize the greatest flaw in your logic. You may have fixed them, but what about us? What about the beings we are supposed to raise? How can you expect to create a world of peace when the system we are using to build it is broken?"

"How are we broken, Saira Ta'u?"

"We, as Peacemakers, were monsters long before the Council was, hiding from our own flaws and calling it the mark of a sophisticated system."

"We have never believed ourselves to be perfect," the Elders said.

"We did," I said. "*I* did, though I could never admit it to myself. We thought we had learned all the lessons. We thought we had all the answers, when, in truth, no one can know it all. We'll know it all at the end, when every civilization has crumbled and vanished and the stars blink out. We're dangerous. You cannot let creatures that perceive themselves to be flawless lord over the development of fragile races."

"We cannot continue to exist where it's safe," I added. "You send us down to the planet and let us live as humans, but not really. How can we ever truly understand and be good—how can we raise someone else if we do not ourselves experience their pain and suffering? We demean them when we let them die of war and infections, but we can leave and forget. It's not right."

I realized then that the Elders—all of them—were focusing on me. They were all listening.

"You thought you would fix the Council," I said. "But they tore you down just as easily as they did the rest of us. Did you ever expect that it would be one human girl who would save us all? Did you ever think her flaws could trump your calculated perfection? It was because we do not know how to suffer. We cannot call ourselves good when we do not face and deal with our own evils."

Slowly, the eyeless Elder's face changed. The corners of his mouth curled upward.

He was smiling at me.

"Saira Ta'u," he said, and I could hear some of his voices giggling. "After all this time, have you not realized that it was always about the girl?"

I stared at them, not comprehending.

"Perhaps not that girl," the Elder said. "Perhaps another human, but we always knew that it would be one of them."

"I don't understand," I said.

"You are right," the Elder said. "We know how to teach the lessons of lesser planets, but with our power and knowledge, we forget that we too are faulty creatures. We marched toward this fate for millennia, never realizing how far into the dark we had traversed until there was no turning back. We would destroy ourselves because we cannot recognize or handle our own flaws. This was always the fate of higher beings, Saira Ta'u. We must always strive to make ourselves … better. The growing—the humility at the sheer magnitude of existence—can never stop."

"Our role as higher species is to raise lesser species," the Elders said. "But we needed them to save us from ourselves. We needed them to be our teachers. To do that, we had to let go and let fate decide. It was up to other beings to determine if our way of life was to be saved."

I shook my head, confused.

"It was the chips," I said. "Jo'sha told me—"

I stopped. It had taken Jo'sha nearly fifteen years before he could speak to me. It had taken all the courage he had to beg my forgiveness in the part he had played against humanity. He had been ashamed when he told me that he had stayed with the Peacemakers, even after all the lies and manipulation he had endured. I didn't understand his reasoning, but I understood that he was driven by the insurmountable need to atone for his actions, so I did not judge him.

"He truly believed that everything you told him to do was to save all of us—the humans as well as the higher species. Had he known, he never would have sent me back to Earth. He never would have hurt or used any of us. He had no idea that it was you from the beginning."

"We told him the truth he needed to hear."

"You preyed on his emotions. You lied to him. You used him to get to my brother. You used their love for me to get them to do exactly what you wanted, and that was to manipulate and use me to get to Jillian. All you wanted was her microchip."

"The microchip meant nothing."

"Jillian standing in the Council's chamber was an accident," I replied. "It was never meant to happen. Jo'sha's orders were to get the chip and return her. Every Peacemaker hidden on the *Allisandre* was working to get the humans home. Jillian would have been sent back to Earth if it weren't for the Council. It was Pask and Pashka who—"

Again I stopped as comprehension came to me. It suddenly made sense, though I didn't know how it was possible.

"You knew what they were doing," I said. "You knew they were letting us keep our emotions."

"It became evident," the Elder said. "Over the centuries, countless Gangers responded to emotional stimuli from their past—stimuli that had never happened in their current lives. We see everything. We remember everything. We knew."

"I always thought I ended up in the cell with my brother because someone knew he would help us. They knew he would protect my friends, even when they came for me. That wasn't it, was it? I was put in that cell because the doctors were there."

"The doctors were disenchanted with our way of life for decades," the Elders said. "They were keenly aware of our flaws. It was always their desire to make us realize our shortcomings."

"You never thought to strip their emotions after what they saw," I said. "Just as you never thought that twenty minutes on the planet as an Impersonator could make enough of an impact to warrant having emotions removed."

Still, there were too many moving parts in this intricate plan for it to work. It *couldn't* have worked.

"The Council had you in chains before they took me from the Earth. None of us could have known that the events that would lead to that day in the Council's chamber were going to happen. *How?*"

"We told many truths to many people," was their response. "There were people who knew to stop the humans from going to Earth. There were people who knew where the doctors had to be."

"They almost died saving me from the Council," I said. "If they had, all would be lost."

"There were always more chances for failure than success," was their reply.

"But you did it anyway," I said in disbelief.

"The chance of saving all we hold dear was worth the risk of destroying ourselves."

I stood there as the words sank in. What could I possibly say to that? They had gambled with the lives of countless people. And for what? A lesson? Had it truly been necessary?

It took me some time before I realized that my eyes had drifted to the walls. I was watching the images flash by, almost too fast for me to make them out, but ...

It was the first time I had seen humans in decades, and I could not take my eyes off them. As I watched the faces dance by, I felt a longing. There were men, women, and children. They were rushing here and there. Most of them worked in fields, others in factories, and still others in various other workplaces. The planet was green and thriving, the water clear and blue.

It was beautiful.

"When is this?" I asked, my eyes fixed on the screen.

"Now," the Elders said.

"Why am I here?" I whispered, my eyes not leaving the walls.

I felt them calling to me. I felt a tug in my second heart that I had not felt in years.

"Jillian Carter has passed away of advanced age. She was—"

"Ninety-seven," I said.

Marie had died a decade earlier, surrounded by family and friends. One of them was an adopted daughter, a daughter who had grown to be a leader on Earth, who stayed by her side through the night, holding her hand until she passed away in her sleep. Time had claimed Kaitlin as well. Jillian was the last.

Jillian stayed on the ship with me for six days. The universe still whispered about the human who was barely more than a child and how she ended the greatest evil the Higher Planets had ever wrought. Children learned about the senseless violence that was rained down on the planet Earth, how billions of humans and thousands of Peacemakers lost their lives when the pulse cannons and bots were set upon the planet, and just as they learned for the first time what true repulsion and shame felt like, they also learned about the humanity of Jillian Carter. She was a symbol that would live on for as long as our worlds existed.

It was because of her that the Peacemakers left. For three days she begged the Council and the Elders to let the planet heal in peace, to let them see what humanity could do on its own—to let them see how good they could be. Much to my amazement, they listened. On the fourth day, the alien infection set in. I stayed with Jillian, Pask, and Pashka in a medical unit as they treated her until we also fell ill from a human bacterial infection. Evolution had not caught up with us yet. Our biology wasn't compatible and wouldn't be for centuries, and as advanced as our technology was, there was only so much our nanobots could do to protect us from each other. On the sixth day I carried Jillian into the transport room and we said our goodbyes. There were some nights, as I was falling asleep, that I swore I felt the warmth of her forehead against mine as we said the alien goodbye first, then the warmth of her cheek against my neck as we said goodbye as humans. A split second later, we sent her home to Marie, whom she stayed with until the end. I told myself that we had no choice, but I missed them both every day. I missed Tori. I missed my mothers, fathers, sisters, brothers, nieces, and nephews from so many lost families.

I closed my eyes and felt the weight of their words settle in. I had not seen or spoken to any of my human friends in over seventy years, since I had put them inside transport rooms and watched as a beam of light took them away. The Peacemakers had sworn to leave the planet alone for the first few decades after the Cleansing. With no human Gangers, there was no way for us—for me—to go to them. Until only two decades ago, no alien had made contact with the planet Earth, and even now the Peacemakers came back and interacted with the planet with the utmost caution. They had promised.

Because of Jillian.

Those who had stayed with the Peacemakers updated me on the planet's progress every few years, but I never went back. I couldn't. It was three days after Jillian was sent home that I took my past lifetimes back. The creature who emerged from that was not one that any of us had ever known. There was no going back to either of my realities—to the human friends on Earth or the Thellessian family on Maegora—after that. I hadn't even seen my brother, though I missed him dearly.

I had felt the absence of my friends for so many years, and now they had both been laid to rest. A chapter of my life was closing, and it was both sad and comforting.

"They both lived happy lives. They both had families. Their children, grandchildren, and great-grandchildren are all well," the Elders said.

"Yes, I know," I said quietly.

There was a long silence as I watched the people come and go on the walls.

"You were right," the Elders said.

I watched the humans, waiting for the Elders to explain what they meant.

"We have a request to ask of you," the Elders said.

"I am no longer a Peacemaker," I replied.

"We do not ask this of you as a Peacemaker," the Elders said. "We do not wish for you to be a Peacemaker."

"What do you want me to be?"

"Something better."

"How do I know that what you are about to tell me isn't just another one of your truths?"

"Because we are leaving, Saira Ta'u," the Elder said. "We made our choice and played our role in this world's fate, and for that, we must not be allowed to play a part in its future. We shall leave, and a new Peacemaker ship will raise humanity, and they will do it right."

"And where will you go?"

"To our homes. We have served our purpose to its completion. There is nothing more for us to accomplish."

I didn't know what to say. The idea of the Elders leaving a planet was unheard of.

I wondered if they knew how to live outside their chamber. Could they even live without each other after millennia of sharing one mind? What could life possibly be like after seeing and experiencing all they had?

"You have searched the universe for a planet untouched by us. You will not find one," the eyeless Elder continued. "But we believe there is a better way, and that is why you are here."

I nodded, urging them to continue.

"You were right about the cycle. We have learned from our mistakes, and now it is time to do what is right."

"And where do I come in?"

"Jillian Carter has a great-great-granddaughter," they said.

The humans moved on the screen—smiling, laughing, building friendships and families.

"We believe she could use a friend—one that she shall keep."

I understood.

Slowly, I turned and faced them. I felt the beat of my second heart quickening. I felt a tug in my chest as I saw the look in the eyes of those who looked down at me.

They were sending me home, too.

"What's her name?" I asked.

"Allyson."

EPILOGUE

"**M**ommy?" she heard a little voice say. Laina rolled over, her amber eyes opening slowly.

"Mommy, we would appreciate it if you would wake up now, please," said another tiny voice.

She saw their faces peering at her expectantly. One child had the same blue-black skin as her own, but Dorain's shining golden eyes looked back at her. The little girl had Dorain's royal-blue skin and Orna's amber eyes. They sat on their knees beside her, waiting patiently.

"The starshine is still dim, my loves," Laina said softly, lifting her head to get a better look at her children. They were hardly ever up at this hour of Maegora's rotation, yet there they were, with a look of deep thought upon their faces.

"Do I hear the children? Are they awake?" Orna said, sounding as if she had only just awoken. Laina could hear the soft fabric rustle as she rolled over. Her face, a paler blue than hers or Dorain's, appeared over her, eyeing her and the children curiously. A ray of starlight caught her face, causing the white and silver flecks in her skin to glisten.

Zaizair and Alairan glanced at each other, looking guilty.

"We're sorry for waking you," Zaizair said, his gaze downcast.

"Daddy is being very sad," Alairan said. She glanced over her shoulder. Laina followed her gaze out through the openings of the white bedroom wall, the gaping holes in the great porous stones revealing the world outside. Beyond the confines of their dome-shaped home, she could see the white sands of the beach, just barely glowing in the dim light. The red waves beyond weren't visible, but she could hear them crashing against the shore, a comforting, rhythmic rumble in the background.

Laina glanced up at Orna with a look of compassion in her eyes. Orna glanced down and met her eyes, her own reflecting a gentle understanding. She nodded.

"I think we had best go to him, don't you?" she said.

They each took a child by the hand and led them out to the beach. Down at the water's edge, Dorain was sitting in the sand, the red waves lapping at his feet. They sat down next to him, each taking a side, and nestled up against him. In the dim light, the planet had developed a mild chill, and it was nice to feel warm skin pressed up against them at this hour. The children crawled into Dorain's lap, looking up at him curiously. They were over a century old, but still so tiny in comparison to their father! He pressed his forehead against each of theirs, then tucked each child into the crook of an arm and held them between himself and their mothers, where it was warmer.

"Why are you awake?" he asked them in a gentle voice.

"We heard you being sad, Daddy," Alairan said. She sounded tiny and young in comparison to her parents, but her voice held behind it knowledge and understanding. It reached out to her father, offering a child's comfort.

"Yes," Dorain said. "Daddy is very sad today."

"Can we help, love?" Orna asked, placing a hand on his knee.

Dorain looked out over the water. In the distance, three stars hung just above the vast ocean. Because of the way the light came through the atmosphere, they took on different colors: the smallest appeared green, the middle star was pink, and the largest star, the one that led the others across the sky, was a strong yellow. The white sands, speckled with precious stones, caught the light coming off of each of them and split them. Looking down the beach, you could see the sand shimmer and sparkle with all the colors of light. Even the red waves would play with the colors if the stars were positioned just right.

"I spoke with Joshua—Jo'sha," Dorain said quietly, catching himself at the end. "I forget that he's going by Jo'sha again."

"Is he well?" Laina asked.

"He thanked me again," Dorain said, his eyes lingering far out into the distance, "for giving him the opportunity to raise her."

Laina's eyes lit up warmly. "He made such a good father!"

"He wept," Dorain said, his voice barely above a whisper. "He already misses her greatly."

"We all do, my love," Orna said sweetly.

"He says they buried her with Rocky, Emilee, and Derek. She was laid to rest right beside Ryan," Dorain said. "They kept them all together."

"I'm sure it is a great comfort to their children to see them all together," Orna said. "And you know how Sarah missed Ryan."

"Yes, of course," Dorain said, nodding.

"And what of Adam?" Laina asked.

"He is in good health," Dorain said.

Dorain shook his head, his eyes cast downward. "He looks so old. And to think that he was the youngest!"

Laina rested her hand on his shoulder and gave him a gentle squeeze. "We all know that human lives are shorter than ours," she said softly.

"I know," Dorain said. "It's just—"

He fell quiet, his eyes looking far out again, beyond the three stars that burned low in the sky. His eyes scanned the sky, looking for something. They fell upon a patch of starlight, and he looked out and out and out, watching something too far away to be seen.

"Did I do the right thing?" he whispered.

Laina took his face in her hands and forced him to meet her eyes. "My love, you gave her everything," she said gently.

"Did I?" he asked. "If I hadn't—"

"If you hadn't, she would always be lost," Orna said. "Her place was with them. It always has been."

"I know," Dorain said. "It's just—I never really thought—"

His mind wandered, a memory floating just behind his eyes. The power of it reflected in them.

"She was so small," he whispered. "I carried her in my arms as if she weighed nothing. She was—she cried when I said goodbye. I saw the tears fall down her cheek as Joshua held her on his hip. She was so happy, and yet—"

"You both knew that was goodbye," Orna said. "We all did."

"Will they send her ... other form to us?" Laina asked gently.

"Yes," Dorain nodded. "Her wishes are being fulfilled. Her human form was laid to rest amongst her brothers, sisters, and her partner. They shut down the life support machines on *Moga* shortly after the human form died. She'll be coming home to us soon."

The children squirmed restlessly in Dorain's lap. Their faces looked somber as they took in the anguished expression of their father.

"My loves, do you understand what we are talking about?" Laina asked gently.

"Yes," Zaizair said. "Aunt Sarah died."

"And do you understand what that means?" Orna asked.

"It means we don't see her anymore," Alairan said.

"But can we still see our cousins?" Zaizair asked, looking up at Dorain hopefully.

"Of course," Dorain said. "I think they will be quite pleased to see you, although right now they are sad."

Dorain's expression fell. His eyes grew glassy. He bent over and pulled his children closer, holding them tight.

"It's okay, Daddy," Alairan said, taking his face in her hands and pressing her forehead against his. "No one needs to be sad. Aunt Sarah's life was happy."

"Yes," Dorain said. "It was, wasn't it?"

They sat on the beach for hours, watching the stars rise in the sky. When the largest star reached its zenith, Dorain rose to his feet, Orna and Laina at his side. The children raced each other along the ocean's edge, splashing water as they ran.

Their laughter carried across the glimmering sands.

ABOUT THE AUTHOR

Alyse N. Steves is a Ph.D. student in the Genetics and Molecular Biology program at Emory University. She is a graduate of Kennesaw State University, where she received a B.S. in Biotechnology. She spends her days working in a research lab and her nights writing science fiction and fantasy stories. When not writing or conducting experiments, Alyse dotes on a menagerie of pets and spends time with her family and friends.